FACING
THE
SUN

Also by Janice Lynn Mather

Learning to Breathe

FACING THE SUN

JANICE LYNN MATHER

SIMON & SCHUSTER BFYR

NEW YORK LONDON TORONTO SYDNEY NEW DELHI

SIMON & SCHUSTER BFYR

An imprint of Simon & Schuster Children's Publishing Division
1230 Avenue of the Americas, New York, New York 10020

SIMON & SCHUSTER BFYR is a trademark of Simon & Schuster, Inc.
For information about special discounts for bulk purchases, please contact Simon & Schuster Special Sales at 1-866-506-1949 or business@simonandschuster.com.
The Simon & Schuster Speakers Bureau can bring authors to your live event. For more information or to book an event, contact the Simon & Schuster Speakers Bureau at 1-866-248-3049 or visit our website at www.simonspeakers.com.
Jacket design by Lizzy Bromley
Interior design by Hilary Zarycky
The text for this book was set in New Caledonia.
Manufactured in the United States of America
First Edition
2 4 6 8 10 9 7 5 3 1
Library of Congress Cataloging-in-Publication Data
Names: Mather, Janice Lynn, author.
Title: Facing the sun / Janice Lynn Mather.
Description: First edition. | New York : Simon & Schuster Books for Young Readers, [2020] | Audience: Ages 14 up. | Audience: Grades 10-12. | Summary: "In this Caribbean-set story, four friends experience unexpected changes in their lives during the summer when a hotel developer purchases their community's beloved beach"—Provided by publisher.
Identifiers: LCCN 2019048734 (print) | LCCN 2019048735 (eBook) | ISBN 9781534406049 (hardcover) | ISBN 9781534406063 (eBook)
Subjects: CYAC: Friendship—Fiction. | Real estate development—Fiction. | Family life—Caribbean Area—Fiction. | Caribbean Area—Fiction.
Classification: LCC PZ7.1.M3766 Fac 2020 (print) | LCC PZ7.1.M3766 (eBook) | DDC [Fic]—dc23
LC record available at https://lccn.loc.gov/2019048734
LC ebook record available at https://lccn.loc.gov/2019048735

FACING
THE
SUN

1

1

KEEKEE

Light filters through the trees and onto the sand, onto us. Eve and Nia toss a beach ball between each other, trying to avoid the thick bar of seaweed that snakes between shore and water, while I sit on the sand. Faith and Toons are calf-deep in the sea. It's Friday, but it could be any day, any year. We're always here. Pinder Point isn't much— the sand is more gray than dazzling white, the water gets choppy often, and outcroppings of rock appear and vanish with the tides, so jet skiers don't come here to stunt. Then again, all we need is someplace to kick off our shoes, to wet our feet, maybe our hair. I recline on my elbows and let myself sink into the sand. "Heads up!" Eve hollers, and I duck as the ball just misses my head. I look past Nia at my brother, who's trying to pick Faith up and toss her into the water. Her long, bare legs scissor the air as she squeals in unconvincing protest. I open my mouth to ask him why he's all over her today.

"Ay! Beach closed."

I turn to see a guy on the sand behind us, hands on his

hips. He wears a T-shirt tucked into snug jeans and a baseball cap shields his face.

"Y'all deaf?" he shouts. "Beach closed!"

Toons lets go of Faith and steps forward until he's face-to-face with the guy. Baseball Cap matches him—same height, same lean build, maybe even the same age—and blocks his way. "Who you think you is, bey?" My brother's upward-tilted chin warns of trouble.

The guy doesn't speak again, but I feel his body tense, as if his muscles lie under my own skin. Toons moves to the left; the guy mirrors him. Moves to the right; the same. Then Baseball Cap reaches down for a plastic bottle of water, his eyes hidden by the shadow of his brim. Tilts it up to his head, Adam's apple lifting and falling five, six, seven times. A twist of his fingers and the bottle crests through the air, then lands softly on the sand.

Toons turns and walks toward where it lies. The rest of us are frozen in place, watching. He bends down, reaching to pick up the crumpled plastic, but when he straightens up, I see a glint of perfect pearly pink in his hand. His arm draws back, then forward. A conch shell, almost as big as my head, sails through the air. Our gaze arcs as we watch it soar above us, then start to descend, heading straight for Baseball Cap's head. He ducks just in time, and the shell smacks into a tree trunk behind him and cracks in two.

Then we run.

NIA

My feet pummel the sand, glasses bounce on my face. My heart hurls itself against my chest as I run. The other four are almost at the guava trees, Faith in front, then Toons, with Eve close after, and KeeKee, who can outrun us all but isn't, because I'm falling behind. I look back; he's gaining on us, on me, the sharp *huh huh* of his pant so near I can almost feel his breath on my neck.

"Hurry up, girl!" KeeKee looks back, caught between moving ahead and staying behind, for me. She zigzags and I follow; my foot splats into an overripe guava and my flip-flop sole skids in the slick. I barely regain my balance in time to duck under a low branch in our way. Now he's almost beside me—my legs are on fire and I can't push any harder. KeeKee reaches back and her fingers graze mine. I hurl myself forward and as we lock hands, she yanks me between tree trunks and over old leaves. I can't think, only push, as together, our legs fly. KeeKee pushes a branch aside too fast for me to avoid and it whacks me in the face. I feel an odd lightness as my glasses fly off, and the world blurs.

We spill into the yard and up ahead, the blue truck puffs exhaust as it idles under the hog plum tree. Faith and Eve are already in the back. Toons waves KeeKee and me in as we scramble up, just as the guy rounds the end of the path.

"Let's go, let's go!" Toons yells. The truck speeds away, like Pinder Street is longer than eight houses on each side of the narrow road. At the intersection, the truck veers right and we bump into each other. Then it accelerates again and the wind muffles all sound. The only things clear to me are the rise and fall of KeeKee's breath as we lean into each other and the tickle of Toons' leg as it grazes mine.

Eventually we drop to a steady cruise. Faith says, "That

was close, boy." She keeps doing something with her hair—fiddling, pushing it back—and turning her head toward Toons. Eve hums low. Her soprano notes vibrate my insides.

KeeKee leans closer and whispers, "What you think that was about? You heard anything about the beach?" Her forehead is furrowed with concern. I hesitate, wondering if there's a way to braid the truth that will soothe her. But she's already moved on to her next question. "Where are your glasses?"

"They got knocked off," I say.

"Victim to the chase. We'll go back." The truck slows, then turns around in the middle of the street. My mother would not approve, not of a three-point turn on a curve, not of riding in the back of a truck, not of being in a car with Angel and her boyfriend, definitely not of the flutter in my chest and the dampness on my palms when I think about how close Toons is to me. Toons shifts slightly, and now his whole leg presses against mine. Then he leans forward, snatching whatever Faith has been fiddling with on her head, and bats her away as she tries to wrestle it from his grasp. I squint as he settles the thing on his face. Shades. My skin is cool, now, where we touched. KeeKee elbows me gently, then lifts her chin, eyes on Faith and her brother.

"What?"

"Hey, Toons," KeeKee calls. "How's Paulette? Your girlfriend?"

I can't make out their expressions, and before he can answer, we speed up again, and wind roars in our ears. We loop back onto Pinder Street and Faith raps her knuckles on the glass to the truck's cab. Sammy stops the truck and

Faith climbs down easy, her legs slim and muscled in shorts I'd never be allowed to wear. Eve jumps out after her and we glide to the end of the road.

Angel leans out of the passenger window as we pull into the yard. "Y'all come out. We got a run to make."

"Drop me off by the mall." Toons stretches out in the space vacated by Eve and Faith. KeeKee climbs out like a gecko, easy, sideways and lithe. Angel beckons KeeKee over to the passenger-side window. As KeeKee leans in, she raises a shoulder to rub her cheek and the motion makes me think of a heron preening itself, effortless and smooth.

"Davinia!" My mother's voice rings out from across the yard.

"You in trou-uble," Toons sings out low. KeeKee looks over at me. We don't trade words—we don't need to. Her eyes tell me everything I already know. She's got me.

I climb out and scurry over to my side of the yard. My mother stands in the doorway, her arms folded. "Davinia?" she says again, her tone so tight a gymnast could do backflips along it. In the background, the kitchen radio is on, blaring out the news.

"Hi!" I step inside, trying on a smile that fits my mouth like last summer's size. "You weren't looking for me, were you?"

"Don't you *hi* me. Whose truck did you get out of just now?"

"Um—KeeKee . . ." Even half blind, I can see my mother's face shift into a full-on glower. "Her mummy's friend."

"Friend?" She spits the word out like the bitter scab on a

fruit's skin, then sighs, looking down at my feet. I imagine the grains of sand on my calves, a smear of squashed guava and shards of pine needle and tall grass telling tales of where I've been. She looks back up at my face, tilting her head to one side. "Where are your glasses?"

"Um . . . they dropped."

"You better go pick them up, then. Do I look like I have money for a new pair?"

"I think I dropped them in the classroom."

Mummy huffs in frustration. "School's locked up for the weekend now. Better hope they're still there come Monday." She marches to the back of the house and the wooden floor shudders under her sure step. "You'll have to make do. Hurry up, I want us in Rawson Square when the protest starts."

I fumble around in the kitchen drawer for my old pair of glasses and cram them on. The glasses I lost aren't even new, I've had them almost three years, so this pair is probably from when I was nine or ten. The arms strain against my face. The lenses are scratched, but the house clicks into some type of clear—square table stacked high with books, chairs tucked under the skirt of the yellow tablecloth, sink polished to its best shine in the light filtered through the thin floral curtains, a garden of tiny daisies strung against windows that let in a steady billow of breeze. The view is imperfect, though, the world slightly curved at the edge of my lenses, my eyes unused to the outdated prescription. On the fridge, the last issue of *Pinder Street Press*, my neighborhood newsletter, rustles, as if the baby-blue paper is alive, then falls back into place. I grab the tape recorder from its perch on the counter beside the radio and cram it into my purse. Mummy reappears, sliding her feet into her loafers. I push my school shoes back on. I feel her gaze on my back as I step outside again and imagine my missing glasses looking down at me from some secret high place, smug with freedom, just out of reach.

KEEKEE

"Put some laundry on for me, babes," Angel says from the truck's passenger seat. "Dark load." She lifts her eyebrows ever so slightly, perfect crescent moons.

"Whose?" I avoid looking at Sammy, his seat tilted back behind the steering wheel. He stares across the street, squinting into the bush, like he can see through the trees and to the beach. He scowls, as if trouble's coming in on the tide.

"Iris. She need her delicates." She blinks her lash extensions one time more than is necessary, though Sammy's still looking away. He's too dense to catch on to anything even if we laid out the whole box full of pads and tampons and condoms and lined up all the girls in the neighborhood to collect their stashes, even if we stapled every receipt together and smacked him across the face with it. "It's *urgent*."

"If it's urgent, she could do it herself."

"Hey. Don't backtalk your mummy." Sammy doesn't bother to look at us as he inserts himself where he hasn't been invited. He clamps a hand over Angel's leg like she's a Guinness in a bar short on beer. *Love you*, Angel mouths at me before I step away. I duck under the clothesline, heavy with stiff-dried clothes. The hem of a skirt grazes my elbow like an oversized moth and I swat it away. Sammy wouldn't be rushing to Angel's aid if he knew where a third of the laundry money goes. I slip around the back of our house and onto the path again. It still vibrates with the memory of our racing feet, the air thick with our fear.

I scan the beach for some sign of Baseball Cap. I didn't catch his face, coward-shaded under the brim. *Beach closed.* Like he owned the place.

There's no one on the sand except me. No sign of Nia's glasses, either. I step farther out onto the shore, though I won't find them here. The sand is still indented from our footprints—Faith's small and slim, Toons' large and close, Eve's wide ones trailing behind, Nia's and mine overlapping with each other so sometimes it looks like two girls and sometimes a single being with oddly shaped hooves. Growing up underneath each other, you get to know footprints like shadows, like the shape of someone seen from behind, like a voice.

I walk along the beach until I'm in line with Eve's daddy's church. The roof to the low green building is crumbling slowly, but it still casts shade on the porch that wraps all the way around like a story so long it never really ends. I head toward the steps like I'm going in, then veer off and pull myself up into the guava tree on the south side, my toes gripping the bark. A long, smooth strip peels off under my feet and I kick it away. My fingers find holds, my arms pull me up into its canopy. There it is, right where I left it, wedged in the cleft where a branch separates into two directions; a freezer bag zipped tight, and a sun-bleached exercise book that used to be red, tucked safe inside. I open the bag, flip open the book, and find the pen holding my place, its clip tight around the form, folded in half. I lean my body against the tree's trunk and let my legs dangle over either side of the branch. A heron passes overhead, its croaky call pulling my attention after it like an invisible trail over the sand, and then over the water. It lowers its legs as it nears an outcropping of rock that juts out of the sea, and I let out a long breath I didn't know I was holding.

I unfold the pieces of paper. The letterhead blares at me: *NewBeat Summer Arts Program Application.* Out here, I've filled it all in. Kimberly Grace Hepburn. Age: 16. Current school: East Gardens High School. GPA: 2.8. I flip the page over to the side that says *Art medium and sample of creative work.* I've already written in *poetry*, but under that is nothing but a sandbank of space. If I want to go, I have to get out a net and catch the words, pin them down to the page. I return the pages to their hiding place and lower myself to the ground.

Beach closed. The shout echoes in my ears.

These are not the words I want.

FAITH

I turn my music off as I pull up to my house. The driveway is empty—Daddy's working late again. I'd give anything to be back on Pinder Street, in that truck, sitting across from Toons, our knees bumping, nothing more on my mind than the flush that comes from running and the feel of his skin against mine. I'd even be glad to stay out here behind the wheel till evening comes, until Daddy pulls up behind me. Let him be the one to go in first. Let him call out my mother's name like a wish. Let him pray for an answer.

The car whirs oddly as it idles. I sigh and turn off the

engine. It isn't the only thing awry in my life. I walk up the driveway to the front door and slide my key into the lock, slow. Daddy's been threatening to fix the front door, but I like the cheerful squeak it makes as I open it, an announcement other than my voice. A warning of someone trying to escape.

From somewhere in the house, I hear a sound. "Mummy?"

No answer. I lock the door behind me and venture deeper in. I check the cool, empty kitchen that smells of— nothing. Then I look in the sitting room, under the dining table, through my room, and the side room opposite, where Daddy sleeps. In the corridor, her portrait catches my eye, a head shot from her last year in dance school—wide eyes, long, elegant neck, a subtle smile. I carry on to the master bedroom, the last place she could be.

"Mummy?" Empty bed, sheets tossed back, closet open, shoes strewn, bureau drawers vomiting clothes onto the floor. "You there?"

The bathroom door is closed. I try the handle and the door swings open.

My mother is perched on the toilet, her panties around her knees, teal skirt pooled around her ankles. She glares up at me from an open book. "What? You can't knock?"

I stare at the cover. *Tropical Desserts of the Bahamas.* "Sorry, I was just—"

"Pineapple cake or guava pie? How I supposed to decide when y'all keep interfering?"

"Only me and you home—"

"You wanna close the door and give me some privacy?"

What I want is to throw my arms around her, to hold her

tight—this proper her, this rare quicksilver fish of a mother, before, in a turn, a twist, the light changes and she is gone. This is what mothers do, right? Pick out cake recipes? Even on the toilet, it's kind of normal. She humphs, then turns the book upside down.

"It's not a show, Faith." She holds my gaze as she reaches for a shampoo bottle, then raises it in the air, launching it at me. I shut the door just in time.

"Sorry." I press my back to the bathroom door, closing my eyes against the mess of the room. Behind my eyelids, I can see the cookbook, cracked open for good toilet reading. The title inverted as she reads, as if she moves through life on her head. The pie on the front cover set at an odd angle, half upright, half fallen down. *No,* I reassure myself. *Everything's fine. Everything is just as it should be.*

2

EVE

I wipe my feet in the scraggly grass by the front door. I've dusted off most of the sand, but I can't get rid of the low, sick feeling in the pit of my belly, as if I've eaten too much green mango at once. I pull my keys off my wrist. I've had my own set since I was five; Daddy gave them to me on a string decorated with a long strip of straw he'd plaited, the way his mother taught him to. I used to wear the string like a necklace, hidden under my school uniform, the straw itchy against my skin, the three keys comforting with their metallic cool. When Daddy went out on church business, and Mummy was on bed rest with Esther, I used to let myself in. I'd come in and give her a kiss, then take Ruth outside under the window where Mummy could hear us, and play.

Now I know all the things that could have gone wrong back then—someone could have snatched me from the side of the road, run me over on the faded crosswalk. I could have gone to the beach and drowned in two inches of water at low tide, been attacked by stray dogs that were part gentle pot-cake, part pit bull. None of that happened, though, because every morning and every night, Daddy prayed for me. I turn the key and ease the door open. I only hope that, all these years, he was praying for our church to be protected too.

"Evie?" Daddy calls as feet thunder to the door. Joe and Esther jostle each other out of the way, green dish towels swathed around their heads. Esther has my comb in her mouth.

"Hey, what y'all doin?" I block them with my arms. Joe ducks between my legs and out the open door.

"Our hair salon on fire, we have to go!" Esther gives me a hug, then wriggles past me after him.

"Why they get to go out in the yard?" Ruth complains from the table, where she's surrounded by schoolbooks. A stack of church publications sits at Daddy's spot at the table, but he's on his hands and knees, Junior bouncing on his back.

"Look, big sister home!" Daddy slides Junior off and sends him toddling to me. "Phew. My knees can't take this."

"Tired?"

"I'm fine." Daddy stands up, rubbing his back. "How was your afternoon?"

"Better than mine," Ruth cuts in, glaring up at me.

"Where you coming from?" Daddy settles at the table and glances over Ruth's page. "You missed question eight."

"Daddy, you see she look like she been on the beach? And I been stuck home—"

"If you had done your work in school, you wouldn't have extra homework now."

"This ain no fair!" Ruth kicks a chair under the table, and Daddy snaps his fingers at her.

"Watch that attitude. Take your books in the yard, do your work there if you want some fresh air. But if it isn't finished to my satisfaction—"

"I know, I know!" She gathers up her books and runs outside.

"Bet you she's going straight over to her friend's house." Daddy shakes his head. I sit across the table from him, then set Junior down on the floor to crawl around. "Something on your mind?" Daddy asks.

Daddy can read me that way. Always has. "We were down by the water. Me, Faith, Nia, KeeKee, and Toons."

"Oh yes?"

"We got run off the beach."

"By who?"

"Some guy telling us it's closed. How is that even possible? I thought it was a public beach."

"If a thing looks like it has value, someone's gonna claim it." Daddy brings a hand down to his knee, frowning as he rubs it.

"What happened?" I ask, almost glad for the distraction. An aching body after a day of work is a familiar problem.

"Just a little twinge. What happened with this guy at the beach?" Daddy leans forward, inviting the rest of my story out into the open. It plays over in my mind: Toons' eyes meet mine, pause a second. Then he lets fly.

"Toons threw a conch shell at him."

"Did it hit him?"

"No. He ran us off the beach and when we cut through KeeKee's yard, Sammy and Angel were there in the truck."

"That was lucky."

"Yeah. The guy was *mad*. Sammy rode around with us for a little bit and when we got back here, no one was on the street or anything. I didn't wanna go back to the beach and see if he was still out there."

Daddy scratches his cheek. "Are you worried he's coming back?"

"Kind of. I mean, who is he? How could the beach be closed, and why's he the one telling us to go? He didn't look that much older than me."

Daddy fiddles with the stack of booklets, tapping them so they're stacked one on top of the other, neatly. "Well, when you see this person again, best thing is try to make peace with him. Never pays to have an enemy."

"So you think he'll be there again?" An uneasy feeling passes over me. Does Daddy know something I don't? Why is he so dismissive about this? Maybe if he'd been there, seen how this guy was so urgent, so sure, so defensive of one little stretch of sand on a rocky beach with water too rough to be turquoise-clear. He didn't just chase Toons for almost hitting him with a conch shell. He chased all of us, chased us hard, like someone who had something big to lose.

"I really can't say, Eve." Daddy reaches across the table and squeezes my hands. "But try to let this all go, at least for now. You're home."

I nod, but I don't want our talk to end yet. "I don't know. I feel kinda responsible."

"Responsible?" Daddy looks surprised.

"I feel like I should have stopped Toons."

Daddy chuckles. "Well, now, unless things have changed since I was a young man, I don't think a fleet of stallions could have stopped Toons from throwing that shell, not if he'd already decided to."

"But he . . . he kinda . . . looked at me for a second. Like he needed permission or something. And I didn't do anything."

"Ahh." Daddy smiles, a knowing smile that takes a second to click with me.

"No, not like that!" I protest, but it's too late.

"So you got a little crush!" he whispers, looking over his shoulder.

"Daddy, no. It's not like that."

"Okay, okay." He grins, then turns serious again. "But Toons has a girlfriend, right? If anyone was gonna stop him, it would have been Paulette."

The house phone rings and Daddy starts to get up.

"I got it," Mummy calls from the back. He settles back down and looks at me, expectant.

"Paulette wasn't there. Anyway, he was focused on Faith."

"The plot thickens."

"It's *really* not like that. I just felt like I should have helped him do what's right."

Mummy pokes her head out of their bedroom. "That's Mr. Collie for you."

Daddy nods. "I'll take it up here in a second." He drums his fingernails on his stack of booklets. "Eve, not everything is your responsibility. You set a good example and try your best to be a positive influence. When it comes to what other people do, sometimes you have to know when to let go. Listen, let's not mention this business with the beach further." He glances down the hallway and I understand. I won't say anything to Mummy.

"Here come my little ruffians," he says louder, his tone playful as Esther and Joe race into the room, rounding the table for the kitchen and stampeding toward the back door. "Stay in the yard," Daddy calls as they scamper outside again. He pushes his chair back. "Anything else on your heart today?"

It still bothers me. I think of our church—the building old but dignified, the porch always swept clean, the sand around it clear of garbage and fallen leaves. If something's happening with the beach, what does that mean for us? Daddy looks at me, patient, expectant, but also tired, the skin under his eyes dark. He's been out in the sun all day, on his feet all week, and he has to take that call. If the church there was in danger, he would have heard. He would have said. As if he can read trouble on my face, Daddy smiles, a shimmer under the fatigue from his day. I try to push the worry out of my mind, to grab hold of that glint instead.

"No, Daddy," I say, making it true as I smile back. "Nothing else."

NIA

On the bus, Mummy sits ramrod straight, as if good posture will earn us a cheaper fare.

"You read today's newspaper?" she asks me.

"Yes . . . there was a shooting off Blue Hill Road. Mall renovations are almost finished. The minister of health says people need to be more active to reduce the incidence of diabetes." I rattle off the headlines without even thinking, but she nods, satisfied. I turn to the window. As we head down Soldier Road, my mind goes back to another time I took this bus downtown.

I am ten. It's spring break, KeeKee's by her grammy, Eve is at the church with her dad, and I'm stuck in the house all day, sticky with boredom, while Mummy tutors kids all day. At the table, she explains a math problem to Mr. Rahming's granddaughter, Paulette, for the third time. I ease a handful of change off the counter, then slip out the front door.

On the porch, brisk sea air urges me onto the grass, up our dead-end street to Queen Elizabeth Drive, and onto the first bus that comes. I drop my coins into the driver's hand and sit near the front. I ride to the end of the line, then follow an old woman with hair the pale lilac of periwinkle blooms. She goes into the library and I sit on the benches that circle the old trees outside. Two policemen lead a boy—he has a man's height, but his face is soft and scared and scattered with bumps—up the sidewalk to the courthouse while a woman wails after him, "He didn't do it! Y'all listen to me!" I glimpse his hands behind his back. Silver cuffs glint beneath the sleeves of a long T-shirt; his fingers curl up limp, like he's asleep.

I follow the street down to the water. Tourists meander across the road without looking, as if brightly printed T-shirts and flip-flops can stop oncoming cars. In the straw market, women, wide, thin, and in between, call out invitations: "Straw hat for the beautiful lady!" "Get your hair braid?" Their voices are cultivated, sunny and high. When the visitors are out of range, their tongues revert to the rhythms I know, gossiping, cackling, confessing, sighing.

A barefoot man peddles early scarlet plums by the bagful and I dig in my pocket for a dollar. He grins with a perfect set of gleaming white teeth and tosses me the bag of fruit, breaking into laughter that lifts like a kite when I fumble the catch and the bag spills its treasure onto the split sidewalk. He springs between stopped cars to hand me another bag. The whole world is music: a Mack truck's horn blares bass as it glides through a red light; a spat breaks out between two girls who toss intricate freestyle cusswords (carry ya crusty panty—at least my ma taught me how to squash out my shirts, with ya cheese and onion armpit) until a woman sets down her half-woven basket and steps in, scolding them for rowing in the street like both of them are her own children. The air dances over the hot asphalt and it seems only I am still, blown here like a leaf following the orders of that sea air. In Parliment Square I lean into the cool concrete base of the big white statue of the woman on the throne, suck the yellow flesh off scarlet plums and spit out the knobbed seeds till Mummy finds me, her face a whole summer storm.

Mummy nudges my foot with hers. "Head in the clouds." Her tone only scolds a little.

"I was thinking about that time I took the bus down here."

She shakes her head. "I don't know what got in your head for you to run away."

"I wanted to get out and see," I say.

"See what?"

"Anything. Anyway, if I hadn't, you wouldn't have made me start doing *Pinder Street Press*."

"Look at you, trying to get credit for acting out," Mummy says, but she smiles. Then she leans closer, scrutinizing my face. "Those glasses are way too small, you know. And the lenses are so scratched." She sighs, and the lightness between us is in danger of being weighed down. I switch topics fast.

"Guess what happened today?"

Mummy turns to look out the window. We're stopped on Shirley Street now. The roads are always busy on a Friday afternoon, especially late. "What?"

"This guy showed up on the beach and told us to get lost."

Mummy's head snaps back as she stares at me. "He showed up where?"

Maybe I shouldn't have opened my mouth. At least she's not thinking about how we're short on money. "Right on the beach by us," I say, and brace myself for Mummy to call me on lying about how I lost my glasses.

"What did he look like? What did he say exactly?"

"I dunno, just a regular guy. Twenty or something? He just showed up and started shouting for us to get off the beach because it was closed." I roll my eyes. "Like you can close something that's in the open air."

"Who else was with him?"

"Nobody. It was just me and KeeKee with Eve and Faith and Toons, minding our business. Why?"

Mummy presses her lips together. "You'll see soon enough," she says as the bus swings onto Frederick Street. We clamber off and hustle along Bay Street.

"Where are we going anyway?"

She picks up the pace as we near Parliament Square. "I heard it on the four o'clock news, but I didn't think they'd be out by us already."

There's a smattering of applause like a small crowd has gathered up ahead. "Just tell me!" I half-shout, and then I stop short, we both do. In the square, where I ate scarlet plums, a few dozen people stand watching three men and two women with placards raised above their heads: they read NO TO BIG DEVELOPMENT and HOTELS OUT!

"We oppose this proposed development and the loss of important beach access, coastal habitat, and community infrastructure," one of the men shouts. "We call on the government to reject this proposal." I look at Mummy. Her tightly pressed lips tell me this is about us, about our little beach. About what happened earlier today.

"Get your recorder." Mummy edges closer to the man who spoke. She stands a little straighter, leans forward, and waves at him. "Excuse me, can we talk to you?"

I slide my hand into my bag and fumble past the folded-up piece of paper. As I pull the tape recorder out, I wish I was back on Pinder Street with KeeKee in the yard or hanging around Mr. Rahming's store. Anywhere but here. I'm not like Mummy. I don't want to ask this loud stranger all kinds of questions. But the man has lowered his placard and walked over to us, and Mummy is waving me over to stand beside her. Mummy nudges me forward and it feels like I'm wearing someone else's too-tight shoes as I step onto a pathway I don't want to walk down.

I take a big gulp anyway. "Can I ask you some questions about what's happening here today?" I say, and press record.

KEEKEE

Tap-tap-tap. Water drip.

Tap-tap-tap. Spoon curve on cup lip.

Tap-tap—my eyes fly open as my ears scan for sounds again. It's Saturday night, when the pop and zing of firecrackers, music blasting from a passing car, laughter from a house a street over, are almost guaranteed, even this late. Beside me, Angel stirs in her sleep, then settles again. Through the open window, not even a tree shadow shifts shape in the moonlight. Clouds are low, and it's oddly quiet tonight.

Sniff.

A tiny lift of air through a nostril, the sound of a person hiding who wants to be found. I slide off the bed and lift a corner of our tired curtain. To one side is the clothesline, bobbing in time to a light breeze's beat. To the other, the melt of overgrown bush. Too still.

Tap-tap-tap.

In an instant, Angel is up, soundlessly rolling off the bed, soft feet finding the way even before her eyes adjust. I follow behind her in a klutzy din—sweaty soles damp on tiles, cotton nightgown's swish. She opens the front door. Night spills in, washing up a new victim: a girl, no older than me, shadow long, shoulders hunched like a wind-battered tree without roots. Her thin body curves away from Angel's outstretched arm. We understand—this one cannot be touched.

I heat water to just before boiling, then brew tea while

Angel wets washcloths to let the girl wipe herself off. Fear, sharp and animal as pee, mingles with Lipton's bitter steep. While Angel rummages for clothes, I stir in a thick shot of cream, then return the can to the fridge. I hold the steaming cup out to the girl. At the edge of the room, my mother breathes, waiting.

A hand darts out. Three lines traverse the thin wrist, raised scars like young, green twigs. The lowest one is so fresh it's still scabbed. Broken people come here—women with wet faces, men with black eyes and bloodied lips, girls walking alone who creep away by morning, boys whose soft bodies shake in the dark. Once, we woke to the sound of a cat, but when we opened the door, a baby girl was there, a twist of human rope connected to her belly, snaking out into the night. A woman came and took her and I never saw either of them again, but I know that baby's out there still, old enough to be running, by now.

Angel never asks questions, so neither do I, just boil water, pour it over bags of dried leaves, lay digestive biscuits on a plate while she patches their faces with rubbing alcohol and ointment, mashing a balm of part silence, part whispered words, to comfort the cuts we can't see. I don't make a sound at the sight of that carved-up little wrist, but she sees me seeing, feels my breath draw in, and in an instant there's a low whine as Toons turns over in bed.

I let go too soon, or the girl does. Hot tea splashes my legs and I clap a hand over my mouth to keep the scream in. The cup clatters onto the floor.

"You're all right, sweetie." Angel steps between us as the girl slides back toward the wall. Toons' bedroom door opens and Angel shoos him back in. "Only me and my daughter and son here tonight," she tells the girl. "Nobody ga hurt you."

I open the freezer, take out an ice cube, and dab at the burned spots on my legs. Tiredness has my head fuzzy—did my fingers slip on the mug, or did the girl mean to scald me? I'm sure I was holding the mug, sure I felt her grasp the handle and start to lift it away. Would someone really do that? Can someone hurting that bad do anything but hurt others too?

I wait on the sofa while Angel convinces the girl to sit, back against the wall, fingers around a fresh cup of tea. Angel stoops over to speak to her and her nightdress slips down over one shoulder and reveals the long, smooth, raised scar that cuts across her back. She adjusts the gown quickly and straightens up again.

I trace a finger over the sore patches where the tea landed. If Baseball Cap was the one tap-tap-tapping the window, demanding help in exchange for Toons almost splitting his head open with that shell, would we take him in? Would my brother get to lie in bed then too? If I were handing Baseball Cap tea, would I pull my hand away from him too fast too? Or would I be like Angel and whisper kind words, never mind the tender spattered spots on my skin?

3

KEEKEE

Pinder Street totes soft breezes and ocean birdcalls. There are stray dogs and dusty children darting between yards, dub blaring from a speeding car. Conversations blast out tinny from phone speakers; people yell back. For a place far east of everywhere, our corner beats fast.

But when I turn onto my father's road, with its old-paved asphalt bleached white by the sun, I step into a different Nassau. Here, there is yellow pine forest for miles. It seems monochrome at first, but if you stop and look, stubby palms begin to show themselves, their fronds like hands waving; little ferns and sharp sisal plants push up out of rocky ground, laying low. I wonder, not for the first time, how it would be to melt off the road and into that forest, to keep moving until the bag eases away and my shoes disappear. Moving until my feet are done walking and my arms stop their swing, until birds hover around my hair, then dive in. Until sunlight streams right through my body. Until no one I'm responsible for knows how to find me.

"If I walked out, could I become a pine?" I say, as the words take shape in my mind.

"If I walked out, could I become a pine,
legs fusing and feet unfurling pale roots the color of
my palms?
Would my toes curl and shoot into the soil
and pull up food?"

As I speak, I drop my bag onto the cracked street, sinking down to sit. I look out, and up.

"I would
reach up my arms and feel the tiny twigs shoot out
from where
I had elbows. My hair would turn to needles that,
dropping, would let my only babies and
a few friends grow.
If I walked out, could I become a pine
among the pines, standing tall and aloof,
sun reaching through me and
my closest kin, casting shadows up to the sky?"

Someone coughs behind me and I turn.

"My little poet," Dad says, and I get up, hugging him.

"You heard me?" There is always that small bit of shy I find grown up when I go to Daddy Sunday morning, replaced by a wide grin and free laughter by the time I leave in the afternoon. But like jasmine weed on a fence, it snakes up again by Wednesday, calls and texts too weak to keep its leaves from spreading open, its tendrils from catching hold of my heart.

"Heard. Felt. Loved." Dad picks up my bag and grunts as though it's filled with concrete blocks. "You gonna put that one down on paper for the camp application?"

"Um . . . I haven't decided," I say, stalling. Mercifully, he changes the topic.

"So, y'all fighting on the beach now."

"You heard about that?"

"Word travels." He strides toward the house. He's not tall, but he holds his back extra straight, extra sure. He doesn't ever look like he's rushing, but sometimes I feel like I have to hurry just to keep pace. "You see they protesting it down-town, now. You keepin' outta that?"

"Of course."

"Good. I don't want you getting in problems. Who started it?"

I roll my eyes. "Faith."

"Why her?"

"Toons gets stupid around her and he don't think straight."

"Isn't he with Paulette?"

I nod. The way he talks, you'd think Dad knew these people from when they were small. Maybe he does, from my stories. Maybe he knows them better than he knows me.

"Well, once y'all made it away safe."

"Nia almost got left behind," I say.

"She did? She's that slow?"

"The guy was fast." We're at the house now. Dad turns up the driveway, stepping over and around fallen guavas that litter the ground, half-nibbled by critters that have hidden themselves, for now. I breathe in deep and feel at home. The fermenting scent of guavas is one thing Dad's place has in common with Pinder Street.

"Don't get into it with those people." Dad unlocks the door and the smell of cake barrels out. "You know that's private land."

"Since when?"

"Always. They left it open, and it sat empty so long nobody thought they'd ever build out that way. Now the owner sell it, everyone up in arms."

"It's not empty. The church is still there, and there's activities and meetings there pretty much every day."

"Church? Oh, that's what that old place is now?"

"Always was. You'd know if you ever came through to see me." I kick off my shoes and welcome the quiet. No Toons thundering in, no Angel laughing and Sammy murmuring. No *tap tap tap*. It's bliss.

"Not always, babes. Used to be a bunch of things. But times change. Anyway, listen." He steps into the kitchen. "Back to the matter at hand. You fill out the form for camp?"

I follow him, inhaling the scent of butter and slow-roasted sugar. The room is alive with sunshine, the sink piled high with bowls and spoons. "That's duff you makin?"

"Guava pound cake." He opens the oven door and slides a knife into the loaf's soft center, then eases the blade out, holding it up to the light. "It's an opportunity. You like to write, even though I've never seen any of these mysterious poems on paper." He drops the sticky knife into the sink, then closes the oven again. "Five more minutes."

I cross my arms and lean back against the counter. "You ga be there?"

"I already told you," he says impatiently, "I'm on the admissions committee, not teaching."

"Cause if my one and only daddy was there . . ."

"I'm serious, KeeKee." His voice is firm.

I don't get my father sometimes. He'll be smooth and easygoing one minute, then all business the next. "I don't think my poems would work."

"You have any of them with you?"

"I left them home."

"You should have brought them," he says seriously, missing my sarcasm. "I'd drive you over there, but this cake . . ."

There it is. There's always some excuse why he can't come to Pinder Street. Suddenly the spacious kitchen feels too small. "I could go in the studio?"

"Sure."

As I step out the back door, he lets out a sigh that fills the air and pushes out past me, following me through the grove of trees to the shack he uses as a studio. Let him be disappointed. He's not the only one.

I push the door open and sink onto his favorite carved stool. I've been sitting on it from the time I needed to be hoisted up onto it. I run my hand over the smooth sides, left pinky finding the knot in the wood that used to be a tree, right forefinger slipping into the old split. He might as well have come out and said it: Angel won't let him come around. If someone wants something bad enough, though, they go ahead, even without permission.

Why doesn't he get me? Why doesn't he understand that when I put my poetry down on a page, the words wilt and flop sideways, flowers cut and left out of water too long? Maybe if he came to see me at home, he'd understand that there's more, too—that there's weight to leaving behind a world of people who count on me, who need me to serve them grits in the morning and do their laundry in the afternoon, make tea for them when they show up broken in the deep of night. How could he really know if my poems are good when he doesn't know where I come from? Does he even know *me*?

NIA

It's still and hot in the kitchen. Around us, Pinder Street is fragrant with Sunday meals, the scent of baked chops, ribs and rice, roasted potato, macaroni, and coconut bread drifting in through our windows. Our heat is ironic; the oven is empty and stone cold. I turn back to the old gray computer monitor, but I just can't focus on the protest story with the smell of all that food cooking everywhere but in our house. I get up, leaning on the counter.

"Mummy, when we getting more gas for the stove?"

My mother sets down a plate of sandwiches on the table. A rubbery finger of sausage pokes out at me from between the bread. I open the cupboard. Two cans of tuna, a tin of corned beef, tea, salt, a little rice, that washed-out fruit cocktail with desperate chunks of pear and peach suffocating in sugar syrup. The arms of my old glasses press into the side of my face. I slide them off. Maybe if I squint, the options will look better. A jar of mayonnaise catches my eye from the back of the cupboard. I grab it like a life raft.

"Hallelujah."

Mummy looks over at me, then down at the jar. "What you mean by that?"

I flash her a smile. "Just feeling holy on a Sunday afternoon."

"Put it back." Mummy slides the hot sauce in my direction and selects a sandwich, nibbling at the crust.

"But Mamma-Jamma—" I start, hoping the silly nickname will coerce her to give in.

"If you open it, it'll spoil too fast."

"That bread old and hard!"

She licks her fingers as if she's devouring a plate full of sticky barbecued ribs and points to the cupboard. "Back."

"Sandwich look like concrete block," I mutter.

"You need to be saying 'yes ma'am' like a respectful young woman. None of this backtalk and Mammer Jammer pass the hammer business."

I shove the jar away. "Joke as stale as this food."

"Hush." Over her shoulder, the radio plays a dreary love song. I can't ignore the dull ache in my belly. Slam bam it is. I slump back into my chair and take a sandwich, then look over at the arts camp pamphlet on the side of the beige filing cabinet. I push the glasses back onto my face and the front of the brochure clicks into focus. A circle of girls on a beach on the front taunts me. I bet *they* wouldn't be eating stale sandwiches for Sunday dinner. My gaze slides to my bag, where the application is waiting to be filled out.

"Nia?"

I look up at my mother at the other end of the table. "Yes ma'am?"

"I asked if you're almost finished with the paper for today. Mr. Rahming's niece is coming at three for me to help her with her reading."

I turn back to the monitor, glowing white. "Pretty close." My eyes drift over to the pamphlet again. "Mummy, you thought any more about if I could go to that art camp this summer?" I force my voice to sound casual.

She reaches for the newspaper. "Why would you want to spend the summer away from your friends?"

"Well, KeeKee's applying too," I say. My mother scratches her chin and turns to the business section. Something about this is odd. She doesn't *like* my friends. "It's a chance to experience more of the Bahamas," I add, trying to sound patriotic.

"Come." She tosses the newspaper down. "Pass the brochure, let me see."

I spring up out of my chair too fast to be nonchalant and snatch the pamphlet off the cabinet so fast the magnet holding it in place flies across the room. "It's just a short ferry ride away—"

"Where is it, exactly?"

"Somewhere on Paradise Island. They have dorms and it's all girls, you do creative arts—"

"I don't know what other type arts there are," she interrupts.

"Culinary arts, maybe." I rummage in my schoolbag for

the application form and rest it on the table beside the pamphlet.

"Since when is cooking an art?"

I bite back an argument and focus on the matter at hand: get to this camp, out of the house, and out of this neighborhood.

"They do writing, painting, sculpture, dance, theater— you have small classes in your own specialty, and they have an on-site farm where they grow their own food—"

"Organic and tended by angels, no doubt." My mother scans the page. "Only one page on this application?"

"You include a sample of your work to it so they can see. That's the most important part."

"And I suppose you'll be submitting the newspaper." Mummy glances up at me. "I told you it would come in handy, one of these days." She flips the paper over to scrutinize the back. "Who's judging the submissions to this seasonal nirvana?"

I ignore her sarcasm and push on. "It's a whole committee. Mr. Lewis from the *Nassau Journal*, Mrs. Strachan from the university's art department, Ms. Morris from the art gallery, Mr. Wright, Mrs. Symonette—"

"Mr. Wright?" She looks up abruptly.

"Um . . ." *Why would you call his name?*, I think, mentally kicking myself as she scans the list of organizers.

"Timothy Wright, architect at Gibson & Associates." My mother scowls, then tosses the paper down. She gets up, her back to me as she opens the cupboard. "That's KeeKee's daddy."

"But it's a great opportunity, it would look good on a college application, I could learn independence and maturity and—"

"And bring world peace, and end global hunger." She bangs a glass down on the counter.

End nasty sandwiches, I think. I bite my tongue. "So can you sign my application for me?"

"Nia, what makes you think I'm sending you out of my sight for six weeks with no one around who I know—"

"But I told you, KeeKee's gonna be there."

"Is that meant to comfort me?" Her voice drifts back to me over the clink of glasses, then the sound of water pouring over ice.

I try again. "That's six weeks you don't have to worry about me—"

"If you think sleeping out with strangers is a way for me to worry less—"

"You aren't even gonna think about it?"

She sets a glass of water down beside me. I don't want a drink. I want out. I want something other than the cloying routine of a Sunday afternoon spent with her and her papers and her glasses of water and her cold sausage sandwiches. I want something more than writing this stupid Pinder Street Press. That's her dream, not mine.

"It's after three," Mummy says, as if she can read my mind. "Let's get the paper finished off, please."

"But—"

"I'm done talking."

I grit my teeth and thump down in front of the computer.

I scroll through this week's stories without really seeing them: something about Danny across the street, who won a martial arts trophy; a summary of the protest we went to in Rawson Square; a school essay on Dame Doris Johnson that I had to tweak into something half fit for other people to read; a piece on the school band playing this Thursday. The paper's always been so everyday, so unimportant. So small. Even the protest seems faraway now. Up the road, the boys shoot hoops in front of Riccardo's house. A trail of kids have filtered into the road, bellies full and feet freed from tight church shoes. How big a deal could what happened on Friday, here and downtown, really be?

Mummy comes and peers over my shoulder, then taps her finger against the screen. "Read this. What you wrote about the protest."

I sigh. "'There was a group of people who got together in Rawson Square to opposition against—'"

"To protest against, or oppose."

"'To oppose against—'"

"Listen, girl. To *oppose*. Start the sentence again."

"Mummy, you ain ga even answer me?"

"Girl, your head too much in the clouds to see news if it knocked you right in the eye. You doing your work or you nagging me?"

I want to snap back that this paper was her idea all along. Instead, I bite back those words. "Please can I go? Please, please, please?" I fling my arms around her neck. "Can I?"

She squirms away, but relinquishes a grudging laugh. "I'll think about it—"

"Yes!" I jump up and down and accidentally knock the chair. "Thank you, thank you, thank you!" I hug her again until she wriggles free.

"Ease up, I said I'd *think* about it."

"And you know you have to decide by—"

"I saw the deadline, Nia. I can read. Now, can you write?"

I bound back to the table. "It's finished," I say, reaching for the form to look at it again.

"The protest?" Mummy slides the application out of my reach. "Oh, forget it. Just print and go get the clothes on to wash so you can hang them up before night."

I smack a kiss on her cheek and send the document to print. The old behemoth at the end of the hall whirs to life with a series of beeps and clicks. While it spits out this week's issue, I sort our laundry and load it into the basket. There's a perfectly good washer just across the yard—brand new and big enough to wash two full-sized bedspreads at once—but it's Angel's, so that's out. Usually, I complain about having to tote a heavy hamper of clothes all the way down to the Armbrister house to use their regular old machine that groans when it spins and sometimes smells of mildew, but today, the load is light. Besides, I don't want to irritate Mummy and make her take her word back. I swing the front door open and almost bump into a man in a suit.

"Oh—sorry!" I step back inside.

"Is your mother in, young lady?" he asks in a no-nonsense voice.

"Mummy!" I call over my shoulder. "Someone here to see you."

Mummy appears beside me in the doorway faster than a

genie from a rubbed lamp. "Can I help you?" she asks.

"Marvin Knowles." He extends a hand, which Mummy shakes formally. "On behalf of our member of parliament for Eastern Heights."

"I know you, Marv." Mummy folds her arms. She holds the hand she offered to Mr. Knowles at an odd angle, as if she plans to wash it as soon as she closes the door. "Faith comes through here all the time. How's Mrs. Knowles?"

Faith's daddy, I think, as he chuckles, a tight, forced sound. "You have a good memory, Mrs. . . . ."

Mummy's lips are pursed, as if she's found something bitter stored in her cheek. "Taylor. What brings you to my doorstep?"

"Just making some courtesy visits through the neighborhood." Mr. Knowles fiddles with the collar of his suit. It fits him evenly, and the fabric looks smooth, not like Eve's daddy's suits, which are always a little rumpled and have an odd shine. "Introducing myself to our constituents."

"Reintroducing. On a Sunday," Mummy says.

"It's always good to see old friends." Faith's father smiles widely. "Just taking a minute to chat with folks about the development up by the beach."

"Proposed." Mummy uses her reporter voice as she corrects him. "The sale hasn't been officially approved yet, has it?"

He laughs like his mouth is full of candy, delighted but also restrained. "You're sharp, Mrs.—"

"Ms." Anything else, Mr. Knowles?" Mummy's voice is stretched thin.

"Actually, yes. We had reports of some teenagers causing

trouble down at the beach. I just want to make sure the parents are aware the property is private land."

"What type of trouble?" Mummy asks.

"I can't really go into the details, but we've heard that the property owner is concerned about the level of security on the premises. They mentioned there will have to be consequences if trespassing continues to be a problem."

"What about the after-school group they have at the church?" I ask. "Don't people have to go on the beach to get there?"

"Yes, and the Tuesday-morning seniors' reading. I suppose you're going to accuse those old ladies of trespassing too," Mummy says dryly.

"I, uh—well, I can't comment on what arrangements have been made for the tenants of the rental property on-site." Mr. Knowles regains his composure quickly. "We want to look out for the interests of our constituents, of all ages." He smiles slick. "We don't want any trouble."

Mummy holds his gaze, her chin slightly raised, and taps the card on her leg. "Was that it, Mr. Knowles?"

"That's it." The man bobs his head. "A pleasure." He strides down the steps, then over toward KeeKee's house, as though he's too important to cut across the grass like everyone else. I carry on down the road to Eve's house. I have no reason to be nervous, I tell myself. I didn't do anything wrong at the beach, unless you count losing my glasses, and Mummy already knows about that. I have a bad feeling about what Mr. Knowles said, but I push it away. None of this will matter, so long as Mummy's in a good mood when she decides if I go to camp. None of this will matter, once she says yes.

4

EVE

All six rows are full at church this week before the service even starts, with the regulars from the neighborhood, some we occasionally see, and a handful of brand-new faces. By the time hymns are over, we've had to set up another two rows of folding chairs at the back and add seats along the walls. It's like people sense the building needs them and are here to fill it with singing, with the attention they give Daddy as he moves to the front of the room. He lowers his head in a brief, unspoken prayer. I glimpse a tiny shake in his hand as he grips the sides of the wooden lectern, looking out at the congregation.

"No doubt you've heard talk. Seen the protests. Felt the shift in the air." His hands release the lectern. He spreads his palms. "Change is coming to Pinder Street."

I brace, waiting for him to repeat what he told me. There's an explanation for everything that's been happening. There's nothing to worry about.

"Developers plan to take over the land, including this entire beach area. Including the spot where we stand."

Murmuring rumbles through the rows. I look over at Mummy. Her face is set in a stoic gaze. Am I hearing right? Daddy told me everything would be fine. Next, he's going to say it won't happen, say that our place here, in this building, on this land, is assured.

"I can't promise to know the future, but I'll tell you this: Now, more than ever, good people need to come together. Good voices need to be heard."

Beach closed. It's true.

He looks down at his notes, his pause a moment too long. His eyes are shut. Ruth leans over. "He okay?" Her whisper is a notch too loud. It feels like things are slowly sliding out of control. Did he know this when we spoke? Why didn't he tell me then? If he found out later, how come he didn't say something to me?

"Amen!" My voice cuts through the quiet, surprising even me. Daddy raises his head. He blinks, adjusting his collar.

"Turn with me to the Book of Luke," he says. I glare at Ruth, then turn my attention back to the front. He was just feeling the spirit, I tell myself, pushing aside the questions that prick at me, pressing hard against the peace I want to feel.

After church, Daddy spends two hours shaking hands and patting shoulders while the younger three run up and down on the sand. Mummy hunkers down at the back, talking to one woman, then another. When everyone is gone, I straighten up the rows and put away the extra chairs while Daddy rolls the windows down against coastal gusts and the fine salt spray they bring. Questions bubble in my mind, threatening to boil over and burst out of my mouth, but something makes me hesitate. Somehow, even after what Daddy said during church, hearing him tell me one-on-one would make it true, would make me have to face that we could really lose our church.

"Thanks for doing that." Daddy's voice interrupts my thoughts. I turn around and see him behind me. He looks tired, as if today has drained him, but his eyes are as warm as always.

"How come you didn't tell me?" My words tumble out.

"I don't want you to worry, Eve. This isn't over. Not yet." Daddy looks around at the room, the chairs lined up like parishioners waiting, then turns back to me. "It's been a long day. We should eat."

Outside, he takes Mummy's arm. I wish I had someone to hold my hand even when I walk a path I've known my whole life. Especially when that path is about to shift. The way is slick with beach pine needles and rough with raised roots. For our family, though, it's as comfortable as our backyard; barefoot, Ruth storms right over the prickly marble-sized cones, with Esther and Joe in tow. Even in my good shoes, my footing is sure.

"Oh!" The cry from behind is sudden and high; I spin around to see Daddy down on one knee, my mother holding on to his arm.

He straightens up. "Missed a step," he says, his face contorted with pain.

"You go ahead and catch up with the rest of them." Mummy waves me on. "Start heating up the food. We'll be there."

I want to stay back, to help Daddy on his feet, but my mother's lips are pressed too tight to invite negotiation.

Back at the house, I put the chicken in the oven, then change out of my black church dress, which has darts down the middle and requires those high-waisted elastic panties like what Mummy wears, just for it to kind of fit. Even so, I feel like a sausage stuffed into a too-small casing. I slip on a loose blue dress and shove my pointy black church shoes under the bed, where I can pretend they don't exist for another week. I hear my parents come in, but when I step into the hallway, the door to their room is closed. I strain to hear their voices, but there is silence on the other side.

"I wanna go on Daddy's shoulders," Joe says, coming up beside me.

"Not now. Take off your good clothes," I tell him.

"Where Mummy?" Esther holds Junior in both arms. Ruth shoves past behind her, rolls her eyes at our parents' door, sticks a finger down her throat, and pretends to gag.

"Come help me in the kitchen?" I plead.

"In a minute," Ruth calls over her shoulder, heading for the front door. "I goin across the road."

That means dinner is on me. I dig a pack of crackers out of the cupboard for Esther and Joe and set them up in the living room, then switch on the radio to the last of the oldies broadcast, letting low, rich singing fill the air as the oven heats. I mix up the coleslaw and take out the potato salad and a pot of rice as the scent of baking chicken fills the house. It was Daddy's week to make the marinade; he's used a heavy hand with garlic and thyme and sour, but there's something else in there, something sweet, and some spice. As I start on the dishes left in the sink from our rushed breakfast, "I've Been Loving You Too Long" comes on. As the water runs over the plates and through my fingers, I hum along. The music, the sweet smell of food, wash over me. It's like Daddy's in the kitchen with me anyway. Like he and I are cooking together.

There's a brisk knock at the door. I dry my hands on the side of my dress and peep out the window. Nia stands on the doorstep with her clothes hamper. A flame of irritation flickers. Really? She has to come here now? I grit my teeth and open the door. "Hey." Over her shoulder, I see Faith's car pull up outside. Soca blasts brash brass like the world is made of nothing but reasons to shake and wine. *Please*, I pray, *turn it off. Or down. At least down.*

"Ooh." Nia sniffs like she's trying to carry our meal away in her nostrils. "You put brown sugar on your chicken. And pimento!" She thumps her hamper onto the floor. "Hey, did Faith's daddy come by here to tell y'all not to go on the beach?"

I look past her at my best friend, who's cut off her car, silencing the music's trumpety-bass blast. She rummages around in her backseat, her behind in the air, her airy white-and-green polka-dot skirt in danger of flashing us if the wind so much as breathes. Why would her father come by to tell us to keep off the beach? If he was doing that, she would have warned *me*.

"We was at church. Why?"

"Hey, what y'all talkin about?" Faith chimes as she sails through the door. She is morning-hibiscus fresh—hair gelled in place, a fresh shimmer of something on her lips, the smell of soap still on her skin. I've sweated ten buckets between zipping myself into the dress before nine this morning and stepping out of the kitchen three minutes ago, and Nia's in a faded, stretched-out tank top, and shorts that have seen a splatter or two. Faith doesn't seem to notice as she drapes an arm over each of our shoulders.

"Your father been to see my mummy," Nia confides, glancing back down the road. "Apparently if we go on the beach, we're gonna be in trouble."

Faith snorts disdainfully as she unwinds her arms. "What, he's gonna ground you? Eve, what happened, you ain shower yet today?" she asks as she sashays into the kitchen.

"This morning." I squeeze my arms close to my side, then turn back to Nia. This is no time to worry about smelling like daisies. "What exactly did he say?"

"He was going on about private property, and not wanting any trouble, and how he was visiting on behalf of the member of parliament, and that there was an issue couple days ago and if people were found trespassing there would be *consequences*." Nia shifts her laundry basket. "You think they'll call the police on us for what happened?"

Something in my belly somersaults. I shoot Faith a questioning look.

"Don't ask me. We don't talk."

I turn back to Nia. "They wouldn't arrest us just for going on the beach. Anyway, we *have* to go through to get to the church. We pay our rent; they can't stop us."

"I guess not." Nia sounds unconvinced. She picks up her hamper again. "You mind if I put this on?"

"Yeah, of course." I lead the way around to the back door and push aside the mop and bucket. "We're low on soap," I say, opening the washer. A stray white sock clings to the inside, crunchy and stale. I scrape it out and drape it over my shoulder to take back inside.

"It's okay." She settles the hamper on the ground. "You know my mummy has her special soap." She waggles a tin that says SENSITIVE and FRAGRANCE FREE. I leave her to it and head back inside where Faith waits, perched on the edge of the counter. She's helped herself to a bowlful of potato salad, and sniffs as I open the oven.

"What we havin today?"

"Baked chicken." I pull out the tray of meat. The sauce is thickening, the top of the chicken getting brown, but unlike Faith, I don't have much appetite. "Why your daddy up here going to people's doors?"

"I dunno." She peers through the window and looks up and down the road. "I don't even see his car. Maybe Nia's making it up." She stretches out her legs, then tucks them under her, stuffing her face.

I feel a pang of irritation. Does Faith have to be so flippant? Her house might not be on Pinder Street, but she grew up on that beach, same as the rest of us, and she's around so often she basically lives here too. She *should* care. "Maybe he parked a street or two over," I say.

Faith licks her fingers. "I'll ask him tonight if he's actually home for a change. But you don't have anything to worry about. I'm sure it's no big deal."

I turn the oven off. "I think we do. They're having protests and all that downtown. They're gonna have some here, too. Church was packed today. My dad even talked about it in his sermon."

"What happens to your church if the land gets developed? That building's Moses-old."

Anger bubbles up in me like vinegar on baking soda. "Same thing as if the dance studio property got sold."

"We own it."

"But y'all would find a new place, right?"

"Yeah, that's true." Her tone is casual, as if we're talking about switching brands of soap. "There's always new places to go. Or the students might all find different studios instead." When I don't answer, she slides off the counter to join me by the sink. She bumps me, shoulder to shoulder, and I catch a whiff of her lemon vanilla lotion. She's smelled like that as long as I can remember. At least some things don't change, I think. This is Faith, after all. My Faith, beautiful, kind-of-crazy Faith who makes me laugh, who helps me let go. I take the invitation she's offering me with that bump, and shift my attention off my fears. "What you up to?"

She drops her empty bowl into the wash water. "Don't even ask. Stuff with my mummy is horrible."

I bump her back. "You wanna elaborate?"

"The new medication was making her drool, so. She's refusing to take it, and it's making her act . . . I dunno. Weird."

I forgive her earlier nonchalance right away. "Does she know who you are?"

"Sometimes. Anyway, I don't wanna talk about that. Tell

me what else goin on through here. Was church exciting?" Her eyes dance with mischief.

"You mean if one of the extra people there was tall and bright?"

"With eyes to die for?"

"Nope. Only time Toons sets foot in the church is when we sing after hours."

"Fine by me." Faith grins. "I like 'em ready to sin."

"Girl, behave!" I pretend to be shocked.

Esther bursts into the kitchen. "I hungry!"

"Hey, y'all ain supposed to be running up and down in here," I say, elbowing Faith as she reaches out to tug one of my sister's puffy plaits. Esther twists out of the way, pinching a chicken wing off the pan. "Look out, that's hot!" I switch off the oven and lean into the dining room. "Joe, call Ruth inside, y'all come and eat."

"Oh, hold on." Faith reaches for her purse. "I got something for you." She fishes out a tiny plastic bag.

I reach in and pull out a small, shiny gold cylinder crusted with rhinestones. "What's this?"

She plucks it out of my hand and tugs the cover off. The lipstick is luminous and red, silky smooth as an unopened flower. "They had them for sale at the mall."

"I can't wear that," I protest. "My parents would have my head."

Faith waggles it at me. "It's gonna be worth it. Trust me."

Before I can answer, there's a thump, a bang, then a cry from deep inside the house—not Junior or Esther or Joe—I know their voices. It's not even a child. I rush out of the kitchen and to my parents' bedroom, but the door is still closed tight. Now it's as quiet as if I imagined what I heard. I go to knock, but my hand freezes inches from the door, as if making another sound will bring all kinds of noises to life, unlock a new, ugly world.

Then Faith is beside me. She stares at me for a second, then raps twice, lightly. When the door opens a crack, Mummy peers out, her forehead wrinkled with worry.

"Eve, you—oh, Faith, hi. Listen"—she turns to me—"make sure they eat, then take them to the church and set up for seniors' meeting."

But it's my Sunday off. The words rise, selfish and eager. I push them back down fast. "Okay." I swallow to keep them there. "Is Daddy—?"

My mother looks back into the room at something I cannot see, then back to me. "Everything's fine," she says, gently closing the door.

"Come on, man, I hungry," Faith singsongs as she leads me back to the kitchen. "You hear what she say. Nothing going on." I can hear Joe and Esther complaining while Ruth samples from the pan, and it's so every-week, so easy, so right.

"Nothing's going on," I repeat as we step into the kitchen, but buzz from everyone else drowns out my words.

KEEKEE

I stand at the top of Pinder Street and take in our little stretch of eight houses either side of the street. It seems tiny now, though there are plenty of secrets hidden here. Before I'm even out of the intersection properly, I can hear Mrs. Armbrister ordering Eve's siblings to behave. Across the street, the AM station blares from Mr. Rahming's store radio. The sign on the front,

RAHMING'S DRY GOODS, is always shabbier in a late Sunday afternoon's light, the split wood extra tired, the peeling paint more obvious. Today, Mr. Rahming has his wife's old rocking chair hauled around to the front. He raises his bent-fingered hand to greet me.

"How's Daddy?" he calls. Even though my father has not once set foot on Pinder Street in my sixteen years, Mr. Rahming always asks after him, as if they are old friends separated by war and water.

"He's fine," I answer, carrying on down past the Armbrister house, cracks in the concrete, shingles still missing from the last storm. Ruth leans against the almond tree outside, too busy playing cute to hail me. Closer to the end of the road, a cluster of figures appear, coming from the beach. I recognize gangly Mark, Amos issuing occasional flutters of smoke, and Riccardo, short and so heavy he walks side to side. Then my brother appears with Paulette, his arm wrapped protectively around her shoulder. They head toward me as I make my way home. Past them, the blue truck is pulled up far on the grass, its front bumper right up against the tree. Great. Sammy's here.

The boys nod and murmur greetings as we pass, then part ways, Riccardo to the Sweeting's house, the other two cutting through the pathway to the road behind ours.

"Where you goin?" I ask Toons when we get level with each other.

Toons shrugs, glancing back at our yard. "Not there." He pokes me with his free hand. "You good, sis?"

I nod and keep going. My bag digs into my shoulders,

and the full clotheslines bob in the breeze, anticipating my attention. I have no choice but to go home.

"Home," I whisper, stepping onto the grass.

"Late shadows fall, long
sun, day full and fat gone
flat like splattered
plum. Night, hurry up
come, let this
Sunday be done."

Across the yard, Nia's mother sits inside, framed by the window, a small girl beside her at the table. Their backs are to me, but their heads lean in toward each other. The girl's only six or seven, her hair in neat plaits. It could be Nia, eight years ago. On the other side, in my house, the yellow lamp is on, its shine straining against the afternoon's glow. Inside, Angel's bedroom door will be shut, the curtains drawn to match the lamp's message: she's off duty. The sign is for me and Toons as much as for anyone else, though. Angel's careful that way, keeps us separate from that part of her life. She's had boyfriends before, but Sammy is the one who's stuck around long enough to get comfortable, for his truck wheels to form grooves in the ground. Yet somehow he's not family, not to me.

Six months ago, when the old washer went, he was the repairman the company sent out to take a look. It was too old to be fixed, but we needed something fast. Next thing you know, the old rustbucket was gone, replaced by a shiny, maximum-capacity front-loading machine, and Sammy was picking Angel up in his truck. The first night Sammy slept over, I stayed outside all night long. I leaned back on the floor of the porch and stared up at the star-speckled blackness. If I held my head just slightly to one side, I could see the sky but not the truck that squatted in the grass, an aggressive dog claiming turf in our yard. I watched the stars, the sky, the slow fading of lights in Nia's house, the radio extinguished at last.

In the morning, I didn't hear the door open, but I stirred to the chatter of the truck's engine. My body stiffened. He had walked over me to get out. The truck scraped over the grass, and when it was gone, Angel drifted out in her pink satin robe, the lace trim barely covering her behind.

"What you think about him?"

I looked up at the sky, its stars hidden now. She'd never asked me what I thought of a man before. "I dunno."

"Well. If he ever try anything funny, you let me know. I'll kick him out so fast he won't have time to clench his cheeks against my foot."

I didn't answer. She poked me with her toe. "You understand?"

"I heard."

"Hey, any space on the line?"

I turn as Nia comes up behind me, lugging a hamper full of wet clothes. "Let me make some room." I drop my bags in a corner of our wash area, then grab the pink hamper marked FAITH and start unpinning the linens. I fold as I go, stacking the towels on top of each other.

Nia squints up from clipping a bra onto the line. She extends it lengthwise. "Whose stuff is that?"

"You can't see the name on the hamper?"

She pulls her old glasses out of her pocket and puts them on. "Oh. Her father been by here, you know?" She takes the glasses off and shoves them away again. "These things give me a headache." She's on to panties now, stretching out each pair till it lies perfectly flat and smooth enough to write an essay on. Whatever. At least I don't have to do *her* laundry.

"Been by for what?" I start on another row of clothes; bras in a rainbow of colors. I don't have to check the tags to know Faith's size. Skinny and athletic as she is, the cup is large. A good part of me doubts it's her real size; she probably wads up socks to fill out her silhouette. That'd explain why there are so many of those balled up every week for me to wash.

"He come talking bout how they ga make trouble for us if we go on the beach."

I snort. "Her daddy know she was out there too?"

Nia drapes her school skirt across a third of the length of line. "Probably not."

"You should put *that* in your paper."

"I told Mummy what happened on Friday. Did you tell Angel?"

"Toons said something, I think. What you said?"

"The part about us getting run off the beach. Anyway, she saw me come off the back of the truck so it wasn't really a secret. Anyway, I can't afford to get in any trouble. Mummy thinking about if I can apply to the art camp."

"Why not just let you apply and decide whether to send you if you get in?"

Nia rolls her eyes. "Since when anything she do make sense?" She moves over to the row I'm trying to clear and sprawls a blouse out across the line. She's just about caught up to me.

"True. Hey, you gettin paid for your clothes to take up room?" I complain.

She reaches into her basket and pulls out a handful of wet socks. "Just these, then I'm done. So anyway, now I have to wait while she look at the application, then decide if she want let me go away that long."

"Yeah, well, I have the opposite problem. My daddy won't get off my back about applying. He's all like *you write poetry, you need to go.* He don't even know I don't write my poems down."

Nia says nothing, but I know she thinks I should be glad I have a daddy in the first place. Times like this, it's useless to talk. She's the one who doesn't know her father, so her feelings always win. I unpin the last skirt; it's still a little damp, but I'm done with laundry. What I want is to go inside—not to Angel and Sammy's love shack, but to our home, Angel's and Toons' and mine. I want to stretch out and close my eyes and smell the old-house smell with the new-tide breeze, hear Toons' music through the wall and Angel humming in the kitchen while she clinks and clanks dishes into the cupboard. Those moments when it's just us are what I long for most— moments like that are when poems are born.

Nia pins up her last piece of clothing—she's managed to use three full rows to put two sets of uniform, a few pairs of socks, and a couple bits of underwear out to dry. "So you ain even tryin to get into the camp?"

"Haven't decided. I have a new poem, if I could convince myself to write it down."

Nia leans on the tree where the line is anchored. She doesn't want to head back into her house any more than I want to go to mine. The truck glints behind her as if Sammy himself is looming over her shoulder, listening in.

"You wanna hear it?" I say, half to defy the metal shadow, half to stretch out this moment a little more.

"Always," she says, as if I'm offering her cake.

"Twilight
moon bright
curtains lift, dark birds in flight."

The second I start to speak, the application, the closed curtains, the truck, even Nia—they all fade away.

"Ocean calls
through the walls
bare tree stripped down, still stands tall."

I close my eyes and there, behind my lids, behind the words, I find it. Peace. Home.

"Feet on sand
hand in hand
walk to where the sea meets land."

The words are being born all over again, and my body

is agreeing *yes this is the way to go, up here, breathe there, pause, speak.*

"Love's bliss
first kiss
stay until the morning mist."

There is a moment of even more perfect silence, the way cleared by the fallen words. My whole body is calm, is sure. I belong here, in this space left behind by my poem, and the words have opened up the possibility of more poems after, and more, and more.

"I love it." Nia's voice is all awe. "'Twilight, moon bright.'" My words in her mouth make me open my eyes. It feels wrong to my ears, but I push the thought out of my mind. She's my best friend. I can trust her with this. "Wish I could write like you."

Around us, everything is still here. Truck, line, basket of Faith's clothes, curtains drawn, closed door. Yet it's all different—smaller, as if I can put my arms around it, lift it up and set it down where I need it to be. "It's not writing."

"You know what I mean."

A clothespin glints up from the grass. I bend down to pick it up. "What you usin for your application? The newspaper?"

"That's Mummy's thing, not mine. Hey, imagine if I printed one of your poems in the paper."

"Um, you better not."

"Yeah, I know. You like it when your poems live on air."

I smile at her as I clip the pin in her hair like a bow. We're so different, some moments I ask myself how we could even be friends. Then she'll say one thing that shows how much she knows me, not my life, not my secrets, but the pure, distilled, original me.

The door to the house opens and Sammy sidles out toward the truck.

"New daddy!" Nia calls, her voice a little too loud for her joke to stay just between us.

"Don't even." I glower at his retreating form as he climbs in and ignores us, starting the truck up.

"Keeks, you sure those things dried through?" Angel calls from the doorway. Her words float out like jasmine, heavy, thick, sweet. Like she doesn't care if the whole neighborhood knows she and Sammy were together in the room.

"Pretty much."

Angel sails out in a short-sleeved shirt and a mini skirt and glides between us. Her arms are full of wet clothes. Delicates. I recognize the slick strap of a satiny red camisole, tangled up around something made mostly of lace. She swivels around and examines the clothesline.

"Pretty much ain good enough. If we send the people home with things half done, they won't come back." She drapes her lingerie over the strong point where line meets thick metal frame. "Sunday night is our night to have the line."

Nia slips away, guilty or fearful, or both. Angel sets about rearranging what my friend hung up so badly, snapping the clothespins impatiently back into place. "I don't know what wrong with that girl's head. Think she owns the world."

"The clothesline is the world?"

"Smarty-pants." Angel snaps a damp T-shirt at me. I dart out of the way and duck behind her to make space on the other side of the line. "I need a place to hang up my things, is all."

I look away and close the wooden clips over each end of a lacy thong. Everyone has underwear, obviously, and it's all clean, but a part of me wishes she could tuck it on the back line, a little less in plain view. I move on to socks. Nia's mummy never has her hanging racy underthings three feet from the road. "Nia want know if Sammy's my new daddy." Beside me, Angel shakes out a deep purple cat-print contraption. Its satiny black ribbons flutter, giving off water and bits of grass.

"She need to stay out of grown people's business. Look, Paulette coming." Angel peers over my shoulder. I turn to see her strolling up the road, in our direction. Toons is nowhere in sight.

"I got it." I slip over to the covered patio area, where the washer is crammed under the awning. I reach behind the detergent for the stash. My fingers find the easy slick of a plastic wrapper. I pull it out and the pink square winks at me. I peek at the seal, and there it is, a trio of condoms folded up and tucked into the pad. If you weren't looking for them, you'd never know. I reach for the hamper of clean clothes Paulette's picking up and slide the secret between two shirts.

"I don't know where that boy is," Angel's saying as I join them at the line. Paulette gives me a smile as she takes the hamper. "Now make sure you hide that," Angel adds. "I don't want Mr. Rahming on my case."

"Of course."

A creak interrupts us. Across the yard, Nia's mother steps out of their side door with a bag of garbage in her hand. She stares straight ahead as she passes us on the way to the bin.

"Say good evening, girls," Angel says loudly. She shakes out a bloodred thong. Paulette laughs nervously and slinks away. I wish I could do the same. Nia's mother marches past us again, her head high. "Can't forget our manners. We girls never know when we might need each other around here." Angel's voice rings out, bell-clear and foghorn-loud. "Right?"

"Mummy!" I elbow her, but Nia's mother doesn't seem to notice as she disappears back into her house.

"What?" Angel tosses her pink hair. "I ain shame."

"You actin like Nia's mummy comin to us for . . ." I nod after Paulette, who's halfway down the road by now.

"And if she did, I wouldn't be shame then, either. We ain doin nothing wrong, remember? Somebody gotta make these things accessible."

I turn back to the line, and a breeze lifts a curtain of nylon lace into my face. *I know*, I want to answer back. *But how come it has to be us?*

EVE

When we're done eating, Faith is the first one to push her chair back. "That was good." She pats her belly. "Wanna watch something?"

I try not to look at my parents' empty chairs at either end of the table, the matching pair of unused knives and forks, their napkins still folded, untouched. "We gotta go down to the church for a bit. You could come too."

"Nah." Faith stands up. "I'll try catch my daddy home. I need him to look at my car, it sounds kinda funny."

"We gotta go back to church?" Esther whines.

"Shhh." I look down the hallway. "They tryin to rest."

"Okay, see you tomorrow," Faith calls as she slips out the door. We've been friends long enough for me to know that an afternoon of moving chairs around the church isn't her definition of fun, but I wish she could have just stayed, for me. If I can't have good company, I think, I'd rather not drag this pack of kids behind me to whine and complain the whole way. I fish around in my church bag and take out a ten, then wave it at Ruth.

"Take them by Mr. Rahming's store for an hour?"

She examines my offering, then hauls Junior up onto her hip and herds the other two out the door. I clear the table, then reach for the phone on the kitchen counter. In the silence, I pick up the receiver and dial Toons' number. It goes straight to his voice mail.

"Hey, it's, um, Eve." For an instant, I feel treacherous, and not for foisting the little ones off on Ruth. What would Faith say if she knew I was calling her crush? Then I push the thought out of my mind. If she hadn't been so eager to get out of here, she might be seeing him too. "Heading there now, if you free."

I push the church door open and find the building empty. Toons probably has something else to do. I rearrange the hall, set up a long table, line chairs up on either side, fill four bowls with water for fresh hibiscus in the morning. Most churches have pews and a set sanctuary. Ours has rows of folding metal chairs for the weekly service, and changes shape to fit whatever people need. Weekdays, it houses seniors groups and youth meetings and small study sessions, and for special occasions, it can do anything—open out for kids' parties and dances, get classy with tall candles and long tablecloths for fund-raising dinners, dresses up for weddings. Daddy's pulpit is the one constant, anchored at the front. It always makes me feel like this place is watched over, protected.

I turn off the lights. Familiar shadows stretch out over the room and fade into the floors and walls. Some people say a church isn't the building, it's the members, the spirit, the calling, the souls. Those people haven't been in our church, where old wood walls and the high, echoey ceiling hold the congregation together, hold a family together. My parents and I lived here, once, in the side rooms, when a good turnout had a half dozen people, when the service sometimes happened right on the wide porch, with the wind lifting Daddy's words to the sky.

I start to sing, quiet at first, *I've been loving you a little too long* growing louder, till my voice reaches the ceiling, making the windows tremble, knowing every spider-hiding crevice, every crack in the wall.

The church is packed and nearly rocking, thick-heeled shoes tap and stomp, hands clap and drums rumble and brass instruments blare joy and sass. I shift and tiptoe as I strain to see around jostling backsides and swaying bodies, but I can only catch glimpses of Daddy at the pulpit, and the heads of other children bobbing in between the adults. A row ahead, Nia turns and waves, her smile made of sunlight. Then she crosses her eyes and sticks out her tongue. Ms. Taylor flicks

Nia's ear and leans down to scold her. Beside me, Mummy shifts and fans herself. Her belly is large with Ruth. Then I feel a tap on my shoulder. I turn and see Faith behind me. She stands on a chair, and the folds and flounces in her dress bounce to the music. I drop to my hands and knees and crawl under my chair. She stretches out an arm and I take hold, climbing up. Yes—now I can see, through the bodies. Faith's big sister is on the end, singing and clapping, and her mother's eyes are closed as if she's in a world all her own. Now I have a good view of Daddy and the choir and the band. His hands are raised as the trombone player flares, bare brass horn twists a loose note that makes me want to squeal and twirl around and cry all at the same time. Below us, KeeKee emerges from under the same chair, and then Nia, and we jiggle and sway and dance, feet on the seats, our fingers woven together, palms sweat-sticky and soft. Our arms swing wild and high and if we bump the people in front of or behind us, they don't seem to notice or care. I don't even know what we're singing, but when it ends, the pianist freestyles a bridge to another, twirls and flourishes make the air around us ornate, and the other musicians follow along as we ease into "It's a Grand and Glorious Feeling." I look over my shoulder, out the open door, hear the ocean's lift and crash, waves carrying the song.

I let my voice fall. Silence settles over me, thick and complete. A board creaks and it might as well be thunder. I stiffen, listening. Footsteps start on the verandah, then stop.

"Not too bad." Toons' voice stretches out in the dark. "Need to work on your pauses, though."

"How about you work on your timing?" I toss back as I step out onto the porch. "I didn't think you was coming."

He steps into view, then turns back, as if someone trails him in the dark. "Yeah, sorry," he says, but offers no explanation. "You soloing or . . . ?"

I want to explode with yes, but I wouldn't dare sing that song with Toons, not at the church, not in the dark, even though it wouldn't be the most scandal these walls have ever heard. He and Paulette have been together for three years now. Mr. Rahming doesn't let boys in the house when he's home or at the store, which is always, and KeeKee says Angel has rules too—girls can come by the house, but they're not allowed in Toons' room. Three years is a long time for a guy like Toons. I'm sure they've found all our neighborhood's hidden corners, including the ones under this roof.

"Next time. So, you saw that guy from the other day? The one who chased us?"

Toons drums lightly on the porch banister. "Nope. I ain been down in the daytime since then."

"I told my dad about that."

"You told Pastor?"

"I tell him everything."

"Everything?" His voice is thick with disbelief.

"Almost everything. Anyway, I feel like it was kinda my fault."

"How come? You ain put that shell in my hand."

"Yeah, but I didn't stop you either."

Toons laughs. "Come on, man. That guy was beggin for it, with that attitude. I couldn't wait to throw that at him. Wild horses with a fleet of placards ordering me to cease fire couldn't have stopped me."

"Yeah, but . . . I should have tried. I feel funny about it."

"How?"

"Like trouble coming."

"Oh, Eve," he says, sighing, and the laugh is gone from his voice. Before I know what's happening, he's close, pulling me into a hug. I know how he means it, a friend hug, a brother hug. I know he's with Paulette. But something about this—pressed together, arms around each other, his smell, the echo of soap, cologne sprayed hours ago and faded to leave room for something like bay leaves and sunshine and a little salt and sweat—it's too private, too close. I don't trust this warmth seeping over and through me.

Then he lets go. "You good, little sis?"

I laugh to myself. It was nothing, I tell myself. Toons is totally unaware, or if he knows, he doesn't care. He starts to tap out a beat on the porch's wind-worn railing, soft, slow.

Thump . . . thump . . . thump . . . thump.

It's dark. I start humming along. My lips are sealed, but the lyrics blast in my mind: *You are tired and you want to be free.* And when the wind changes, just a little, and blows so I can't hear myself, only feel my core shake, I dare to sing the chorus, so soft no one could swear it was there. *I've been loving you a little too long . . .*

FAITH

Daddy's car is gone when I stop by after leaving Eve's. I ride around, stop at the mall, watch a movie alone. It's almost nine when I get back again. The house is dark, the windows open.

He's still not home. I let myself in and close the blinds, then turn on a few lights.

"Mummy?" I peer into her room. From the hallway's glare, I can see my mother's shape under the covers. She shifts soundlessly. If there's one thing lonelier than coming home to an empty house, it's being ignored when you know someone hears. *She's having a day*, Joy would say. *You can't take it personally.* She doesn't seem to understand that not taking it personally sucks just as much as accepting that she doesn't even notice me. I walk down the hallway to my room. I mean to wash my face, brush my teeth, put on pajamas, but instead, I fall asleep.

Even before I open my eyes, I know something is wrong with the world's sound. The distant squeal of a siren too crisp, too clear. The air feels overly fresh, almost chill, even though it's late May. It's almost as if I'm outside. I lie still in the dark and strain to hear anything else. Stillness—then footsteps, too heavy for my father's, too sure for Mummy. I sit bolt upright. They sound like they're coming from inside.

I reach for something heavy, but all my fingers find is my chemistry book on the nightstand. I tiptoe into the hall and pause outside my father's bedroom. "Daddy?" I whisper loudly. No answer. In the dim light, I can see his bed still neatly made from the morning. Across the hall, my mother's room is empty too. Carefully, I come around the curve into the living room. My heart thuds against my chest.

Our front door is flung open. A thin guy stands in the foyer, backlit by the streetlamp. His face is obscured, but I recognize the build, the set of the cap on his head. It's the same person who chased us off the beach two days ago. "Are you Faith?" he asks.

"I have a gun," I lie, but my voice comes out a squeak, and higher than it should be. I raise my textbook, ready to hurl it as hard as I can. My heart pounds so loud I feel it in my ears.

"Hey." He raises his hands in defense. "I brought your mother home. The man from the store said she lives here."

I fumble for the hallway light and snap it on. "Mummy?" My voice is weak.

"She's outside in the golf cart. Your front door was wide open, you know."

I open my mouth to call for my mother again, but no words come. *Stay calm*, Daddy would say. *No sudden moves.* I swallow, forcing my words to comply. "Mummy?" I call again. My voice shakes. He steps back out into the night and I follow cautiously. The golf cart, parked beside my car, is empty. It takes a minute to separate her body from the shape of the jasmine bush. Her head is bent forward like a cut flower left too long out of water, hair a tangled nest.

"See? You back home." He speaks to her as if his voice will calm her. She steps forward, and into a puddle of streetlight. Nightgown too thin, and nothing underneath. Her feet are bare, legs unshaven, sand stuck to her calves and ankles and toes. She seems so small. I rush forward and grab her arm, tug her toward the house. At the front door, she wrenches away from me.

"I ain no child," she mutters, as she stumbles inside.

I turn back to the guy. "Thank you," I start to say, but he's already back in the golf cart and pulling onto the road again. I shut the door and bolt us in, then put on the chain. I know I should guide her to the tub, wash her sandy feet, comb out her hair, lay her head on a fresh pillow slip, tuck clean sheets around her shoulders. But something holds me back and all I can do is lean against the locked door as she totters back to her room, alone.

I'm coming home as fast as I can. That's what Daddy said when I called the first time. Then *You want me to get Joy to come by?* I sit on the sofa and wait while night drags its arms around the opal face of the living room clock. There are no numbers on it, only a space where *11, 12, 1* should be. It leaves you to guess. To make up your own ways of telling time. Would Daddy burst through the door at Half Past Dawn? Or would my sister beat him at a Quarter to Who Actually Cares?

Joy wins, rapping on the door three times a few minutes before six, huffing out through her mouth sharply. "Faith," she says, hugging me tight and smelling of toothpaste and sleep. She steps out of her high heels and onto the sandy floor. "I bet you didn't get any rest. Why you didn't call me first?"

"She's sleeping," I say, and step away from her embrace. My eyes are burning. I don't want her comfort anymore. "I gotta go shower."

When I'm done and dressed for school, I step out into the hall.

"You really can't keep doing this, Mummy." Joy's voice drifts out from Mummy's open bedroom door, cheerful and fake.

"It's funny in here." My mother's words are flat.

"It's fine," I hear Joy say. "You lucky someone brought you home."

"I had to go lock up the studio. When I went, I couldn't get in."

"Mummy, the studio hasn't been there for eight years, remember? It's a church now."

"Church?" My mother's voice is incredulous, as though she's never set foot in the building since Mr. Armbrister took it over full-time. As though we didn't used to put on soft dresses and shiny shoes every Sunday, for a while, until things started to change. As though she's always been this way. Tears start to well up in my eyes.

"Yes, Mummy." Joy's voice is protective, persistent. Annoying. "You know the minister there. Faith's best friend? Her daddy."

"That's our studio." Her voice is insistent now. "I taught there yesterday. You forget, eh?"

I push the feeling down, but it only makes me feel sick to my stomach. I head for the foyer so I don't have to listen to Joy trying to reason with Mummy. If she actually lived here herself, she'd know there's no point. I unlock the door and step out into the morning. The sky is pale and new, soft blue as a Sunday dress. It's too early to leave for school, but I can go by Eve, go get breakfast. I let myself out and climb into my car, turning the key. It coughs twice, then catches, and I lurch out of the yard.

5

EVE

"Can we stop for grits?" Ruth squeezes past me to open the front door, her voice already rising to a whine.

Joe pokes his head around the corner, his shirt on inside out. "I can't find my pencil case."

"Where'd you leave it? No, Junior, sit back, sweetheart." Mummy frowns as she bends down to strap Junior into his car seat, the light smell of baby powder rising from her bodice. She insists on driving us to school, even though it's fifteen minutes away on foot. I'd rather walk there myself, slip in a little morning silence, but that's never been an option.

"Look under the sofa," I call as he disappears back into the living room. "And fix your shirt."

"I want grits too!" Beside me, Esther's breath is pungent from the tuna salad I threw together for breakfast, in between corralling lunches and spooning mashed banana into Junior's mouth. Mornings are always crazy, but today is different. Mummy only left her bedroom a minute ago, hurrying out and closing the door behind her. Daddy's been out of sight since he got up after dinner yesterday. I could hear the two of them talking last night when I got up to pee; then their voices fell silent behind their door, as if they could sense me.

"You all hush," Mummy says now, dusting bread crumbs off the front of Esther's dress. She hoists Junior's baby bag onto her shoulder. "Ruth, unlock the car so y'all can start getting in."

Ruth jams her feet into her shoes. "I don't have the keys."

Mummy rolls her eyes, then shoots me a pleading look. I wish for once she'd make Ruth pull her weight, treat her like she's thirteen instead of three, but there's no point getting in an argument when we're trying to rush out the door. I scan the kitchen. The key hook is empty, and they're not on the table. I don't see them in the living room either, although Joe is there, emptying the contents of his pencil case onto the floor.

"Someone took my eraser," he announces.

"Put your stuff away," I say. "We're leaving in ten seconds." I pause outside my parents' bedroom, then tap on the door twice. Nothing. I ease my way in.

The room is empty, the bed unmade. A gap in the curtains gives enough light for me to see the keys on the chest of drawers. I grab them, glancing at the bathroom door. Daddy must be in there. Should I call out? No, I'll just go. We're already late.

Retching, spattering. Then the wet sound of food being brought up. Then heaving.

"Shit!" Daddy spits out the word.

My legs are frozen. Did he . . . curse? I realize too late that my fingers are loose on the keys. They fall, jingling as they land.

"Gina?"

His voice shakes me into motion. He can't know that I'm in here, that I heard him. I grab the keys and run out of the room. On the way out the front door, I snatch Joe's abandoned pencil case off the floor, then stumble outside. Mummy reaches out for the keys and our hands touch, her fingers familiar and warm. I open my mouth to ask her what's really wrong, why Daddy's hand is shaking at the start of a sermon, why his knees are buckling. Why he's throwing up in the bathroom so hard he swears.

"But how come Daddy tired?" Joe asks, before I can even get out a word.

"People get tired." Mummy hoists Junior into the back, while the others climb in. I watch her face for a sign of guilt at this lie; obviously, Daddy's more than just tired. But her expression is blank as she clicks the car seat into place, then settles herself behind the wheel. She starts up the car and it coughs a few times, then groans into service.

"How come big head get to sit in the front?" Ruth complains, digging her knee into the back of my seat.

"A virtuous woman," Mummy says, backing out, "speaks with wisdom. Where is that from?"

"Proverbs Thirty-One!" Joe crows proudly, as though he's been studying the traits of a godly woman.

"That's right," Mummy agrees. "Wisdom, Ruth. Adjust your attitude accordingly."

Esther rustles around in her backpack. "I forgot my math book by Ms. Taylor."

"Man, you ga cause all us be late!" Ruth sucks her teeth,

suddenly concerned about tardiness. This time Mummy doesn't answer, easing toward the end of the street, passing the two little girls who come to Angel for breakfast every Monday and Wednesday, one of them five or six, the other not yet four. I peer through the windshield as we slow outside Nia's house. Faith's car is parked at the end of the road and Toons is rummaging around under the hood with Mark, examining the car's inner workings. Faith stands by the clothesline, a scowl on her face.

I hop out of the front seat even before Mummy's fully stopped outside, and hurry toward Faith. "You okay?" I call as I get closer.

"It cut off twice." Faith looks tired, and her blouse is untucked. "I called Daddy and he didn't answer."

Toons nods at me. I'm sure there's more to all this—she wasn't just cruising early morning for fun. Even the sight of Toons all sweaty and studious under the hood isn't enough to lift her spirits. I rest an arm on her shoulder. Faith's expression softens and she leans into me.

"Sucky start to the day," I say.

She looks like she might cry. "And it started last night."

I know what that means; something happened with her mum. She'll tell me about it later; for now, I want to ease things for her. I lean my head against hers. "Come with us."

Faith breathes a sigh of relief. "Space in your car?"

Internally, I chuckle. There's seven of us—there's never any space anywhere. It feels good to find a reason to smile, to forget what I heard at home. "Just suck in your gut. We'll find room."

Behind us, KeeKee jogs up, holding out a container of food to Faith. "Angel sent this for you."

"Thanks." Faith takes the dish, then grabs her bag out of the backseat.

"Faith, honey, you need a ride?" Mummy calls out the window as we reach the car. "Ruth, move over, let Faith slide in by you. Eve, you didn't get the book?"

"Oh—sorry." As I turn away, I can't help but roll my eyes. Couldn't Ruth have gotten off her butt while I was helping Faith? I suppress my annoyance as I knock on Nia's door. It only takes a minute, and Esther gives me a grateful grin when I hand the book to her through the open window. As I get back in, the smell of scrambled eggs and butter-laden grits greets me.

"Listen," Mummy says quietly as she turns the car around. "You good to get some stuff from Mr. Rahming after school?"

"How come?" I ask. Behind us, the younger ones are squabbling over Faith's food, Junior squawking like a baby bird, even though he was nursed and ate an egg before we left.

"I don't like how," she lowers her voice, glancing into the backseat, "certain people carry on when we go in the Tropi-Save. And I got something to do with your daddy this afternoon." Is her voice more serious, or am I imagining it? She checks the rearview mirror again, this time so quickly I'd miss the lines that crease her forehead if I didn't know to look. I want to ask her what it is, to tell her what I heard in the room, to ask her what's really going on. But behind us, Joe is kicking the back of the seat and Ruth complains that Esther is elbowing her, and Junior swipes at the spoon and hot grits end up on Esther's dress and Mummy has to swerve to avoid hitting another car after she turns around to scold them in the backseat and now just isn't the time.

"So, you'll go to the store?" Mummy asks, when we're on our way safely again. She depends on me, same as always, and now, I really have to keep stepping up.

"Of course, Mummy," I say.

NIA

A familiar tan car is parked in front of my house when KeeKee and I come home from school. Of course—Monday afternoon. Mummy's most meddlesome friend is over to talk politics and solve the world's problems over undersweetened iced tea and soggy food store cookies. Normally I go right inside to ditch my uniform for shorts and a T-shirt, but today, I follow Kee-Kee across the yard.

"Mrs. Jones here." KeeKee deposits her bag on top of her washing machine. She takes her phone out, checks the screen, then drops it back into the bag. It clunks, barely cushioned, against the machine's metal cover.

"Save me. What you doin now?"

"I goin down by the beach."

"Okay, okay, don't beg me for company. I'll come."

Her phone dings, a delayed complaint against being roughed up. She reaches back into the bag and rolls her eyes.

"Who is it?" I ask.

"My daddy."

"What happened?"

"He's nagging me about doing the camp application. Cut-off date is the end of next week."

"KeeKee, that's you?" Angel's voice wafts out like the scent of cake from an oven.

"I can't even get a minute by myself?" KeeKee snaps.

"What's your problem?" I ask.

"Somebody always want something from me."

"So . . . you don't want me to come with you?"

"KeeKee!" Angel's voice is more persistent now. "I hear you out in the yard. I need you to cut up onions for the tuna salad."

"Why people can't just go away!" KeeKee's anger spikes without warning, her eyes lit up with fury, her voice a hard bark that makes me step back.

"Fine, forget it," I snap, and stomp toward my own front door. When I turn around, she's long gone, even the bush around the path to the beach settled back into place. I feel unsettled, a tower with a concrete block chipped out at its base. KeeKee doesn't get angry at me. What does she have to be mad for, anyway? Her mummy calling her inside? Or her daddy texting her? Having your mummy nag you is just the way things go, and a daddy who tries too hard to reach you is a problem I'd love to have. *Whatever*, I think, and ease the front door open. The radio blares, blending with the conversation in the kitchen. Lucky. If I step light, I might be able to get in without Mummy and her prissiest of friends noticing.

The protest is to begin at six p.m. sharp, the announcer says.

"Think I should let her go?" Mummy's tone is hushed. I

freeze, listening; she's got to be talking about art camp.

A full police presence will be in effect, according to Chief Carey.

"It's a mistake, if you ask me," Mrs. Jones says, her voice shrill. I step closer, careful to avoid the squeaky floorboard by the wall, and try to keep out of sight.

This is the first of several events planned leading up to the government's decision, which will be made on Friday.

"It has to happen sometime." Mummy pauses, as if she can just about smell me, and I get the feeling this is about more than just the camp.

"You been carrying the secret of how that girl came about for too long," Mrs. Jones says, as though there are several methods of having a baby and I might have been dropped off by a migrating heron or left on her doorstep like a bag of bad-luck chicken bones, as though Mummy never actually *had* a man anywhere near her. I hold my breath, willing them to keep going. My father is the one thing Mummy never wants to discuss. I take another step forward and the floor groans under my weight.

"Nia?" Mummy calls. So much for hearing anything good. I step into the kitchen, where Mummy and Mrs. Jones sit at the table.

"Afternoon." My voice comes out a little too loud. "Hi, Mrs. Jones."

"Didn't hear you come in." Mummy and her friend look at each other. Clearly they'll trade comments on this later.

"Yes, ma'am." I set my bag on a chair. When in doubt or danger, extra politeness always helps.

The proposed hotel development would see the end of an era of beach access for the Pinder's Point community, where locals have used the coastline daily, one of the only neighborhoods where grass-roots families occupy properties adjacent to the water.

"Are we going to the protest tonight?" I make my voice sound eager as I slip the recorder into my bag.

Mrs. Jones tucks her purse onto her shoulder, then pushes a plastic bag on the counter toward Mummy. "I have to go meet my husband. No, sit down, I know my way out," she says, then looks me up and down. "What happened to her glasses?"

"Listen." Mummy rolls her eyes. "Don't get me started."

After the door closes, Mummy gets up and turns off the radio. "We need to talk." Her voice is stern. My mind races—did I do anything she might have found out about? She takes her glasses off, resting them on the table. Glasses. Maybe that's it.

"I checked, but I can't find my glasses," I say.

She furrows her brow but doesn't say anything else. That wasn't it. If I'd been sneaking around doing anything, I'd be scared. But if there's one thing I'm sure of, there's no trouble I could be in, seeing as all I ever do is go straight to school, come straight home, or head out with Mummy, tape recorder in tow. Maybe she's about to tell me the answer to the thing we never talk about. Maybe today is the day I'm going to hear about my father.

"I know you're waiting to hear about this camp."

I sit down. "You decided?" I try to make my voice casual.

"I don't make decisions like this lightly," Mummy says, and I feel it right away like a weight in my belly, a swallowed stone.

"You're not letting me go."

"Fifteen—it's too young to be away from home all summer."

"Kids a third my age go off to summer camps all the time. And it's not all summer, it's just six weeks!"

"You're getting to be grown now, and—"

"Grown?" I'd burst out laughing if I wasn't so mad. "I thought I was too young—"

"You need to understand." Mummy's voice is flustered. She knows I have a point but it doesn't matter anyway. It never does. "I can't have you sleeping out by any and everybody."

"Mummy, they have teachers and chaperones everywhere. I can show you on their website. They—"

"I don't know their teachers and chaperones."

"This ain *fair*!" My voice pitches to a shout as I shove my chair back. I know losing my temper will only make things worse, but I can't hold in my disappointment, my anger, my need to be free. "It's an all-girls program! What kinda trouble I could get up to?"

Mummy's voice is so quiet when she answers that I can barely hear her speak. "There's plenty trouble a girl can get up to anywhere."

"You don't even care!" I ram the chair back in under the table. "You didn't even think about it! You never meant to let me go."

I grab my bag and run into the backyard faster than my heart can keep up with. I expect her to call me back, but the only sound is my feet on the path. I hate her. I hate this place. I wish I had Toons' conch shell now. Wish I could let fly and watch it explode through the window glass. Send her running and screaming. Tear her out of this house and her secure little bubble, leave her scared and exposed while I escape.

The sand on the path is soft and dry against my feet, pulling me in farther. I could run till it becomes thick, then hard with seawater. Keep running. Never stop. I reach the place where the path spills out onto the beach and stop abruptly. Chain link fencing stands between me and the soft expanse of sand, its diamond design extending as far as I can see, left and right, barricading me out, or in. Breathlessness catches me. I lean my back against the fence. It gives slightly under my weight. I slide down, feeling my bottom sink into the dusty, pinecone-studded ground, and wrap my fingers around the fence's cold metal. This is as far as I'll ever go. I look up at the limitless sky. The clouds above me blur as my eyes fill with hot tears. Then I hear words. KeeKee's voice is clear above me, floating down. A bird in the middle of nowhere, singing just to sing.

"Dark birds in flight. Ocean calls through the walls, bare tree stripped down, still stands tall."

I stand up, trying to pinpoint where she is out here.

"Where the sea meets land . . ."

She is over to my left, where the fence is laid tight to the trees. I step slow, trying to avoid crunching leaves. Fallen guavas rotting on the sand squish between my toes as I ease myself around and between branches. There she is, over the fence, up the guava tree, resting in its arms.

"Until the morning mist."

It happens almost without thinking. I slide my recorder out of my bag. She makes a small, impatient sound, and I freeze.

"No, don't go like that," she mumbles to herself; she hasn't heard me. I hit Record and it's meant to be. She begins reciting her poem from the start. I lift my recorder toward the singsong of her voice.

". . . dark birds in flight, dark birds in flight . . ."

The recorder's slow, vibrating whir is a tiny heart beating in my hands. I don't know what I'm going to do with this poem in my hands. I just know I need to have it. I have no choice but to reach up and grab hold. Hang on tight and let it fly me somewhere better. Somewhere that's not here.

FAITH

"Sorry I can't give you a ride home." Eve's smile is apologetic. She and I walk in unison, our steps coordinated, even though she trails siblings behind her like a badly behaved tail. She has Joe's schoolbag in one hand. It bumps against my leg with every step.

"Joe ain keeping up," Esther announces, and we stop while Eve waves him toward us. I slip my hand into my bag and check my phone again. I reread Dad's last message to me at lunch. Can't get away from work. Joy's still there, she can stay till after school when the studio opens. A new message pings in. Locksmith installed a new lock, code 8735. Thanks for helping out while your mummy's not doing so well.

"You heard back from your dad?" Eve asks.

I pass my phone to her and she reads through the message, then hands the phone back without a word. It's one of the things I love about her. When there's nothing to say, she doesn't try to concoct a script, doesn't prod me into sharing more than I want to. We walk without speaking for a minute, till my thoughts are together.

"'Not doing so well,'" I repeat. "You think he serious? Like she has an upset tummy." I shove the phone in my pocket.

Eve leans in close and sidesteps Joe as he executes a fake karate move. "Watch your feet," she warns him, then looks at me. "You wanna come with us? Since you're walking."

I shake my head. "I'll just go by the dance studio early."

"Okay. Well, I better go so we can get home. I think something's going on."

"Still?" I search Eve's face. If she's really worried, she's hiding it well; there's only the faintest rumple in her soft brow, and that could be from Esther swinging off her arm. "Your mummy said everything's fine."

She shakes herself free. "Yeah, she *said* that, but . . ."

"Your parents are like the happiest couple in the universe. What you think they have to hide?"

She turns back to look at the others. Ruth has drifted off to walk with her gaggle of friends, and Joe is chasing another boy around, screeching like a hog about to get slaughtered. Not that I've actually seen a hog slaughtered, but I can imagine. "Daddy ain been out of the room since yesterday when we got home from church, and Mummy said they had an appointment today."

"She probably meant they were gonna, like, do it."

"Eew."

"How you think they got all a y'all?"

"I don't know. Osmosis." Her lip is turned up in disgust. Eve seems so young sometimes. "Anyway, it was something different," she says. "Something new."

I shift my bag on my shoulder and turn toward the parking lot. I might as well get going, if I'm gonna have to walk to the studio. "Probably just worried about everything that's going on with the development and all that."

"Yeah." She sounds doubtful.

I'm about to tell her to quit looking for problems, that everything's fine, when something catches my eye. A shiny green car, a very familiar-looking car, cruises through the parking lot, dub blasting through the speakers till they shake. Eve does a double take.

"That's your car?"

I squint. My car hasn't been that shiny in months. "Maybe Toons actually got it fixed. I'll call you when I get home."

She nods as I turn away and weave through the milling students. Sure enough, as I get closer, I can make out Toons behind the wheel, seat back so far it's almost horizontal. In the backseat, KeeKee is sprawled out, feet propped up by the window. Nia's in the front, jigging up to the music. The car eases toward me and slows to a crawl, and I feel a rush of relief. My heart does a backflip at the sight of Toons in my car, sitting where I sit. As the car reaches me, he lowers the volume, hanging out of the window. His grin is wide, a long dimple creasing his left cheek.

"Hey, miss, you want a ride?"

Nia grins from the other side of the car, teeth bucked forward like an overeager bunny. "We takin your car for the rest of the week!"

Jealousy pricks me like an oversized mosquito. Who told her she could get comfortable in *my* car? "Wonder what your mummy would say about that."

Nia's smile melts away fast. She opens the door, climbing out. KeeKee keeps chawing like a snacking camel, and doesn't even glance my way. Whatever. If she's the price I have to pay to stretch out this moment with him, so be it.

Toons leans the seat back another fifteen degrees. "It's running fine now."

"What was wrong?"

"I just tweaked couple stuff." He jingles the keys as they hang from the ignition. "So?"

"So?"

"Get in."

"You just gonna keep driving my car?"

He lowers his foot onto the accelerator, revving it. A couple boys from our grade turn their heads, grinning. I roll my eyes but hide my smile as I walk around to the passenger side. Nia steps aside awkwardly as I get in.

"KeeKee, you walkin with me?" she asks. KeeKee hoists herself upright, then climbs out. A bag of chips dangles from her fingers. Our eyes meet. I'm sure I detect a smirk, which I ignore.

"I'm good." I slide in and slam the door shut.

"Hope she at least says thank you," KeeKee tosses over her shoulder.

"What's her problem?" I ask, settling into the seat. Toons turns the music up again.

"Y'all girls," he says.

It's tempting to light into him about his cocky little jabs. *Y'all girls. Tweaked couple stuff*, like I can't understand big mechanical terms. But sitting this close, just us two, it's more tempting to lean over. I can't think of a single excuse to touch him that wouldn't be weird. "Thanks," I say.

"No big thing." He clips a corner. "So tell me. Where you need to go? Straight home, or . . ."

"Or where?"

He grins over at me and I almost melt right there. "Hey, I don't get behind the wheel often, so, you leave it to me, you could end up anywhere."

"I have practice at the dance studio at four, but I got some time."

He follows the curve without slowing down. "So we joyriding."

"Don't burn too much of my gas, hotshot," I say. It's meant to come out teasing, but I kick myself as soon as the words leave my lips.

"I put in ten dollars." Toons glances over, his eyebrows raised. He thinks he's got me. I see it then. The way his eyes pause on my face, slow. The way that dimple hovers, just on the edge of showing itself. Could he like me too? Maybe? "Ah, I actually rendered you speechless." He grins, so wide and smug the dimple is obscured.

"You put in regular or supreme?"

"Regular."

"I only run on supreme."

"And yet you ain think to put in some supreme oil, or top up your tires with superior air."

He's got me. I lean back, looking at him out of the corner of my eye. "Well," I say finally. "Look who swallowed a thesaurus."

The dimple appears, lingering for few seconds longer. Then a more serious look crosses his face. "You need to let your daddy or someone tune your car up for you regularly, though. You don't want it to cut out on you in the bush someplace."

His words catch me like a kick in the gut and in an instant, last night replays in my mind. That tilted feeling as I wake, certain the world is wrong but not knowing why. Huddled by the front door, waiting, watching, my eyes burning with lack of sleep, while the clock drags its fingers around till dawn, Daddy nowhere in sight. It's after three now, but nothing's really changed. My mother is still not the mummy she used to be, and Daddy's still missing in action, and in a few minutes, Joy will be leaving the house to head to the studio, and what happened last night could unfold all over again. I shouldn't be out cruising; I should be at home with her, watching her. Keeping her safe.

Toons reaches over, fingers on the back of my wrist. "You okay?"

"Yeah." My voice comes out strained, a thread pulled too tight. I will him to keep his hand where it is, to drive longer, to drive with me like this forever. I turn my head toward the window, welcoming the breeze on my face, letting it blow the unwanted thoughts away. We're past where the trees are thick and right where the seawall and the road meet. We pass a bench with an old woman sitting on it, a dog curled at her feet. Feels like I haven't been out this way in ages. I ease the window down, and warm breeze greets my skin. The air calms me, starts to make it feel possible that life is normal, that everything is okay. A few more turns and we're on the far end of the island where the driveways are paved better than the street, where homes are set so far back they can't be seen from the road. The car slows and Toons eases it onto a stretch of gravel by the seawall. Casuarinas touch arms above us. We sit, listening to the sea turn itself over on the sand, stretching its fingers up the shore, pulling them back. His hand is still on my wrist. I reach my other arm out the window, letting the breeze run through my fingers like water.

Neither of us hears the other car coming until the last minute, as it swerves behind us. He pulls his hand back as if I'm made of fire. I lean away. Just like that, he's someone else's boyfriend again. He pulls over to let the other driver pass. When the car is out of earshot, I clear my throat. "Thanks. For fixing it, and the gas and all that. How much I owe you?"

"You don't owe me anything." He taps the steering wheel. "You probably got someplace to be."

"I have dance practice in half an hour." I don't want to leave. I want what we had a moment ago.

"I should get you back, then." He starts the car up again. I catch sight of something on his neck. An ant marches along his skin. I reach out without thinking, and pinch it between two fingers. His face close, curls on his chin a soft bristle I can already feel on my cheek. He's holding his breath. I dust my fingers off out the window, setting the ant free. When I lean back into my seat, I hear him exhale softly again. We don't talk the rest of the way back to the neighborhood, but I can feel his breath all over me.

6

EVE

The last dish is washed up from dinner, my own homework done and Joe's and Esther's both checked, when the phone rings.

"Somebody answer that," Mummy calls from the bedroom. I pick up.

"Hello?"

"Good night, is Eve there?" Toons.

"Yeah?"

"Come practice?"

I hear the younger ones pestering Ruth to read them a story from her English anthology. I look up at the clock. After eight. It's well past dark. My eyes dart over to the church's activity schedule on the fridge. Tomorrow morning is the women's meeting.

"You there?"

"Yeah. Okay."

"Cool." The line goes dead. I hang up too. "Hey, I gotta go straighten up at the church," I say, and grab the keys to the building. I run a finger over the key for the gate in the new fence. It gleams bright silver. I shove it into my pocket. Ruth barely even looks up as I step out into the night. The air is like boiled milk sat too long, so still and warm it's almost formed a skin.

"Peaceful out here tonight." Daddy's voice catches me off guard. I turn around. I can just see his outline, sitting under the tree. His face is hidden in the dark, but I can make out a few papers in his hand.

"Off to the beach?" he asks.

"Yes. I'm gonna—"

He waves my explanation away. "I trust you. You're a good girl."

I look back toward the windows, lit up orange from the lamps inside. A good girl compared to who? Faith? I try to push away the memory of her sliding into her car, Toons behind the wheel.

Daddy shifts, then groans quietly.

"Daddy?"

He looks over at me, waiting.

"You all right?"

"What makes you ask that?" His voice is soft.

"I thought I heard . . ." I don't want to say. How do I ask if I heard him vomit today? Then swear? It's not so much the word, though I've never heard Daddy swear before. It's the loss of control. He must have been hurting, really hurting, to let himself curse.

"Have faith, Eve. All will be well."

It's an answer and it isn't. I'm used to Daddy being straight with me. I want to push through my fear and make him tell me what's really going on. I wait, giving him a chance to add more, giving myself a chance to gather my courage.

"Church may not be there much longer."

"Much longer?" Relief floods me that the subject's naturally changed. Then comes dread as his words settle over me. "I thought it wasn't for sure they was gonna start building out here." I know I've spoken too loudly from the way he sits up straighter, glancing toward the front door. He waits, as if hoping for Mummy to stick her head out the door and start talking about cake or dirty laundry or homework that needs to be checked. But no interruption comes, and he leans back into the chair.

"Developers offered the government a pile of money. They couldn't pass it up, apparently."

"Aren't politicians already rich?"

"The deal is done. Been done from spring. The people just don't know it yet."

Nia's words on Sunday replay in my mind. "I heard Faith's father was coming through the neighborhood telling people not to go on the beach or there'd be trouble. Do you think he knows anything? Maybe you could talk to him?"

"Him? He'd sell our house out from under us if he could." The first hint of disgust slides into Daddy's voice; then it's gone. "All things work together for good, Eve. You believe that. Don't you?"

I hesitate. "I guess so."

Daddy coughs, then suppresses it. "Times change, Evie. Things change. You can't let your faith be one of them." He clears his throat. "Anyway, just know I appreciate you."

I want to take a step toward my father, but it's as if a force is all around him, keeping me from coming close. I can't answer, can't think, can't breathe. Everything around us is on pause, suspended in midair. I stand there a long time. Long enough for Junior to begin wailing and stop, long enough for Ruth to boil a kettle and for it to sing. Across the street, Paulette comes out and waves at me as she turns up toward the main road, heading to her night classes at the college. She disappears. Above us, stars begin to emerge and greet each other. Angel's boyfriend eases down the road in his truck, his headlights a muted yellow. Then it's dark again. Daddy starts to snore, his head tipped to one side. The papers he holds slip, shifting in his sleep-slackened hand.

That small sound unfreezes me. I step closer and lift the papers from his loose grip. I'll put them inside, then go. Toons will be waiting. As I push the front door open, a bar of light falls across my face and onto the pages. It illuminates a letter on top. *Dear Jacob Armbrister, this is to inform you of outstanding moneys owed for the following services. Radiation treatment—*

I stare at the page. I must have read wrong. But the word is there, bold as day. *Radiation.* Cancer. He has cancer. I pull the door closed again, plunging myself back into darkness that's thicker, more complete, now. When my eyes adjust, I shove the papers under Daddy's chair. More questions flood my mind. What kind of cancer is it? How far along is he? When is he going to tell us about it? Why didn't he tell me?

I can't wake him up for answers. I can't even let him know I saw. If he doesn't want me to know, it must be bad. I start walking toward the street. When I reach it, I run. I don't care that my breasts jiggle, that my shorts ride up between my thighs, that my legs rub together. I don't care who sees me. I push myself to go faster, willing the hammering of my feet on the road to drown out my mind, to stamp out what is coming. From what is already here.

Toons is in the church when I arrive. He's humming "I've Been Loving You Too Long," testing it out, the back of his shirt hauled over his head like a hoodie, insulating the sound around him. I watch from the doorway as he lets his voice rise, riding the notes. I try to see what's so good about Toons. What would make a girl like Faith, a girl who could get anybody, look at him when she knows he's already with someone? He's tall, like Daddy. His skin is smooth. Otherwise, there's nothing uncommon in his wide eyes, his nose, the twist of beard sprouting from his chin. Isn't there enough to go around in the world? On the island? Enough boys? Enough beach? Do we all have to want the same people? The same things?

He stops abruptly, midmelody, as if he can feel me watching. "Hey, little sister." He hauls the shirt down off his head, shaking the fabric back into place. "Eve? You okay?"

I hold up a hand while I catch my breath. I don't want to talk. I don't want to think.

"Sing," I gasp. Then Toons is beside me, a hand on my shoulder.

"What happened? Tell me."

Radiation. Shit. Radiation.

"Nothing. Let's sing."

"Why you outta breath?"

"I ran here."

He frowns. "How come?"

"No reason. Let's start. I'm fine. Really."

He looks doubtful, but he goes along with me. "I been doing something different," he says. "Trying a little harmonizing. Listen, tell me what you think."

I listen, and while he sings, his voice shining alone, I look around at the walls, the ceiling I've known my whole life. The rafters that have always been there for my voice, for so many voices, to bounce off. *The church is not a physical structure.* But my father *is* physical, and like the church, he's weakening. Like the church, he may not always be here.

"Why you want keep me in suspense?" Toons says, and I realize I've zoned out.

"Sorry."

"You in love, ay?" he asks, and smiles. There I have my answer. This part of Toons—the eyes that see something wrong, the words that won't stop trying to make you feel warm, feel right—would have any girl wanting him near her. Especially when everything else might be taken away.

NIA

In my bedroom, I pull out the copy of the NewBeat application I rescued from the garbage. With shaking hands, I start to fill it out. In the space that says *special talents*, I pen in *writing*. Then I add another word. A word that would set me apart, that would make me special. *Poetry.* At the bottom, I pause at the line reserved for a parent's signature, then I scrawl in *Tanya Taylor* like I've seen Mummy do a million times.

My heart pounds out a guilty drumbeat as I press Play on my recorder. Should I do this? I'll just listen. There's no harm in hearing her poem again.

Then KeeKee's words swirl around me. They move me. They make my fingers lift a pen, force me to write the words, quick and sloppy, crammed tight into the space. My heartbeat speeds up more and more, making me feel alive, making me wish I could be her, could create something like this. "*. . . ocean calls through the walls, bare tree stripped down still stands . . .*" If I could write like this, I would use my words to weave me a pair of wings and fly me out of here. But until then, I think, maybe these borrowed feathers will do.

KEEKEE

I wake up to find Angel still asleep beside me. I reach over for my phone. There's a bunch of new texts from last night. The first is from my dad. I can check over your application this Sunday. Deadline is end of next week. Just try, Keeks. I thumb the screen to send an answer, then stop. What can I say? Not the truth, that writing my words down turns them tangible, vulnerable, something a committee of people in a room I can't see can tear apart and reassemble all wrong. Even worse, someone might put it together perfectly right. Too right. Hear the rhythm of syllables knocking together like waves on the bottom of a boat, get rocked into taking it for themselves. Written down, a poem becomes land, a thing that can be fenced off and taken away. I close Dad's text. Better for it to stay like water, free.

The rest of the texts are all from Toons, telling me he forgot his keys and begging me to let him in. I tiptoe out front and open the door quietly. Toons is stretched out on the porch.

"Hey." I rub the sleep out of my eyes. "I only just saw your texts. Who'd you go to see last night anyway? Doesn't Paulette have class Monday evening?"

Toons groans as he gets to his feet. "Mind your own business, and thanks for not helping," he grumbles, stepping around me. I check my phone again—I have to get moving or I'll be late. I sprint to the bathroom, but I'm moments too late: the door closes in my face.

"Toons! I gotta get ready for school."

"Yeah, and I gotta pee," he shouts back. Shortly after, I hear the sound of the shower turning on.

I grab my clothes and head across the yard. I tap on Nia's bedroom window. The curtains part and her face appears, her eyes barely open. Guess I'm not the only one who overslept.

"Can I shower over here?" I ask.

She lets the curtains fall into place. A second later, her side door opens. I creep in. "Your mummy up?"

Nia puts a finger to her lips, then points at a thin strip of light from under her mother's closed door. I follow her into her room and she takes out a towel and washcloth. "She been on the phone since six this morning," she whispers.

"Talking to who?"

"I don't know. She closed her door a little while ago."

"Maybe she has a boyfriend."

"I wish."

In the bathroom, the shower is ice cold, even after I run it on hot for a few minutes. The brisk water wakes me up all the way. It's invigorating, once the initial sting is gone. I reach an arm out and realize I forgot to bring soap. I reach a little farther to get the hand soap on the counter. I take two pumps, not too much, and rub my hands together. Rose-scented bubbles froth up my hands.

Morning light, garden
bright, petal fragrance red and white.

I towel off, bracing myself to dress fast out of habit. With Sammy around, I've perfected the art of getting ready quickly and without anything showing. But this is Nia's house. There are no overnight visitors. The only danger is Nia's mummy needing to get in the bathroom, and I can hear through the wall that she's still on the phone. I take a few pumpfuls of lotion and rub it into my arms and legs.

"No. *No*, I really think if you give me a chance . . ." I hear her say. I haul my skirt and blouse on. A chance for what, I wonder? "That was years ago," she says, sadly, then, "and I have excellent references." Her voice is small.

I jump at the sound of knocking on the bathroom door. I do up the last button, then open the door. Nia looks more awake now, her hair already combed. "You done?" she asks.

"Yeah, thanks. I better go." I step out into the hall.

"You don't wanna wait while I get ready? We can go to school together."

"I wish you'd just give me a chance." I hear the words clearly, from Nia's mother's room. Didn't Nia hear that too? But she looks back at me, so sure we're the only two people in the house with something to hide. Maybe my best friend heard it and is embarrassed to acknowledge it in front of me. Or maybe she just doesn't want to hear what's askew in her home.

"I have to put some clothes on to wash," I say. "I'll see you there."

EVE

At school, Faith finds us on our way to the grade two classrooms. She's got her usual spring in her step, and an extra glint in her eye. She tugs Esther's plait gently and taps on Joe's head before nudging me with her elbow, falling neatly into step.

"How come you look so tired?"

Guilt washes over me. "I was up doing homework," I say.

"Oh. So, guess who I was with yesterday?"

"Oooh, you got boyfriend?" Ruth chimes in.

"No one invited you to this conversation," I say, then turn to Faith. "Who?"

"Someone tall."

"And?"

"With a pretty complexion . . ."

Esther twists to look up at Faith. "Someone I know?"

I poke her. "Turn around."

Faith rolls her eyes. "Someone—"

"It's a boy?" Esther asks, too enthusiastically.

I shoot Faith a look that says *Put this on pause till these kids are in class.*

"We was hanging out," she whispers anyway. "After school."

"Mummy say Eve can't have a boyfriend till she eighteen," Joe interjects cheerfully as we arrive at their class blocks, grade one on the one side, grade two opposite. He extracts his hand from mine reluctantly; Esther is already engulfing her teacher in a hug.

"Eve don't want no boyfriend," Ruth says, trailing away from us.

"Y'all be ready at three. Wait inside, don't go on the playground," I call after the younger ones. Faith takes my arm. "So what happen, now?" I ask. "Who you was with?"

"Toons!" she exclaims.

Something flickers in me. What were they doing together? "You and Toons?"

"That was him in my car after school yesterday," she whispers, suddenly discreet. "And I think he like me."

Ruth's words play back in my head. *Eve don't want no boyfriend.* What is it about me that makes people think Faith and I are so different? If I told her about evenings at the church, what would *she* say? "So what—y'all together now?"

She pretends to look offended. "It was the first time we hung out like that."

"What about Paulette?"

"We didn't do anything. You my friend or my judge?"

"I'm not judging, I'm just saying—"

"Well, we didn't do anything."

"I hope not. You know he's taken, so."

"He may want something better." She shrugs, trying to look nonchalant, but a wide grin gives her away.

"Better than Paulette?"

"What you tryin to say?" There's an edge now to her voice. She drops my arm.

I want to say something reassuring, something best-friend-shaped. "It's the truth."

"Thanks a lot." Faith pouts. "You're supposed to be on my side." She turns off toward the field, heading for the bleachers. I keep going to our classroom, wishing I could have explained what I meant. Wishing even more I could understand it all myself. What makes one person better than the other? And what if Toons decides one day he wants someone better than Faith? I wish I could ask Daddy these questions, but he has bigger things on his mind, and Mummy would just wave it away, tell me not to worry about it till I'm out of school. I slip into the classroom, take out my book. I chew on the end of my pen, trying to get the words to come. *You and Paulette are both equally as good*, I write, but the words sound flat when I read them in my head. Truth is, neither of them deserves half a boyfriend. And there's another truth, riding under the surface of this one. A question I don't want to even acknowledge, let alone ask.

How good am I?

As the bell rings, Faith stalks in, back straight. Heads

automatically turn. After all, she's a dancer. Her body is a tool she's trained to use. It can steal a boy away from his girl. It's what gives Faith the fierce glint in her eye. It's why no amount of snatched songs in dark rooms could ever give a girl like me a chance with Toons.

7

NIA

I sit at the desk, scanning over the Thursday issue of *Pinder Street Press*, when Mummy comes home, a food store bag in her hand.

"Don't print it yet, I want to look over something before you do," she says, and reaches into the shopping bag to pull out a block of cheddar cheese. "I thought we could make macaroni tonight, as a treat."

"We're out of gas."

"Not anymore." She rustles deeper into the bag, fishing out a carton.

I'm not in the mood to be pacified, but I'm actually hungry. "You got eggs?" I ask. "And cream?"

"In the bag. Fresh broccoli too."

She must have spent two weeks' worth of grocery money. I don't even know the last time we cooked like this. Mummy heads into the kitchen. I abandon the computer and follow her. What's the point in being mad? I have to eat either way, and at least it isn't a cold sandwich with sausage from a can. She takes out the grater and I prepare the glass dish while she washes an onion and sweet pepper. It's been a long time since we fixed food together, real food, things that involve heat and slicing and flavor. Tonight, our kitchen will be the one producing tempting aromas that windows and walls can't contain. She starts chopping while I grate. The cheese unfolds into dozens, hundreds, of orange ribbons. If I had my way, I'd make the world's craziest macaroni, skip ordinary cheddar and get my hands on Swiss and fancy Parmesan that comes in a wedge. I'd pick up feta, crumble it with my own hands.

"You ever tasted feta?" I ask, breaking the silence.

"Feta?" Mummy frowns as she gets down the oil, passing it to me. I reach for a pot and pour in a circle, twirling it, watching it thin and spread with the heat. "It's salty, I think." We work in perfect rhythm, moving with and around each other, building toward a single task. The onion fries, its fragrance rising into the air, declaring our news to the neighborhood: We're eating well tonight.

"So, did we win the lotto?" I pause in grating. Mummy leans over and runs her fingers through the cheese. Her hands are small, her fingers ending in delicate points, her nails neat ovals trimmed low. I try to imagine the man who once held that hand. I must have his fingers; mine are thick and strong, my palms bigger than most of the boys in our class.

"The Higgs boy? He got top marks on his last set of tests, and his parents gave me a little something extra."

"That's great, Mummy. I thought maybe you had a new boyfriend or something."

She looks over at me sharply. "We don't live like that in this house."

"I was joking." I wrap the rest of the cheese, then tuck it into the fridge. "You ever had Camembert?"

"No." She says it like such a thing would be ridiculous. "Speaking of papers. Before you print this evening, I want you to give more balance."

"Balance how?" I stir the pot. The onion has started to go slightly dark at the edges.

"Turn that off."

I lower the heat and stir it again. Another few minutes would let it caramelize perfectly.

Mummy reaches across me and snaps the burner off abruptly. "You don't remember what you wrote?"

"That was couple days ago."

She picks a copy up from the stack on the table. "Let's see. Here we go. 'The people who were protesting complained that Pinder's Point provides important beach access to local residents. A hotel would cause that to be lost. This is important because the Point is Nassau's only beach community where everyday people still live so close to the water.'"

"Yeah, so?"

"If they put up a hotel out here, it could be something good, too. The neighborhood needs new life. More jobs for young people. Like you, in a couple years."

I screw up my face. "You couldn't pay me to work in a hotel."

"Work is work, Nia." Mummy opens the can of evaporated milk and pours it into a measuring cup. "There are people around here who need a job. Badly."

I sigh. "I get it. You don't like my story."

"I don't like that you only told half the story." Mummy's voice is more serious again. "You should have included the developer's point of view, or at least why some people want the hotel to be built. There are always at least two sides, sometimes more. You know that."

"So, I was supposed to go house to house and ask people what they think? Hey, how many eggs do we need?"

"Just take out two."

I reach for the carton. Why do we have to talk about the stupid paper? I don't want to argue. I want to caramelize onions and watch cheese melt into cream. I want to smell macaroni getting crispy edges in the oven. Next door, Angel laughs.

"If there was a hotel out here ten years ago, things might even be different now. Might have cleaned up this neighborhood," Mummy continues.

"It's not dirty. Anyway, I like how things were before."

"What about opportunities? You don't think those matter for the kids through here?" She shakes her head, impatient, and reaches for the eggs. "Look at Toons. All he does is lie around that woman's house. Coming in all kinda time. You don't think he could do better?" For a moment, we both hold on to the egg package, a Styrofoam bridge between us.

"'I don't really care.'" I pull my hand away. "Toons isn't my boyfriend."

Mummy sets the carton on the counter. *"I don't really care."* She twists her voice into a squeaky-toy parody of me. "History is happening right around you and all you care about is boys and running up and down like you're wild."

"I care about going to camp, but you won't let me do that, so . . ."

Mummy ignores my bait and cracks open an egg, then scowls into the bowl at a tiny speck of red. She pours the egg into the empty can, then reaches for another. A sharp crack; her movements are so sure. Spill into the bowl. Another perfect red dot. She pushes the bowl away, disgusted. "Blood in these eggs. I have to take these back to the store." She pushes the carton into the bag and reaches for her keys.

"Ain ga wash your hands?" I mutter.

"What's that?"

"Nothing."

Mummy takes a wet wipe out of a pack in her purse, like that shows me who's really in charge. "That's the problem with you, Nia," she says, opening the door. "Always got something to say, except when it matters."

When she slams the door behind her, the whole house shudders. I look down into the bowl at the egg, vulnerable without its shell, yet holding together, in a way. Carefully, I reach in and lift off the specks of blood. I'll show her. I turn on the fire, and the onion begins to sizzle again. I whip up the egg with a heavy hand of the milk, and season it with salt, pepper, and garlic powder. I boil the pasta, then add that into the pan with chopped broccoli. Finally, I add the eggs and let it cook slow, until it's set, smothering it with grated cheese. It looks and smells amazing, I think. Pity Mummy won't even get a taste. While it finishes off, I print the usual twenty copies of the newspaper. So what if she doesn't like what I wrote?

I wedge the papers under my elbow, grab a stack of

small plates and the pan, then step outside. I march over to KeeKee's house, where Angel and Sammy and another man and woman lounge near the front.

Angel sees me coming and tilts her head up, sniffing. The other woman smiles broadly, flashing a gold tooth.

"Good afternoon," I say, loud and clear. "Any of y'all would like a copy of my newspaper?"

Sammy peers up from his hand of cards. "What you got there, princess? Don't smell like paper to me."

Princess. The word is a drop of honey flicked onto my skin. I let myself look him straight in the face for a second. "Frittata."

"Fri-what?" The woman's tooth glints as she takes a newspaper.

"I don't know what kinda funny food that is," the skinny man says. "Y'all playing or what?"

"Don't mind him," the woman says. "I'll try it."

She helps herself to a slice. "Ooh, hot!" She sets it down neatly on her plate, licking her fingers.

"This looks nice. You need to teach KeeKee how to make this," Angel says, taking a piece too.

"Hey, don't forget me." Sammy reaches over, his hand hovering over the dish. Finally, he reaches for a piece closest to my hand. His finger just brushes my wrist as he lifts the slice away. "Look real nice," he says. His eyes meet mine and it feels like he's noticing me, not the dish. Is it my imagination? No one else is looking, the women too busy tasting, the man scrolling through his phone, and I can't be sure. It's just my imagination, I tell myself, and smile back, so I don't seem rude. When I turn around, KeeKee's at the door.

"Hey," she says.

"Hey." My mind goes to the poem, to her words trapped on the thin reel of tape, to her rhymes, printed out in my best handwriting. I think of the application, filled out, folded up, hidden in my bag. Is it my imagination or is she looking at me like she knows?

"What wrong with you? You comin in?"

"Yeah." I look over my shoulder, but there's no sign of Mummy yet. I follow KeeKee into the soft clutter of her home. Pairs of shoes socialize near the entrance, Toons' sneakers bumping toes with KeeKee's dusty penny loafers and a risky pair of bright-green heels that must be Angel's. The kitchen counter houses the black-bottomed pot and misshapen foil pans they use for breakfasts, with that moon-shaped lamp pushed up under the window. Its bulb is dark, for now.

"Your mummy out?" Her way of asking why I'm here in the evening, when I'm not allowed over, let alone inside.

"Yeah. And I made food." I hold out the half-empty pan of frittata and she shakes her head. Something's up. Does she know? How could she?

"I thought you came for your glasses." KeeKee slumps onto the sofa. "I still haven't seen them." She inspects the pan, then settles back into the cushions. "Egg in that?"

"Yeah, and—"

"I'm not hungry."

I set the dish down on the coffee table. *Curtains lift, dark birds in flight.* The words to KeeKee's poem flutter against my mind. Outside, the clink of dominoes is tempered with laughter and conversation. KeeKee sighs. Does she not want me here? "What's up?" I ask, trying to sound nonchalant.

"I just feel off."

"Your period coming?"

"It ain that. Like too much things gone down around here and it's just stuck in the air. You know?"

I don't. To me, not nearly enough happens. If it did, maybe I wouldn't feel so desperate to get out, to be anywhere but here. But I want to feel like KeeKee and I are sharing something. "I get it."

KeeKee carries on. "This girl came here a few nights ago. Like round our age. She look like she hadn't eaten for weeks, not properly. She was jumpy, like any second someone was about to hit her. She had these scars." KeeKee uses a finger to draw three diagonal lines across the insides of her arms.

"What you think happened? Somebody did it to her or she did it to herself?"

KeeKee shrugs, as if it doesn't really matter. "Couple weeks ago Mr. Roberts's son been here and slept on the couch cause his daddy locked him out for stealing his wallet."

"You weren't scared to have a thief stay here?"

"What was he gonna take? Anyway, I just feel it."

"Feel what?"

"Bad vibes. Everywhere."

The room is starting to feel hot. I look over at the windows, but they're already cranked open. Outside, KeeKee's mother and her friends chatter, laughter rising and falling in uneven waves. I don't want to talk about all this. I want what they've got. Freedom at the end of the day, the clink of bottles that have them wafty and loose. "You got any more nail polish?" I ask, trying to change the subject.

KeeKee looks down at her hands. "Yeah, but we'd have to take it off before school tomorrow."

"I don't care."

She sighs and gets up, heading for her bedroom. "My dad won't ease up about this camp application either. I wish he'd just get off my back already."

I wait for her to say more, to show some sign that she knows, but she just opens the rhinestone-encrusted glass box on the bureau. We perch on the edge of the unmade bed, dragging bright-orange and banana-yellow polish across our fingertips, erasing the naked pink and white of our nails, emblazoning color across our lives.

"Nia Taylor!" Mummy's holler breaks through the stillness.

KeeKee looks over at me. "Busted."

"Nia, honey," Angel calls through the window, "time for you to go home."

"Don't forget these." KeeKee holds up the rest of the newspapers, still unfolded. A translucent grease mark stains the ones near the bottom, a smudge of nail polish on the one at the top. I get up carefully, so I don't smudge my toes, and make my way outside. Mummy stands off, apart from the action, a priest glowering over a gambling den. As soon as she sees me, she turns back to our house, knowing I'll follow. Behind us, the atmosphere thaws again. The big woman chuckles as she settles her domino tile onto the table.

"Ahhh, beat *that*!" Sammy smacks a tile down hard, making the bottles on the table chatter like nervous teeth. I turn back to see their faces lit up under the porch light's glow.

"Get in here," Mummy snarls.

I hold up the rest of the papers—I know I'm pushing my luck and I don't care. "Don't you want me to finish handing these out?"

She swats at me as if I'm a fly as I slide in past her, and I twist out of the way. "I *told* you not to print that yet! And who sent you over there? I can't leave the house now without you taking off?"

"All I did was go next door."

Mummy snorts. "That's all you did."

"I made a frittata and I wanted to share it."

She stares me down, and for the first time, I realize I'm almost as tall as she is. She purses her lips, then shakes her head. "I can't deal with you." She pushes the fresh carton of eggs onto the counter and walks past me, heading for her room. The way she dismisses me so easily—like I'm not even worth a fight—makes me snap.

"Maybe my daddy should deal with me, then."

She whirls around and stalks back to me. "Don't you try to change the subject. You know you don't have no business over there. And wasting food—"

"Angel gives food away all the time."

"So what, now you want follow after Angel? Want to have men sleeping over every other night like she don't have a young daughter in the house?"

"She only has one man sleeping over, and nobody's doing anything to KeeKee. And at least over there they actually help people instead of just writing stupid stories no one even reads," I say.

Mummy grabs up the carton and smacks it down on the counter, hard. Yolk oozes through the holes in the box. "You are a *child*! You don't know how this world works. You think you know everything, but you don't!" Her voice rises, then falls off. "You don't know."

We stand there a minute, Mummy, me, and the box of broken eggs. Laughter from across the yard seeps in through the mesh screens. Mummy looks over toward the window. For a moment, she looks terribly small.

Then she pulls herself up to her usual height, and scoops the mess into the garbage. I turn away and walk down the hall to my bedroom with the door that can't close. I lie down in the dark. This is the only world she wants me to have. I reach for the recorder and slide my headphones into place. I close my eyes and press Play, letting KeeKee's poem unfold, letting my mouth shape the words, letting the words drown out this world. A world built on the lie that Mummy is perfect and that I'm not the product of a secret she won't share. That my whole experience is a mistake she believes I'm destined to repeat.

FAITH

"Good work today, girls," my sister says at the end of Thursday-afternoon practice, clapping her hands together. A couple of the girls shove past me briskly, bumping me out of the way. I square my shoulders and stand firm. This is *my* family's dance studio.

"How you doing?" Joy asks me, pulling me into a sweaty hug.

"All right."

She lowers her voice. "Mummy was really out of it today. Daddy know how bad things are?"

I step back. "I dunno. Ask him."

"I asked the neighbor to look in on her this afternoon, but I don't think she should be home alone. He's been working late a lot, hey? Is he home this weekend?"

"No clue."

Joy runs a hand over her head. "Maybe she shouldn't be home at all."

"So where's she supposed to go?"

Joy opens her mouth as if she has more to say, then checks herself. "Want a ride?" she asks instead.

"No. I drove here."

She frowns. "Daddy told me your car had to get serviced."

"It's fine now."

"I don't want you driving if it could just cut off on you, Fay. Daddy ain here and I have classes till nine. Who's gonna come for you if it breaks down again?"

"It's fine!" My voice comes out sharp-edged. I fumble to soften it. "Someone fixed it for me. I gotta go." I sling my bag over my shoulder and head for the door. Joy's too fast, though; she steps in and blocks my path.

"What's his name?"

I look her straight in the eye. "I didn't say it was a *he*."

My sister holds my gaze a moment, then tosses her hands up. "Fine, whatever. You wanna stay and help me tidy up for next class?"

I don't answer, just throw my bag in the corner and reach

under the counter for the spray bottle and cleaning cloth. Wiping fingerprints and smudges off the mirrors that line the walls is still better than going home. In the reflection, I see Joy sweeping behind me. She whisks the broom over the wooden floor, stepping back, forward, humming under her breath, so seamless, so natural I don't think she even knows she's doing it. *Last summer in the kitchen, spilled bucket, wet mop, my mother's bare feet on the soapy floor going forward, forward, back, back, doesn't miss a breath as she trills, "Charleston, Charleston," her laughter spills out like clean water, fresh, clear, my legs ache to keep up with her even though we're the same height now. I skid and she grabs my waist and we both slide across the floor, cackling so hard our stomachs ache. She catches hold of the counter and we careen to a stop, our faces wet with sweat and mop water and tears and as she straightens up, she is graceful and perfect. Still a dancer inside.* I look away from my sister's reflection, grab the cleaner, and spray it again and again, until I can't see her anymore.

"Mummy was amazing." Joy appears beside me, so close her arm hair tickles mine. The past tense irks me. I move away, scrubbing at the glass.

"I know."

"She was always shy, and a little dreamy, but that was just her way. That's what I thought for a long time, anyway. She could dance better than me, too. I wonder if she still can."

"She can." This time I don't care that my words come out hard.

"I blamed myself for the longest time. All those years we

were together, I never knew anything was wrong with her."

I toss the cloth back under the counter and throw the cleaner down after it. Why does she do that? Make our mother into a freak? I grab my bag and storm outside, letting the door bang shut behind me. My hands are shaking as I unlock the car and climb in. *Don't follow me. Don't.* I turn the key in the ignition. There's a tap on my glass. I stare straight ahead.

"I know it's hard, Faith. She's my mummy too. I love her." Her voice, muffled through the window, goes high and funny. She wipes at her eyes. "But I can't change how she is. My job now is to look after you for her."

I roll down the glass. "I'm good, thanks."

"There's more than one way to be taken care of, Faith."

"Okay. Got it."

"Just be careful. Don't let yourself get caught up in any bad situations. With boys, I mean. She wouldn't want you— going about, you know what I mean?"

"Do *you* know what you mean? I don't see anyone around here interested in you. When's the last time you even went on a date? 1903?" I feel a wave of satisfaction as shock, then hurt, registers on her face. "I gotta go," I say, and start to reverse.

"Faith, I'm not finished—"

I rev the engine, relishing its roar. I put it in drive and swerve onto the road. I don't think, I just go, letting the speedometer climb to thirty, forty, fifty, sixty. Instinctively, I'm heading away from home. Perfect. I follow the road's curve all the way to Pinder Street, then turn down. Mrs. Munroe's old dog skitters out of the way just in time. At the end of the road, I slam on my brakes and turn the car off. I need space. I need air. I need to move.

My feet can't find their way to the beach path fast enough. I push myself to full speed right away, arms pumping, stumbling over dry sand, regaining my footing, jolting my joints— all the things a dancer shouldn't do. Motion without emotion or flair. I lean forward, pushing myself harder till I run smack into a fence. My mind starts to question—when, why? I shut it off and start to climb, feet fitting into the diamond-shaped spaces easy. I get to the top, then jump onto the softness of the sand. I run again. I pass the church and keep going, push my body until I can't go any faster. Finally, I slow to a walk, letting breath flow into me steadier, steadier, till I feel normal again. As normal as I can be.

Three months ago, though her last episode feels like yesterday. The doctor leans forward. "I don't want you to keep getting your hopes up." I turn toward the face I hardly recognize—sunken skin, chapped lips from being licked too often, hair with perm three or four months too grown out, and those eyes that, for as long as I can remember, could go from blue holes, dark and swimming-deep, dangerous and refreshing and full of life, to black holes, to vacuums that can pull you in.

I force my mind back to the present. I face the ocean. Tide is high, the water churned up to a murky blue. Agitating waves form angry peaks. In the distance, I see someone sitting on the stretch of rock that juts into the water. Wait a second. I squint. Toons. I smile, then push away the pang of guilt that follows. Going home won't make my mother any better.

Anyway, I deserve to be happy, no matter what Joy thinks.

I climb up onto the rock. It's like walking on broken glass, but I hobble over it and plunk down beside Toons, shoving my sore feet into the sea. "What you doin here?"

He takes a swig from the bag, then points down at a swirl of faint red drifting into the blue. "What happen to you?"

"Actually, it feels good." It's not a lie, I welcome the sting. It tells me I'm alive. That the world still makes sense. Salt water in a cut *should* hurt.

"I thought y'all dancers was more careful with your tools." Toons pulls his feet out of the water altogether.

"Skin can heal."

"True." Toons lifts a bottle to his lips.

"Little early to be drinking."

He eases a bottle of Vitamalt up for me to see, then drains it.

"Poser," I tease.

"Masochist."

"Pretty big vocab for someone who ain doin nothing since they got outta school."

"Present conditions don't define my whole timeline." On his tongue, the words are rhythmic, slick.

"Smooth." I try to sound sarcastic. Never pays for a guy to think you're too impressed.

He tosses the bottle into the water. It bobs on the waves.

"And you litter, too?"

"Ain like it's ours."

"What?"

"Beach. Rock. Water. Why should I care about something if it's only getting taken away?"

When I look over at him, his face is calm. All except his jaw, lined with curly brown hair. Then I'm thinking of my hands cupping his face—rough hair half-scratching, half-tickling my palms.

"What you care for anyway? You got your nice house to go back to, end of the day."

His words hit me like a slap. I pull my feet out of the water. "I been out this way from before you came along."

Toons looks at me as if he wants to say something but can't find the right comeback.

"Not to mention, my mummy grew up here, so if anyone's an outsider, it's you," I add, for good measure.

He stands up, then before I can say another word, stretches his arms over his head, leans forward, and arrows his body into the water, piercing the blue. The ocean swallows him and panic surges over me—I went too far, broke the unspoken rule of people who grew up together, who know each other's most vulnerable parts. Then he surfaces.

At first, he does freestyle, body propelled on the strength of his arms. Then he switches to the butterfly, arms lifting, body undulating so smooth I almost forget to breathe. He reaches the bobbing bottle in half a dozen strokes, and I wish he had more distance to swim. He freestyles back, pulls himself up beside me, and sets the bottle between us with a purposeful clunk. He glances my way for a second before he looks out over the water and I see it in him, that spark, the fire that lives in a dancer's heart.

"Happy?" His lips tilt up in a grin.

"You ain scared to drown?"

He leans back. "It's just water. Anyway, this *my* beach." He sneaks another sideways look at me. "Even if I'm an outsider." He reaches for the bottle and lifts it to his mouth, forgetting it's full of seawater. He splutters. "What the . . ." And then he laughs and I catch it and we're both laid out on the rocks, our guffaws echoing off trees sky waves water each other, and my sides ache and I can't feel my cheeks. I haven't felt this free, haven't laughed this hard since . . . And then, for the second time this afternoon, I'm thinking about Mummy dancing in the kitchen. I can't go there, I have to be here, be now, be happy. Toons sits up, still chuckling. I straighten up too, and lean over fast, brush my mouth against his. He pauses, then kisses me back. Salty. Sweet.

He pulls away first, smile gone, and gets up. "I can't be—I'm with Paulette."

I stand up too. Paulette. I didn't think about her. *Exactly,* something whispers in me. *You didn't think. For that three, five, fifteen seconds, you could just be.* "I gotta go home," I say, and turn away from him, stepping over the rock, knowing he's watching me.

I walk the whole way back, grains of sand lodging into the cuts on my feet. Maybe I deserve it. Maybe I should feel sorry, feel guilty. Instead, all I feel is relief. There's something else I can turn my mind to now. From the memory of my mother's eyes, from the fading echo of her laugh, and the space that's left behind. That kiss, and this water, and the piercing of these rocks, they all tell me what matters most: I am here, still, and I am alive. I can feel. I'm still a blue hole.

EVE

When I get Toons' text, I make it to the church fifteen minutes before he says he'll meet me there. I push the door to the women's bathroom open, check that all the stalls are empty, then slip my hand into my pocket.

I pull it out. The tube of lipstick lies in the palm of my hand, glittery and magical, even closed. It opens with a satisfying pop. I roll the lipstick up and examine it. It has a slight orange tinge. I imagine wearing it would make me feel as perfect as a tree-ripened mangola eaten on a quiet stretch of beach, out of reach of sticky little hands and begging mouths. I hold it up to my face. Would it really match my skin tone? I've seen Faith wear this color, but she's a few shades lighter than me, and with her attitude, she can pull off anything. Still, if she picked this color for me, it must be a match.

I take a deep breath, then stretch my mouth into an open-lipped grimace and stroke a layer on. It glides on smooth, made for me. I stick a finger in my mouth, close my lips around it, and pull it out. Then I check the outer edges of my mouth. Everything is perfectly in place. I step back and look at myself. A woman stares back at me. An ordinary woman—oval-faced, high forehead, razzy hair—but a woman regardless, with glamorous, full lips that scream *bold*.

I turn to the side and suck in my tummy. Maybe Faith was actually onto something. Under my T-shirt, my heart starts pounding. Here, away from prying little eyes, it seems possible that another me exists. A me that doesn't constantly have someone hanging off her hip or arm or neck. Those red lips glint at me from the mirror, daring me to try more. I roll up the sleeves to my shirt, then tuck the shirt up so it bares my midriff. I push my lips out in a pout, turning to the other side.

"Not bad," I say out loud.

The door swings open and Toons bursts in.

"Hey!" I scramble to pull my shirt down but it's too late, he's already seen me.

"Oh, shoot—sorry, sorry. I didn't think nobody was here!" He backs out, hand over his eyes. I grab a piece of paper towel and scrub the lipstick off my mouth. "Sorry," he calls again from the other side of the door.

In the mirror, a ridiculous reflection frowns back at me—now my lips are stained like I got messy with a watermelon Blow Pop. I wet the paper towel, but somehow I end up with a faded smear across my cheek. I rub at the stain with the back of my hand. Stupid, stupid, stupid idea. "What you doin in the women's bathroom?"

"The men's is locked." He sounds repentant, humiliated. It makes me feel like I'm an elderly aunt he surprised on the toilet. "I didn't mean—I hope you weren't—"

"It's fine." Now my hand is smeared red. I give up and toss the lipstick into the garbage. It stares up at me from the fresh bag, ready to declare my experiment to the first deaconess who comes in.

"I didn't see anything, don't worry. I mean—nothing personal," Toons continues as I fish the lipstick out of the garbage and look around for a spot to discard it. The plastic spider plant on the counter catches my eye. He's still babbling through the door. "I didn't even think to knock, you coulda been changing, good thing you wasn't doing anything like—private."

Good thing, I think as I shove it under the dusty nylon leaves. *That would have been embarrassing.* I splash water on my mouth, then push the door open.

"Oww!" Toons backs away from the door, holding the side of his face. Just when I thought this couldn't possibly get more awkward.

"Sorry. You ready to practice?"

"Yeah." He turns around and leads the way to the main part of the building. Walking behind him, I pick up the planty, fishy scent of ocean. There's a smudge of dried salt on his arm. He's been swimming and couldn't even be bothered to shower. Even better. I'm making myself up like Bozo the Clown and he couldn't even rub soap on his pits.

"Ready?" he asks, stopping at the first row of chairs.

I nod, rubbing my hands over my face to clear away these ridiculous thoughts. I came here to sing. We should do that.

"I'll sing solo, then you come in on the chorus?"

"Yep."

He nods and I close my eyes. I start humming, and his voice melts all the awkwardness away, like forgiveness. Makes us new. Time moves differently, with music, we are at the chorus already, and I let my voice free. Our words lift and tumble and twine, taking leads, giving way, till our overlapping words line up in perfection, sync and balance, tune toning and rising and raising the roof till it threatens to break free, loose our song all the way to heaven. Then a hard buzz breaks in. I keep going, but it buzzes again. Toons stops abruptly, reaching into his back pocket. As he takes out the phone, he motions for me to keep going. The screen illuminates the dim room and I stop singing too.

"Sorry, my girl's looking for me." A guilty grin creeps over his face as he leans against the wall. "Just let me answer her."

"Which one," I mutter, as I suppress a sigh and fold my arms, waiting. I sit down and my foot bumps into something. I reach under the chair and bring up a hymnal. "I'll put this away," I say, getting up, and he nods, not taking his eyes off the screen. I walk to the back of the hall, my mind racing. This is where I'm supposed to pipe up. We're in a church, a place where lies are shunned, where truth reigns. I set the hymnal down on the stack of its brethren, then walk back. He's still hunched over his phone, a half-smile lifting his lips. "It's wrong." I blurt out the words.

"Wrong?" He leans against the wall, crossing his arms. "This is almost the same as we did it before, only—"

"I mean with Faith."

He frowns, putting the phone down. So something *can* hold his attention after all. "All I did was fix her car."

I shake my head again. "She told me something's up with y'all two." My heart pounds in my chest, the words too loud in my ears. "You shouldn't be fooling with her."

He shakes his head, and suddenly, I know who he was with when he went swimming, why he didn't have time to shower before he came to see me. Correction: before he came to sing.

"Eve, you reading into things that ain even there—"

"I live in a two-bedroom wooden house with a mummy and daddy who like each other enough to make five children in seventeen years. I know when something's going on between people."

"Well, okay. You ain had to bring Pastor in it like that—"

"You know what?" I cut him off. "I can't do this with you anymore."

"What? Come on, sis. Just practice with me, man. I need this. I know you do too." His face is wide open, his voice a song all its own. I should stick to my word, walk away and go home. But this building's being sold and this might be one of our last times to stand here and sing together. That's as much the truth as anything else. He snaps his fingers to the rhythm, so sure I'll give in. I know Toons doesn't see me like Paulette or Faith, doesn't think of me like that. And yet, he is here and wants to lay his voice beside mine, under mine, over mine, twist our tunes together. Plait them like straw, wear them smooth.

Snap.

Snap.

Snap.

Snap.

As I bring my fingers up to the keychain at my neck, I start to hum again. And in my heart I hear my voice shouting, *You* do *like him like that. You're just as bad as she is.*

FAITH

The thrill of that kiss evaporates the minute I pull into the driveway. My father's home. I get out and slam my door shut.

Inside, his shoes are neatly lined up. Pity he couldn't be so attentive about everything.

The house is closed up, lights turned on, creating the appearance of some type of normal. From upstairs, I hear a television. In the distance, water runs.

"Hey!" Daddy emerges from the kitchen, his dress shirt's sleeves rolled up. He opens his arms.

I sidestep his embrace. "I'm going in the shower."

"No hug for me?"

"I didn't think you even lived here anymore."

"I've been home for a couple of hours now. didn't you see my message?"

"It's not just today."

"I know. Your sister—"

"I was here by myself." I want to tell him how it felt to hear a strange man's voice ring out through the house, how my fingers were slick on the textbook, how alone I was in the house after, just me and the gaping hole where my mother's mind should be. But part of me doesn't want him to know how small I felt.

"Joy tell me she had it under control."

"Yeah, *okay.*" I start down the hallway.

"Faith." Daddy reaches out and I wrench away.

"Why are you even here?" My eyes sting. He's ruining everything. I would have just come home, heated up some of Joy's pumpkin soup, peered into my mother's room, curled up on my bed, fallen asleep with the memory of Toons' lips on mine. I pause when I hear singing coming from upstairs. "She's up there by herself in the shower?"

"She's taking a bath. It's not that bad, she can take a shower alone. She's alone most of the day."

I'm so angry and so sore, I can't even speak. My cut-up feet are aching now. It was stupid, walking out on those rocks. How am I supposed to be ready for practice again in two days? I'm already behind the other girls; next class I'll just look dumb. I turn and head upstairs, away from him. I step into my mother's room. The running water has stopped now. I look into the bathroom.

She's in a tub near overflowing, her clothing strewn across the floor. When I come in, she looks over, but she doesn't seem to see me. When we were little, she would hold me in seawater as clear as her bath while Daddy somersaulted and did half-submerged handstands. Our little triangle was complete.

I step over her vacated clothes and sit on the edge of the tub. She turns her head toward the light, examining the wall over my shoulder.

"Carla?" She calls my aunt's name.

"It's Faith," I say softly. I swing one foot over into the tub, then the other. My feet smart as the water ripples, then calms, taking me in. She lifts a hand, letting water trickle down from her finger, a string of beads. The hand falls, plunking like a dead weight. She raises the same hand again and pats the surface of the water so light it barely makes a splash. Something thumps against the window—my mother startles, kneeling up in the water. I stand up and look out. A pair of fleshy legs, splayed out wide, the underside vulnerably pale, the toes grotesque and long.

"It's okay." I try to sound reassuring. "Just a frog." As I step back from the window, the mirror captures my eye. In the reflection, I tower above her while water drips from her bare body, as if I am the mother and she is the child. I turn away to see her looking at the reflection too. I wonder if she sees what I see. If there's enough of her mind left to understand why it's wrong.

8

NIA

I wait outside the classroom for KeeKee. Through the slats, I can see her with her bag open, head down as she slides one of her pouches into a girl's hands. The girl tucks it into a pocket, then walks out fast, arms folded across her chest. KeeKee follows a minute later. We fall in step with each other, heading away toward the gate.

"Pads or condoms?"

"Shh. You aren't allowed to speak about such things."

"Please. Mummy ain here." I crane my neck to look at the girl. She's a grade below ours—is she sleeping with someone, or does she get her cycle already? "Which one?"

"You know that's confidential." KeeKee is serious as she turns to look at me. "Why? You finally got your period?"

"No. And thanks for the reminder. You really ain't ga tell me?"

She sighs. "It was pads."

"I knew it."

She grins smugly. "Or was it condoms? I forget. Stop ogling the girl, you can't tell who's doing it by looking, trust me. I don't know why you so nosey anyway, you don't have no use for either one."

"I wish," I sigh.

"You're not missing out, from what I hear."

"Hear from who? Toons?"

She makes a rotten-fish face. "We don't talk about that type of stuff."

"Of course *you* don't. You wouldn't care if you died in a nunnery, hey?"

"Nope."

"He don't tell you who he likes?"

KeeKee gags as if a large hairball is lodged behind her tonsils. "Don't tell me you have a crush on him too."

"We could be like sisters."

"We're already like sisters. Anyway, you don't want Toons. Believe me. You know I saw him all snatch up with Faith out on the rocks day before yesterday, and then that same night I catch him sneaking in the church to meet Eve?"

"Eve? She too prissy for that."

"Girls ten times prissier than Eve come looking for things all the time."

"So she ever came to you for—" I start, and KeeKee elbows me sharply, looking pointedly at the gate. "What?" I follow her gaze and see Mummy at the entrance to the school, her giant purse over her shoulder, her arms folded, legs planted like tree roots. Students stream around her, waves around an awkwardly placed rock. "Oh, man. I forgot I have an appointment today."

"Hi, Ms. Taylor," KeeKee says as we reach my mother,

then leans in and whispers, "Good luck," before she slips away. I'd give anything to be KeeKee, going home to drop a few clothes in the wash, then skip off through the rest of the day, free as a bird.

Mummy looks me up and down. "Ready?" She leans forward, tweaking my collar. I pull away.

"To get poked and prodded for nothing?"

She leans in. "Did you wipe off your underarms and put on fresh deodorant?"

I glance around at the students sauntering past us. Earth, swallow me now. "Can we just go?" She heads for the bus stop and I follow several paces behind. My legs are heavy, and my backpack is gaining a pound with every step I take. The only thing worse than being met at the gate by my mother is going to the doctor with her for the fourth time this year for her to ask yet again why my body isn't doing what she thinks it should.

Mummy gets on the bus and sits on the left. I find a spot on the other side of the aisle, two rows back. I can tell she's annoyed from the way she shifts her body in the seat, but more students crowd on and there's no space to move even if she told me to. The girls on the other side of the aisle jostle each other, and one almost bumps into her. She turns toward the window. Even from behind, I know her eyebrows will be drawn together so that a deep furrow has formed, like someone's pinched the skin that way. Her lips will be pressed together as if she's been asked to swallow a mouthful of aloe. She turns and looks at me, as if to make sure I'm still there, and her face is fixed exactly as I knew it would be. The bus lurches into motion and a boy in front of Mummy stumbles as he waves to a friend at the back, almost falling onto her. I see her hand go up, a reprimanding finger raised, as she chides him. I slide down, wishing I could disappear. Seems like she was never young.

There are four people ahead of us at the clinic. The air conditioner is on full blast, raising goose pimples all up and down my arms. Mummy opens up a notebook and starts jotting something down.

"I'm bored." I lean over and rest my head on my forearms.

"Start your homework."

I sit up in the chair, unzip my backpack, and look down at the jumble of math, English, history books. Nope, nope, nope. Not in the mood. I look up again. Through the glass door, I see a convenience store across the road. "Can I go get something to drink?"

I expect Mummy to complain that I should have refilled my bottle at the water fountain before we left school. Instead, she reaches into her purse and hands me a five.

"Pick up something for me, too." She closes her bag up again. Her fingers fiddle with the buckle closure. Why is she nervous? We're here for me, not her.

"Bottled water?"

She reopens her book. "Get me a Coke."

I hide my surprise as I step back out into the heat. Mummy never drinks soda, especially not something caffeinated and strong. Oh well. We all have our secrets, I think, as

the door closes behind me. *Okay, Sunshine Convenience &
Snacks. Entertain me for the next fifteen minutes.*

"Hey, your bag open," a girl calls as she passes behind me.

"Thanks." I reach around to close it. Someone shouts
across the road, hailing a passing car, and I look up. Then
I see the plain white sign with green letters: GIBSON & ASSO-
CIATES ARCHITECTURE. KeeKee's daddy works there. I look
down into my open backpack. A corner of crumpled manila
envelope peeps up at me: the application. I cross the street,
pause outside the convenience store, then turn right toward
the staircase leading to the second floor.

I make my way up the stairs and along three doors until
I'm standing outside the office. My heart pounds. My bag
feels light, as though the envelope could float right up and
into the office on its own. It's meant to be. It has to be. At the
door, I pause. I half expect to see Mummy behind me in the
glass, but the reflection only shows me, backpack over one
shoulder, glasses too small for my face, arms hanging awkwardly at my sides. I catch myself furrowing my eyebrows like
Mummy does, and rearrange my face so I wear a calm smile.
Above, a mockingbird calls once, urging me on.

The door opens and closes without a sound. Inside, an
older lady sits behind a desk, thumbing through the *Bahamas Herald*. I look around the room: thin gray office car-
pet, drawings of prim houses lining the walls. Plaques glint
from the wall opposite me. *Timothy Wright, in honor of outstanding architectural contributions*, the nearest one reads.
KeeKee never told me her daddy got all these awards. Did
she ever go to any of the ceremonies? Is he rich? Is she rich?

In an instant, I feel like I don't know my best friend at all.

The lady turns the page and catches sight of me. "Yes?" She pushes the newspaper aside. "Can I help you?"

"I—um." I step up to the desk. Maybe I shouldn't send this form off. What happens if I get accepted? Mummy's already said I can't go. And KeeKee's definitely getting in. What do I tell her when she asks what I submitted? What if, worse, her daddy shows her my application?

"Yes?" The woman's smile is impatient.

I'm doing this, I decide. "I have an application to hand in." I set my bag down and reach in for the envelope.

"We've already hired our summer interns."

The envelope is pinned, half crumpled, under a book. I tug it out too fast and the tape recorder thumps onto the floor, the back popping off with a clatter. "It's for the art camp." I lean down to gather everything. It's a sign, I think. I shouldn't be here. But I have to do this. I have to show Mummy that I can get out from under her thumb. I have to show myself. I separate the envelope out from the debris and stand up. As I do, I come face-to-face with a short balding man with bright-green glasses perched on his face.

"I've got it, Louise. This must be one of my kids. I'm Mr. Wright. Most of our applicants just put it in the mail or slip it in the tray." He nods at a wire basket labeled NEWBEAT SUMMER ARTS PROGRAM CAMP. "But you made quite the entrance."

My heart is all the way in my mouth. KeeKee's daddy, live and in the flesh. He has her smile. She has his eyes. This was dumb, I should have mailed the application a week ago when I wrote it out. "Poetry," I blurt out as I shove the recorder into my bag. I straighten up and shake his hand.

"Ah, a writer."

"Yes, I like to write all kinds of stuff." Now I just sound like I'm lying. Can he see right through me? I'm sweaty. Why didn't I put deodorant on like Mummy said? "You have interesting glasses," I add.

"Thank you." KeeKee's father adjusts his glasses on his nose. "They're new." I see him noticing my pair, scuffed and scratched and tight on my face. I look down. His shoes are shiny, dark brown dress shoes laced tightly. I wish I wasn't in dusty Mary Janes with the front of the left sole starting to come loose. Does he notice that, too? He must be wondering why someone so awkward is in his office, trying to get noticed for camp. What if I do get in and he sees me there with KeeKee? The whole idea is crumbling to bits. Why did I even come here?

"I'd love to see that application," he says kindly.

There's no backing out now. I hold out the envelope to him and he takes it.

"Thank you . . ."

My mind races. I can't tell him my name. If he finds out, when he finds out, I'll have to deal with it. "Denise," I say.

"I look forward to reading through your application, Denise." He smiles my best friend's smile, then goes back into his office, tapping the envelope in his hand.

My best friend. What have I done?

As I step back out into the heat, my heart pounds. A sick feeling washes over me. There's no way I win. If I get in, Mummy still won't let me go. Even if she did, I can't write poetry. I can barely write in regular sentences. Worst of all, if KeeKee finds out what I did, she'll never forgive me. Thoughts swirling, I dart into the store, grab the first two drinks that my hand falls on, then head back into the clinic. Only one person left.

"Line was long?" Mummy reaches for the soda.

"Huh?" My head swims. KeeKee's daddy is going to read that application. He's going to see that the name on there isn't Denise. What if he recognizes her poem? Does he know her poetry? Why don't I know this? I'm a terrible friend.

"I thought you were getting me a Coke."

"They were out." The lie feels insignificant, weighted against the knowledge that I just betrayed my best friend.

"Davinia Taylor?" the nurse calls. "You can come."

Mummy pushes the soda into her purse, then heads for the corridor, so sure I'm behind her she doesn't stop to look. I follow her into the examination room. My heart sinks when I see this doctor is a man. He has a bald patch already forming at the top of his head, but his face is young.

"I'm Dr. Albury. Come in, sit down." He gestures at the chairs opposite him. Mummy plunks herself down like this appointment is all about her. I sit too.

"I brought my daughter in to see you," she begins, launching into the familiar spiel. "Nia is fifteen now, and I'm concerned about her development."

The man's expression doesn't change, but his eyes flicker over my body like it's a page in a textbook. He looks back at Mummy. "What are you concerned about exactly?"

"She should be fully into puberty by now, but since her

breasts began to develop at ten, there hasn't been much change."

I lean back in the chair. Do they have to talk about me like I'm not here?

"Well, has she—Nia, have you—had your first period yet?" He looks between the two of us, unsure who to direct his questions to. I don't want to talk about blood and breasts with this man. At least the last doctor was a woman.

"No," I mutter.

"She hasn't seen anything," Mummy pipes up, her voice drowning out mine. Great. She can talk. This appointment is for her, anyway.

He studies my chart, then looks up again, this time straight at me. "You've been to see a few doctors about this now."

"Five."

"Most of your friends probably started seeing their periods too."

"She—" Mummy begins, but the doctor holds up a hand, cutting her off. He points at me.

I straighten up in the chair. "Yes, but I don't care. I don't need it now, anyway."

He takes out a form and checks a few boxes. I can almost feel the steam rising off my mother, but she doesn't speak.

"All right, Nia," he says finally. "You obviously have entered puberty, it's not like you look the same as when you were eight. Right?"

"Right."

He signs the paper, then hands it to me. "I'm sending you for some blood tests, and that will tell us whether this is hormonal, or whether there may be another factor."

"Like what?"

"Stress can affect the body and suppress nonessential activities, like bleeding. Your body doesn't need to reproduce to survive, so if you're under extreme stress, that may be causing a delay. However," and now he looks at Mummy for a second before turning back to me, "your records show you've been to six clinics over the past year, so I'm assuming you ruled that out long ago."

Mummy's voice is a tightrope she dares him to walk. "She isn't stressed."

The doctor opens his mouth, then changes his mind and smiles.

"Aren't you going to examine her?" Mummy asks.

"A physical exam won't tell us anything new," he says, "unless your question is whether she's—been active as yet. Though a conversation could answer that for you."

"My daughter isn't—she doesn't—come, Nia." Mummy stands up abruptly, snatching the paper for the blood test out of my hand. She's out in the hallway before I can even get my bag onto my shoulder.

Outside, Mummy scowls. "That was a waste of time. We don't need to come back here."

"I like him."

"Let me go in the store," she says, as if I haven't said a word. "We need corned beef and bread."

"I'll wait outside," I say, as Mummy disappears through the doors.

"Hey, princess." The voice is familiar; I look up and see

Sammy. Here, of all places. He smiles. "You on your own?"

"Waiting for my mum." My heart surges as if it's going to launch itself right out of my body.

He smiles. A normal, neighbor smile? Or is there something different in his eyes? He's kinda . . . old, isn't he? I brush it off. I'm sure he's just being friendly.

"You out here on assignment?" Sammy's voice jostles my thoughts.

"Assignment?"

"For your newspaper."

"Oh. Yes." It feels like a better excuse than to tell him we just came from the doctor to find out why I don't menstruate yet.

"You should interview me sometime. I'm a big deal, you know."

"Really?"

"You got a pen and paper?"

Something about his words don't feel just . . . polite. I look up at his face. He wears a half-smile and he's eyeing me that way. The way I imagine I look at Toons. Like I'm a sugar-coated, deep-fried snack. I don't know how to feel about it. Except I feel a warmth in my belly—someone's noticing me, not just someone, a guy, an older guy. A guy with strong arms and warm eyes that see me. I open my bag and take out the bottle of water, feeling around for something to write on. I pull out the recorder.

"Give me that." He says it like an invitation, his voice low, as if there's already a secret we share. My legs are jelly as he slips the recorder out of my hand. His fingers touch mine, warm on warm. Then he murmurs his phone number into the microphone. Then he looks over his shoulder, almost casual. My eyes follow his gaze. The grocery store's automatic doors are still. Sammy leans forward, lifts the flap of my bag open, then tucks the recorder inside. We don't touch, but the shift of my books is like fingers against my belly. Suddenly, Toons doesn't matter anymore, not when there's someone grown, someone mature, someone who actually notices me. "Call me," he says, then slips around the corner. A moment later, the store's automatic door opens outward. Mummy bustles toward me like she means business. As she gets close, she pulls a bag of chips out of her shopping bag and hands it to me.

"I know these doctors' visits aren't fun, but we'll get to the bottom of things." She hugs me quickly. I squeeze back and pray she won't feel how something in my body is beating its wings, fighting to take to the air. Pray she won't see my feet just half an inch off the ground.

KEEKEE

I can just imagine the woman. She wears the same tired, plastic, overblack wig eight days a week. She wears stockings a shade too light, and wide, self-righteous penny loafers, like she's too moral for heels. She has a bust that moves as a single unit. She cuts her eye at you just for being a girl, like she sprang into womanhood by some other path. Egg hatching. Plucked from a tree.

"There's always a fuss," she shrills over the radio in Mr. Rahming's store, "when time come for things to change.

They did it with the Paradise Island Resort, they did it out west. And now some years on, people forget about that and apply for jobs there, living off wages from these places. And them who ain benefiting is the ones who looking for handouts from the same government they complain about. You understand me?"

I slam tins of corn and peas onto the shelf, metal chattering on metal furiously.

"What's cooking your grits tonight?" Mr. Rahming asks over the woman's voice.

I glare over at the radio. I wish he'd turn the stupid thing off. "Nothing."

"You're on *Callback Live*," the host says, the woman's tirade finally over. "Folks, if you're just joining us, we're discussing the development at Pinder's Point. The government announced earlier today it has approved development of two six-story hotels and twenty-four cottages on the premises. Call in, give us your take on this. Do you go out to the beach there? Are you in favor of the jobs a new hotel could create? Do you live in the area? Let us know your thoughts, our lines are open."

Mr. Rahming eases up out of his chair. "You heard the man, KeeKee. Lines are open. What's on your mind?" He looks over at me. "What you say, Kim?"

I wish I could look Mr. Rahming in his eye, explain to him that everything feels wrong. I wish I could tell him about last night, seeing my best friend strut across the yard with that dish of eggy mess in her hands, her chest pushed out almost to the ocean. About watching her grin up with Sammy. About her coming inside after, lying on my bed, like I couldn't sense there was something she was trying to hide. About everything that's going on with Toons and Faith and Eve, how he's carrying on like Mr. Loverman while these girls act like they don't have basic sense. About how our whole lives are falling apart around us and no one seems to be thinking about that, or thinking about much of anything above the waist.

"Speak up, now. What's wrong?" Mr. Rahming tries again. "This hotel business got you tense?"

Before I can answer, Amos strolls into the store. He leans on the counter, and I get up to refill the cooler.

"Evening, Pops." Out of the corner of my eye, I see him grab a tin of spaghetti and an energy drink. "Spot me tonight?"

"On your tab."

"Thanks, Mr. R." Amos tucks the containers under his arm and steps out as a girl in snug jeans and an even snugger top strolls by. "Hey, sweetness," Amos calls. The girl turns her head, giving him a haughty look, then keeps going without a word. If it was me, my store, my world, I'd call Amos back and make him return those things. If you can afford to be catcalling, you can afford to pay for your crappy processed dinner yourself. I've seen the book where Mr. Rahming keeps track of unpaid grocery bills. The whole thing is blank inside. He's helped everyone out more times than they can count. He bailed out Riccardo, when he was arrested for being in a car with a guy who shot someone. He bought a new pair of shoes for Toons when his got stolen the second week of school and he was too scared to go home in bare socks. I've seen him slip extra tins of corned beef and sweet corn in a bag for Eve. In the last storm, he sent his nephew up to Nia's house and let him nail planks over the windows and trim back overgrown trees in the yard.

"Do you ever get tired of people coming to you?" The question surprises me as it comes out.

"Well, that's a hazard of owning a store." He hoists a box of cooking oil onto the countertop.

"People who don't have money."

"Ah." He starts unpacking the bottles, neatly pressing a price sticker onto each one. "That's the hazard of doing right. You do it once, people hope you'll do it again. Gets to be addictive."

"People are just . . . assy sometimes. Don't you want to just let them stew?"

Mr. Rahming leans back, considering this option. "I don't know what good that would do. That would bother me at night. The smell of stew burning when I'm trying to sleep. Especially ass stew." He looks over at me. "Philanthropic life wearing you out?"

How can I explain without saying things I'm not supposed to repeat? "I feel like it's a waste of time."

"Those breakfasts y'all serve up is a waste?"

"Not so much those."

"Or opening the door to whatever troubled soul is passing through and needs shelter and a place to lean their head?"

"It's more like the nonessential stuff."

"Ah." He nods as he prices the last bottle of oil. "You think people should get their own rain gear."

"Rain gear?" I laugh in spite of myself.

"That's it, isn't it? Child, you might as well accept that. That's something people need. And they ain ga stop needing it either."

"How do you know about us giving away rain gear?" I ask, still laughing.

"I've lived on this street seventy-nine years. You think there's anything I don't know?"

"People have time to"—I try to stretch the analogy—"run around in thunderstorms, but no one cares that we're losing the beach."

"How you know they don't care about the beach and the weather same time?"

I don't want to joke anymore. "No one's doing anything about the important stuff because they're too busy getting mixed up with stupid boys who too lazy to go buy a pack of condoms."

Mr. Rahming glances at the clock above my head. "Speaking of which, almost time for tonight's meeting." His eyes drift across the street to Eve's house. Through the open windows, I can see a small crowd forming in their living room. "You sure you don't want to come? We can close the store down."

"What's the point? It's not like we can change them selling out."

"It's not over yet, KeeKee. But you stay here, if that's what you want. If you change your mind, just turn the sign around to Closed. And listen."

I look at him, a thin little man with small, sharp eyes, his back upright even as he leans on his cane.

"You never been in love, I take it," he says.

"With what?"

"With a person who makes your brain stop working right. When I met Mrs. Rahming, she was set on staying a spinster and running her mother's seamstress business. Things change. In the meantime, be careful and be kind. Especially in uncertain times. People need it extra, these days." Mr. Rahming pats my shoulder, then steps out into the evening air.

A minute later, the door tinkles open again. I look up as Paulette comes in. She slides behind the counter, beside me.

"Granddaddy here?"

"You just missed him."

Paulette reaches under the counter, pulling out two textbooks and a pen. "You talked to Toons today?"

"Not since this morning. Why?"

"Something's up with your brother."

"Something's always up with him."

She shakes out a plastic shopping bag, sliding the books in, then straightens up. "It's like he's here, but not here."

If there's one thing I don't want to do, it's talk about what type of boyfriend my brother is with the girl he's cheating on. "Hmm," I say in my least-interested voice. "Weird."

She leans across the counter. I can smell the almost-spent mint of her chewing gum. "You saw him with anyone else?"

I want her to know, but I don't want to be the one to tell her. Why should I do that dirty job? I choose my words carefully. "He hasn't said anything."

"Can you talk to him?"

"I guess."

"Thanks." She drops her voice lower. "You got any . . ."

I don't have to ask which one she's looking for; Paulette always has her own pads. I unzip my schoolbag, reach under my books for one of the other pouches. She tucks it in her back pocket, then hands me a dollar. The store grows too quiet, too still, and she leans over, turning the radio back on. They're done with their debate now. A song plays about being a man's number one girl.

"I got to get to class," she says, hoisting up the bag. "If you see Toons, tell him call me?"

I don't answer as she leaves, only head to the back of the shop to dust the stock, to keep myself busy. I don't get it. If she really doesn't trust Toons, why would she want to be close with him that way? If times are changing, why do people keep making the same mistakes?

NIA

When we get back to Pinder Street, cars are parked up and down the road.

"What's happening?" I ask.

Mummy sighs. "They approved the development, and now people are up in arms. There's a meeting down at the church. Listen, I want you to go ahead and get started on your homework. I want to go hear what's happening."

"I'll come with you. I don't have that much homework."

Mummy's already turned away, her face hidden by the shadows. "If you don't have homework, you can start on next week's newspaper."

"Shouldn't I write something about the meeting?"

She carries on into the yard. "We have bread on the counter, and you can make a cup of tea. I don't want you wasting time at that stove," she says.

I drag my feet down the street. Bread and tea doesn't put

much hustle in my step. I hope KeeKee's home too. I should tell her about the doctor's visit, though what I really want to talk about is Sammy. As I get to the yard, I hear music coming from across the way, music unlike anything I've heard before. Neither church music nor island music, it lacks drums but seems heavy and sticky and sweet, like guava duff sauce, sugar beaten and pearlized with fat, spun with jeweled fruit puree, laced with rum. There are brassy instruments, but they are not a clamoring celebration. They are a series of slow, aching groans, somewhere between agony and delight. There are no voices. They are not needed. That music is dessert at the end of a hungry night. I step closer, leaning into the tree, and listen. I want some. Both houses are pitch dark, but the music comes from KeeKee's house.

Near the back of her house, I see movement. Someone's dancing. She sways slow, her arms raised, feet on tiptoe, a circling ankle, an arched neck and bent back and undulating hips. Deep in the shadows, a male voice murmurs something. My heart races. Is it him? The dancer turns and the moonlight catches her features. Faith. Why's she dancing for Toons?

In the dark behind me, someone inhales hard, and I almost jump out of my skin. KeeKee strides right past me without even realizing I'm there. It's like I don't even exist. She marches toward Faith, who's so caught up she doesn't hear or see her coming.

"Get out our yard!" KeeKee's shout is so loud and so hard I wouldn't believe it's her if I hadn't seen it, heard it, for myself. Faith stops abruptly, hands planted on her hips.

"What's your problem?"

"You know he has a girlfriend, right?" KeeKee pushes

herself right up in Faith's face, her chin jutting out, defiant.

"Well, that ain your business." Faith doesn't back down.

"It ain like that." Toons' voice. Relief washes over me.

"You even worse," KeeKee barks at him. "You got her out here looking like a ten-dollar show."

"You would know," Faith snaps, grabbing up her phone. She scurries out of the yard like a swatted dog caught waist-deep in a Sunday roast.

"I can't even believe you." KeeKee turns her full wrath on her brother now. "Your so-called girlfriend just been in the store, begging me to talk to you."

Whatever Toons says is too hushed for me to hear, but that's not my focus. Right now, I'm terrified of KeeKee. I've never seen her like this. Furious. Righteous. Vicious. She seems to know everything. What would she know if she looked at me? Would she see everything I've done? I slip away as fast as I can, unlocking the front door so she won't see me around the side of the house. As I close the door behind me, the racing of my heart slows a little. It's fine, I tell myself, welcoming the dark of our empty house for a minute before I fumble for the switch and flip it. It clicks, but no light comes on. Great. I feel my way to the kitchen and reach for the switch in there. Still nothing.

I open the fridge. A deeper darkness greets me, stale and tepid and dank. From across the yard, a long rectangle of light stretches out, taunting. When I turn, I see light coming from KeeKee's room. It's not a power outage after all. It's just our house that sits in darkness, brewing hidden things.

9

KEEKEE

Two mornings after the whole Toons-Faith shenanigans, I wake up with a headache. I wish I could sleep in, but I'm out on the couch because, of course, that had to be the night Sammy came over too. I get up and get dressed, then head out to the line, squinting against the overzealous sun. Nia's door opens and she comes out in her pajamas.

"Hey."

I unclip a pair of rugs from the line and shake them out. "What you out here for? You look like you ain even wake up yet."

"I could talk to you? Before my mummy wake up?"

I eye her. Since when does she ask permission to talk?

"Keeks," Angel calls through the open door. "You put on the sheets for Mr. Munroe?"

I roll my eyes. "Not yet."

"And don't forget, Sandra coming by for her wash." Angel disappears and I turn back to Nia. I'm not in the mood.

"Talk, then."

She fiddles with the ends of her backpack. "I don't know if I should tell you."

"Just spill it, man."

"Oh, and Ms. Gibson needs her uniform early this week." Angel's singsong breaks into our conversation again.

"Arrrrrgghhh!" I ball up the clean towel I'm folding and fling it on the grass.

Nia bends down and picks it up. "Your mummy got you all over the place today."

"What's that, KeeKee?" Angel coos.

"Nothing," I shout back. I yank the washer open, stuffing the dingy white sheets into the machine, then reach for the hamper of towels. "Yeah, so what you say?"

"If I tell you, you can't tell no one." She leans in. "I think someone likes me."

Seriously? The last thing I have a stomach for is batted eyes and swooning. I reach for the drawstring bag and stuff the clothes in. I remember Mr. Rahming's words. *Be kind.* If I can't manage that with my own best friend, the rest of the world is officially screwed. I try to stuff my feelings down like those clothes. I measure out a scoop of soap. "Who?"

"You sure all that could hold?"

Toons saunters into the yard. I lean on the door, cutting my eye at him. "You wanna do it?" I snap at Nia. The door clicks into place and I straighten up, then start the wash. Toons continues on his way without so much as looking at me. Then I catch Nia gazing after him. "What you lookin at him like that for?"

She looks away guiltily. "Like what?"

"Oh, please." The washer is filling, obediently. In half an hour, I'll be caught up, hanging stuff out to dry. What will Nia be doing? Anything she wants. "Hold up, this ain about him, right? If you tell me you sleeping with him too . . ."

"Too?" Nia makes a face as she hoists herself up to sit on the machine. "Okay, so we could talk bout *that* later. But it ain about him." Under her, the machine stops filling, sighs, then clicks and starts agitating. She swings herself off, following me to the line. I start unclipping Mrs. Sturrup's pale blue pharmacist's uniforms, folding as I go. "What you think about older guys?"

"Older like who?"

She looks at the blue truck parked under the tree, so quick it's almost a reflex.

"Sammy? You crushin on Sammy?" I drape three pairs of pants over her shoulder as she weaves between the clothes. "Gross."

"Really? His lips are like . . ."

"Crusty." I shake out a pillowcase, cracking her back to reality.

"You know how to kill it." Nia turns to look at the washer, which is clunking as it agitates. "This thing too full or what?"

"It does that, must be something with a zipper in it."

"Oh." Nia slides down, straightening her clothes. "I was just joking, you know. About Sammy. It's not him."

A car stops in front of our house, a girl getting out. She unloads three baskets and waves at us. "Morning, KeeKee. Your mummy say you could squeeze us in. That's all right?"

I bite my tongue. "Sure!"

"My sister in town from Miami, and our washer broke down last week." She pops the trunk open. More? Seriously? The tilt-bump of the machine elevates.

"KeeKee!" Angel's voice carries over the noise. Nia backs away.

"Look out!" I shout too late, as she bumps into the clean hamper. Everything I just folded tumbles out onto the grass. For a second, I stand there, frozen.

"Sorry," Nia says, slinking home. Toons strides out of the house, slaps the washer off, scoops up four baskets at a time, then balances a fifth on his head. The woman giggles as he staggers over to the washer.

"KeeKee, you might as well let him do the wash," she says as he bounds over to me again, rescuing the rest of the clothes on the grass.

"Take a break, sis." He waves me away. "I got it."

I don't know whether to yell at him that I don't need his help or throw my arms around him in gratitude. Instead, I just nod, then hurry out of the yard as fast as I can.

As I get closer to the water, my frustrations start to drain away. At the end of the path, I come face-to-face with the fence. It's grown overnight. Now a heavy coil of barbed wire loops along the top. Between the fence's crisscrossed hatching, the tide is half in and half out. I can't tell whether it's coming or going. Maybe it's stuck in between. Like me.

I lean against the fence, then sink down to the sand, resting my head against the metal.

Times change, Dad said. No hint of how they change or what we do in those shifts. How we keep hold of what we once held dear. Angel's no help either, and Toons hasn't even noticed anything's going. Hasn't had time for anything except girls, which isn't new, exactly, just exaggerated. As if legs and eyes and hands matter more than the beach. They're not so different, my father and Toons. Love a place, a person, the way they want to. And then not. And yet, I remember when my brother was different. Remember when this place meant everything to him.

In my mind, my mouth, words awaken, slipping out into the air.

"New life
new love
new space and
same view from above
if only you can get up high enough
and stay there."

My words settle, moths startled to find themselves in daylight. They open and close their damp wings, drying out in the sun. Words feel rusty, as if I've not used my tongue in weeks. What if, when this house, these trees, are gone, I have no rhymes left in me? Maybe Toons has the right idea. Maybe, sometimes, you have to let one thing be replaced by another. Using my finger, I trace out the words to the poem on the sand at my feet. The sand is dry, is soft, too far from the water to hold shape.

The spinning in my head slows, then stops. I look up at the sky, at the snippets of treetop that persist, free. For now, they are here. For now, I have my words. I stand up and shake the sand off myself, ready to go back and face the yard. The mess. All the things to be done. When I get to the end of the path, I round the corner and bump right into Toons, a towel slung over his shoulder.

"Where you goin?"

"I was just comin back."

"And I tell you go take a break? Chill, girl." He drapes an arm over my shoulders and walks us back down the path.

"I was scared Nia wanted me to set y'all two up," I blurt out. Toons looks over at me, his head cocked to one side. His eyes hold promise and mischief. No wonder he has half the street wrapped around his finger.

"Nia? Hmm . . ."

I swat him away. "She ain interested in you. How much girls you need?"

"I'm just sayin, I had to consider it. But Nia's your best friend."

"Yeah, well. She have a crush on Sammy."

He makes a face. "If she want go old, she might as well check Mr. Rahming."

"Ha-ha."

"But you sure you was supposed to tell me that? I thought y'all was into keeping y'all secrets. Or is this like the whole blood is thicker business?"

"It ain that. Obviously, we're not—"

"Don't say it." He stops, all the laughter drained away from his face. "Me and you is blood in every way that counts." He doesn't look away until I nod.

After a moment, I sigh. There's laundry waiting for me back at the yard. "Let me go finish—"

"Washer full and laundry on the line."

"Really?" I nudge him with my shoulder. "Look like you good for more than getting into trouble with these girls."

We get to the fence, and Toons gazes up at it, then shrugs, as if the metal wall can simply be dismissed.

"Angel talk to you bout Sammy lately?"

"Not since she asked if I like him."

"When?"

"I dunno. A month?"

"And what you said?"

"I said not particularly, and she asked why. I couldn't answer so I left it. I can't put my finger on it. It's just something."

"And everything." Toons looks up at the fence, then eases his feet out of his flip-flops and slides them into two holes in the fence. "Ah well. Laundry done, he in the yard, and sea won't swim in itself."

I look down at the sand, where my words still lie, hidden. Alive, but, like invisible moths, impossible to trap. I look up at Toons, already halfway up the fence, then reach for the metal. It's cool under my fingers and sways against my weight, and his. Near the top, he tosses the towel over the barbed wire, creating a safe way for us to clear the top. Looking up at my brother's back, finding a way over and out seems so easy.

"Hey," I call up. "Wait for me."

FAITH

"Left and right and back and turn," Joy calls from the front of the class, clapping her hands once for every move. From the middle of the room, I can halfway avoid her gaze as she counts out time. I turn left; on my right, Nadine turns the other way and we collide.

"Oops," she says, barely missing a beat. I grimace as I regain my balance, scrambling to catch up while I try to ignore my feet's burn and sting. The turn is killer, spinning balanced on the balls of my feet, which feel like they're about to split open. "I see sloppy rotations, ladies, come on, it's Sunday, you all should have some energy! Shoulders back, light, light, we are not in cement sandals," my sister trills over the music. "Lift, lower, lift, lower, arms up, stretch, arch, and spin, spin, spin—finish, hold."

It was stupid, marching over those rocks like a superhero with no life goals. In front of me, Carmen extends her leg, nearly hitting me in the face. I stumble to the side and bump into another dancer. She catches herself before she over-balances, but still shoots me a withering glare. When class is finally over, I grab my stuff, then slip out the side door while Carmen goes over to talk to Joy. No doubt she's whining about me.

I drive to Pinder Street, hoping to catch Eve so I can complain to her. She's a few houses down, headed for the end of the road and trailing siblings. I pull up alongside her. "Where y'all goin?"

"By the church," Esther pipes up. "Daddy send her for a book."

"You wanna come?" Eve adjusts Junior on her hip.

I hesitate. That'll take long: I should go home, check on Mummy. Plus, my feet are in more agony, now that I'm off them.

"Come with us," Eve pleads. "I need big-people conversation."

"Me too." I check the time. Five-thirty. "You plan on being long?"

"I can just run in and out. Why, you in a rush?"

Mummy should be okay another few minutes. "No, I can come."

While I park the car, Eve sends Esther and Joe ahead. After I get out, Eve hugs me, Junior still in her arms, his little body warm and smooth. As we near Toon's yard, I feel myself tense, but thankfully, neither he nor KeeKee is around.

Eve looks over at me. "How are your feet?"

"Horrible. Stupidest thing ever."

"Was it worth that kiss?"

I consider. "Ask me when I'm not Quasimodo."

Eve slips her straw keychain over her head and unlocks the gate, then holds the gate open for the rest of us to pass through, then closes it behind herself, leaving it unlocked.

"At least they still let you have access," I say.

"That ain a favor," she points out. "We paid up till the end of this month."

I haven't been in Eve's church in what feels like years. When things with my mother started getting too noticeable to ignore, Daddy stopped coming with us, like he was ashamed. When she drove herself to the airport and then forgot why she'd gone and where she'd parked the car, I hid her license and passport so she wouldn't get lost too badly. Standing in the shadowy hall, the pulpit in the same spot I remember, under the window facing the trees, the rows of folding metal chairs lined up five on one side, four on the other, I get the feeling I've stepped back in time. Like my mother might come around the corner, look at me, and smile wide. *Hi, Fay.*

Esther and Joe race past me and outside, toward the water. "Don't get too much sand on you," Eve warns, disappearing into the storage room. While she rummages around for the book. I sit on a chair in the back row and soak up the feeling of home. When I stopped coming, things were already changing, but she was still my mother. Sunday mornings, we would sit in the backyard instead, barefoot in our nightdresses, naming the ants, counting clouds. I would show her the moves I'd learned from Joy and she would applaud, her eyes alive. Then she'd twirl on the grass, showing me her own version of the steps. If our laughter woke my father, he never said. And then, she wasn't my mother anymore, but I was already in the habit of wearing my Sunday-morning nightgown till almost noon.

"Got it." Eve emerges, clutching a dusty paperback. She wipes it off on her skirt. It leaves a grayish smudge on the pleats. She spreads out a blanket on the floor and I settle Junior on it. Outside, Esther and Joe are digging in the sand. Their laughter floats in, magnified in the open space, as though there are a dozen more children with them. I slip off my shoes and socks, stretching my toes on the floor. It's only a little gritty, as if the sand has respectfully stayed outside, preserving sanctity, sparing the old scuffed floor a few new scratches.

"Remember when Joy's dance school used to be in here?" I ask.

"Of course." Eve sits at the out-of-tune piano and rests her fingers on the keys, coaxing out a few notes. "Mrs. Munroe used to play for the recitals."

"She used to murder that piano. You know she's the reason that thing sounds warped now. Oh, man, that recital we did when somebody's dogs got loose on the beach and came running through here and she didn't see till it came up behind her and jumped on the piano bench?"

Eve bursts into giggles. "I thought she was gonna die! And when we had the talent show and Mr. Rahming was singing while Paulette tried to tap-dance, and his dentures fell out in the chorus?"

Soon we're both laughing so hard our voices bounce off the walls and echo off the ceilings, lighting up all the corners the afternoon sun forgot.

"What y'all laughin at?" Esther asks from the doorway. Eve turns around.

"Just remembering all the jokes we had here."

"I hungry," Joe complains.

Eve closes the piano and picks up the book. "I should get this to Daddy."

Now that I'm here, I don't want to go yet. "Can I stay and close up for you?"

She hesitates. "Daddy don't like people in here after hours, now that the fence is up. He thinks it might cause trouble."

Maybe it's the memories, maybe it's the happiness that still hangs in the air. Maybe it's knowing this place won't be here much longer, and realizing I want it to be. "I'll be like half an hour."

Junior's starting to fuss. Eve picks him up. "I guess it's okay, for a little while," she says finally. "Just turn the bottom lock when you finish, and secure the gate."

Alone, I walk through the place—the pokey kitchen with a fridge that hums and a microwave that's older than me, the storage room with its bookshelf and sagging sofa, half a dozen folding tables stacked against a wall, along with extra chairs, down the hallways, back to the sanctuary. At the back, there's enough space to dance, I realize. I ease my shoes and socks off and examine my feet. They feel worse than they look. Maybe dancing on these floors, where my mother once taught, is what I need, in my soul if not in my soles. I close my eyes as I move through a few warm-up stretches. I should be heading home, I know. But this place won't be here much longer, and right now it is, and my mother is always fine, even though she never is, and Daddy should be there anyway, and I'm not far away, and it's just a moment to stretch, to redeem myself, to remember that I can balance, can move right, even on feet that hurt.

I rise onto the balls of my feet, arching my back, lifting my arms. I let no music play, let the sound of the waves sing me on, count me down. There is room to lift and twirl, no one to bump into, no Joy trying to catch my eye. I leap and spin and when I finally stop, through the windows, the day is gathering its pinky-orange skirts together, and making room for the night. And then I turn and he is there in the doorway. Barefoot and wet from the sea, sandy footprints tracked onto the worn wood floors. Toons.

"Hey."

From my back pocket, my phone buzzes, sudden, urgent, and I know I should answer it. Joy. Well, she can wait. I drop it on a chair and turn back to him. "Hey."

"How you get in here?"

"Eve."

"Oh." He licks his lips and I taste salt spray. "She here?"

"No. I supposed to lock up when I finish."

He looks out over the sand, then back at me. "This used to be your mummy's studio, right?"

"Used to be."

"Her and your big sister." He leans against the wall, a half smile tilting his lips, and I look away. That smile is trouble. That smile is what got my feet all cut up. "Your mummy used to get everybody to do the Independence Day dances."

I look up at Toons. "You remember that?"

"Yeah, man. One time she came down to the shop, all of us was out by the court and she bought everybody orange Fanta and hot cheese puffs and told us we had to come help her out because all she had was girls."

"For real?"

He shakes his head. "I can't make that up. I was like eight that year, and it was right before some stuff went down. There was Ms. Elaine in this bright-pink leotard and green leggings,

I thought she looked like a hibiscus bush in bloom, barefoot on the basketball court, teaching us the moves."

Heat rushes through my body and I feel like the world outside is spinning like a top let loose, but somehow in here there's a spot I can make contact with, keep myself centered now. "Y'all were in tutus too?" Toons steps closer, then sits down a few feet away from me. He looks outside, as if someone might come through the door at any time. "Your mummy was real cool. Some of the big boys was out there and they was acting all hard, standing off to the side, pulling tricks with the balls and whatnot. Let me tell you what she did. She pointed at me."

"At you?"

"She was like, 'Lil man, come here, you know how to scull? Come here, lemme teach you.' Then she showed me." He jostles his shoulders, forward, back, arms coordinating. His legs are crossed but I can feel the folded memory in them, itching to be let loose. "And then—oh, man. She dropped into a split, then spring back up and she hit this break dancing move like—you can't even imagine."

"What?"

"I serious! She gone in a one-arm handstand and tilt her legs to the side like she about to cartwheel, then spring back up, spin, and scull again." He wipes his brow, shaking his head. "She had that court full. Three minutes, she had dead-hard guys elbowin each other to be like, I could beat that."

I shake my head, a grin spreading through me. "She really did that?"

"Yeah! Ask Angel. You was a little young, maybe, but that stuck in my mind. Your mom's like a legend."

I close my eyes. I want to remember her like that, and I halfway do, but sometimes the present crowds it out. Her vacant eyes, spilled skirt. I open my eyes. I can't. I have to hold on to this gift Toons has given me. Something I can unfold later, shake out and wrap around me. Lean into, like an embrace. Feel warmth beating through it. "Nobody else through here remembers her, you know? Not like that."

"They do. And if they don't, they're probably just scared to, cause things are different now." He stretches out his legs. "People don't like to talk about what they don't understand."

"You don't seem to mind."

"Maybe I understand."

"What, your mom's crazy too?" I've never said that word out loud before. It's instantly too sharp, too much clatter in my ears. But I've spoken it now; it can't be unsaid.

"That year? When I was eight? I didn't live through here yet, ya know. I used to come through because Angel would keep me sometimes when my mummy needed some—I don't know. Needed a break, I guess you could say. She had this boyfriend at the time, he was into some things, and he got her into them too, so she was—I dunno. Not right, but right enough to know it. You know that kinda way?" He closes his eyes, leaning back into the wall.

"I do."

"Yeah. When things got . . . like, too off, she would send me up here to Angel."

"You must have missed her."

He scootches over so he's sitting closer. Close enough

that if he stretches his leg out, his foot will touch mine. I focus on that foot. The second, third, and fourth toes almost the same length, the nails oval and smooth, new-flower-petal pink. Conch-shell pink. Kissed-lip pink.

"I was mad at her. I felt like she kept picking anything, everything, but me. Something she could drink or smoke or whatever. That guy. Some type peace and quiet I thought she got when I was out the house. I didn't miss her till I moved in with Angel for good."

Dusk is stretching out around us now, cocooning the room. I get up, my feet silent as I step lightly over to the hallway. The first switch I flip drops us into a thin, billowy twilight. I can still see his outline, see the soft wink of his toenails as he shifts his legs. I sit again, a bit closer.

"Did she die? Your mom?"

"No. Yeah, but no. She dropped me off by Angel one night and, like, that was it. After that she didn't even try anymore. I used to see her sometimes, just walking, spaced right out. I think she in Freeport now." His voice is forced casual, but I hear the way his words catch just a little, snag on grief. I reach out, just to try to set him loose, and my fingers find his.

"Sometimes she doesn't know me anymore." I blurt the words out even before I even realize I need to say them.

"Your mummy?"

I nod. "I look at her and she's just gone. Who she was in that story, in the pink and green, busting out on the court? She used to be like that all the time. But not anymore. We live in the same house but she's gone—" And then the grief that caught him grabs hold of me and I'm crying and he's holding me like he's seen the mother that's replaced Mommy and the empty that starts deep and pours out fast and never seems to run out. He doesn't say it's okay or that she'll get better, he doesn't say anything, only squeezes me tighter and lets me cling to him like a long-held note. I rest my head on his chest until the sobs fade and his fingers soak up my tears like sand drawing seawater in. Everything goes still when he moves his mouth to mine.

Words on pause. Nothing but quiet. Hands fumble, wood floor hard against my side. The warmth of him close against me. My breath catches. It's about to happen. I should have a condom or something, but my pockets are empty, and then I'm not thinking about pockets or condoms, or empty eyes or vacant gaze, I'm just here, and it's the purest, most perfect place to be.

"This okay?" Toons murmurs, and his words prick a pinpoint of clarity in my mind.

"I don't have any . . . you know."

"It's okay," he whispers, "it comes natural."

"I mean, like, protection." The words are clumsy in my mouth. I don't want to be talking, to be thinking, to be sensible. I want to turn my mind off, to set it on the waves, let it be carried straight out to sea.

"Oh . . ." His voice peters out. He checks his pockets. "Oh, man."

I can feel the grit of sand under my back. I start to sit up. "Should we go get—"

"Probably," he agrees, his voice a pillow, a comforter, a whole bed.

"In a second," I say, and pull him in close again. Somewhere between mind and mouth is a question, I can't quite dismiss: *And what about her?* Then his mouth is on mine again, cutting off my words before they can be breathed, and I want it—the world without thought, the floating on waves, on air. His fingers glide up my back and he's kissing my neck, and I bliss out on all of him. And it's comfortable and familiar and perfect, like walking barefoot down a beach you've always known, on low-tide sand. It's dark now, and I can't tell if my eyes are open or closed and it doesn't matter. Nothing does, except being with him, being understood, fully. Finally.

I wake with a jolt, and sit up. It takes a moment to remember where I am, and why. Toons' shirt is draped over me from the waist down. He lies on his side, facing me. I can't make out his face. It must be after eight. I have to get home. I feel around for my underwear and shorts and yank them on.

"How she got through the gate?"

The voice—a man's—comes from outside. I freeze, in the middle of putting on my T-shirt.

"Look, out there, see someone out by the water?" a second man calls. I shake Toons' shoulder, pressing my fingers to his lips as he startles awake.

"Pastor, you stay here, we'll go get her."

"Shoot!" Toons springs up, hauling on his shirt and pants. I'm already out the door. I stumble down the stairs and into the night. There are three men moving fast, flashlights casting beams across the sand and somehow I know they're here looking for my mother. Tide is way out and the beach seems never-ending. I can't see where the water starts, but I know it does. And if she gets to it . . . My mind is racing. She's out there. I have to bring her back.

"Elaine!" Mr. Armbrister's voice carries across the beach. "It's Jacob. Stay where you are, we're coming out to get you."

"Stingrays come in close at night," one of the other men says, quieter.

"Mummy!" The word bursts out of my mouth as I hurry after them. Mr. Armbrister turns around, waving the other men on. He reaches out and stops me.

"Faith—don't go out there, the reefs are too sharp, it's dangerous." He stops to catch his breath. "They have flashlights, let them go. They'll bring her back safe."

Out across the sand, my mother shouts. Her voice is furious, wild. They've almost reached her and one shines his light right on her. She slips and goes down with a howl. The men call to her—don't they know they're making it worse? I start running again—I see her better now, she paces and sways, dips and lifts onto her toes. "Mummy!" I call again, climbing up onto the rocks. Toons calls out behind me, but I don't look back.

The wind shifts and throws back the sound of a name I haven't heard since I stumbled into the kitchen on much smaller feet and caught my parents about to kiss. I look back to see a golf cart speeding across the sand. It stops and my father jumps out and starts running along the slippery reef. "Laney!" The weather is picking up, wind and rock turning sea to salt rain. Somehow he passes me, shouts something to the men. He reaches her, shifts one way, then the other, then lunges and grabs at her. My mother struggles against his arms but he holds her tight and the other men join in, helping him restrain her while she howls. Together, they half-carry, half-drag her back. When they pass me, his face is hard-poured concrete set against her screams. All her words are gone; it's just sound now.

Joy comes up beside me, sobbing, holding me, while they force Mummy into the golf cart. Nurse Pratt, who works at the rebab center's psych ward, is there too, giving orders. She takes out a needle and shoves it into Mummy's leg, and my mother goes quiet. Joy and I make it back to the gate and up the path, then to the road where the car waits. They load her into the backseat, a sack of potatoes gone limp.

"Come," my father barks. I look over at my car. Then get into the back beside the potatoes.

"Faith." Joy, her voice from far up. "It's gonna be all right."

And then we are moving, my seat belt off, and I can hear Eve, *You better wear that, how you's drive.* No, sister driving, homes blur and we are on Pinder Street or the main street or our road, everything looks the same.

"Where are we going?" Underwater words. I lean over, forehead to the window glass's cool, and it moves and air rushes in, slap to the face.

"Hey, window!" Daddy scrambles for the controls on his door.

"Put the child lock on!" Joy swerves, looking back, then rights the car. The window goes up. Beside me, movement; Mommy's hand twitches, her eyes half-closed. Then still

167

again, only the shallow push and pull of her breath. Drool trickles from the side of her mouth.

We turn through a big set of gates painted ghost blue. Past rows of cars, under an arch of trees. Then slow at the front of a building. HOPE SPRINGS REHABILITATION. Two men hurry out in yellow scrubs and the back door opens and hands on my arms, shoulders, a minute. Someone shouts *other side* and they're gone, and arms pull Mummy out and away. My father follows as the building's doors slide open, swallow her whole, slam shut.

"It's best," Joy keeps saying, "it's for the best," but I know it didn't have to happen. I should have been home. I should have stopped her from coming. I should have known.

EVE

When Daddy leaves the house, he doesn't say where he's going and I don't ask, just finish up dinner and listen to Esther read her book to me while Ruth cleans the bathroom and Mummy helps Joe through his math homework. When the rice is done steaming and the curried chicken is finished, I turn the fire low and stick my head around the doorway.

"You want to wait for Daddy to get back, or go ahead? It's eight-thirty."

"He's by the church." Mummy taps Joe's page, squinting at the words. "Let's read it together. 'If you have three apples and your friend gives you two, how many apples do you have?' Just look outside, see if he's heading back yet."

I leave Esther in the kitchen to watch the stove and push my feet into my school shoes. As I step into the yard, a car flies past. It looks like Faith's dad's car. I glimpse two heads in the front, and two in the back. Did something happen back at the church? Is that why Daddy went there?

"I'm gonna go check at the beach," I call through the window, then start down the road.

"You hear what happened?" Mark calls as I near his house. His car's engine runs while the hood is propped up, a work light illuminating its insides.

"No. That was Faith and her daddy?"

He nods. "Her mummy gone up there, clean out her mind. Just going crazy out on the rocks. Lucky she ain drown."

I pick up my pace. How come Faith didn't call me? Why didn't Daddy let me know? At the end of the path, the gate is open. I step through and out onto the sand.

The church stands in darkness; Daddy must have gone someplace else. Shadows hide the building's age, but as I sit down on the steps, they groan with the fatigue of people walking over them all these years. I plunk down on them anyway. The old wood will have to bear weight a little longer. It feels wrong that Faith went through something so awful and I wasn't there to help her. Where are they taking her mother? Will she get to go back home? My throat thickens, thinking about Faith. She must be falling apart right now.

I let myself into the church and flick on the lights. Right away, I feel that something is wrong. Did Faith's mother have a breakdown in here? I walk into the sanctuary and right away I see.

Faith's phone lies on a chair at the back of the room.

Nearby, a crumple of clothing is strewn on the floor. Cotton. Plaid. I bend down and pick it up.

Boxer shorts.

I tie the underwear in a knot and cram it into the bathroom garbage, then fill a bucket and grab a mop. As I slosh water over the floor, I feel myself shaking. I can't believe she would do this. Here. Now. Am I missing something? She wouldn't do that. She's not into church, not that I care, but even so, she wouldn't actually have sex on a church floor. *My* church floor. A part of my mind adds, *with my Toons*, but I push that thought away. It wouldn't matter who she was with.

Outside, the wind howls, its breath sliding under doors, around closed windows, finding the building's secrets and threatening to blast them wide open. I run more water and mop the floor again. I lose track of time as the wind sings. I sing back, to fill the minutes, to clear my head and calm myself, to hold this rickety frame together.

"She all right?"

I drop the mop as I turn around and see Toons standing at the entrance to the sanctuary, hands jammed deep in his pockets.

"You had to do it here? How could you?"

"It wasn't like that. We didn't mean to—we was just talking." His voice is small. "What happened with her mummy? Where they took her?"

"I don't know—probably the hospital." Outside, the wind has dropped, leaving behind an eerie still. Toons leans into the wall, knuckles tapping, as if he has extra rhythm in him he needs to shake out. "Why are you here?" I say. "Just go."

"I came for—" He steps forward and picks up Faith's phone. "She texted from her sister's phone and asked me to get it."

"Nice y'all so close. Though not close enough for you to stay and find out what happened to her mother."

"Don't be like that." He sits on the piano bench, kicks the leg once. "Can we just—you wanna sing?"

"Sing? Boy, you out your mind?"

"I don't know what else to do."

Footsteps hurry up the creaky steps and the door bursts open before I can answer.

"Evette Armbrister." Standing in the doorway, Daddy seems taller than usual. His stern tone tells me that he's already been here. That he guessed the same things I did. "I need to speak with you." And he blames me.

From where he is, I know he can't see Toons. "Hi, Daddy," I say. I step past the bucket of dirty water. "Can we go in the storage room? I need to get a cleaning rag."

"Sand and water isn't what I'm worried about." Ahead of me, Daddy sounds disappointed, tired. In the room, I move to close the door and he stops it with his foot. "That young man out there can hear everything I have to say."

"Daddy, I didn't—" I start, and he cuts me off.

"I don't even know where to begin. I asked you to come down and get me a book, and you left the gate open. Because of your carelessness, Faith's mother was able to come right through, and apparently your friends are using this place like their playroom. I saw Toons leave the church not two minutes after Faith came out. I trusted you with the key not only to the church, but the key to that gate these people went and put up. You know how contentious that thing is? You *know* it's a miracle they even let us keep coming and going freely. They could have kicked us out anytime."

"They didn't break anything, I checked," I try to reason.

"That's not the point." One hand is balled into a fist that he smacks into the palm of the other hand. "You realize that girl's father wants to tell the hotel we're responsible for her mother getting out there? That if the gate had been locked, the premises would have been secured and she couldn't have found her way onto the beach?"

"The fence wasn't even here two weeks ago! She could have come out here then!"

"You're not getting it." He starts to pace up and down the small room. I want to beg him to calm down, to tell him the stress isn't good for him, but it feels like everything I say makes things worse. "I trusted you with something important and you let me down. I don't care if your friends sneak around and make out or whatever it is they were doing in here. They make their own choices, they have their own problems at home. That's between them and their parents. But I thought there was an understanding between you and me. That I can lean on you, and you can come to me. That there's honesty between us."

"Like how you been honest about having cancer?" The words blurt out of me before I can stop them. Daddy pauses in his pacing and looks at me. For a second, I see bare vulnerability. Fear. Then he looks away.

"Finish up in here, I'll wait for you outside." He bangs out through the front door.

In the the sanctuary, Toons sits on the floor, head in his hands. I nod at the side door and he gets up, slipping through and away, into the night. I dry the floors, then straighten up the chairs again. When I'm done, I turn off the lights and lock the doors. Just beyond the steps, I can make out my father's shape on the sand, standing, back to me.

"Daddy." I try to make my voice grown, try to speak calmly, try to show him he can confide in me. "I saw the bill for the radiation. Mummy won't answer me when I ask her what's going on. Can't you just tell me?"

Daddy doesn't say a word, just leads the way back. At the gate, he holds out a hand. I slide my plaited necklace over my head and take off the key for the gate. He locks the gate, then puts the key in his pocket, and we carry on up the path, together but miles apart.

10

KEEKEE

"The trees have eyes
in their branches and
breath under their leaves.
They see what people cannot see."

I lean my back against the trunk, whisper my words to the sky, let them fall to the sand. I feel like I'm not in the right headspace today. What comes next? My mind is blank. There's a sound below me and I look down to see Eve and her siblings head into the church with Faith. I lean back and revisit my words, turning them over in my mind, in my mouth. When I see Eve and her brothers and sisters leave, I tell myself I'll spend just fifteen more minutes, then get down and head home. Just as I'm getting ready to climb down the tree, I see Toons coming. He heads into the church. They must be talking in there. As it gets close to sunset, I finally clamber down. As I pass by the window of the church, I catch sight of them. Toons and Faith—holding on to each other like they're the last two people left in the world. I sprint back toward the house.

. . .

The TV buzzes, its drone interrupted by Sammy chomping carrot sticks. In the background, Angel runs onions through the food processor. I sit on the floor with my back to the wall, staring at my English exercise book on my right side, my phone on the left. It's not the homework—it took me half an hour to finish my essay on how a lunch program at school could improve attendance and grades. It came so easily I wished I had another essay due. That's the problem. I love playing with words, stretching them, letting them bounce off each other, holding up one so it mirrors another. Poetry makes essays seem like a well-seasoned snack when someone's offering to pick up dinner, plus ice cream and two types of cake. A whole six weeks for poetry is a dream. So why can't I just fill the form out? Why can't I write a few lines down?

I tap my pen against the paper. *Think*, I tell myself. *Come on, think. If you don't want to be stuck here all summer doing laundry while Toons romances the whole neighborhood, think.*

Angel scrapes out the processor. Sammy cranks the volume up a notch.

Sweaty evening,
straining, believing
to catch the feeling

I scrawl the words down. They stare back at me, flat, all wrong. It's stupidly rhymey. What is this, preschool? I turn the page. Fresh start. I pick up the phone. After nine. I scroll through Daddy's texts. The latest one reads: Deadline's

tomorrow, don't forget. Like he'd given me a chance to do that.

The front door opens abruptly. Toons slams the door behind himself and stomps past on his way to the bathroom.

"Evening to you too," Angel calls after him. She clanks a tuna can against the side of a bowl, emptying the contents out. I look back down at the page again. The words are all wrong. I turn to a new page.

> *Seawater rising, moon*
> *surprising, I*
> *am despising . . .*

"Bet you they ga make a fuss about what gone down with Elaine tonight." Angel raises her voice to be heard over the TV. Sammy doesn't answer.

Not despising.

> *Moon rising, lies disguising, fences sprout like*
> *weeds, surprising—*

"Can't blame other people if she crazy." Sammy sets the carrot bowl on the floor with a clatter. "She didn't turn that way because they put up a fence. And you went to school with her?"

"In here loud," I complain, hoping they'll take the hint.

"I wouldn't say she was crazy. She was always a little different . . ." Angel's voice trails off. I look back down at the page. It waits, expectant.

> *Disguising why they really try to—*

Toons marches out of the bathroom, a towel wrapped around his waist. "Y'all ain got nothing better to do than talk bad about other people?"

"Here we go." Sammy gets up and heads outside. Angel drops the empty bowl into the sink.

"Who you talkin to like that?"

"Both of y'all." Toons' voice is raised, and getting louder. "You don't know that's somebody's mother?"

"Arrgh!" I fling the book away from me. It bounces off the edge of the sofa and splats, open, behind my brother.

"You hear them?" Toons turns to me, holding his hand out, accusing. He steps back, right onto the book, and doesn't even notice. "You ga let them talk about your friend's mummy like that?"

"I just want all y'all to shut up so I can focus for three minutes." I snatch the book up. My words stare back at me, pathetic. Mocking me. I rip the page out and ball it up.

Toons plunks himself onto the sofa. "On your period, ay?" he mutters. I hurl the screwed-up page at him. It bounces off his head and he yelps like I socked him with a rock. "You lettin her get away with that?" he complains to Angel.

Angel shoves the tuna into the fridge. "I don't know what wrong with either one of y'all tonight."

"He out here talking bout people period," I snap back. "Ask him where he comin from so late. Which girl he been by? Hmm, so many to pick from."

"Shut up, snitch."

"Enough." Angel snaps off the TV. "KeeKee, what happened? Why you so edgy tonight?"

"Why you startin with me? The golden boy can't do no wrong? He don't have to do nothing round but come in late and pick fights, and you still turn around and treat him like new egg."

"I don't do nothin? Who help you hang up them clothes? People memory short."

"Exactly. I just supposed to do it, but when you get involved, you want a gold star. I wish I could finish school and do nothing but sit on my backside all day and chase after tail all night."

"Okay, y'all," Angel interjects. "Come on, why we arguing?" Her peacemaking only fuels my rage.

"You make him like that. You don't know he running round with three different girls?"

"Three?" Toons jumps up from the sofa. "You don't know what you talkin about."

"What three?" Angel begins, and a rap at the door cuts her off. Toons hunkers down deeper in the sofa like he's trying to shape his bony backside to its angles. Angel holds up her hands, dripping with dishwater and soap.

I suck my teeth. "I gotta answer the door now too?"

"Ooh, so hard," Toons mocks.

Angel takes a step toward the door. "Hello?"

"Evening. Mr. Armbrister here."

She dries her hands on her T-shirt as Toons retreats down the hall to his room. She opens the door. Mr. Armbrister wears a deep frown. Eve stands with him, but off to one side, as if she'd rather pretend she's not there at all.

"Evening, Pastor," Angel says.

"Sorry to bother you, Miss Hepburn," he replies, and despite my mood, something in me softens. "Is Toons in?"

"He just came out of the shower. Something happened?"

"Seems he was spending some time at the church with Faith. Alone."

Angel looks over her shoulder toward the back of the house, but Toons is ensconced in his room now. "Tonight?"

He nods. "They shouldn't have been able to even get in"— Mr. Armbrister glances over at Eve—"and I've dealt with that, but it's not appropriate, disrespecting the space that way."

"Anthony!" Angel shouts for Toons. He emerges in a red shirt and dark jeans. "KeeKee, give us a moment, please," she says. I know she means out of earshot, but I go to the sink and plunge my hands into the water, pretending to start the dishes. "Mr. Armbrister says you were up in the church?"

"Sir, me and Eve don't do anything like that, we just sing."

"You and *Eve*?" Angel exclaims.

Mr. Armbrister turns to Eve. "You've been sneaking around with this boy too?"

"Just to get a break, Daddy, like he say, we only sing." Eve looks like she might burst into tears.

"The acoustics in the church are so excellent, Mr. A," Toons tries to explain, and a rush of guilt washes over me. He really sounds like he's telling the truth.

"I'm sorry for the interruption, Miss Hepburn." Eve's daddy sounds like thunder, like her singing is as bad as anything Faith did. "Clearly I have some things to sort out under my own roof."

As they leave, Angel smacks Toons in the back of his head. "Boy, what wrong with you? You don't have any sense in your head?"

"Me and Eve never—"

"I'm talking about you and Faith! What happened to that nice girl up the road?"

"I . . ." He shoots me a furious glare, like somehow I got him in this mess. "I didn't plan it, it just happened."

"All the time I spend teaching these girls around here to be careful and take precautions, meanwhile my own son running round like King Solomon in the harem?"

"Well, sorry I couldn't be perfect like *her*!" Toons pushes back inside and disappears into his room.

"I hope at least you were careful," Angel shouts after him. She stands in the doorway, looking out into the night. "I can't even believe y'all children."

"Who *y'all*?"

"You knew all this was going on and didn't tell me?"

"How I get in trouble?"

"I know you stay sneaking round, watching and listening."

I toss the sponge on the counter. "He goes running all about the place and I get in trouble for nothing?"

"You supposed to help me!"

"You let him get away with anything."

Angel lowers her voice. "Cut the boy some slack. I'll speak to him again about taking more precautions." She shakes her head. "I sure missed this one."

There's a sound from the hallway. Toons stands there, a backpack over one shoulder. "Sorry to disappoint y'all." His voice is a sarcastic hiss. "Since I letting everybody down, how about if I just get outta here one time?"

"Toons," Angel begins, and he ducks past her out the door.

"You lettin him go out again?" I ask.

"KeeKee." Angel sounds tired. "Leave it alone, now."

I don't want to leave it alone. It all feels wrong, the way she reprimands me for what he did, the way she expects more of me than she does of him. "I don't see—"

"You wanna go out too?" Angel steps out of the doorway, gesturing into the night. "Be my guest."

Except I don't. I just want things to be fair. I know Toons got into trouble, even if it should have been more, and Eve, too, even if she really was only singing with him all those times in the church. But somehow, I still feel empty. Angel goes out, closing the door behind her, and I hear her under the tree, telling Sammy he should go tonight, let her sort things out with us. I flop onto the sofa. The house is quiet, finally, but what's the point anymore? I catch sight of the crumpled ball of paper, pathetic and small. That's what I get for trying to capture my words.

FAITH

I lie in my room, the night around me awake with silence. I can't get my brain to shut off. The howl of wind. *Laney.* Clunk of untuned piano keys, Toons' hands on my arms, on my waist. What felt perfect before has me tender now. I shift, looking for relief. *Stay out of trouble. Hope Springs. My fault.*

I am twelve when the pigeon flies in the open door. Daddy swears at the bird, throwing books while it flutters, its eyes darting, wings opening dangerously, unaware that the safest thing it can do is fold in its breakable parts and keep still.

"What y'all let this bird in for?" Daddy keeps saying. The bird beats its wings, finding screen, ceiling, wall.

181

"It's okay, Daddy," I answer, but it's Mummy who goes to the closet for a sheet.

"You do it." She hands it to me and I unfold it and toss it at the bird, but I miss and it keeps flying up, landing a few feet away. On the third try, just before the fabric settles over it, I catch sight of a tiny dark eye and see a mixture of understanding and fear, a knowing that I could save it or crush it, the glint of hope. I put my hands around its small body, the sheet between it and me, and the wings flutter slightly, its feet scrabbling against my hands until it finds a way to grasp my fingers with gentle claws. Walking to the French doors, I hold the small, exhausted life a moment longer than I need to, then step out into the sun and pull the sheet away. Stunned, it struggles, then realizes it's free. Its wings are white underneath as they lift it away.

I hear her again, the lopsided scream twisting out of her throat, her wild arms fighting against being caught, being carried away. Stretching. Longing to fly.

There's a creak down the hall. *Is that her?* I wonder, then remember that she's gone. The house groans again, settling, reordering itself. I feel trapped in here—no phone, no car. Blue walls, luminous in the dark. *Laney.* Daddy snores from the other room. How can he sleep? I lie awake and remember how he was different before too. He told jokes, though I can't think of any of them now. He could swing me around, ordinary things flying by as if they had wings. He would walk up to Mummy, kiss her cheek, and wring out a twisted sheet of a laugh, damp and crinkled and long. I would find a way to squeeze between them, a small grove of legs. His hands found me every time, picked me up, and I would be at the core of both their kisses like I was the heart that made them beat.

I have to get out of here. I stand up, slip my keys into my pocket, then tiptoe down the hall. Soundlessly, I let myself out. Stepping outside from the air-conditioned big house, the night air is like tepid bathwater. I walk toward Pinder Street, walk the way my mother must have gone to get to the water.

The roads are still, and the lit windows of the houses I pass seem far. I check behind me, but I'm alone on the street. I turn onto QE Highway and pick up the pace. My feet are in agony all over again. My mother must be stronger than I realized, and more determined. The walk feels like it's going on forever. The homes peter out and I'm on the vacant stretch between my neighborhood and the high school. Headlights illuminate the road behind me, distant and sudden. Someone's turned onto the street and is heading my way. They're coming closer, high beams on. I look back and squint at the blinding light. Right behind me now, and slowing. My body tenses, ready to run.

"Faith?" A girl's voice calls from the passenger side. No. Oh, no.

"Hey, Paulette." I almost choke on the words.

She leans forward to look past the plump woman in the driver's seat. "What you doing walking after eleven? Get in."

The pounding of my heart tells me I shouldn't be on this dark road alone, but I can't catch a ride with Paulette, especially not tonight.

"I'm okay." I try to sound casual.

"Girl, get in the back. You crazy?"

That word is like being kicked in the gut. But her face is friendly, concerned. She doesn't know what went on at the beach tonight.

"This is my friend from my biology class," she continues. "Ms. Bain, this is my neighbor, Faith."

Ms. Bain nods. "Come on. We can't leave you out here like that." In the distance, another set of headlights has appeared. "Hurry up," she says. "I don't like to stop in the night."

I get in and we pull off. The headlights behind us are gone now.

"Where you headed, walking this late?" Paulette turns back to look at me as she speaks.

Why does she have to be so nice to me? "I have to go back and get my car. Long story."

"Good thing we passed you." She reaches into her bag and hands something back to me. "Gum?"

I take a stick and unwrap the slim strip of foil from around it, hating myself.

When we reach Pinder Street, they stop just behind where I parked. I scramble out, fumbling over a thank-you. As I walk to my car, I pause—something isn't right in the air.

The SUV comes out of nowhere, black paint, black tints, lights off, squeal of tires on old road—and flies past us toward the dead end. It swerves into KeeKee's yard, but it doesn't stop, plowing through the clothesline, then slamming into the bushes at the back. Four men burst out and scatter, one to the yard, one to the front door, two down the path.

"Get back in," Paulette hisses, and I scramble back into the car while we watch one of the men hammer on Toons' door. *Open this door*, he shouts, *open this door.* Then the two that went down the path reappear dragging someone between them, someone kicking, someone struggling. Toons. Paulette gasps.

"Stay in here, don't get out," Ms. Bain whispers, holding Paulette back as they open the rear of the SUV and shove Toons in like furniture. He must be gagged—he struggles, but there's no sound. Then, fast as they came, they are gone. Ahead of us, toward the water, smoke rises.

NIA

Pushing past Mummy to the backyard, the street behind us painted red. Fire truck's lights, KeeKee's mouth a drowned-out scream, Angel on the ground. I hold on to KeeKee, who holds on to me. Her tears on my shoulder are hot rain.

"He ain do nothing!" she keeps sobbing. "What they take him for? He don't bother no one!"

Women haul Angel up and get her inside, but we are caught in the crowd. Where did all these people come from? There are only eight houses along here. I hold KeeKee's hand like when we were small, my fingers a protection, a promise to her. Two of the members from Eve's church push toward the path. "They're using seawater to put the blaze out," someone shouts. "That building's finished." It's hard to pick out faces or recognize voices. All that's preserved is one big message: someone cut a hole in the fence, broke in, and set the church on fire.

Somewhere in everything, fingers close over my shoulder, the same spot where KeeKee's tears fell, and pull me away.

"Back to the house." Mummy's voice is insistent in my ear.

"I can't leave KeeKee." I look around frantically, but she's disappeared.

"Back." Her hand on my elbow, tugging me against the grain. Inside, our house is too close, too quiet. Voices push against the edges of the windows.

"But KeeKee's my best friend—"

"It's not a debate, Nia. It isn't safe." Mummy locks the top lock, then shoves the key deep into her pocket. "KeeKee's with her mother, where she needs to be."

"How could they do that? How someone could just take Toons?"

"Best thing we can do is go to bed. Nothing more left for this day." She won't look at me. It's like he isn't worth getting excited over, like she doesn't even care.

In my room, I fume. I want to be outside, standing with KeeKee, seeing the firemen come back down the path, hearing how bad the damage was, listening to what the police say, trying to make sense of what I saw through the gap in the curtains— the SUV speeding past our window like grass was highway, men in black clothes, faces covered, Toons struggling to get away.

Slowly, the voices die down. The fire trucks pull off, giving way to a silence that's too still, too thick. Every few minutes, there's a muffled sob. I hear Mummy moving around out front, then talking, hushed.

Hypocrite.

When I wake up, everything is quiet, and as it should be, the bedroom door propped open slightly, the hulk of the printer a large, docile pet half asleep, half-guarding, Mummy's snores drifting in, soft and deep. Then after a second, it all comes back and nothing can ever be right again.

Wind picks up, a low, slow, defeated gust. I reach for the window, cranking the louver down to seal off air. The sound comes again—it's not wind, it's something isolated. Something alone and broken off from the things that used to tie it down. I peep through the curtain. Grass, bush, nothing moving. There it is—it's coming from the street. I slip out of bed and through the house. From the front window, I can make out a pile of clothes leaning up against the porch railing. Wait. No. A person. It's a person. They shift again, lifting their head.

I drop the curtain, my heart pounding. Is it safe to open the door? What if it's a setup, what if the men in the SUV are back and when I open the door, they jump in and grab me? The sound comes once more, an awful, broken groan. I have to do something. I look again. No cars, no light, no sound. I tiptoe into Mummy's room. The air is thick and still, double dark with her curtains drawn tight and the streetlamp hidden from view. I give my eyes a moment to adjust, till I can see her. She lies on her back, facing the door, one hand over her belly, the other behind her pillow. I reach for the key on her nightstand, easing it off carefully. She snorts once, then turns her head the other way.

I run into the kitchen and grab a flashlight from the drawer. Then I slip a hand between the fridge and the wall. My hand finds the cool wood of the cutlass handle. Armed with it, I unlock the door, moving slow, coaxing the key to click into place quietly. I open the door.

"Hey," I whisper. "Can you hear me?"

A strange sound tears through the air, rearranging my

words. A sob cut short, choked off. I step out into the night and turn the flashlight on. *Toons.* In two steps, I'm beside him. He struggles to push himself upright and yelps, then cuts off the cry. His left eye is swollen shut, his lip split.

"Can you lean on me? I'll walk with you."

"No." Toons half-sobs. "I can't go home. If they catch me . . ."

"Come in our house," I whisper. He hesitates. "Mummy sleeping."

I sling the flashlight around my wrist and help him to sitting, then standing. He whimpers in pain. Then his whole weight is on my shoulder as he leans. I steel my legs and we stumble inside.

"Nia?" Mummy calls from the hallway, then sees both of us in the glare of the swaying flashlight. What—" She stops short. In seconds, she lights a match, and the room opens up with the tiny flame. Then she puts it to the kerosene lamp. In the brightness, she gasps.

"Go in the bathroom, get a clean washcloth and wet it." She guides him onto the couch while I do as she says. "Put the cloth on his face," she orders when I come back. He flinches as the rough terry cloth touches his skin.

"Don't tell Angel I here," he pleads. "I don't want them hurt my mummy or my sister."

"Who's them?" I ask.

"I don't know, but they beat me up bad. Drive round and drop me in the bush."

"Did you walk back here?" Mummy asks.

"Yes—oww."

"Take this and let him go in the bathroom and get cleaned up." Mummy holds out the lamp. "If he isn't out in five minutes, come get me." She disappears into the kitchen.

I wish I was like KeeKee, used to helping people in trouble. Then I'd know better what to do. I try to copy Mummy and give directions. "Can you stand?" I ask Toons, and he struggles to his feet. "Use the wall. Rest on me." I suppress a grunt as he leans on me, and we stagger back to the bathroom. I put the toilet seat lid down, then help him to sit and ease off his shirt. I used to dream of being this close to a boy. It's coming true, but like a dream, everything is odd and sideways-slanted, put together wrong. Then Toons raises his left arm and he yelps like a kicked puppy, then brings a hand to a bruise on his side. He leans on me as he steps out of his jeans. Muddy shoeprints stain up and down the leg, as if he has been used as the street, as if someone lost their way on him, then found it again. I smell urine, embarrassing and sharp. I swallow hard to make way in my throat for words again. "You could get in the shower? You can take your boxers off there."

He ignores my hand, leaning on the counter as he steps into the tub. He draws the curtain between us. "Don't tell anyone." The water hisses as it moves through the pipes. He gasps at the shock of cold on his skin.

"I won't." Another thing I can't tell KeeKee, I think. "Let me get you a towel," I say, and hurry for Mummy's room. She's on the landline, her voice urgent.

"You can't do something? Okay. No, I understand." Now resigned. "If you can't help, you can't help." She hangs up, then sighs, the sound swallowed by the dark. "Yes, Nia, what you need?"

"Um—what towel can he use?"

"Any one." Her voice is impatient. I reach for the third drawer, then pull out the first one my hand finds. As I turn to go, I hear her dialing again. I pause in the doorway. "It's Tanya," she says. "She's fine, but I need you to help."

The shower cuts off before I can hear anything more. I tiptoe back to the bathroom. "I got something for you to dry off with," I say. Toons' hand emerges from behind the curtain, and he takes the towel.

"Nia, look in my bureau, at the back," Mummy calls from out front. "Find some clothes you can give him."

Men's clothes? I wonder, but when I check all I find is old T-shirts and pairs of her shorts, I choose a looose faded green shirt that smells stale from being packed away too long. There are no pants that would fit him, though. I bring the shirt to her as she yanks cotton, Band-Aids, and alcohol out of the cupboard next to the fridge.

"I didn't see any pants."

She heads for the bathroom. "Find some," she calls over her shoulder. Mine won't fit him either. I look out at the clothesline. The grass is chewed up with tire tracks, but the laundry on the line hangs still, strangely undisturbed. In front is a mix of children's uniforms and women's blouses, but behind is a row of men's clothes. I tiptoe out through the side door and unclip a pair of tan pants. Back inside, I knock on the bathroom door. Mummy opens it.

Toons is sitting on the closed toilet, Mummy's best towel

wrapped around him, up under his arms, his head low. His teeth are chattering. I set the clothes on the counter.

"You okay?" I ask.

Mummy helps him ease the shirt on, then tugs him to standing. "He's in shock."

"You don't think we should get Angel? Or take him to a hospital?" Through the closed windows, I hear a car ease up to the house. Its headlights are off. It's the men from earlier. They came back.

"I have someone here who can take him for help. He doesn't want his family to know where he is, in case these thugs try to come back." Mummy takes Toons gently by the arm, guiding him into the kitchen. "You stay here. Put his clothes in a plastic bag. I'll deal with them," she says. "And Nia?" She looks at me straight in the eye. "Anybody ask, nothing happened here tonight. He's in danger. If you care about his life, you can't say a thing, especially to KeeKee. Understand?"

I nod. For once, we agree.

"All right, then." Mummy turns away. The door closes behind them. The porch boards squeak once, then night takes them up, bears them away. Alone in the bathroom, I reach for the clothes, abandoned in the tub. If Toons is in trouble, it'll be easier to find his clothes if they're dirty, if they're still stained with his—with everything. I fill up the bathroom sink with hot water and plunge the clothes in. The jeans take on water like a boat with a leak, growing dangerously heavy and hard to move. The shirt, ethereal and flimsy, wafts through the water, going whichever way my hands tell it to. The underwear twists between, hiding itself. I empty and refill the sink until the rinse water finally runs clean. I wring the clothes out and put them in a plastic bag on the floor.

When I come out of the bathroom, Mummy is back, sitting at the dining table. She turns her face toward me, then looks away, as though she's seen a ghost, as though she sees it still, where I should be.

KEEKEE

Two or three different neighbors offer to sleep here, but Angel shakes her head. "We all right," she keeps saying, as if repetition will make it true. Instead, that silence settles in, stretching over the house, wrapping it, warping it, until there would be no way for my brother to find his way home if he was led right up to the front door. At first, I sit upright on the sofa, watching the front door, listening, willing him to walk through it. As the minutes turn into hours, I can't stay there anymore. I stand in Angel's doorway. The light from the living room lamp illuminates her body curled up on the bed.

I turn to face the open door to Toons' bedroom. Did Toons really set fire to the church like the police say? Is that why those awful men took him? Outside, a car's tires crunch along the sandy street. I jump up and hurry into his room, but by the time I reach the window, it's gone. I sit down on the edge of his bed, willing my brother to find his way out of that car. To make his way safely home.

11

FAITH

I lie awake, feeling the itching burn between my legs. Daddy moves around the house with heavy footsteps. I hold my breath, listening. If I wait long enough, I'll hear something else in the background—the whoosh of a toilet's flush, a book falling to the floor, anything to tell me last night was a dream and my mother's right here, like she should be. She will sneeze and fill out this deflated, lopsided house. Then there's a soft sound, half cough, half clearing the throat. *It's her.* I sit up slowly, let myself believe yesterday was a dream. If she is here, the evening wasn't real, and neither was the night. I open the door.

"Faith." Daddy stands right outside my bedroom, hand raised as if he was about to knock. "It's almost eight, you got school." He is showered and dressed, his collar turned back, his shirt buttoned up. He has circles around his eyes, as if, despite the snoring, he didn't sleep at all.

"I'm not going."

"It's not a debate. You think I'm leaving you home alone after Saturday? You were supposed to be home with your mother. Instead you out, not answering your phone, and I get a call from Mr. Armbrister telling me you were in that church with some guy?"

"It's not my fault! You aren't even home half the time," I shoot back. I stalk past him into the front room. My car keys are gone. "Where are my keys?"

"I look like a fool to you? I'm not letting you sneak out again. You'll get them back when I can trust you."

"That ain no fair! How am I supposed to get to school?"

"I'll take you myself. You got fifteen minutes to get ready."

I reach for my phone and realize I don't have it. Toons was supposed to get it for me. If he never made it back to the church, it was in there when the fire started. And if he did make it back, does that mean he set the place to burn? Nothing makes sense anymore. Then something clicks. "Who told Mr. Armbrister I was with Toons?"

"You think that's the point?" Daddy leans his head back to look at the ceiling. "Get ready for school. I'm finished talking." He starts to make his way to the kitchen.

"You know who took Toons?" I call after him.

He stops and walks back to me. "Is that the little boy you've been running around with? You bold, asking about him after we watch your mummy get carted away. You better not bring no baby around here. Your mother may not understand, but that would kill her anyway."

I swallow the lump in my throat and raise my chin. "He could be dead and you wouldn't even care. You don't care about Mummy, or me either. Or anyone." I wait for Daddy to yell at me. Instead, he closes his eyes, as if he is remembering too. Then he opens his eyes.

"Get ready for school. Staying in the house won't bring back your mother, and you don't need to stay home for no boy."

Mummy's gone. I turn around and walk away, to the bathroom. Toons is the one person who could make me feel better, and he's nowhere to be seen. The itching intensifies, making me want to scream. Reminding me that everything bad happening is my fault.

KEEKEE

Up the street, life unfolds as if today is normal. Mr. Rahming sweeps in front of his store. Eve's family is being herded into the car. Riccardo and Amos are laying low, but Mark is half under his car. The stereo blasts an old Buju Banton album, defiant, joyful, raising rhythmic Cain. Here, it's a different story. The yard is chewed up, tire tracks spun out and doubling back, the grass on edge, each jagged blade a tooth. A splat of red discolors the road in front of our house, a period at the end of a sentence no one wants to say. Behind me, under the tree, the same police officer who came last night to take a statement is talking with Angel again.

"I'll do my best to help," he says, "but between you and me, I was told to leave this alone."

"What you mean leave it alone?" I hate hearing the tears in Angel's voice. "He's an eighteen-year-old boy and we *saw* him get taken. You expect me to leave that?"

"I understand, miss, I have a son myself. That's why I came out here a second time when you asked. But what I'm telling you is, I got orders from above that this wasn't no random thing.

I was told he was continuously trespassing on the property, and the developers got some guys to scare him off. And there's reason to believe he may have even set the fire to the church."

"But he didn't come home. That's more than just scaring. And why would my boy set fire to the place where he and his friends hang out?"

"Officially, we'll file a missing persons report. I'm just—I want you to know what they're saying. I'll take additional statements from people along the street. I just don't want you to get your hopes up." He glances at the water. "These people are powerful."

Toons is dead. The words cross my mind like clouds across sun, clear as any rhyme.

"KeeKee?" Nia is beside me. She looks as tired as I feel. Her front door is open behind her. She reaches into her bag and pulls out a foil package. "Breakfast," she says as I open it. Bread, a layer of green between the slices. A diagonal cut. Flash of red from within. Blood and grass.

"Tomato sandwich with basil," she says. "I used extra black pepper."

I scrunch the foil around it and shove it in my pocket. "Thanks." Behind her, I glimpse movement. Her mother passes the open door, watching.

"He's okay. He's coming back." Nia looks at me, this twist of hope wrapped all around her, as if she just knows my brother's blood isn't on the street, but in his body, warm with life. As if this sandwich will make me see it too. We start walking, and I let her keep talking, let her voice comfort me. "He didn't do it," she continues. "He would never start a fire. Did the policeman say anything? I didn't hear them talk about it on the news. You should go to the papers. I bet they would do a story."

"You don't have to wait twenty-four hours," I say.

"To report him missing?"

"I thought you had to wait. You don't."

"So that's good, right?"

"It means even the police can give up after a day. He isn't coming back."

Nia bites her lip, searching for something to say. "He's coming back," she repeats, finally. "This is his home. He has to come back."

In the school yard, word has spread. I can tell by the way students huddle in private groups, talking low, turning to look at me, their eyes avoiding mine. In our classroom, I sit at my desk, back to the wall. Nia stays beside me and I flip through my textbook, letting the whisper of the pages fill the silence.

"Hey," I hear Nia say, and I look up and see Faith coming toward us. "I heard about your mom—"

"Yeah." Faith cuts her off the way I wish I could do to other people. "I need to talk to KeeKee. Can you . . ." She looks over at the door.

"How about if *you*—" Nia starts.

"Two minutes."

My friend hesitates, then nods, heading outside. The classroom is empty now, except for me and Faith.

"It's about Toons," she says.

"Yeah, and how the hotel developers took him."

She looks surprised. "He didn't come home last night?"

"No, and the officer who came by this morning said he was told to leave it alone. He said the hotel people wanted to shake him up. Except it doesn't take all night and into the next day to scare someone a little bit. You gotta ask your dad what he knows."

Faith looks disbelieving. "I'll ask him. I don't think that's true, though. What would they take him for? He didn't do anything."

I think back to that night. What was in his backpack? I can believe he would have cut a hole in the fence, but could he really have set a fire? "He didn't say anything when y'all were together?"

She looks surprised, embarrassed, even, as if her and Toons and whatever they did is important right now. "He wasn't mad or anything. We were just talking about old times. Our mothers. I don't think Daddy knows anything, but I'll find out." She leans in close. "I need a favor, though. Can you help me go to the clinic?"

"My brother didn't come home last night and you came to ask me about the clinic?"

"It's just—I need to go."

"I don't believe you. You don't even care about Toons. For all I know, you could have set that fire yourself, and he's the one who got snatched."

"I wasn't even on Pinder Street till after there was smoke," she protests.

I look her dead in the eye. "You know where my brother is?"

She stares back, her face fearful. "No, KeeKee, I don't!"

"You know how to drive and how to get Toons to cheat and to sneak around and to get himself beat up and taken away. I think you could figure out the clinic on your own."

"You supposed to help people!" Her voice cracks as she speaks. "You gonna help me or you gonna judge me?"

I know what Angel always says, that we don't ask questions, we don't give our thoughts. I don't care, not anymore. "You gotta be either stupid or brain-dead to sleep with somebody else's boyfriend and not even use something."

"What's your problem?" she asks, spinning around to face me. We stare at each other, eye-to-eye. "What did I do to you?"

"Toons is gone, and you're the reason. You on your own."

As my words hit her, I can almost see her shrink a few millimeters. We stand there for a moment, her eyes on her folded arms, me staring right into her face, daring her to look up. Something white-hot rears up in me, begging to be fed, let out.

She swallows, her eyes locked on mine. Narrows her eyes. Then she looks away, taking a step back. "I didn't cause Toons to get locked up. I didn't. I thought he loved me, okay?" She hurries out of the classroom before I can find a way to get hold of the thing in me, find a way to use it to make her pay for what she did. Make her admit it's her fault Toons got taken away.

NIA

All day through school, I feel Toons with me. Bruised face looking over my shoulder at my math answers, shaking hands reaching for half my sandwich at lunch. I take my seat beside

KeeKee in French class, the phantom Toons sitting in front of us, silent and bleeding, the truth I cannot speak. He is so large I can't believe KeeKee can't see him. His sobs rattle in my ears through the listening comprehension exercise, distracting me until Monsieur Kemp says *"Posez vos stylos et changez de papiers."*

KeeKee leans over to me to swap papers. She whispers, "I didn't get to tell you before Faith cut in this morning—Angel spoke to the police again. I don't think they're gonna help."

He's okay, I want to blurt, *I don't know where he is, but he's okay.* But it's a choice between calming my best friend's fears and saving her brother's life. "Toons will come home," I say. I try to make my voice steady, honest, trustworthy.

Then Monsieur Kemp begins reading out answers and I look away without a word, marking her paper, the pen moving over the paper steadily, reliably, sure. Wrong, wrong, right, right, right.

FAITH

Eve finds me by the field at morning break and plunks down next to me on the bleachers.

"You all right?"

I have to get through another five hours of school, so I steel my face. The itch down below is almost unbelievable. It'd serve me right if I caught something. I squeeze my legs together. "I'm fine," I say, hoping it can be true.

"You wanna talk about it?"

"Nope."

"How about the other thing?"

"Even less so."

Eve leans back. "So, I got in trouble."

"For what?" I look over at her, welcoming the distraction.

"Daddy found out you and Toons were . . ." Her voice trails off. "According to him, it's my fault."

"Oh, so you came here to throw that in my face."

She sits up. "I didn't say that."

"KeeKee did."

"Well, her brother got beat up and abducted right in front of her."

"I care about Toons too. I saw it too, Eve. I was right there. And not only that, now I'm pretty sure I have some type of . . . disease."

"Disease? Why?"

I slump forward. "So, we didn't exactly use . . . like, protection. And don't lecture me about how I should have known better, because it already happened. I can't go back in time."

Eve looks confused. "KeeKee gives condoms away for free."

"You don't have to point out the irony. Anyway, now I feel like I'm on fire and I'm pretty sure I have an STD."

"Why?"

"It's like I'm on fire."

She frowns. "Maybe it's a urinary tract infection. My mother gets those."

"It's not when I pee. It's, like, all the time."

"Yeast? I dunno. Doesn't it take longer to feel an STD?"

"I don't know."

Eve leans her shoulder against mine and I almost melt with

relief. After everything that's happened, not a single person has asked how I'm doing. But Eve's touch is pure comfort—letting me know she's still on my side. I throw my arms around her and she hugs me back briefly, then pushes me away.

"Don't go giving me your syphilis," she says with a straight face.

"Not funny!" I say, but I crack a small smile. Eve giggles and I push her so she half-tumbles off the edge of the bleacher, laughing even more. Then I'm laughing too, even though nothing is funny and I really might be sick, and we both know it, and she's the only person I care about who's not disappeared from my life literally overnight.

"Just go to the doctor," she says, climbing back onto the bleachers.

"You wanna come with me?"

She shakes her head. "I'm on lockdown now, for 'taking advantage of my parents' trust.'"

"They're acting like you were the one doing it in the church. Anyway, that church was the only place you ever snuck out to, and it's burned down now, so . . ." After I say it, I wish I'd chosen softer words.

"Ask KeeKee," Eve says, but she doesn't sound offended.

"Already did. She passed."

Eve stands up, waving her arms. "Hey, Henry!" she shouts across the field. A boy in our class jogs toward us. "Let me borrow your phone."

He slips his hand into his pocket and passes it to her.

"Can I bring it back in ten minutes?"

"Just leave it on my bag," he says, heading back to the field.

"Well, look who's got game," I tease.

"Ha-ha." Eve dials a number, then waits. "Hi, is this KeeKee's mummy? No, it's Eve from down the road. Faith was wondering if you could take her to the clinic this afternoon, if you're not too busy. Okay, thanks." Eve sets the phone down. "She'll be there. She said wait by the bus stop after the food store at three-thirty and she'll stop for you."

I know I should thank Eve, but for a minute, I feel frozen. With amazement at how she keeps going, even the morning after her family lost their church. How she found a way to make me laugh when I couldn't even imagine a smile. How even after knowing her for twelve years, she can still make my jaw drop with shock. Instead of trying to twist my mess of emotions into words, I let myself sit there with her. Feel how it is for someone to really, truly know you, not just in traded stories, pressed bodies, close space, but in years and tears and misplaced laughter, in unspoken words, in actions that make the stopped world start to slowly spin again.

By three o'clock, though, the lightness has dissipated. I head straight for the bus stop where I'm meeting Angel. I have seven minutes to get four streets over and two streets down. And I'm scared. The heat is making me sweat, and the itch is even worse. I pick up the pace and my bag bounces against my side as I jog across the street to the bus stop. A number 26 slows down for me. I wave the jitney away and the driver speeds off and leaves me in a cloud of black exhaust. After a few minutes, the blue truck pulls up and stops right beside me. The passenger window rolls down.

Angel pops the lock, fiddling with the radio as I open the door.

"Hey, girl," she says casually raising her sunglasses and smiling at me. She doesn't look like her son was abducted less than a day ago: She has on a light green strappy dress with a yellow scarf around he shoulders. She looks and sounds as if we're going to get ice cream. *What if what you need is more than a trip to the clinic and a ride back home,* a small voice in me wonders. I push the question out of my head.

"Hi." I hold my bag on my lap. It's burning now. How did it get this bad this fast?

"Don't be nervous," Angel says. "It's nothing to be afraid of. In and out. The tests are over before you even know. They take samples and you're done."

We drive the rest of the way in silence, and she eases the truck into the parking lot. Angel looks over at me.

"You want me to come in with you?"

"No." I let myself out. "Thanks. It's okay."

Inside, three people sit waiting. I walk up to the counter. One woman stares at a computer, while the other flips through a drawer of patient files.

"Excuse me." I try to make my voice confident, but it shakes as I speak. The woman at the computer looks up. Her face says that she spends all day dealing with problems she couldn't care less about, and I've come here to vex her at the end of her shift. She looks me up and down and I wish I wasn't in school uniform. "I came to get tested."

She presses her lips together as if she knew as much. "What kind of test you come for?" she asks, as though they offer a billion different kinds, as if she's not sure whether I want to pass a geometry quiz or get graded in my ability to recite times tables.

"For the STDs." There's a fluttering in my chest as I say it, but I keep my face stony.

"Pregnancy test also?"

I nod.

The woman slides a clipboard across to me and I scribble in my name and date of birth. She scans it, then pushes it back to me.

"Parent or guardian?"

"What?"

"Your parent or guardian." She taps the paper with a long, bright-pink fake nail.

I swallow hard and straighten my back to make myself as tall as I can. "I'm seventeen."

The woman rolls her eyes.

"You could consent to open your legs, but till you turn eighteen, you're a minor."

I snatch the paper up and turn away. My eyes sting with hot tears. I barrel through the waiting room and reach for the door, just as it swings open from the outside. Angel reaches out and touches my arm. Her fingers are light and soft, like a blanket being laid over you on a cold day when you have cramps, like soft TV in the next room and soup bubbling in the kitchen, like light rain outside. I wish I could stop and lean my head against her shoulder and soak in that soft. Did Mummy ever touch my arm that way? I struggle to remember, but all I can think of is a slack mouth and empty eyes. I wish I could hold on to Angel instead of that memory. I wish Angel was my mother.

"They giving you trouble?" Angel looks into my face, reading me. "What happened in there? You can't be done yet."

I pull away and run for the truck. She *isn't* my mother, and what kind of person am I if I even thought something like that? I yank at the door, but it doesn't let me in. I pull harder, and when it stays shut, I press my head against the window and squeeze my eyes so tight they might implode. I don't want her to see me crying. I don't want anyone to see me. I wish I could just disappear. I wish I'd never been born.

The truck beeps and the doors click. "It's unlocked now," Angel calls after me. "Wait here."

I get in and slam the door hard. The windows are up, the tints strong enough that no one can see me hammer my fists on the dash, no one can hear me scream. *It's not fair*, part of me wails. Another part whispers, *That's what cheaters get.* I hate myself. I hate Toons. I hate Angel—why didn't she make her son carry something? She's probably in there talking about me with those women. Telling them I don't have a guardian. Telling them my mother is off her rocker, locked up in the crazy house.

The passenger door opens.

"Come, they won't hassle you," she says, "I made sure of that." When I don't move, she tilts my chin up with her hand. "Go back in there and hold your head high. Go take care of yourself."

Those blank eyes in my head again. She should be here. She should be standing beside me.

"We're all hurting today, Faith," Angel says, softer now. "I know you care about Toons, and I was close with your mom too, when she was still herself. She'd want you to do this. Come on. I'll go in with you."

Together, we walk back into the clinic. When the nurse calls me into a room, Angel looks at me and I shake my head. "I'm okay now," I say.

"I'll wait for you in the truck." As she turns to go, her scarf slips off her shoulder and I glimpse a long wide scar. Smooth damaged skin sprawls across her back and disappears into the back of her dress. What happened to her? Whatever it was, it must have been awful. And yet here she is, trying to help me, I think, as she disappears through the door. In the room, I squeeze my eyes shut while they take a vaginal swab. Then I have my blood taken and get a cup to bring into the bathroom for a urine sample. Like Angel says, I keep my head up. Like she said, it's over fast.

"I gave them my number for the results," Angel says on the way back, easing into traffic. "Three days. You heading home, or . . . ?"

"I'm staying by Joy," I say.

She nods. "I remember where her house is."

"Thanks for bringing me today."

"I needed the distraction. How's everything at home?"

I don't have the energy to fake it anymore. "I wish I could just crawl into a hole and never come out again."

"Amen." Angel turns onto the road to my house. "If you ever need anything, you know where to find me."

"Thanks."

"Tell me something." She slows outside the house and slips the car into park. "Your dad is involved with that new development. Can you ask him about what happened with Toons? Two of the men went up the path last night, and maybe they have surveillance cameras. I know he didn't have anything to do with that fire, but we can't get proof."

"We don't talk much," I say, "but I'll try."

Angel nods. "Yes, try. It's important, okay?"

I nod as I get out, and close the truck door. "Thanks." I hear Angel roll her window down. She waves me around to the driver's side. I stand there and brace myself for a mini-lecture on being safe.

"I know it's hard," she says instead. "But just cause your mum isn't with you in the same way doesn't mean that she's gone."

It doesn't make sense to me, but I don't want to offend her. "Uh . . . okay."

Angel nods, rolls up her window, and backs out. I turn up the driveway and head for the door. Too bad those words are just a bunch of hot air, as worthless as Toons whispering *I good*. My mother's been going for years now, and I watched the last of her drain away right in front of me. I can't pretend she's still here.

12

EVE

Daddy is out when we get home from school. The younger ones swarm around Mummy while I rinse out the lunch containers. The house feels too light for everything that's happened. Right now, it feels like a good gust of wind would send it flying away. Outside, Mrs. Munroe's grandson pedals past on his little sister's bike. The girl trails after him on foot, scolding for her turn. Mr. Rahming steps out of his store and starts sweeping the faded driveway with a bent-bristled corn broom.

"There's a meeting tonight, remember?" Mummy's voice behind me snaps me back to attention. "Can you clean up the floors? Some people may stop by here afterward."

"That's still going on?"

"Just because they burned our church down doesn't mean our work is done," Mummy says. "It's been three days now. We have to move forward."

I grab our mop and pass it over the entry, then the kitchen and dining room. When I step out to empty the bucket, a mourning dove coos above my head. Its mate answers softly.

A few yards away, Mark whistles off-key, as he clanks around under his car. With this music in my ears, it's easy to imagine that everything's right on our street. Is it better to pretend everything is okay, or face the truth and search for answers we might never find? I pull the bucket back and let the water fly.

"Thanks for doing that, honey," Mummy calls as I pass through the living room. "With everything going on, we need to carry on like normal, when we can."

I hear it then, the siren's high wail, strobe lights painting the house fronts, the urgent voices, firemen rushing onto the beach. The pat of small hands on my feet brings me back. I scoop Junior up, tickling his chin. "Where Daddy gone?"

"He'll be back soon." Mummy checks the clock. "You all better get your homework done early." She claps her hands. "Esther, Joe, at the table."

"Floor still wet," I call as they stampede by. "Do you think he went to find out who set the fire at the church?"

"I have to go to that meeting?" Ruth's whine cuts right over my voice.

"You're not staying here by yourself," Mummy says, avoiding my question again. I plop Junior into his play yard and slip into the bedroom, closing the door on my family's noise. For now, I decide, I'll pretend everything is okay. Alone in the bedroom, life is messy but peaceful, and it's possible to imagine that things are right again. I gather up scattered clothes, humming as I go. When I lift the spread, I see a shoe box under the bed. I pull it out. Inside is a jumble of makeup—discs of eye shadow and lip gloss tubes.

Nestled on top is a rectangular compact. I flip it open and a palette of eye shadow stares up at me, pinks as hot as the heart of a hibiscus, dusky purples, new-leaf greens. Carefully, I stroke a finger across a square of color, then rub it onto the back of my hand.

The doorknob rattles. "Hey, open up!"

Ruth. I spring up before she gets louder and open the door. "Shhh," I say as she pushes past me.

"What you got it locked for?" Ruth shuts the door behind her. "Hey, who said you could go in my things?"

I pass the compact back to her. "Mummy know you have these?"

"You tellin her?"

"Not if you let me try it on."

My sister's face blossoms into a wide smile that makes her look like Daddy. "Let me get the good stuff." She opens her underwear drawer and pulls out a little stack of colorful cloth bags.

"Hey, are those the ones KeeKee hands out?"

"Yup." She pulls the drawstrings of one open and empties eye pencils, mascara, and lipstick onto the bed.

"How you got the bags?" I ask.

She shrugs. "I asked KeeKee. What, you never got any stuff from her?"

"Why would I? We always have pads under the bathroom sink." As I glance over the jumble of wands and tubes, my eyes fall on a familiar package, crusted with rhinestones. "Is that my lipstick?"

Ruth opens another jar of eye shadow and tilts it toward

me. "Finders keepers. You can use some though."

I shake my head. "Uh-uh, too bright."

"Bright isn't bad." She dusts my lids with a soft brush, then selects a wand of mascara.

"What's that, green or yellow?" I giggle, and she laughs too, and pulls out the tiny brush caked in plain old black.

"Look up," she orders, as she gently guides my chin down an inch. I look up and my eyes fall on a light brown splotch on the ceiling, but my mind is focused on the periphery of my view, where Ruth is making micromovements I can just barely feel. The only sensation I've ever registered through my eyelashes has been subtle, private—a roll of my eyes when Mummy tosses yet another task my way, a look shared with Toons a fraction of a second too long as our voices blend into each other, colors melding just right. Now I can add this shared one of Ruth, so close her breath tickles the fine hair on my face. "Hmm, not bad," she says.

"Let me see." I start to reach for the mirror on the bureau and she stretches out and passes it to me. I peer into the glass. Large, wide eyes stare back at me; my face seems like it belongs to a different person. To a girl who might have some-where to go. Who might have someone to look back at her a second longer than before. I lower my lids and tilt my head from side to side. The ocean shimmers from my face, delicate sparkles glinting like sun on slight waves.

"Eve! We need to go down for the meeting in an hour. Can you put on some rice and throw together a tuna salad?" Mummy's voice carries from out front, strident and strong.

"Really?" I mutter. "Now?" I start to get up.

Ruth pushes me back down. "Just let me finish. Blush and lipstick." She opens another jar and strokes a finger against the surface, then rubs my cheekbones.

"Hurry up," I whisper.

"Eve?" Mummy's voice is right outside the door.

"I'm changing," I holler, as Ruth scurries to stuff her stash away.

"Get the younger ones to set the table," she says. "And watch that tone. Don't act like I didn't used to bathe you."

I pump lotion onto a tissue and wipe my eyes. "Better?" I whisper. Ruth looks over her shoulder.

"Yikes."

I squint at the mirror. The sophistication of a minute earlier is gone: brownish pink and garish blue are streaked across my face, mixed with black and globs of white cream. I grab another few tissues and scrub again. Not much better. I need soap and water. Gingerly, I step into the hall: no Mummy, but I nearly collide with Esther, who bursts into laughter.

"Eve face look like the clown who came to the church party that time!" she sings as she skitters past. I ignore her and make a beeline for the bathroom. Out of nowhere, Joe pushes by me and slams the bathroom door in my face. I hammer on the door.

"Hey, you saw me about to go in!" I rattle the knob. It stubbornly refuses to turn. I slap my palm on the door. "Joe! You know you ain supposed to lock this."

"Eve? Put some cabbage and carrots on to steam too." Mummy's voice floats out from her bedroom. I suck my teeth and retreat to the kitchen. Small, dirty footprints prance across the still-damp floor. Fantastic. I wipe them up, then wash six carrots and a cabbage and slice them into a large pot. While the smell of cabbage fills the house, I start to measure out two cups of rice.

"You're it!" Esther screams, and runs into the kitchen.

"Watch it!" I snap at her, and Joe barrels right into me. Rice spills all over the counter and skitters onto the floor. The pair of them freeze, then, as if by unspoken consensus, dart outside, leaving the kitchen door wide open. I grit my teeth as I sweep up the rice and start measuring again.

"Stay out the kitchen," I shout out into the yard. "Y'all making more work for people in here."

"*Makin work for people in here*," Joe mocks, darting in again. More muddy footprints. Amazing.

Ruth pokes her head into the kitchen. "You could tell Mummy I have a test to study for tomorrow? I don't want go to this thing."

Anger flares up in me. The church is a part of our family, as much as the living, breathing members. I've known that place from before I knew her, and our parents have known it, loved it, even longer. Doesn't Ruth even care that it's been destroyed? Doesn't she see Daddy's health is waning too? Meanwhile, all Ruth cares about is *getting out of it.* "You should grow up," I say. *Grow up.* Is that the best I can do? Times like this, I wish I had Faith's tongue.

"Grow up or shut up," Joseph chimes, and swings a foot at me. Before I can snap at him, my nose picks up burn. I spin around and lift the lid off the veggies. Smoke and a vile smell belch into the room. The bottom is totally charred. I grab the pot off the fire and dunk it into the sink. Ruth peers over my shoulder.

"Smells like roasted farts," Ruth offers cheerfully.

"Thanks a lot. I don't even think we have more cabbage. Shoots, man!"

"Eve said a bad word!" Esther chirps from the living room.

"I said *shoots*." How did she even hear me?

"Honey?" Mummy's voice trails out from her room. I grab the bag of carrots out of the fridge and pretend that, for once, she means one of the others. I wash and chop them, then toss them into a fresh pot, then turn the rice down. I open four cans of tuna one after the other, drain off the water, then dump them into a big bowl and slop in mayo on top. "Eve? You want make sure these children eat before we leave?"

A thud comes from the living room; Joe begins to wail.

"I ain do nothing!" Esther calls out quickly.

"Eve?" Mummy calls. "Check on them, make sure they all right."

I bite my lip as I push the tuna salad aside and head for the living room. How come I have to work like an adult but my parents won't tell me the truth about what's going on? And what's my mother doing now, anyway? Why do I have to run around after all these kids? Isn't that *her* job?

NIA

People funnel through the gash in the fence and make their way onto the sand in front of the burned-out hulk. Tiki torches planted in the ground light the area with glowing orange flames, and flashlight beams slice the night. I find a spot for myself near the back of the crowd, beside KeeKee. We edge close to each other, but neither of us says a word as we stare at the hollowed windows and blackened walls of what used to be the church. I lean into KeeKee and feel the warmth of her arm against mine. The meeting is in full swing, with people taking turns to say what they think is the solution for the neighborhood, but it already feels like we've lost everything that made this place ours. It's not just the building; this isn't the same sand we joked around on, before the trouble began. In the moments before the guy in the baseball cap came along, this was a place we could kick off our shoes and socks, flop down and joke, roll our skirts up and wade knee deep or deeper, till nothing else mattered or even existed, for a while.

"We couldn't stop the church from being set on fire, and we can't stop this hotel from going up," Mr. Rahming says. "We have to accept that times change, and accept it peacefully. We had some good memories down here, let's not let it end sour."

"I don't agree with that." A woman I don't recognize raises her voice over the low buzz of chatter. "It's not final till they actually start to build. That's what's wrong with people, y'all want to give up before y'all even start. I brought all my kids out here to swim at a safe, quiet beach where they could play and have a good time away from the crowds. I think it's worth fighting for."

"How are we supposed to do that?" a man calls out just in front of me. "The land is privately owned. Matter of fact, all of us are trespassing just by being here. Y'all didn't hear about the boy who got arrested last night?"

"He wasn't arrested, he was taken. Those weren't police."

Riccardo's voice comes from off to one side. "Know what you're talking about before you open your mouth."

"All right, all right, friends," Mr. Armbrister breaks in. "Let's keep the tone respectful."

Even here, at this meeting, where everyone's supposed to be on the same page, no one agrees. There's no point to any of this, just like there's no point to that stupid newspaper. Why did I ever go to that first protest with Mummy, when writing about it couldn't stop what's happening now? Beside me, KeeKee shifts, something in her body uncomfortable. Is it worse for her if people talk about Toons or pretend nothing happrened, I wonder.

"You wanna go?" I ask her.

"No!" KeeKee's voice is filled with horror, with surprise, as if she can't imagine walking away. But the same weird shift that's made everything out here all wrong is affecting me and her too. I don't feel the same way, and I don't understand why she wants to stay in the place where her brother got beaten up and abducted just yesterday.

Across the crowd, Mummy is engrossed, taking notes frantically, like history is being made and we're going to capture it in our homemade publication on eight-by-eleven-inch sheets of paper folded in two by hand. Looking around, I don't want to be here. It's not just the tension growing in the air; something about it feels as false as *Pinder Street Press*. We really don't have any say in what's happening, same way as no one actually reads what I write. Why are we grouping together in front of a burned-out building, pretending our voices, raised in the night, can actually make a difference? It's done. The only reason security guards aren't ordering us away is because they've decided to let us have this moment. To me, the beach is already lost. It's no longer part of Pinder Street.

"See you back home," I whisper to KeeKee, then weave through people to the edge of the crowd, and up the path again. I walk around to the front of my house, then sit down on the porch and stretch out my legs, drink in the quiet like cool rosemary tea. At least here still feels sort of right, if I don't think about Toons lying in the dirt in front of me. If. If. Footsteps rustle in the grass and I look up to see Sammy standing there, like he's come to rescue me from the thoughts I can't push away.

"Mind if I join you?"

My heart speeds up. Where did he come from? Did he come back here just to talk to me? "Sure."

He sits down on the porch and leans back on his elbows. "Couldn't take that crowd anymore." As if in reply, a voice in the distance rises to a shout.

"Yeah, me neither."

"What you usually do in the evening? Like if there wasn't any meeting going on tonight?"

"Well, my mother makes me write that newspaper, so. Mostly that, I guess."

"That's kinda cool." He looks at me sideways, as if he's analyzing the situation. "Or a chore."

"The second one." I don't tell him that, with our electricity off, the newspaper's on hold anyway.

"What would you rather do?"

"I dunno. Go out, I guess. See something different."

"Such as?" He leans forward, interested.

"Well, like the airport. I mean, I wouldn't just go there to look. I'd wanna travel."

"Ever been on a plane?"

"Not even once."

"What's the farthest you've been?"

"Farthest I've been," I echo Sammy's question. "Paradise Island. When we were eleven, KeeKee and I went over for a day with my mummy and Mrs. Jones. They had live musicians in the Festival Square." I smile as I remember that afternoon. *Late light fading fast, the square clear except for people crossing through it to and from stores that sell jewelry or expensive straw work or sleek clothing. Near the water, musicians play—keyboard, electric guitar, a drum set. A couple sways, and a few tourists join them. KeeKee looks at me and her smile spreads to my face and we have no choice but to hold hands and break apart and laugh and twirl, then whirl and spin until the world blurs and we collapse, giggling, into each other. The music changes and the dance floor fills out, tourists with faces flushed red in the hot evening, laughing women out for the night who don't miss a chance to shake. I wiggle my hips like they do and KeeKee giggles and imitates me, except she's so bony she looks like a lanky rag doll wriggling without bones. Then a hand closes over my shoulder.*

"What this nastiness is you're doing?" Mummy's voice cuts through the music, and the song comes to an end and I know I'm in trouble, in deep, but it was worth it to feel free.

I sigh. "I'd be glad even to go back there."

"Someone should take you. So, what you wanna do when you finish school?"

I look up at the sky. It seems so high, so far above my pathetic little wishes. Sitting here, next to someone who actually wants to know what I think and where I want to go, I start to see the possibility of attainable goals.

"Well, my mother wants me to be a reporter."

"Tell me what *you* want."

"What I want? Well, I love food. I don't know. I think I want people to pay me to eat really fancy food. Expensive stuff."

"Caviar."

"I read about this dish one time, they call it tiramisu. It's creamy and has coffee and chocolate and cookies and cocoa powder. I want that. But I don't get how you make the cookies soft, but not soggy. And how do you get it in layers that just stay, so you can slice it?"

"Bake it, I guess."

"No, you don't bake it. I looked it up, and . . ." I look over to gauge how bored he is. "It's a bunch of different steps. I really like nice food."

"And what would you do after you have that nice food?"

"I don't know. I guess I'd want to remember it somehow. Maybe I'd record my adventures." I pat my pocket.

"Ahh, your trusty recorder." He holds out a hand. For a second, I wonder if he wants me to hold his hand. What would that feel like? Warm? Sweaty? Firm? "Can I see it?"

"Oh." The heat of embarrassment washes over me as I pull the recorder out. Sammy reaches over, fast, and slips the recorder out of my hand.

"Let me hear what you got on here," he says, his voice teasing.

"Nothing important," I protest, reaching over, and my arm brushes his. He's all the things I imagined: warm, firm, the hair of his arm tickling mine as he moves the recorder from one hand to another, holding it out of my reach.

"Ooh, you got secrets on here? Let me hear."

His finger finds the Play button and, a millisecond before sound erupts from the speaker, I remember what I recorded on the tape, and shout, "No!"

KEEKEE

Words turn over in my mind, but I can't separate them out in the press of people at the meeting. A few minutes after Nia leaves, I slip away too. The fresh air soothes me and the breeze opens out my crumpled parts. I wish I could close my eyes, could lean back my head against the trunk of a tree while I listen to the water push and pull.

I step into the backyard. I freeze, bristling—is it Toons? I turn, but there's nothing but a thin scrap of cat loping through the grass, peering, once, back at me, then darting onto the street. I turn back. There, on her front porch, Nia sits on the step. Sammy sits beside her. My stomach squeezes in against itself. *You tell me*, Angel singsongs in my head, *if he ever try anything funny. You let me know.* The weight of those words in my mind keep me there, watching as he reaches over, snatching something from her. I'm about to pounce out of the shadows when I hear her giggle. Instead, I freeze. Because I know Nia, because I feel her bones in my body, her inhale in my

blood, and her bones are saying *go on* and her breath is saying
please and now he's got his hand on her arm, play-fighting like
me and Toons would. She squeals in a way that makes my head
want to turn away. No, this isn't how me and Toons wrestle.
The way she smacks at his hand weakly is too familiar, too exaggerated. She could get that recorder back easy, an elbow to the
ribs, if she wanted to.

Sammy grabs both her wrists in one of his hands, and she
squeals *no!* and twists and I know she could break free, but
the recorder matters less than his skin on her skin. There's a
purposeful click, then words spill back from the machine—an
odd strangely familiar voice.

"... *on sand, hand in hand, walk to where the sea meets* ..."

My voice, my words, my poem, my blood, my bones,
the stuff that holds together my body, on her recorder, in his
hands. And it's awful. It's awful. The voice is like stones, each
word sinking, emotionless and bland. I can't sound like that,
I can't, that isn't me.

The recording ends with a scuffle of fingers or clothes
over the mic. The night is hollow again.

Sammy hands the tape recorder back to her. "Ask me,
you still better off with a good phone."

I don't move. I can't. Underneath the awfulness of my
words being played back in the night is something else, something I don't understand, something even worse, because my
Nia, my best friend, would never steal from me. Especially
not the one thing I value the most. Especially not now, in the
middle of everything. Except she did.

I might stay there for bones-long years more if not for

the sound of voices carrying. The meeting's done. I can't go to the beach to clear my head, can't even stand on the path and strain to hear the waves. Our house is off-balance without Toons there. I move across the yard toward her. My heart pounds so hard it feels like it's propelling me forward. Her back is to me as she reaches for the door.

"You stole my poem." My voice shakes as I speak. Nia turns around, her eyes wide.

"KeeKee, I didn't—"

"I heard you!" I don't care that my words come out loud.

"I didn't mean to. I'm sorry."

"You just took it by mistake? What you plan on doing with it?"

"Nothing, I . . . nobody was supposed to hear it. I just like your poems so much. I didn't steal it. I wanted to borrow it. That's all." Nia looks at me like she's afraid, like I'm the one who could hurt *her.* How could she? I've never done anything but be her friend. I don't believe her, and suddenly, sharing this space feels too suffocating, as if there's too little oxygen to go around. I stumble back down the stairs and around the side of the house and bump right into her mother.

"Watch it!" Her mother's voice is surprised, but softer toward me. She sees my face and hesitates. "Something wrong?"

"Nia was talking to Sammy at the house by herself." The words pop out without planning, as if they live and breathe on their own.

"What?"

"I saw them here and he was touching her."

Her mother glowers, pushing past me without another

word. I should feel something from having told on Nia, but instead I am numb, so numb I barely feel the buzz of the phone in my pocket. I reach in and pull it out. A new text. My heart almost leaps out of my chest.

Safe, it says. From Toons.

I call back right away, but it goes straight to voice mail. I try again and again, then text back **Where are you? When are you coming back home?** I push my way through the press of bodies making their way back to the street, searching for Angel. *He's alive,* I tell myself again and again. *He's alive.*

NIA

I close the door behind me and lean my head against the steady wood. *It's better,* I try to tell myself. *It's better KeeKee knows. At least she only thinks I recorded her.* The thought of her finding that out that I used her poem on my application makes me want to spill my dinner over my shoes. *She doesn't know, though. Yet.*

I breathe out sharply and step into the house, feeling around for the matches and lantern. My fingers close around the box. I slide it open, take out a match, and strike a tiny, reassuring flame. Then the front door flies open. Darkness again.

"Were you with him?" Mummy's voice hits me like a slap.

I keep my head down, make my voice steady as I strike another match, but my hands shake as I hold the glimmer up to the light. "Him who?"

"Get in the bathroom now."

My legs are cold oatmeal as I walk down the hall. Did KeeKee tell her? Did she see Sammy with me? Mummy follows me without a word, and that scares me even more than her rage. I start to close the door and she steps forward, blocking it.

"Mummy, I—"

"That's a grown man! You have *no business* with him!"

"We wasn't doing nothing, we just talked—"

"He didn't have his hands on you?"

KeeKee told her. If Mummy saw that herself, she'd have been here in half a second. I feel a sting of betrayal. "We were just joking around—"

Her words are a cutlass, hacking mine off at the root. "Undress."

"I wasn't doin nothing like that, I swear. We was just talking, it was just for a second."

She makes a low noise of disgust at the back of her throat. "You think you grown, but you're nothing but a child. For crying out loud, Davinia. You don't even bleed. You didn't hear me? Undress!"

"Mummy!"

She raises a hand like she's going to strike me and I duck. The bang as she smacks the counter is almost worse than being hit. "Now!"

In the lantern's dancing light, I push down my shorts. I am careful not to pull my underwear down at the same time. I take off the shirt and deposit it on the counter, leaving my bra on. Part of me hopes that, by being tidy, being slow, my mother will change her mind.

"If I see blood in your panties, girl. If you slept with that man. . . ." She lets her voice trail off.

"Mummy, please don't make me—" I start to plead, and she silences me with a look.

I pull the underwear down to my knees. I stare at my toes. I don't need to look to know the seat of my underwear isn't stained.

"Wash off." She turns away. "You still dirty, if you ask me."

I close the door and pull my underwear up again, fast. My face is hot, my tears hotter.

"And you ain to so much as speak to them people over there." Mummy's voice booms from the other side of the door. "Don't even breathe in their direction."

I wait in the bathroom and listen out for my mother banging around in the kitchen. She's as gone as she will be, for now. My hands shake with rage as I pull off my underwear. Chastity, virtue, virginity, don't matter what you call it. To her, it's my whole identity. I step into the tub and wrench the tap on hard enough for it to break, but it resists me, smugly remaining whole. I yank up the knob to bring water through the shower head and the blast is numbingly cold. I don't even flinch—I feel like I'm on fire. This hot rage, slack, vicious, and immoral as hell—none of it is me. It's all because Mummy thinks slack can rub off like chalk, like ringworm, that it'll pass from Angel to KeeKee and infect me. Standing here, I *wish* I was that girl. Wish I was bold enough to do what Mummy's accusing me of. Instead, I'm invisible, in here, locked away, just like she wants. I open my mouth and let out a tile-rattling, water-warbling, eye-squeezing, belly-queasing, smoke-rising, mother-silencing, blinding scream.

FAITH

Eve's house is a hive of church people—deacons and stout women and all their different children pile in to applaud her father. Mrs. Armbrister sits beside him like a bodyguard while Eve rushes around distributing glasses and mugs with iced tea and punch and water. I catch her on the way into the kitchen.

"You wanna get out of here?"

"What?" She looks up with a coffee cup that says *World's Greatest Dad* in one hand, an ice cube in another.

"Let's go for a ride."

Eve drops the ice into the mug and rummages around the collection of plastic bottles on the countertop. "I thought you weren't allowed to drive."

I pull my car keys out of my pocket and jingle them. "I took these off Daddy's nightstand. He won't miss them."

"I can't go." She sloshes punch into the glass and the cubes crack in irritation. "You want a drink?"

Just the thought of the sticky-sweet juice makes my itching flare up. I shift from one leg to the other; it's like a fire in my pants and it's not like I can scratch anywhere in here without some churchy person coming around the corner and seeing me. "No. Come on, man. Walk with me down by KeeKee. They could pour their own drink for two minutes."

A woman pokes her head into the kitchen. "Any napkins?"

I feel the bristle coming off Eve as she snatches a roll of

paper towel off the top of the fridge. I take it from her and hand it to the woman, then stand in the doorway with my hands on my hips. "What happened to you?"

"Nothing." Eve opens the fridge and bangs a jug of water on the counter so hard I'm amazed it doesn't break.

I swipe the glass away from her. "Tell me or I ga pour this whole thing down the drain."

Eve sighs, slumping against the fridge. "Something's wrong."

"Yeah, no shit."

She shakes her head. "With Daddy."

I turn and peer through the crowd at where Mr. Armbrister sits. I can't see his face, but I'd bet it's tired. It's after nine and his house is full of people and anyway, I'm tired too. A woman in jeans and a red T-shirt shifts to the left and I have a clear view of her parents. Mr. Armbrister's eyes are ready to tell all these people to go home so he can lie down, but his mouth is stretched into a smile and Mrs. Armbrister holds his hand. From all the way across the house, I can feel the warmth in that grip. Eve's lucky to live in a house where her parents stick close like that. "He looks okay to me."

Eve brings her eyes up to meet mine. "It's cancer."

"Wait." I put the glass down and grab Eve's arm, pulling her to the far end of the kitchen. "Cancer?"

She starts to nod and I hug her, try to drown the buzz of the house out for her, to be an oasis for her, even for a minute. She squeezes me back, hard. "Do you know what kind?"

Eve lets go. "They won't tell me anything. I saw the radiation bill and I keep asking what's going on, but they're just pretending it's nothing."

"That's ridiculous. It's not like you're five and won't get it. And everything you do around here?"

"I just want to know he's gonna be okay."

I reach for the top cupboard and rummage around the extra pots until my hand falls on the long, cool neck of a bottle of coconut rum. I pull it out. "Let's go."

Eve's eyes widen as she shakes her head. "Where you goin with rum? Anyway, I can't do that. Too many people here."

I loop my arm through hers. "Exactly." I pull her outside. The instant the door closes behind us, the crowd is worlds away. I crack the bottle open and take a swig, then pass it to her. She hesitates, then takes it and takes the world's smallest sip. "That one's for your daddy."

Eve puts the bottle up to her mouth again. "And that's for your mom."

I take a chug. "And one for Toons."

She takes it back. "And the church." This time she drinks longer, then splutters, coughing. I do the same, welcoming the rum's sickly-sweet bite.

Across the street someone clears their throat. "You girls all right?" Mr. Rahming calls. Eve shoves the bottle behind her.

"Yes, sir!" she shouts back, and we fall into each other giggling. "You think we're drunk?" she says, not exactly quietly.

"Shhhh. Not in three minutes." I cover the bottle, flopping down on the grass.

"How's your mummy?" Eve's voice is serious again as she

sits down behind me, her back pressing against mine. I lean into her safe, solid body. I let her ground me.

"I don't know. They still have her in that place. Daddy said he doesn't want me seeing her till she's stable. Till she's 'settled in.' Like it's a comfy new apartment or something."

"Wouldn't seeing you be good for her?"

"I don't even know anymore. I feel like I let her down."

Eve doesn't answer, and I wonder if she thinks I let my mother down too. After a minute, she speaks again. "You got a new phone yet?"

"No. I don't even wanna tell Daddy I lost it. Guess I'll have to wait till Toons comes back."

The soft rise and fall of her back against mine. Then, "How was the clinic?"

I let out a long sigh. "So humiliating. Angel was cool, though."

"Wanna walk down and see if she got your results in yet?" She stashes the bottle behind the hibiscus bush. "I want to get away from here a minute."

The air around us feels heavy again, as if liquor and laughter can't shake the weight of all that's gone wrong around us for long. As we get close to Mark's house, music plays quietly from his car radio. I recognize it, an old calypso, "Yes Yes Yes."

Bare ground, bare feet, bare music blares through the night. Bonfire light, clapping hands, Mummy in the middle of a circle, laugh loose to the tune, this tune. I have no choice but to let my feet get light, to shimmy my shoulders, to waggle my head. Eve's laugh wakes up again and I hold my hands out to her.

"Girl, you're ridiculous!" she says, grabbing my hands, and we whirl, slow, then faster, then faster, and even years of doing it in dance doesn't stop the world from spinning, from me feeling like I might twirl forever, until gravity breaks its hold on me and I fly up, above the clouds. "Stop!" Eve shouts, laughing harder, harder. "Faith, you're *crazy!*"

I let go, stumbling away, as I fall back to earth. "Don't you call me that."

"I—no, I didn't mean it like that—"

"Only one way anyone ever *could* mean it." The street settles back into place and I take a step away from her.

"You're taking it all wrong, I just meant—" She reaches out to me and I shove her hand away, getting my balance enough to start walking toward Toons' house again.

"No!" I shout at her as she tries to follow. "Just go back. Leave me." Behind me, I hear her wait. Then her footsteps start to recede.

At Toons' house, I close my eyes and pray to anyone who will hear that Angel will answer the door. Across the yard, Nia's mom pushes her curtains aside, scowling in her sleeping cap and nightie. *Let her look, then,* I think, but when I knock again, my knuckles are softer against the wood. The faded yellow fabric at the window moves aside, then drops back into place before I can see who it is. The itch is getting worse after the short walk down the road; I sneak in one quick scratch and hope no one's looking.

"It's Faith," I call.

KeeKee flings the door open. "You don't have a home?" She spits the words out at me, the hard seeds to a bitter fruit.

I take a step back. The fire is rising now. "I came for Angel."

KeeKee looks at me like I'm nothing, like she knows what I came here for, like she knows the results of my test. I have something bad. I can feel it. Toons never looked sick, but sometimes that's how it is. Maybe Eve is right. Maybe I am crazy. Syphilis crazy. I might have AIDS. I might even die.

"I don't feel good," I moan. Things are starting to lean to the side, to slowly spin.

"Angel's out." KeeKee starts to close the door.

"You have to help me. Can't you check her voice mail or something?"

She heaves a mighty sigh, yanking the door all the way open, so hard I stumble in.

KeeKee pokes at her phone, listening. Then she puts it on speaker.

"The tests for Faith came back clear, except for a yeast infection. She can try one round of over-the-counter cream, that should do—"

She ends the call, the voice vanishing, and shuts the door in my face. As I step back out into the night, I wrap my arms around myself and start back up the road. The rum is kicking in, and every step feels like an effort. As mad as I am at her, I'm going to have to go right back to Eve's and ask her to let me stay overnight. *Everything's clear, I'm fine,* I say in my head, over and over. *I'm fine.* A voice deep inside me answers back, as loud as if I really am out of my mind. *But nothing else is.*

13

KEEKEE

It's Sunday, and past noon, but all along the street, people bustle along like we're deep in a late-afternoon party that will last through the night. Today is the last protest, and I guess it will be more like a celebration of the church's past life than a political appeal, at this point. For now, the landowners seem to have backed off, as if they're letting us have our last bit of fun before they swoop in and remind everyone who's boss. I look through the window at Paulette under the tree, quietly plaiting Eve's hair. Ruth and Faith play cards.

Angel looks at my phone for the thirty-seventh time this half hour. "Nothing more?"

"Not yet." I know she's hurt Toons didn't contact her, too, worried that he didn't say where he is, what happened that night, why he hasn't come home. She squints against the sun, then turns back to go lie down again. I hear the creak of bed-springs as she settles herself. I look across the yard. It's not been easy to avoid Nia, but I've pulled it off by getting to class just as the bell rings and leaving exactly on time at the end. That's about to change.

I duck under the bare clotheslines and knock on Nia's door.

"Yes?" Nia calls back.

"It's me."

She appears at the door, opening it a few inches. "Did you tell Mummy about me and Sammy on the porch?"

There's no point in denying it. "Yeah. And?"

"How could you do that to me? You knew she was gonna freak out."

"Now you know how I feel."

"KeeKee, I already told you I'm sorry—"

I hold up my hands. "I don't care about that. I came for the recording."

Nia looks away. "I can't give it to you. I have something else on there."

Seriously? "It's mine. I want it. Now."

"I gotta go anyway, I can't let Mummy see me talking to you."

"She can't see *you* talking to *me*?"

"I'll explain later." She closes the door quietly, leaving me standing outside, fuming.

"Hey, KeeKee," Paulette calls.

I walk over to them.

"How you doin? The police have any leads on Toons yet?"

I cut my eye at Faith, who avoids looking my way. "Just that they think the developers had something to do with it."

A door closes, and a moment later, Nia's mother marches past us.

"So listen, y'all, who here think they may apply for a job at the hotel when it opens?" Paulette asks. No one answers. "Oh, hey, Nia. You come to join us now that your mummy gone?"

Nia rolls her eyes. "She has me locked down."

"Yeah, wonder why," I say, purposefully not avoiding her gaze. Instead, I catch Eve and Faith trading a look that says *What's up with them?* Paulette doesn't notice.

"I didn't even want to get out of bed this morning." Paulette doesn't notice as she adjusts Eve's head to start a new braid. "Every day that goes by, it's less likely he's coming back."

"He's coming back," Nia pipes up.

Eve looks over at her. "I agree. We have to believe the best, right?"

I turn my gaze to Faith. "So, did you ask your father if he thinks anyone to do with the hotel would have had it out for Toons?" All eyes turn on her.

"He . . . he said no," Faith stammers.

"Remember, he came through a few weeks back and was knocking on doors, telling us we better keep off the beach if we didn't want any trouble?" Nia looks over at me as if throwing her two cents in is going to put us back on the same side.

"Yeah, you mentioned that," Eve says. "But why Toons? I was on the beach too, and Faith . . . all of us were."

"It was after that day," Nia continues, "remember, Toons threw the conch shell at the security guard?"

Paulette looks over at her. "I didn't hear about that."

"Yup, there's a lot that happens along here that people don't know about," I say, looking up at the sky.

"I just pray Toons comes back safe," Eve says hurriedly. "Faith, you wanna deal for Fish? I have another deck in my pocket, we could all play."

Across the street, two little girls are jumping rope. An idea forms in my mind fast. I wave them over. "Can we borrow your rope?" I ask.

"Oh yeah, now you're talking!" Eve perks up even more as the girls hand me the rope.

"Remember when we used to skip?" I say. Everyone falls silent then, looking at me. "After school and on weekends."

"*Bluebells, cockle shells.*" Eve's voice is soft.

"*Evie, ivy, over.*" Nia finishes the line. I can feel how eager she is for me to look her way. I'll look her way, all right.

"Hey, Nia, wanna do double?"

"What song?" she asks, already on her feet.

"I'm gonna improv."

"Oh yeah!" Paulette finishes the braid off and wipes her hands on her pants. "Who's gonna turn?"

"We can do it." Eve looks at Faith, coaxing her up. I hand her the end of the skipping rope. She smiles at me as our hands touch, and I see how tired her eyes are, how they don't seem happy. She leans forward, her breath warming my ear. "He comin back, KeeKee. I know it."

Heat boils in me again, bubbles rising. Who are they to care? To want him back so badly? Who are these girls who whisper and sneak around, singing and dancing and pretending he's theirs? My heart thumps so fast my chest might explode. I slip my flip-flops off. Nia does the same, then smiles, hopefully, like there's a world where jump rope could fix the biggest betrayal possible. I know her, know the spaces between her teeth, know the one dimple in her left cheek that shows when her smile is forced, the one on the right that appears spontaneously. I know the way the lines on her hands are etched, the shape of her toenails and how they curl upward when they grow too long, know how her voice goes high when she's mad or excited or about to cry. How did I not see she was capable of this? Because I'm an idiot, that's how. Realizing that makes me even more angry.

"One . . ." *How could she steal from me?*

"Two . . ." *How could she flirt with Sammy?*

"Three . . ."

We jump, and as the ropes swing, we move in unison, feet leaving the ground and hitting it again in perfect sync, and I don't speak at first, not because I'm trying to build anticipation, but because this is the last thing we will ever do together as friends and a small part of me wants to make it last.

"Let's go!" Faith calls. It's time.

"Sapodilly, sea grape, sugar cane galore
gov'ment sellin off our land
but y'all do even more
Like to bat your eye with people man
and take every kind of things
if words were jewelry you could thief
you'd have a pocket full of rings."

Words spill like water fastdripping, pouring, gushing, don't think, just speak and in the background giggles lift, then fall off and the whole time I don't stop.

"You don't have no talent
you ain got no sense
what you make is always fake
cut you down like that fence.
Find a bridge and leap off
get hit by a car
go jump in the ocean
and carry your psycho ma!"

I jump out of the rope. It smacks Nia on her ankles as her feet hit the ground. She looks as if I've slapped her across the face.

"Steal *that*." I spit the words in her face.

Faith drops her ends of the ropes, her face crumbling like someone just tore her world into tiny pieces. She runs to her car, fumbling to unlock it, sobbing. Her key falls into the dirt and she squats down to pick it up. Eve scrambles after her, but Faith pushes her away roughly and wrenches the door open. Even after she clambers in and locks herself inside, we can hear her sobs. Eve tries the doors but Faith doesn't let her in.

Paulette gathers the rope up out of the dust and hands it to the bewildered little girls watching. "What's your problem?" she snarls at me, disgust in her voice. "That was low."

"I didn't do anything to her!" I protest. The fury inside me has settled for the moment like a starved pit bull taking a rest on its chain. When I turn, I see from the wilted look on Nia's face that my words have landed where I meant them to. Instead of satisfaction, though, I feel an awful silence fall over the porch.

"Why would you do that?" Eve looks at me like she can't understand what type of creature I am. Before I can explain, the door behind us opens.

"Excuse me?" Angel's voice slices through the air. I want to answer, but no sound comes out. "What did I just hear?"

Paulette slowly starts to plait again. Nia slinks off the porch, disappearing around the side of the house. Eve lowers her head so far Paulette has to stretch to reach her hair. Angel steps out onto the porch. She has on one of her flimsy dresses, fabric you can see through if the sun hits right. Great.

"KeeKee." She points at me. "You don't have nobody's business out in the street like that, you hear? And to talk about Faith's family."

"Faith? I meant Nia—"

"We don't do that." Angel cuts me off. "This neighborhood small. Everybody know who daddy look at who ma, who sister and who cousin together, who on they period and who miss and who need to get put on the pill. We all know. But y'all girls are sisters. You can't afford to turn on each other. You see how me and her"—she gestures at Nia's house—"can't stand each other, but we still bring up y'all two girls side by side. You don't see us pulling hair and slapping faces. You're sisters. All of you. Don't forget it." Angels storms back into the house.

"I was talking about Nia," I say finally.

"Faith's mum had a breakdown the same night everything went down with Toons," Eve replies quietly. "I thought you knew."

The sobbing has finally subsided to intermittent heaving.

Faith tries to start up the car. It coughs a few times, then catches. She revs it and pulls off. Eve borrows Paulette's cell phone and walks off to use it in private. Paulette goes to the hose to rinse her hands off. I sit alone. I feel the anger still stirring in me, mixed with guilt. If only the insult had landed where I meant it to. If only it was Nia who I'd destroyed.

FAITH

I park the car at the house but sit in the driveway, idling, my head resting against the steering wheel for a minute. KeeKee hates me and maybe I deserve it. I should have asked Daddy if he had anything to do with Toons disappearing. I should have done a lot of things. But there's one thing I know I didn't ask for, and that's having a mother whose mind shifts reality around like a kaleidoscope. I did nothing to deserve that.

Inside, the curtains are shut, only a little afternoon light draining in through a gap. That filtered light shows me everything I need to know—since I left this morning, everything's changed. Her hot-pink sneakers are missing from the shoe rack. All her shoes are—the yellow flats she wore to appointments, her teal house slippers, her orange flip-flops. The purple vase isn't on the table. It's as though she stepped through the portal to a different universe and vanished. I step into the living room and the thick smell of beer hits me. Abandoned bottles are lined up on the coffee table, the tops scattered over the floor.

"Daddy?" My voice is swallowed up in the still, stagnant air. I pick up the bottle closest to me. Liquid moves in it when I tilt it, and I lift the bottle to my mouth. Tepid beer dribbles into my mouth and I almost gag. My arm draws back, then comes forward, moving me in an involuntary dance as I hurl the bottle against the wall as hard as I can. The smash is music I have to hear again. Lift another. *Crack.* Another. Again, until the house cries brown glass shards and beer. Five bottles. Six. I pick up the last one and hurl it at the photo of my mother hanging on the wall, like a dart at the bull's-eye. The second it hits the floor, the glass shatters. "No!" I stumble over, grabbing it up, but it's too late, a spiderweb of cracks is scattered over her face. Then I hear movement behind me. I turn to face my father.

He walks over the broken glass, apparently feeling nothing, bends to pick up her picture. He cradles it, brushing it clean.

"She ain broke," he says again and again. "She ain broke, baby."

I step away from him and he collapses onto the sofa. I want to believe his slurred words but as I run through the house, the beer-stained photo is the only trace of my mother I see. I lock myself in my room and sit on the floor, press my back to the door. When the doorbell rings, I ignore it. It rings again. "Daddy?" I call. No answer. I get up and go back out front. He's passed out on the sofa now, snoring. I open the door to find Joy standing outside.

"What took you so long?" She steps in, looking around the dark house. "Y'all don't like light in here?" I can tell she's trying to joke, but her voice is worried.

"How come you're here?" I'm not in the mood to laugh.

"Eve called me. Where's Daddy?"

I point at the sofa. She walks over and pokes him a few times, then shakes her head. "I've had enough, Faith. "

"Meaning what?" I turn to walk back to my room and she reaches out and touches my arm.

"I called in a favor on the way over here. I got you into a camp for the summer. You need to get away from this house. And Daddy needs some space to get himself together after—everything." She squeezes my hand. "I'm worried about you, girl."

My mind is a jumble of thoughts. Escaping for the summer, not having to confront Daddy, getting to start over someplace different, around people who don't know every ugly thing in my past, sounds like the best option for me. Joy follows me to my room and together, we pack a bag—school uniform, toothbrush, cosmetics, dance clothes, pajamas—so I can stay with her for now.

KeeKee's words echo in my head. I push them down. For now, I can only afford to think about the future. That means leaving all kinds of things behind—my mother, my father, my car, Pinder Street and everything that happened on it. I take one last moment to take in the dark tomb of my house, then close the door on that part of my life. I get into Joy's car. As we drive off, I don't look back.

EVE

After I hang up from Joy, I sit on the bed where Faith squeezed in beside me last night. I feel guilty. Aren't I as bad as KeeKee? Didn't I use that word too? I didn't mean it like KeeKee did, but does intent matter anymore?

When the street gradually falls quiet, I go out again.

There are just a few stragglers still heading down the path. Even Mark's car is silent, its hood down, its doors closed like folded wings. At the space in the fence, the security guard with the baseball hat stands, looking resigned. I step past him and move to the area where everyone is gathered. I stand off to one side, and that's why I see Daddy, approaching the crowd from the burned-out church, his feet steady in the uneven sand. He stops to stand in front of the group, waiting for the chatter to die down. Quiet begins to spread through the ranks.

"Brothers and sisters," he begins, "this is the end of the line for this building. Church, meeting hall, a place where we have danced and sung, laughed and broken bread together. We will no longer gather in these walls, but we will not be broken by these events. Our community will still stand." The crowd bursts into cheers again, and, there, squinting against the sun, his face shining with sweat, he looks strong. He'll be okay. He has to be. Bad things come in threes, and we've already met that quota. Faith's mother broke down, Toons was taken away, and the church was set on fire. Daddy will be healthy. Our family will be okay. I turn to face the way he's facing—the sea of people behind me, the ocean before. The sun scales the sky, its light white-hot and eager, blinding me.

14

NIA

After Mr. Armbrister gives his last sermon on the beach, a party erupts. Speakers appear, powered by cords run in from the street. Folding tables pop up and people tote foil pans of macaroni and rice, green salads, barbecue ribs, boiled corn, chicken wings. In a minute, the sea is littered with people splashing and wading, smaller kids laughing as breaking waves rough them up and roll them over on the sand.

"Forty-five minutes," Mummy warns, a plate of meatballs and oxtail balanced on one hand. "Then you better be back at the house." I get something to eat, but it lands in my belly like rocks. I keep glimpsing KeeKee here and there, avoiding me. If she would just talk to me, maybe I could explain. But what would I say? As soon as my plate is empty, I head back. It's not worth being even one minute late. Mummy will have a speculum and a pair of binoculars ready if she thinks I got up to anything. As I get close to the house, I hear Mummy's voice raised. Who is she talking to? I duck down, creeping under the kitchen window.

"You stayed away for fourteen years, and you choose

now to come back?" Mummy's words are megaphone-clear.

"None of that was my idea," a man answers her, his voice lower, but just as firm. "She came to *me*."

"She couldn't come to you, she doesn't know you exist, except as *that* one's father."

"I came here to offer her a chance. The girl who showed up in my office is so passionate about her art that she came to my office to apply for that camp in person. I realized when I saw her address." I know that voice, I realize. Mr. Wright, KeeKee's father. What is he doing here? I feel dread in the pit of my stomach. He must have realized the poem I submitted was KeeKee's.

"I told Nia she wasn't going to that camp, and she deliberately disobeyed me."

"Children don't act out for nothing." KeeKee's father sounds accusing. "You're too strict with them, they rebel."

"I suppose that's how you and that woman raise that girl together." She talks about KeeKee like she hates her. Does she hate her? Does Angel hate me? I don't dare to ask the real question, the question I'm afraid I know the answer to.

"I'm not gonna let this go," Mr. Wright says, louder now. "Look at this place. Electricity is off, there can't be more than a few days' worth of food in the cupboard. I wouldn't even speak about those glasses, they look like she's been wearing them since she was eight." He drops his voice. "I helped that boy out and I didn't breathe a word to Angel. Let her try the camp. Get her in a new environment."

"Me and her already went through this. I told her no to that camp from the time she brought it up with me, weeks ago."

"Don't make me take this to court." He lowers his voice again, but his words are arrows meant for my ears. "She's my daughter!"

My daughter. He said *my daughter.* I struggle to make sense of what I heard, but it can only mean one thing. Mr. Wright is . . . my father.

"Nia, come in here, please," Mummy calls. I realize at some point I stood up, and I'm standing level with the window. I open the door and step inside. Mummy stands with her back to the window. She looks as though she just lost a war. All these years, it never occurred to me that when my father finally came into my life, he would tear it apart. "I thought it over," she says, as if I didn't just overhear all that yelling. "You'll go to that camp."

Mr. Wright steps forward. "Nia. You'll have a wonderful time. Your application—it blew the judges away. Ms. Rose is running the spoken and movement arts and she can't wait to work with you." He hugs me, beaming. Why didn't I just use the stupid newspaper in my application? What will I do for six weeks in a camp where everyone thinks I'm a poet? He lets me go. "I have to speak with . . . I have to go." At the front door, he slips on his shoes, then turns back to me again. "Congratulations, Davinia." He smiles, a small, careful smile, but his words are like a knife he has no idea he even holds. "You've earned it."

KEEKEE

I don't stay on the sand long. With all these people here, the beach isn't mine anyway, and thinking is impossible among the crowd. When Angel finds me and tells me she's going to the house, I make my way back too. The clotheslines hang, still, empty. The afternoon is breezeless, as if the sheer press of people has drained away all movement from the air.

"You should go back out there." Angel's voice is a feather blowing across a fresh asphalt road.

"I'm tired," I say.

She smooths the collar on my blouse. "Today was bad, but it'll get better. You have to believe that. And meanwhile, life has to go on."

I open my mouth to say that I know, that life *is* going on, that right now it's just going on a little farther away, that maybe that's best, when I feel something shift. The band misses a beat, the singers falter. Spoken voices rise. Angel hears it too, turns her head toward the yard. There's a knock at the door. Angel gets up and I hear her talking with Nurse Pratt, who passes her two bags full of supplies for pouches. Nurse Pratt's voice fades away, but Angel doesn't close the door.

"What you doing here?" she asks. Her tone sounds odd, as though she's seen someone she thought was dead and buried long ago.

"I was in the area."

I freeze for a moment, then turn around. My father stands in the doorway, hands in his pockets, the sun casting a glare off his glasses, obscuring his eyes. My father here. To see me. On Pinder Street. I scramble up and run to the door, throw my arms around him. He smells of bay rum and office paper. "You finally came! How come? Did you come for the protest? You wanna go get some food?"

"KeeKee," he says. "We need to talk."

"About what?" I grab his arm, tugging him back outside. "We can talk on the beach, this might be the last day you can see it for real." The sound of a door opening. He turns and we both watch as Nia rushes out of her house. Something's in her hand. A flat black folder. His folder. "How come you're here?"

"Nia applied to the camp, in person, actually—and . . . you girls have a lot in common, did you know she writes poetry? Nia!" He beckons her over the last few steps to where we stand. "Tell KeeKee about the piece you sent in. She submitted this incredible poem about birds flying after dark, very lyrical." His words are starting to feel far away as I turn to look at Nia, as it all begins to make sense. She keeps her eyes fixed on the ground, as though if they meet mine, she'll turn to stone. "You should hear it."

"Uh—you left this." Nia holds the folder out.

My father takes it from her. "Thank you, Davinia. I was just telling KeeKee about your poem on the application."

Why is he here to see her, and not me? Why is he putting one arm around her and the other around me?

"KeeKee, I have to tell you something. Nia—well, I'm Nia's father too."

His words hit me like wet cement. It can't be true. Except here Nia is, holding her shoulders hunched like she's bracing herself for a blow, my father grinning awkwardly, looking from one of us to the other. Before I can get any further, before I can even think, a bolt of blue shoots into the yard. The truck door flies open and Sammy charges out.

"What you doin in this house?" Sammy's voice slices through the air.

"Hey, man." My father holds out a hand. "Timothy Wright. I'm KeeKee's father."

Sammy brushes past my father, bumping him with his shoulder. "Angel!" he barks, charging inside. "This man here for you?" His foot catches one of the bags and he trips and stumbles and reams of silver foil packages spill, glint against the grass. He bends down, picking up a ribbon of them. I can't seem to move, to even bend and pick the condoms up. "What the hell is this?"

My father's mouth gapes open. "Where'd all that come from?"

The front door opens. "Sammy, what happened?" Angel cranes her neck. "Timothy? You shouldn't be here." Then her eyes land on the mess.

"This what you doin when I'm out?" Sammy's voice drops, the low slick scuttle of hidden things, things that like damp, dank, that bite.

"It's not how it looks," she begins, her tone laced with honey, and Sammy rushes at her. Outside, from the shore, there is laughter. He lunges to grab her. She ducks out of the way, a small bird's squeak where her scream should be.

"Hey!" My father steps up to Sammy, blocking him. "Leave her alone, man. I'm here to see KeeKee. That's it."

Sammy tosses the bag at her. Panty liners flutter down, so many severed wings. "This where the money goes from the laundry you do in my washer?"

"No!" Angel protests.

"You beyond disgusting," he spits out. He spins around on his heels and jumps back into the truck.

My father hovers for a second, then hurries for the door. Part of me wants to run after him, to tell him everything about Nia is a lie, that the daughter he suddenly wants to claim isn't what he thinks. But the bigger part of me can't believe my father came to see her but never came to see me.

"KeeKee," Nia says softly. How dare she even breathe?

Dark night, my words in flight, trapped in a small glass jar and her hands on the lid. "You knew."

"KeeKee, I swear, I didn't know!"

Angel's wailing leaks through the door in front of me, Sammy's exhaust hangs in the air behind, and in between, us, except we aren't us anymore. "You stole my poem. Why would I believe you?"

"KeeKee . . ." Nia's grabbing hold of me like we're friends, like we're *blood*. I shake her off.

"Liar!" It takes all the breath in my body to draw up that word. "I don't believe anything you say."

"I'm not lying, you know I never knew who my daddy was," she protests, fake tears glassing her eyes.

I dig deep in my belly for the last words I'll ever breathe to her. "I *hate* you!" They tear out of me in a scream. "You take *everything* from me!" Before I turn away, I see it in her face. The melting away, the realization that I know who she really is. That she'll never be my friend again.

My feet carry me down the path. Water bottles, Styrofoam plates, abandoned napkins crumpled into ugly blooms line the way. I step over the garbage. Beyond the fence, the beach is empty, bent placards like injured gulls on the sand. I look over at the building. Fresh plywood barricades the windows and door. I feel like that. Closed off, used, and abandoned. Useless and left behind.

EVE

I wake to old daylight pushing through the curtain's gap, sunshine yellow with age, and a crick in my neck. The bed is empty around me. Elsewhere in the house, Esther and Joe are bickering over something. Panic surges over me—we're never allowed to sleep in on Sunday morning. I get up and step out into the corridor. Outside the closed bathroom door, Junior whimpers to be picked up.

"I gotta pee," Joe whines.

I step around him. "Go outside by the tree."

"But Mummy—"

"Wait or go piss in the bush!" I snap. Joe slips away without a word. I can feel Ruth's stare. Without turning, I dare her to speak a word.

In the kitchen, dishes still from yesterday's lunch, eight glasses from eight elders are lined up. Light catches them, illuminating every chip and crack. The thought of Sunday mornings being like this seems too much to stand.

"Eve."

Over the din in my head, I don't hear Mummy come in.

"Baby, come help me with something outside."

I hear her unlock the back door. Extra light enters the room. Breeze, too. She is waiting.

"Help? Should have gone to Angel long time if she wanted help." I mutter the words. "Instead of having a bunch of kids she can't take care of." Junior lifts a small, fat hand, pointing behind me. I turn to see Mummy in the doorway. Her expression is a mix of hurt and anger. I open my mouth to call back those words and before I can speak, before I can even breathe, there is a death-heavy thump in the other room. The air is so silent for a fraction of a second, so perfect, so serene.

I run into the living room, with Mummy right behind me. My father lies on the floor, his body crumpled.

"Daddy!" Ruth screams.

I stumble back and out the door, away from the fold of his body, the wail that tears up out of Mummy, away from the words, my words, that I cannot reel back in. But I stop short of the end of the street. Trucks and tractors block the way to the beach, to what's left of the church, and before my eyes, the first mighty casuarina falls.

15

KEEKEE

Overbright sun spills in through the kitchen, making the lamp glow. I lean forward and blow dust off its crescent base. Particles swirl in the air, then drift down, mocking me. *Can't get rid of us that easy*, they warn, settling again.

"You should have applied to that program." Angel marches into the room, arms full of curtains. She dumps them on the counter and glowers out the window. "Look at her prancing around out there. Little thief. At least tell your father what she did."

I grab up the dirty linens and tote them outside, avoiding so much as a glance across the yard. "You have as much right to be there as Nia," Angel hollers after me. "At least you earned your way."

Above my head, a mockingbird rides the same two-note ditty as I fill the machine—curtains first, then a green bag stuffed with children's uniforms. I cram in a bunch of kitchen towels for good measure and bang the washer door shut. I shake detergent into the slot at the top, set the machine to start, and try not to look behind me at the high metal fence that divides our property from the mouth of the path. It sprang up exactly two weeks ago, the day after the last protest, right before they started to clear the land. Our half of the yard's been in our family for three generations, and we've never had any type of barricade up, not even between Angel and Ms. Taylor. That's the thing with fences, though—where properties touch, only one person has to create a divide for both to feel the separation. Like with me and Nia. I never wanted to hate someone who was once my best friend. But she built this wall of lies between us, and now, there's no going back, any more than the developers can undo the dredging in the water and take back the truckloads of bleached-white sand they hauled in and dumped.

As I straighten up, the mockingbird falls silent. I look up for a moment, scan the thick foliage for a glimpse of brown and white wings. That's how the vehicle surprises me as it reverses up onto the grass. I jump back toward the washer, my heart hammering against my chest, as it stops just a few feet short of me. *Toons*, my mind screams. *They came to do to me what they did to Toons*. But it's blue, not black, a truck, not an SUV.

"Angel?" I call as Sammy steps out of the truck. Another man gets out of the passenger side, and the two of them head straight for the machine. Sammy reaches behind the washer and yanks the cord, killing the whir-swish of its song. He hauls the door open, pulls out a soggy twine of wet cloth like guts from an animal's belly. He throws it to the side, in the dirt, tilting the machine till it vomits up brown-tinted soapy water.

"What you doin?" Angel runs outside as Sammy and the

man heave the empty metal husk to the back of the truck. "Where you takin that?"

Sammy's knees buckle as he gets close, and he loses his grip, the machine tipping onto its back as it bangs onto the truck bed. The door flies open, then cracks against the side of the truck. "Hold it by the opening." He focuses his gaze on the man.

"You ga break it!" Angel's voice gets louder as they haul the washer up against the truck's cab.

Sammy sneers. He still doesn't look at Angel. "See how she think this her machine? Like she forget I buy this. Like she don't know this mine."

"Sammy, you crazy?" Angel's protest comes out as a shout. "Everything I did for you, now you want carry on like this?"

He climbs into the truck, starting it up. "You ain worth that much," he snarls over the revving engine. Then the truck is gone, leaning left under the weight.

I step over the soggy mess. "It's okay, we can get another machine," I say, hugging Angel as she begins to cry. She pulls away from me, and stumbles barefoot to the empty hole where the washing machine stood. She holds her head as she weeps for it like a lost child.

Another car is coming, like a tropical storm on the heels of a hurricane. Green shine, sharp rims, smooth lines. It stops in front of Nia's house. Angel snaps back like she's been shocked and rushes into the house. Alone, I watch my father get out, look over at me nervously. He raises a hand, then lowers it when I only stare in return. Nia totes a suitcase out, then climbs into the back. Her mother comes out too, and gets into the front. He loads up the bag, then turns to me again. Our eyes meet. This time he looks away quickly, as if breaking eye contact will make him invisible as he settles behind the wheel. Seconds later, they are gone and I am alone in the yard, more alone than I've ever been.

NIA

The boat vibrates with families heading to NewBeat. Everywhere, there are girls with their mothers or fathers a step or two behind them, bags being loaded on, faces shining with anticipation. I clutch the worn yellow case, wheels scuffed and fabric fraying at the edges, and stifle the dorky smile that wants to bloom, then look over my shoulder. I'm not dreaming. There they are. Mummy on one end of the bench behind a book, Mr. Wright on the other, scratching away at a piece of paper with a pencil. Even with three girls squeezed between them, the three of us make a sort of family. *Family.* I turn the word over again in my mind, making sense of its shape.

Then we are moving away from the wharf, Nassau shrinking as we sail out to sea. We go only so far, then begin to curl around the island. In the distance, I can make out the tip of Pinder's Point. From here, the beach is unchanged. I turn toward the open water and warm wind hits my face.

"I'm not teaching at the camp this year, but I have some outings planned for us two." Mr. Wright's voice calls me out of my head. The boat is approaching the first of the two bridges connecting Nassau to Paradise Island. Now it glides through the busy waters, giving me the chance to look somewhere other than at him.

"Like what?" I ask. The gynecologist called and said my results were normal, and anyway, there's no way I'm going to that kind of appointment with *him*.

"For one, the eye doctor," he says thankfully. "I hear you lost your glasses, and I want to replace them."

I look back at where my mother is sitting. Her arms are folded as she glowers out at the passing sea. "Is Mummy coming to the appointment too?"

"She's gonna let us have some space to get to know each other."

Space? Mummy's literally devoted her whole life to making sure I'm never out of her reach. I struggle to read something, anything, from his voice, but his even tone gives nothing away. "I'll be there in the second week of camp to see how you're managing and take you to get your eyes tested." His grin is KeeKee's. How could I have lived all those years seeing my father in her and not knowing? Did she live all those years seeing him in me and never saying so? No, I don't need her in my head, not here, not now. The smile—his, hers—disappears, replaced with a more earnest expression. "You won't miss anything important, I promise."

We're out from under the second bridge, and the boat heads for the far western end of Paradise Island, then dips into a quiet cove. "Why didn't we just take the bridge over?"

Mr. Wright grins at me. "Coming by boat makes the experience more special, don't you think?"

We ease up to a small dock on the side of the island that faces the city. From here, the buildings downtown look so far away. Only those on the coast and a few built up high on rubble, lofty above the homes and trees. I feel a painful pang—will Pinder Street look like that when I return, dwarfed by the new structure? But then the bustle of people disembarking distracts me and I push my fears away. I can worry about the future when it arrives. I hang back while Mr. Wright bustles about like a host, helping parents with bags, directing families to the waiting bus parked just a few steps from the dock. Mummy taps me on the shoulder, her mouth pressed into a stern line.

"You behave yourself." She grips me in a hug so tight it hurts.

"Aren't you coming with us?" I ask, as I hug her back. She feels thin in my arms.

"Gonna ride right back over. Lots to do back home." Then she lets go.

"I'll take good care of her," Mr. Wright calls as he guides me off the boat. He steers me away from the bus where the last families are boarding. "This is our ride." He nods at an SUV with rental plates. Over his shoulder, I strain to catch a glimpse of Mummy, sure she's watching to make sure I get off all right. But she must have gone inside; the deck is empty, as if she was never there. I wish we were getting settled on the bus with the other families. There, maybe I wouldn't feel the gaping space beside me where Mummy should be. "Come on!" Mr. Wright calls as he unlocks the car.

I hover by the passenger side. Am I supposed to get in the front and sit awkwardly close to him, or in the back, like he's my chauffeur? Mr. Wright leans across and flips the front door open. I climb in, grateful that he's made the decision for me. He starts up the car and smiles eagerly. "I figure this way we can get a few more minutes to talk!"

I'm at a loss for words. What do you say to someone who up and decided two weeks ago that it's worth getting to know you? Did he read the poem and think I was worth being his daughter after all? What would he say if he knew it wasn't mine? Would he still want to chat, or would he give me the boot out of the jeep at highway speed?

"I'll go first," he continues. "Why don't you ask me something? Anything. What do you want to know about me?"

"I already know some stuff about you," I say.

"Oh?"

"You're an architect, you have a big studio at home, and you aren't married."

"KeeKee brought you up to date."

I looked you up, I want to say, but her name makes the words dry up in my throat. I turn to the window as we pass a whole row of guest houses the colors of candy hearts.

"I hope all this hasn't created a rift between you two."

"Um . . . not really," I lie.

He exhales sharply as we turn a corner a little too fast. Now there's just bush. "It's definitely weird for me. I owe you an apology. For—not being there all this time. There were a lot of factors, but I have to accept my share of the blame. I should have taken more initiative."

Why didn't you? How could you not? Why would you pick KeeKee to be your daughter all these years and pretend I didn't exist? Questions barrel through my head. I go for an easy one. "Why now?"

"Well. You're almost done with high school. Your mother and I agreed that you'd be ready when you were older."

Ready, like having a father is a cake in a hot oven and a timer has to ding before he comes out of hiding and into my life. "When I first said I wanted to go to camp, Mummy told me I'm too young to be away from home all this time."

"Well, your mother and I may not see eye-to-eye on certain things, but I'm glad we can get to know each other now. I hope these next few weeks can be a fresh start for you. For us."

My stomach clenches. Will he want to get to know me if the truth about my application comes out?

We pull into a parking lot; the bus is already there, girls piling out. We're here.

He turns off the car. "What do you think?"

I get out of the car and take in the two-story main building. Its paint is peeling, and the fountain in front is still and silent, collecting dead leaves, but the driveway is decorated with fancy bricks under our feet. As girls wheel their suitcases across it and down a path leading around back, the wheels click out a rhythmic song. It seems like some sort of fairy world: part-regal, part-abandoned. Part . . . fake. I can feel Mr. Wright watching me, waiting for my approval.

"It's nice," I say, and hoist my backpack onto my shoulder.

"They're renovating the place this season, but we were able to pull some strings and rent out the staff quarters and enough rooms to run the program this summer."

I nod as we walk past the main building. Through the glass doors, I see a man carefully painting the ceiling. An elaborate chandelier dangles over his head. We pass an empty pool, lounge chairs carefully stacked against the wall. Then the path winds through a garden area and opens out to a long, low building. It's less ornate than the one at the front, but it's clean and well kept with neatly pruned hibiscus bushes planted around it. A registration table is opened out under a poinciana's arching shade. It's past its best bloom, just a few red flowers dotting its crown like barrettes. Instead of getting in line behind the dozen or so girls already there with their parents, Mr. Wright slips up behind the two women at the table. I hang back. That lets me see how he smiles widely at them. How he looks right into their faces. One lady points to the line, but the other smiles back, then thumbs through the stack of envelopes and hands him one. He struts back to me, proud of his efficiency.

"Got it." He holds the envelope out to me. "There's a welcome letter in there, and a schedule, so you can follow along with what's lined up for the week. Here, I'll walk with you to your room, let you get settled in."

I feel like I'm seeing this man, this so-called father, for the first time all over again. His shoes, purple and slightly pointed, have somehow repelled the dust of our walk. The creases in his pants legs are as perfect as if he hired KeeKee and Angel to press them, and his pale pink polo shirt is tucked over the type of small paunch you don't get from eating cold slam bam for Sunday dinner.

"I pulled some strings," he says, "and managed to get you the best spot. End room, second floor." He reaches for my suitcase. I look down at his hand. See the neatly clipped nails, perfectly clean, his hands well moisturized. Smooth.

"Are you rich?" I ask bluntly. He pauses and straightens up, then tilts his head to the side as if letting my words filter into his brain. For me, that's answer enough.

"I wouldn't say—" he starts, and I can't stand here with him a second longer. I grab my suitcase and drag it over to the stairs, drowning out his words. The wheels clunk against the step as I heft it up.

"Come on." He reaches for the handle. "Let me help you."

The tears surprise me, and I hardly have time to turn away from him fast enough to hide them. "I'm fine. I don't need any help." Mummy doesn't understand *no* when it's blasted from a mega-speaker, but my so-called father stops in his tracks, all the extra smiles drained away from his face. I haul the bag up the whole flight of stairs, and at the top, I open the envelope and fumble through papers until I find one that has my room assignment: 208. It's at the far end. I brush the tears away and head left.

I push the door open and find a room twice the size of the one I left behind on Pinder Street. There are two double beds, a pair of dressers on either side, a glass door, and a small balcony looking out over the fields. I've never been on a balcony before. I sit down on the bed closer to the glass door, reach over to the nightstand and under the lamp's shade. When I turn the switch, the light blinks on obediently, casting a circle of artificial cheer around itself in a mango-tinted hue.

I settle my suitcase on the end of the bed and lift out the two towels and the set of sheets Mummy insisted I pack. The linens look thin and faded on the bright bedspread. I lay out my five pairs of underwear, two bras, two nighties. The tape recorder is nestled there too. I take it out and set it on the nightstand, under the lamp's glare. Then I pull out the stack of shirts.

Something slips out from between them and lands on the bed. A ziplock bag filled with a foil-wrapped package. I crack open the seal, then rustle open the envelope-sharp fold of aluminum. The smell of canned sausage rises up into my nose, fleshy and metallic. A sandwich from Mummy.

"It took some finagling, but it's worth it." A woman's voice echoes up the stairs and through the open door. "Quiet spot on the end—oh!" She steps into the room and stops abruptly, tall and lean and definitely not old enough to be someone's mother. Something about her long, elegant neck and high cheekbones seems familiar. She frowns slightly. "Hello. Are you sure you're in the right room?"

I shove the foil parcel into my back pocket, then straighten up and reach for my welcome package. "Yes. I'm in two-oh-eight."

"There must be a mistake. My sister's in here, and we specifically asked for a single." She turns around to the door and before she can speak, her sister appears. A loud gasp bursts out of my mouth.

"Faith!"

"Nia? Oh, you can't be serious." Faith looks even more chagrined to see me than I am to see her. She turns right back around and her sister stops her.

"Let me check your papers. I swear it said two-oh-eight."

"I'm not sharing a room with *her*." Faith's voice drips with disgust. I'm not that happy at the thought of six weeks with someone from Pinder Street when I worked so hard to get away from there, but she makes it sound like I'm going to soil the bedsheets and pee in the sink. KeeKee would know what to say to cut her back down to size.

I take a step toward the bed. "My—Mr. Wright made sure I'm supposed to be here."

"Just take me back home," Faith says, ignoring me.

More footsteps, and Mr. Wright pokes his head around the door. "Davinia? Everything okay in here?" He nods at the woman. "Timothy Wright. How are you doing?"

"Oh, *Mr. Wright*, of course!" She stretches out a hand for him to shake. "Joy Knowles. You approached my dad for sponsorship. Assistant to the MP for Eastern Heights."

"Miss Knowles." He takes her hand with a smooth smile. Is that the smile he won Mummy over with, or the one he used on Angel? Did the same smile work on both of them? "So good to meet you."

"Listen, maybe you can clear up this"—she looks over at me—"misunderstanding. I made special arrangements for my little sister to have a private room."

Little sister? I think. What is she, four?

"I arranged for Nia to have this room myself," Mr. Wright says cheerfully, unaware that no one else in the room is smiling. "But if Faith is going to join her, that's even better." He looks from Faith to me. "Faith, you must be here for dance, right? Nia here wrote the most incredible poem for her application. Well, you girls know each other, she probably read it to you sometime."

My heart sinks. "It's no big deal," I say quickly as I see

disbelief register on Faith's face.

"It'll be great to have a friend while you're away from home," Mr. Wright gushes.

Faith folds her arms, leaning against the door frame. "We might as well go back home. I didn't want to come here in the first place."

Joy ignores her and turns to Mr. Wright. "What do you think we can work out? This is a sensitive time for Faith, I don't want her to be upset here." She taps nails on the bureau. They are long, perfectly oval, glistening pink, like her hands are adorned with the inside of shells.

"The girls can share. There are two dressers, and I'll make sure Nia leaves lots of room in the closet for Faith's things. Come on," Mr. Wright says, turning to me, as if everything is settled. "Let's go get some ice."

I follow him out into the fresh air, and deep inside I can make the tiniest allowance for the possibility that I might just like him after all.

In the distance, the registration line is gone, families dispersed to their buildings. Soon, this floor will be buzzing with girls settling in, mothers clucking around them. The hopeful part of me whispers that at least Faith and I have that much in common—neither of us have our mothers here today. Maybe it won't be that bad after all. A gull pulls across the sky, calling, and I look up. It swerves, white wings against the vivid sky, changing its path east. It could be bound for Pinder Street, for our beach. For a moment, I feel like I'll look down and find myself back there, feel KeeKee's arm looping through mine, tugging me to the sand and beyond.

FAITH

Joy stays long enough to help me get my bags half unpacked, then disappears to stock up on snacks. I empty the suitcase, and at the bottom, my fingers touch the sharp corner of something hard and smooth. I pull out my mother's photograph and prop it up on the nightstand. It's supposed to make this place feel like home, but when I look at her smile—secret, small—I remember her slumped in the back of the car, saliva draining from the corner of her mouth, and it's like I'm looking at a memory of someone who's dead. I slam the photograph face down, hard enough that the cracked glass should shatter and break free, but when I lift it up, it still stands, stubborn, in place.

There's a click as the room door unlocks. I shove the picture into the nightstand drawer before Joy comes in, but when I turn, it's Nia alone. She sets a bucket of ice and a big bottle of water down on the table, and avoids my gaze.

"So, you're a great poet now." I zip my case closed and push it into the closet. Nia doesn't reply. "Are your wonderful creations going to be *more* witty than KeeKee's, or less?"

Nia looks at me, startled. "She told you? I didn't think— look, I just wanted to come here. I knew I shouldn't have used her stuff, but I didn't know what else to do."

Her words dawn on me slowly. "Wait—you used your own best friend's poem to get into this place?"

"Well, not all of us have parents who can pull strings," Nia snarks back.

I slam the closet door shut. "Yeah, because it was my dream to spend a summer with one of y'all."

"What did I even do to you?" she asks. I open my mouth, but no response comes out. I pull the nightstand drawer open again. My mother gazes out at me, her face calm, her eyes softly glinting. *That girl ain do you nothin,* those eyes say. I sit down on the edge of the bed. She should be here. It should be her helping me unpack my suitcase, making small talk with the roommate I shouldn't have. If Mummy was here, if she was her, the her in the picture, the her in my mind, she'd tell me to shut up and stop being so spoiled, that she shared a room with four other girls for whole summers when she went to dance camps at my age. I take the picture out and slip it under my pillow, but I hold on tight, my fingers pressed to the frame. I welcome the corner's sharp bite. I guess I don't have any beef with Nia, really. If she stole some poem from KeeKee, it's no skin off my nose.

"Does KeeKee know you took her poem?" I make my voice softer when I speak. Nia must be as ready to bury the hatchet as I am; she flops down onto the foot of my bed and sighs.

"She hates me."

"Well, maybe she deserved it."

"No." She lies back on the bed. "She really didn't."

The sorrow in her voice makes me think of Eve, and how I've ducked all her calls to Joy's phone. I slip my hand into my pocket, lightly touching my new phone. I've never had a number Eve didn't know, but for now, I don't feel like I can be of help to anyone, even myself. And if I can't help Eve, maybe the best thing for me to do is stay out of her life for a while.

"Well, you're here now." I grab a cup and scoop up some ice, pouring water on top. "Might as well make the most of it."

16

EVE

"How much longer?" Joe tugs on my shirt, sighing as he looks up at the clock in the hospital's waiting room. It's after two, long past lunchtime.

"I don't know." I shift Junior on my lap; he's getting restless. It's been over an hour.

"I hungry," Esther whines. "We been here all day."

"I don't have anything to eat. Just wait," I say. Esther heaves herself back in her seat, bumping into Ruth, who's focused on the TV above us. Ruth scowls and pokes Esther with a dusty sneaker.

"Hey." I set Junior down on the floor a minute. "Take your feet off the seat."

Ruth doesn't even dignify me with an answer, but Junior darts across the room. As I grab him by a chubby wrist, a woman shifts in her chair, looking from me to my siblings and back to me. She leans forward.

"Sweetie, you can't control them?" Her whisper is deliberately loud.

I stand up, depositing Junior in my seat. "Watch him,"

I hiss at Ruth as I walk toward the stairs on shaky legs.

"You mean you leaving these children here?" the whisperer says behind me. I spin around to face her—perfect hair, fancy purse on her lap, her whole face an accusation.

"They aren't mine!" My voice comes out louder than I meant it to. The woman huffs. Whatever. I hurry out of the waiting room and take the stairs. At the door to the men's ward, I stop. I want to go into that room. Want to pull my daddy by the hand, willing him onto his feet. Want to bring him home, to let him breathe life and love back into our lives. To tell us what comes next. Tell us he's getting better, that he'll be okay. But what if none of that is possible? What if he's never coming home? Could I delay that reality if I just don't go in?

"Excuse me." A woman squeezes past me and through the door in her church clothes and I remember that today is Sunday. It seems inconceivable that a month ago, we were feasting on Sunday dinner at this time in the day. When we do finally get home, there will be no special dinner—just sandwiches or butter and bread.

The door to the ward opens abruptly, and Mummy comes out. Her already sad face transforms to irritation and disgust as soon as she sees me.

"Where are the others?" she demands.

"I—they downstairs."

"You left them in the waiting room? Alone?"

"There's other people there." The words come out sounding weak.

"I can't even believe you, Eve." She brushes past me and hurries down the stairs. I turn back to the room, daring to look farther in at Daddy, but his face is turned away from the door now, as if he's resting. I get downstairs as Mummy is rounding up the others. "Look at the baby!" she snaps at me, Junior on her hip, already starting to wail. "See how you upset this boy? And you left them here for anyone to up and take. You ain got no sense?"

I open my mouth to protest that Ruth is thirteen and I was looking after her and Esther and Joe when I was that age, but when I see tears in Mummy's eyes, I stop. She turns away from me, leading my siblings outside. As they trail after her, Joe turns to stare back at me, his eyes wide and confused. I follow them to the parking lot. While the rest of them pile into the car, I decide to try to make things better between me and Mummy. Again.

"Mummy, about what I said the day Daddy collapsed—"

"Hurry up and get in."

"I just wanted to say—"

"Now is not the time, Eve." She starts up the car.

"Can you at least tell me how he is? It's been two weeks since they brought him here and started chemotherapy."

She sighs. "He has to see the oncologist again. Then we'll know more. In the meantime, he needs his rest. I don't want you going in there and troubling him." She shifts into drive, the engine adjusting its tone. "Get in the car."

The thought of being in a confined space, with rowdy, hungry siblings and Mummy furious with me, is too much. "I'll walk home," I say softly.

Mummy settles back in her seat. "Go ahead, then. Seems like you're a grown woman now anyway, you do what you like and you say what you want. Apparently you know better than everybody." She pulls away through the parking lot, then out of my sight.

I walk the same way she drove out, then onto the road, then down another, and another. I'm all the way past Bay Street and at the water by the wharf when I stop for a break. I slump down onto the sea wall. The view is so different from the one at the church. There, we see still water over flat sand, sea so shallow you never thought of it as ocean. Here, the water is a deeper blue, always changing, always shifting, hiding what lies beneath. As I sit, memories flash through my mind. Daddy at the pulpit, a hand raised, standing strong, his voice lifted to the rafters. All of us around the table, Ruth laughing with her mouth full, the latest baby squealing with joy. If all that is gone, what do I do now? The long line of us making our way down the path, the first slip of ocean visible ahead of us. Is all of that really gone now? I sit on the wall overlooking the water, staring into the dancing blue. If I look long enough, hard enough, maybe, in the slip of light through liquid, I can find an answer.

I take the bus toward Pinder Street but get off early and walk to Faith's house. I need my best friend. She knows how to joke and curse through anything. Her car is in the driveway, but when I knock, there's no answer. I look in through the window, but the blinds are closed.

A car door slams shut and I turn to see a woman waving at me across the fence. "You looking for the girl who lives here?"

I take a few steps toward her. "Yes, ma'am. Have you seen her?"

"They gone. Mmhmm. Packed up and *psshooow.*" She

skids one hand over the other, her palms moving silently against each other. Her hands are decorated with long fake nails painted brassy yellow. She taps on the fence. A ring clinks against the post.

"Do you know where they went?"

The woman shakes her head. "They don't tell me anything, child. Like to keep to themselves. They too fancy for me. You friends with her?" she asks.

"I'm her best friend."

"What's your name? I'll let her know you came through, if I see her."

"Eve Armbrister."

"Oh, you the pastor's daughter."

Am I? Is he still a pastor if he has no church? Will he ever be well enough to start another one? This is why I need Faith—to help me make sense of this mess. Where is she? The woman stares at me expectantly. "Yes, my daddy was the pastor," I say finally.

"Was? He passed?"

Her words are like a twist of current, wrenching my body out of my control. I turn away from her and hurry out of the yard. Where is Faith? My guts feel like they're tied in a knot my fingers can't ever reach to untie. I have to talk to her. I dial her number. Voice mail. Again. Again. On the third try, it rings twice, then the ring cuts off.

When I get home, I stand outside for a moment. Daddy's chair under the tree seems large, empty. I sit in it, partly to fill the space, partly to feel like he's there. I sit there as the afternoon grows stale with yellow light, but I don't really see Pinder Street around me. Instead, all I see is Daddy, a bus ride between us, but already a world away.

NIA

On Monday morning, the campers meet in classes divided by age, groups of a dozen girls, each in one of four corners in a medium-sized meeting room. Partitions on wheels separate the classes. Faith gives me a nod as she sits in the chair in front of mine. It seems like a few of the girls around us already know each other too. Three of them huddle over a magazine, laughing. Another pair is bent quietly over a sketchpad, doodling in opposite corners. I look around at the other groups. It seems we're sectioned off by age. I wonder how that will work. I'd assumed people who drew and painted would all be together, and writers in another group. Maybe it's better for me this way. If I'm lucky, everyone else will be into art, or dance, like Faith. Maybe no one will notice I can't write poetry.

"Hi, girls," a voice calls. I turn to see a short woman with a wide smile surveying us. I check my orientation papers. This must be our teacher, Ms. Rose. She definitely looks the part, with a shirt that hangs off one shoulder and a long, full skirt that sweeps the floor. She totes a couple of grocery bags in each hand, and huge earrings dangle down to her shoulders. If I had to put money down on the type of girlfriend Mr. Wright would have, I'd say this Ms. Rose is it; Angel isn't the proper type for a man who works in an office and wears spectacles, and how Mummy and he ever—well, that's an abomination I can't even dwell on.

"Good afternoon—" she begins, taking a step forward toward the front of the group. Then her foot catches on the skirt, and she stumbles, just barely stopping herself from falling face-first on the floor. Before anyone even responds, she scrambles to her feet and disappears through the nearest side door. Faith and I look at each other. Even she's too surprised to react.

Only seconds pass before the door bursts open and Ms. Rose strides back in, a huge fuchsia cardboard cutout of sunglasses perched on her face. She pauses, poses in the doorway with her nose in the air, then sashays to the front of our group and retrieves her grocery bags, opening them to reveal fabric and bits of paper, yarn and plastic tubing protruding like guts. Then she grabs a chair, spins it around so it's backward, and plants herself on it, facing us.

"What did you just see?" Ms. Rose studies us, expectant.

A short girl with long braids raises a hand. "Embarrassment?"

"Possibly. Anyone else?"

"Bad acting," Faith mutters under her breath. Giggles skitter through the group.

"Anyone can fall flat—even a teacher," Ms. Rose says, removing the paper shades. "In your creative careers, I'm gonna bet that all of you will fall at least once. But when you do, it's your job to get up and keep going with a little extra flair." She holds the cardboard sunglasses up. "These are my flair. So now it's your turn. Go ahead and use the materials I've got in these bags to make your own. Glasses, jewelry, hat, cape—the choice is yours. Fifteen minutes—go!"

"What she think this is, craft time?" Faith's whisper is

deliberately loud this time. Something whizzes through the air, then clips the empty chair beside her. We stare, speechless, at the dry-board eraser lying on the floor. I suppress a smile. I have a feeling I'm going to like Ms. Rose.

"Get going, ladies," Ms. Rose says cheerfully, propelling us into action. The other girls seem to know what to do right away, picking out reams of orange netting, finding scissors and sparkly paper. Even Faith's sullenness thaws as she starts bunching up tissue paper into a rough rose. I walk from bag to bag, trying to look busy. I glance up and see Ms. Rose laying out papers side by side on the floor—our applications. Panic rises in me like a sudden tide.

Ms. Rose looks up and catches me staring. "Stymied already?" she asks.

"Um . . . I . . . no."

"What's your name?"

"Nia."

Ms. Rose skims the applications, then picks one up. "Here we go. Davinia Taylor. Ah, a poet." She smiles warmly. "Poets are the astrophysicists of the literary world, so I expect you to bring the nebula." She holds my application up and staples it to the partition behind her. Now my lie is right up there for the whole world to see.

I have to do something. I'm here now, and I can't let anyone find out that I don't belong. I rifle through the bags quickly, then settle on a big piece of cardboard. I grab some scissors, then cut out the shape of a mask.

"Eight more minutes," Ms. Rose trills, stapling another application to the partition. Faith actually squeals, bustling back to the basket near the window. Around the room, masterpieces are emerging. One girl's put something together that looks like a giant hat. Another has a cape draped around her shoulders. Faith's rose has unfolded into a tutu in full bloom. I rifle through the baskets one more time—plastic costume jewelry, fabric scraps, dusty bits of wood. I don't know what to do with this stuff. I take a necklace made of plastic hexagon chunks and snip the string so the beads spill out onto the table in front of me. Then I smear glue on the mask and wedge the beads into the goo.

"Time's up! Stop!"

Groans erupt around me, but as far as I can see, these girls have made pure perfection. I look down at my mask. The two halves are lopsided; a third grader could have made it. A bead slides off, leaving behind a snail's trail of glue. *That's what you get*, a voice in my head sneers. *You couldn't make something to save your life. You don't belong here.*

KEEKEE

"KeeKee."

Angel taps on the door. From the crack in the curtains, I can tell that out there, the day is bright, but in here, the dark embraces me.

"You been in there since last night. You're not gonna come out and get something to eat?"

I lean back into the pillows, close my eyes. Pretend I am Toons—still here, still whole. *If you are him, who would be you?* my brain sings. There's no answer. *That's right*, I think. *Nobody.*

"I made soup. I put crackers on the top for you."

Reheated canned chicken noodle, I figure. I can imagine the crumbled crackers sagging into the pale liquid, defeated.

"Come on, KeeKee. You can't stay in there forever." Angel sighs. "I miss Toons, I think about him every minute, but we have to keep on going. Still plenty stuff to do. Three different girls came through here today. You know we almost out of pouches?"

I turn onto my side with my back to the door. I don't care about doing for others anymore. Look where that got us. Anyway, shouldn't she be dying of humiliation after what Sammy did yesterday?

There's a pause, then muffled voices. "Okay," I hear Angel say. "You try her, then."

The next thing I know, I hear another voice on the other side of the door. "KeeKee. You okay in there?"

I get up and crack the door open. Through the gap, my father seems small, out of place.

"I thought you couldn't be here." I start to close the door and he slips his fingers into the space.

"Don't be like that." My father pushes to open the door. "Come on, KeeKee. I want to talk."

I wish I could shut the door in his face, but something in me has to know what he wants to say. "Talk about what?"

He lowers his head a moment, then raises it, looking me in the eye. "Kimberly. I'm so sorry about this mess. I was wrong not to tell you."

I stare back at him. "Is Nia why you never came here to see me?"

He sighs. "Angel didn't want me to come."

"Seriously? You're trying to blame Angel?" I yank the door all the way open. "All this time I thought you didn't come here because of *me*. Because I wasn't good enough for you. And you *knew* she was my best friend, and you never told me. I came all the way to see you every week, all that time and not once did you think to mention she was your daughter too!"

Neither of us hears the footsteps, but suddenly, Angel appears. She's in an old T-shirt, bare from the waist down, except for a pair of old stretched-out underwear. I want to cover her up. My father looks away, pity written all over his face. That's even worse than any look Sammy ever gave her. It's like she's so broken up she can't even take being treated rough. So taken she can't lose anything more. And yet she has that sad bowl of soup still in her hands.

"You're upsetting my daughter," Angel says. Her voice trembles as she points at the front door. "You need to go."

"Angel, I—"

"No!" This time her voice is louder. "Go."

Dad looks at me sadly, then shakes his head. After the door closes behind him, I reach out to her and she rushes toward me. Tears I didn't know were waiting start to fall, but instead of anger, I feel relief as she hangs on to me with her free arm, the soup wedged between us.

"Don't get scalded," she says, pulling away to set the bowl down, and I cling tighter. Even with all the strangers who show up at the door, with all the people she wanted to help, with all the sorrow that came when Toons left, I still matter. Even in frumpy panties, even holding tepid canned soup, she's here for me. She's still here to protect me. She still sees me.

FAITH

At the end of our first day, the rest of the girls gather on the sand for a campfire. I slip away from the group and make my way toward the empty dining area. There's something I can't avoid any longer. I step into the hall and take out my new phone, then dial the number Joy gave me before she left. It rings four times before a cool voice answers.

"Good evening, Hope Springs Rehabilitation, how may I direct your call?"

I slide onto a chair. It feels like my legs might give out under me. "Can you put me through to Mrs. Knowles?" I say.

"Patient's first name?"

"Elaine."

"And what ward is she on?"

Even though no one is around, I don't want to say *dementia* out loud. "I don't remember. Can you look her up another way?"

"Hold, please."

Flutey music begins to play in my ear while I wait, interrupted every several seconds by two beeps and a soothing voice that thanks me for calling, as if I might have forgotten that I'm trying to reach my crazy mother in the loony bin.

"Thank you for holding." The operator comes on again. "That patient is not receiving calls."

"You don't understand." My voice squeaks. "I have to talk to her."

"I'm sorry." The voice on the other end actually sounds regretful, but I don't care. "I'm not authorized to disclose that information," the voice says.

"But it's my mother."

There's a pause on the line. I hold my breath, clinging to the silent phone. And then, a tiny miracle. There is a crackle on the line, and a different voice comes on.

"Nurse Mackey speaking. Is this Mrs. Knowles's daughter?"

"Yes." I can barely gasp in air to form the word.

"And for security, your name, your age, and your mother's maiden name?"

"Faith Knowles, seventeen, and Carey."

"Yes, Faith," the nurse says, "I'm afraid our protocol is that we cannot give out information over the phone to minors."

"But—"

"She had a turn," the nurse says in a whisper. "Last three days. Stopped taking food, unresponsive. She isn't in any condition to talk on the phone."

"But—my father and my sister didn't say anything about that."

"I'm sorry, I can't tell you more than that. If you were to come by, you could see for yourself." There's an accusing note in her voice. I hang up then. I don't need someone to tell me I'm wrong, to tell me I don't love my mother enough. I force my legs to move me forward, toward the side door. I've hardly gone three steps before I'm in tears. If I'd just gone home to be with Mummy instead of messing around with Toons, she'd still be safe. I'd be there with her now, not stuck in this place, unable to see her or even talk to her. She'd still be herself, even a little bit.

"Hey, you're missing everything!" Nia appears out of nowhere. I wipe my face and straighten up, but she's already seen that I'm crying. "Faith? What happened?"

I open my mouth to say *nothing*, to say *leave me alone*, to say anything that will stop her from feeling sorry for me. But here, far from the strange jumble of our house, from Mummy's bright blue skirt and the rhythmic click of all the locks on the front door, from the sweat and focus of dance class, the feel of Toons' fingers on mine, from my little car, even from Daddy's voice floating down the hall as he comes in at night, Nia's round face with the too-small glasses is the closest thing to home. Suddenly, everything around me feels too strange— the orangey light cast from the fire, the bright-lit dining hall confusing the darkness, even the steady croak of frogs from some hidden pond nearby.

"It's just . . . ," I begin, and everything spills out—the way little details started slipping away from Mummy's mind, how sometimes I just want to escape and feel normal, feel like other girls do. How, that afternoon, that's what I did, and how what happened with Toons and what happened with Mummy, what happened with everything, might be all because of me. And as I empty those words into the dark, Nia doesn't speak, just listens, really listens, not to fix, not to find a way out. Just hears me. When, finally, my voice trails off and there's no more to tell, Nia leans over and rests her head on my shoulder. She should make me feel weighed down, pressing into me like that. But sometimes, the world doesn't make sense. Sometimes everything is backward. I close my eyes and lean my head on hers. And it starts to feel that, even if I can't figure a way out, even if there are no answers, at least there's still someone who can hear me.

17

KEEKEE

Bright and early Wednesday morning, Angel opens the front door to take out the garbage and lets out a whoop. I come running to join her. Three baskets of clothes sit on our doorstep, waiting patiently. A note is rested on the top of the middle hamper: *Please iron for my nephew. Will pay double the wash rate. T. Rahming.*

"Sunshine always comes after the rain, KeeKee," Angel says as we bring the clean clothes inside. "Listen, go up by the Armbristers and see if you can borrow an iron, we can work on this together, get it done before noon."

As I head up the road, a few guys pass me on the way to the construction site. They nod and slip in *good morning* between laughing and joking among themselves, none the wiser that they're destroying what meant so much to us here. I turn around to look behind me at the changed skyline, cranes already poised and ready to go. Then my phone buzzes in my pocket. I pull it out. Another text.

Y'all all right? Toons, again. I call him back right away. It rings three times, then goes to voice mail. I text him back.

Fine—where ARE you? What happened? Worried sick, come home. A moment's pause, then my phone buzzes again. This time, a call.

"Hello?" I can barely get the word out, I'm so relieved.

"KeeKee, I'm sorry, I don't want y'all to worry. I'm okay." It's him, his voice is right, he doesn't sound like he's upset or in pain.

"Where are you? What happened?"

"I can't say. I gotta lay low right now. I can't talk long, but I'm fine. Tell Angel I'm good. I don't want to cause problems."

"What problems?" Too many questions flood my mind—I try to focus. "They were saying all type of crap, that you set the church on fire, you cut the gate to get through. But I know that can't be true . . ." My voice trickles off, hoping, praying he can explain it before the call ends.

"That church was already on fire. My camera don't work, but I had Faith's phone and I was recording—these guys burst outta nowhere and grabbed me and I dropped it in the sand, I don't know where. If you can get Faith's phone—"

"Anthony!" a voice calls in a businesslike tone. A woman's voice. It doesn't sound like he's in a bad place, but I can't know.

"Where are you?" I plead again. "Just come home!"

"Find her phone," he whispers.

"Wait, let me get Angel!"

"I'll come when I can. If I can." The line goes dead.

Thoughts swirl in my head, frantic, chaotic, relief and worry mixed together. The beach is totally inaccessible. Even if Faith's phone was there, it would be long gone by now. He's okay enough to talk for a few minutes, at least. He's not hurt. He's alive. But what did he mean *if I can*? I shove the phone away and start walking toward Eve's house again. She'll know what Faith's phone looks like. Maybe she'll even help me.

Ruth answers the door, earbuds in, and lazily shouts for her sister. Eve appears a few seconds later, yellow rubber gloves on her hands.

"Hey," I say. "Can I borrow your iron?" Then I drop my voice. "I gotta talk to you about Faith."

"I don't know where she is." Eve steps outside and closes the door behind her. "She's not at her house, the neighbor doesn't know where she went. I can't get her on the phone, because she lost it, and if she has a new number, she didn't share it with me. Her sister just said Faith's away for the summer and needs some time."

"Well, we have to find her old phone."

Eve frowns. "You were awful to her that day by your house, and I haven't heard from her since."

My face warms with shame. That's the last thing I want to remember, especially when Angel has been so kind to me the past couple of days, and after what Mr. Rahming's done to help us out. "She took it the wrong way," I try to explain. "I told you, that song was about Nia, not Faith."

"And Nia's supposed to be your best friend?" She turns back to the door. "You can get the iron, but I don't want to do anything with you. Sorry." She steps inside, pushing the door half closed behind her. I wait outside for a second. Then I ease the door open. I can't just leave this. I don't blame Eve for being upset with me, but I have to make things right. I have to do what I can to bring Toons home.

Eve's siblings are scattered around the living room. Com-

fortable family mess is strewn around—a sippy cup in front
of the sofa, coloring books and crayons on the coffee table,
a couple of abandoned bowls of cereal on the floor. The TV
blares cartoons. Ruth glances up from her phone, then points
to the back of the house. I head down the hallway. Straight
ahead is what must be Eve, Esther, and Ruth's room. I can
see a few toys on a bed, children's drawings taped to the wall.
The door on the left must be her parents' room. It's a few
inches open. I lean into the space. I can just barely make
out hushed, urgent voices. I take a step forward, straining
to hear. "What happened, Mummy? Did the hospital call?"
Eve's voice is panicked. "Can I do something to help?"

"You and your sharp mouth already did enough." Mrs.
Armbrister's voice is sad, but also angry.

"Why won't you tell me what's going on?" Eve pleads.

"I'll be fine. I'll wash my face." The bedsprings creak, as
if her mother gets up.

I slip back through the house, but I only make it to the
front room before Eve comes out again. Her hands are bare
and she clutches an iron.

"It was hot outside," I say.

"Okay." She looks distracted. As Eve passes the iron to
me, I wonder what she could have said to make her mother so
upset. Maybe Eve isn't the model daughter she always seemed
to be. If we've both made mistakes, maybe we have more in
common than I thought. And maybe I can convince her to
work together with me to try to make some things right again.

"Can you just tell me how Faith's phone looked? I have to
try and find it. I talked to Toons—"

"You found him?" Her face lights up.

"He finally called. He says he's okay, but Eve, he didn't burn down your dad's church."

She looks behind her into the house, and inclines her head toward the door as she opens it. I follow her outside. "How you know? Anyway, doesn't matter, the church is gone now, either way."

"Come on, you know Toons. You think he'd burn down the place y'all used to go and sing?" Guilt flashes across Eve's face briefly. I keep going. "Toons ain gonna come home until everyone knows he didn't do it. If we can find Faith's phone, we can prove it wasn't him, and clear his name. And maybe that will protect him from whoever beat him up."

"If he didn't do anything, why would anyone have it out for him?"

"I don't know," I say. "But they do. Please, Eve. Help me. I didn't mean to hurt Faith."

"And Nia?"

I want to ask her why she'd even care, but I bite back my irritation. "It's a long story," I say, "but she had it coming, trust me."

Eve looks regretful. "I guess accidents happen."

I wonder if she suspects that I overheard her a few minutes ago. "I really didn't mean it," I say again.

Finally, she nods. "Her phone is rose gold, and she has a rhinestone case."

I search on my phone, and together, we huddle over the screen, scrolling through models until she points at one. "There. Toons came by the church the night he went missing.

Faith left her phone, and he came to get it to bring it back to her. That's why he had it."

"Yeah, I know. They were there together, earlier."

Eve nods. "How are you gonna find the phone?"

I take the iron from her. "I'm not sure, but it's gotta be somewhere. Lost things never disappear all the way, right?"

Eve still looks skeptical, and maybe she should. After all, plenty of things are lost and are never coming back. Our beach, her church. Friendships and families. But, to my surprise, she leans over and gives me a hug. "Maybe you're right. Maybe they just change hands. Or change shape." She looks down the road toward my house. "If you have so much work that you need two irons, maybe we can help."

I think back to what I overheard. "Doesn't your mum need you?" I blurt out.

"She might like it if she doesn't have to worry about us for a couple hours. Ask Mr. Rahming if we can borrow another iron for Ruth, and we'll go to your house. The rest of them can come too."

While I cross over to the store, I look back down the road. Sounds of banging and churning are coming from the beach now, the construction site in full swing. Somehow, though, the weight that was on me feels way lighter. It feels like this street might still belong to me.

EVE

At lunch, Ruth takes the others home for sandwiches. I stay to help KeeKee press another four loads of clothes people dropped off through the morning. For the first hour on our own, we work in silence. Then KeeKee bursts out laughing as she holds something up. It looks like a tiny jacket, maybe a child's, except it's too small even for Junior.

"What size is that, newborn?" I squint at the tiny suit. "Are there pants to match?"

"This is for a dog!" She turns it around to show a spot for the tail. "Look, there's four leg holes. Think I should starch it?"

I chuckle. "Depends, whose dog?"

"Nurse Pratt's brother. Well, his girlfriend probably got the suit."

"Never know." The air between us is warmer now. "Can I ask you something?"

"Yeah, of course." KeeKee lays the jacket on the tip of the ironing board and presses the iron against it. "I hope Fifi doesn't mind creases."

"Did Toons really sound okay?"

KeeKee drops the jacket back into the basket and lifts out a white dress shirt. "I think so. I have to tell myself he did, I don't really have anything else to go on. He sounded—healthy. Like he was living life, just not here."

I unplug the iron and fill it with water. "I was worried about him."

"Do you have a crush on him?" KeeKee asks behind me. I take my time setting the iron up again.

"I don't know. He's with Paulette. And then Faith and him . . . you know. Honestly, I guess I did."

"What is it with him?"

I think about Toons, his voice, his smile, the way we sang together. "I mean, he didn't look at me that way, and it's not like anything would ever have happened. But it was just nice to feel . . . special. Like you're worth getting kindness. You know?"

KeeKee is quiet again for a while, our irons hissing, the crisp smell of hot lemon starch rising in the air. "I always wanted to ask someone that. All these girls who come through and need protection and stuff. I just don't get it. We're already special. Why do you need somebody to feel up all over you to make it true?"

"I mean, if people come to you for help, aren't they making you feel special too? They need you and that makes you important to them. We all want that, don't we?"

"Never thought about it that way." KeeKee passes me a hanger and I clip the pleated skirt I've been ironing onto it. "Well, if that's true, pastors are the same as those girls, then. Getting attention and feeling valuable for it."

"Yeah, but pastors are supposed to have a special calling."

"Aren't we all?"

I snort. "According to my mum, I'm basically the devil."

KeeKee looks sheepish. "I kinda overheard you talking to her in the room back at your house. What was that about? You can tell me, I won't judge."

"I said something bad about her the day my daddy had to go to the hospital, and she heard it."

"What'd you say?"

I hesitate.

"Come on," KeeKee needles.

I sigh. "She should have gone to your mummy instead of having so many kids."

"What? Eve, you said that?"

"Hey, I thought you weren't supposed to judge." I

glower at KeeKee as she starts laughing. "It's not funny. I felt horrible as soon as I said it, and now she hates me."

"I know." KeeKee gets serious again. "I just—I can't believe it. I always thought you were a goody-goody."

I shoot her an incredulous look. "And best friends with Faith? Please."

"I guess that's true. Not like I ever say anything *I* shouldn't."

I lean against the wall, stretching my back. "What did Nia do to you, anyway?"

KeeKee puts her iron down and heads to the fridge. She takes out a couple of sodas and hands me one. Before she closes the door, I glimpse the full shelves—yogurt, a container of sliced melon, a mostly full milk carton, a covered casserole dish. In our house, that would all be devoured in half a minute, with people burping and asking for more. "Know what I found out?" she says, flopping onto a chair and opening her bottle. "My lifelong best friend? She's a thief. She recorded me practicing one of my poems and used it on her application for camp."

I choke on my soda.

KeeKee nods. "It gets better. We're half sisters. Nia and me."

I gawk at her. "How is that even possible?"

"Well, I guess my father was busy that year." Her tone is sarcastic, but I hear the twinge of pain in her voice. Now isn't the time for me to feel surprised. I try to imagine what Daddy would say. People were always coming to him with delicate problems, with family secrets, with shame. I try to imagine how I'd feel if Faith stole something that meant the world to me. *Like the church.* Even though she didn't mean to, even though KeeKee thinks someone else started the church fire, I can't shake the feeling that Faith and Toons being in there that night set something in motion. At the same time, I know Faith's been hurting with her mum for a long time. It doesn't excuse her exactly, but it does make her actions understandable.

"Nia must have felt awful," I say carefully. "She must have felt like she didn't do anything well, for her to steal something you created like that."

KeeKee taps her foot against the chair's leg. "Well, that's dumb. She can do things well. I mean, she's a fantastic actress, she had me thinking she actually cared about me all that time."

I try to think of something useful to say, but the truth is, I don't know Nia that well. It's funny how you can grow up so close to someone and go to the same schools your whole life, and even have them come to your house, but not get to know them, really. "What does she do well? The newspaper?"

"The newspaper was her mom's idea—it started out as a punishment years ago, actually. She hated doing that."

"What then?" I say.

KeeKee drains her soda, then sets the bottle down on the counter. "She likes cooking and stuff. But they're always behind on bills so the gas and lights get turned off, and her mother hates Angel, so she couldn't come and bake or anything over here." KeeKee looks over at me. "I bet you'd disown Faith if she stole something you made."

"Well, unless she figures out a way to steal singing, I'm safe." I think for a moment. "I don't know what I'd do if my best friend took something from me. But Nia isn't your best friend."

"Not anymore." She snorts.

"No, I mean she's your sister."

"Half sister."

"Same thing. It's different with family."

"You mean Ruth would take stuff from you?"

"Her? If she had a use for my skin, I'd turn around and find it gone. All my muscles and tendons flapping loose in the breeze."

"You'd just be okay with that? Because you're family?"

"Not okay with it," I say. "It's just no matter how bad you hurt each other, you're . . . stuck. You have to love each other. Didn't Toons ever make you mad?"

She considers this. "We had a big fight the night the church caught fire. That was the last we saw of each other, before . . ."

"See? You and Toons fight but you still love him, right?"

"Yes," KeeKee says, letting out an exasperated sigh. "But what, we're supposed to let people get away with anything because we share the same blood? It's not fair." KeeKee settles onto the sofa, lying back. I flop onto the other sofa and stretch out too.

"Of course not. I still let Ruth know when she gets out of line, but she's not going anywhere, and neither am I. And if she ever needed anything, I'd be there in a heartbeat. It's that way with Faith, too, but different. I don't know what's going on with her, she just up and left. But when she's ready, she'll tell me."

"So what about you and your mom?"

"What do you mean?"

"Well, are you gonna tell her you're mad at her, too?"

I sit up. "Mad at her? No, she's mad at me."

"You must have been mad at her, to say that. I don't know, from what I see, you do a ton in your house, and you said one thing—"

"A really bad thing," I interject.

"Okay, one *really bad* thing, and now she's treating you like dirt."

KeeKee really was eavesdropping, I think, but as her words sink in, I wonder if she's right. Daddy and I have always been close, and things with Mummy and me were never bad before, but the way she's reacting now is as if I've been an awful daughter for years. Even when I tried to apologize, she didn't want to hear me.

"I think I'm more frustrated than mad. I want my parents to take me seriously," I say. "I want them to confide in me, not just lean on me when they want to."

KeeKee lets out a long, weary breath. "That's what I wish Nia had done. If she really didn't think she could get into that camp, I could have helped her somehow. But with your mom, you gotta tell her how you feel. And if she doesn't want to listen, *make her*."

Deep down, I know KeeKee's right. "If I do that, you better find a way to forgive Nia," I say. KeeKee doesn't answer. Instead, she gets up and starts ironing again. I get up too, and as I pick up my own iron, she says a word so soft that for a moment I think I imagined it.

"Maybe."

NIA

Our class is scattered over the grass in silent concentration, bellies full from lunch. One thing I definitely love about camp is the food—there's not a dry sandwich in sight. But the grouper fingers and French fries are churning in my stomach now. Everyone else is huddled over their books, journaling, but my page is blank except for the assignment, copied down from Ms. Rose's dictation: *Write a letter to yourself as someone you dislike, then turn your ideas into a creation of your choice.*

Not only do I *not* have a poem, there's no one I can say I dislike. Mummy, Mr. Wright, KeeKee—I can understand why each of them did what they did. The only person I'm really mad at is me, but I can't write a letter to myself. That would just open up questions with Ms. Rose, and then what would my creation be, a written confession?

"Writer's block?" Ms. Rose squats down beside me. She smiles kindly and I feel even smaller. If KeeKee was here, she'd be killing this assignment. She'd be in awe of Ms. Rose, she'd probably be following behind her every second she could, begging for extra work to do in the evening.

"Um—sort of," I say.

She looks up at the sky, thinking for a minute. "You know, journaling isn't always written down. You could draw something. Or make something. A gift for yourself from a person you think doesn't understand you. It's about perspective, and trying to see things from someone else's view." Ms. Rose looks out over the water. "Maybe it would help you to change your vantage point. You want to go over to the beach? Just stay where I can see you."

Grateful, I scramble to my feet and head for the water. The shore here is raked clean every morning, the bigger hotels farther east on the island looming, ever-present but still out of reach. I think of the men who took Toons, but when I do, I only get more angry with myself. I'm more like them than anyone else. I hurt someone who never did anything to me. I made a big mess on Pinder Street, then just left. I can't stall forever—sooner or later, Ms. Rose is going to wonder why I never actually write any poetry. And when she finds out, what will happen then?

FAITH

I lie in bed with the covers tented over me, phone in my hand. I can't stop the text from Joy. *I've been to see Mummy. It's under control. They know what they're doing at Hope Springs.* My fingers tighten on the phone. It's just past six a.m. I press call. It rings twice, then my sister's voice greets me.

"Why you up so early? Everything okay?" She sounds dazed.

"I don't even know how you sleeping right now." I keep my voice low so Nia doesn't hear. "What's happening with Mummy? How come you didn't pick up when I called last night?"

Joy sighs. I hear her bed creak as she shifts. "I've been up there every day. She's been a bit low. They're adjusting her meds again."

"I don't wanna be here if she's worse. Can you come for me?"

"See, this is why I didn't tell you. You don't need to be

here for this. Please, Faith. Just lay low and stay at camp."

"I want to see her. Come on, Joy," I plead. "She always saw me every day. Maybe it would help if—"

"Look, I didn't wanna say it, but Daddy's really pissed at you. You should have been with her that day, and instead you were holed up with that boy. Then you guys left the gate open and she got onto the beach. And after all that, when she went to Hope Springs, you turned around that same night and snuck out."

"It wasn't my fault!" I protest. "You know it wasn't—"

"Honestly, Faith? I kinda agree with him."

Her words hit me like a foot in the gut. Daddy blames me. Joy blames me. If Mummy's mind was clear enough, would she blame me too?

"She's sick, Faith." Joy's voice is softer, when she speaks again. "You didn't make her sick, and everyone knows that. I just think for now, it's better if you stay at NewBeat. Take some time. Clear your head."

The door to the room opens from the outside suddenly. I don't even say goodbye before I hang up, then toss the covers off. Nia stands by the door, already dressed, her hair brushed, edges slick with water that will only hold it until the sun and warm air dries it. When did she have time to do all that?

"Hey, early bird," Nia says. "Everything good?" Her words are cheerful, but her voice sounds nervous.

I open the nightstand drawer and drop the phone in. I glimpse the edge of the picture frame, and slam the drawer shut before I see anything more. I don't feel like I can speak without something bad happening, something that will leave me naked, something that will leave her pitying me.

"You getting up now?" she asks.

Go away, just go away, I think, grabbing my cosmetics bag. She trails me to the bathroom, lingering in the doorway like a bad smell.

"Want breakfast early?"

I squeeze a line of toothpaste onto my brush. *Ten, nine, eight, seven, six . . .* "Sun ain't even up yet," I say, gritting my teeth. Nia leans against the wall while I brush.

"One of the cooks will give you stuff early if you ask."

I splash water on my face, massage in my cleanser, then rinse. I can still feel her watching me. "You plan on being here while I pee, too?"

"I figured you'd close the door," she says.

I roll my eyes and kick the door shut, then plop down onto the seat. I take my time, freshening up, putting on deodorant, then a spritz of body mist, then a clear gloss, then mousse in my hair. Befriending Nia was a mistake. I don't need someone foot to foot behind me. I need space. I need to clear my head.

"You always take this long to get ready?"

I pull the door open again. "You're annoying."

"What happened? Did you get bad news? Your mummy okay?"

I push past her and into the room. "Are you stupid or what? I just told you last night she's not okay. You think people get better magically overnight? She doesn't have a cold." Nia's face falls and I want to crumple into a ball all over again. She's only trying to be nice. Maybe Joy's right. Maybe I just make things worse. "Sorry." I plop into the chair.

"You wanna talk?"

"Not about that." I look around the room. Light is starting to make the curtains glow. Outside, the day is waking up.
Maybe Mummy's waking too, but I can't know that. According to my sister, I shouldn't know. I have to focus on something. I hear Nia's footsteps as she walks gingerly over to her
bed. She's here. Maybe I can focus on her.

"I couldn't sleep either," she says. "I've been up since four,
so I just got up and got dressed. You know they start working in
the kitchen two hours before breakfast? It's like a whole separate
world that's wide awake while everyone else sleeps. Wanna see?"

"Four?" I turn to stare at her. "What did you come here
on, a scholarship for sneaking around?"

A guilty look crosses her face. "I was trying to think up a
poem for class."

"In the kitchen?" I slip on my purple sneakers. "Did you
come up with one?"

She takes a deep breath. "*I miss you. That is true. Do
dee do.*"

"That . . . is awful. Seriously, you can't ever say that aloud.
Or write it down."

"I know that." She steps outside. "I'll just have to keep
trying. It's Thursday, we've been here four days now. Ms.
Rose is gonna notice if I keep saying I'm still working."

"Why don't you just come clean?" I follow Nia as she tip-
toes down the stairs, then dips around the corner and under
a fig tree. Together, we navigate the network of roots sticking
up like veins on the back of an old man's hand. We pick our
way past the buildings, then cut across a footpath through low

bush. "Where are we going? The dining hall's the other way," I say. Nia keeps going without a word. As we get to the main building, she slips around the side to a door I'm sure must be locked. She tugs it and it swings open obediently. We're right in the meeting room now, the lights dimmed. Ahead of me, her flat leather sandals are so worn the bottoms are smooth, but she moves easily in them, like they're an extension of her own skin. She goes to a door at the back of the room, behind the stage, and holds it open for me. We cut through what looks like a service hallway, and Nia takes a side door that opens to a small room with bare tiles, extra chairs and tables stacked against the walls, and long, wide windows facing east. Through them, morning is softly opening up, pink light rising across the sky. My eyes fall on a small stage at the far end of the room, and I hear myself sigh. I turn to ask Nia how she found this place, and realize I'm alone.

I step up onto the stage and slip off my shoes. A few grains of sand press into my bare feet, greeting my skin. I welcome the grit. I don't have any answers about how to help my mother. I don't even know how to start being a better person, a person my whole family doesn't blame for hurting Mummy. But for now, I have a space where I can stretch out free, where I can let my body lift and soar and spin till my mind forgets, or at least hits pause. I close my eyes. I raise my arms. Then I begin to dance.

18

KEEKEE

"KeeKee, my friend."

Mr. Rahming clears his throat from behind the cash register. "We need to talk."

I set the dustrag down at the back of the store, then come to join him at the front. "Are you sick?"

"Sick?" He laughs, a low, wheezy croak. "I plan on living at least until you get your first gray hair."

"Maybe I'll dye my hair. Then you'll have to live forever."

"It's a deal." He holds out his hand and I shake it. "Now listen." Mr. Rahming's voice is serious again. "It's about the store."

"The store?"

"Remember Mr. Knowles came through some weeks ago?"

"Faith's daddy? I heard."

"Told me this is prime real estate now. Right on the corner of the main street, so it's visible. And with the hotel coming, even better. It's already zoned for retail. It's a gold mine, you see?"

"But . . . you told him no, right?"

"That man offered me a pile of money," Mr. Rahming continues, holding up a finger to say he isn't done yet. "Enough to help Paulette a bit more with her school fees and put something away for the future, and take my money, go retire on the island. I could carry a little rowboat out on the water, just sit and fish and stare out at the sea."

"How could you—"

"I said no." He leans back on the stool, clearly pleased.

"So you didn't sell," I say, relief flooding me.

"No. But I'm still leaving."

I open my mouth to protest, but before I can get my words out, the screen door opens halfway and a little boy pushes his way in. I recognize him as one of the kids who comes to us for breakfast.

"What you need, son?" Mr. Rahming asks, a smile in his voice. The little boy picks up a bag of plain chips and a tepid bottle of soda. "Let's see, what you got there in your hand?" Mr. Rahming leans forward as the little boy slides four quarters over to him. Mr. Rahming takes the food. "This all you got?" he asks, nodding at the change.

"Mummy only give me dollar today."

Mr. Rahming leans back to the fridge behind him, exchanging the soda for a cold boxed juice. "You walking home today or taking the bus?"

"Walking."

"You in luck, then. Only comes to fifty cents. And I got nuts on sale too." He tosses a package of peanuts down on the counter.

The boy gathers up his loot and flashes a huge gap-toothed smile before he disappears. Mr. Rahming settles back on the stool with a small sigh. In that sigh, I hear years of comping children snacks and trading useless junk foods for vaguely nutritious ones, of squinting at inadequate change and pretending there's a deal on. I wonder if all of this has made him tired. Has made him ready to give in. How can that boy's mother let him leave the house but not send him out with enough money to buy a decent lunch? If he'd come through in the morning instead of the afternoon, he'd be one Angel would have loaded up with a double breakfast helping. And in ten years that boy will be chatting up some girl who'll wind up on our doorstep looking for advice on how to use condoms and where to hide them from her mummy. Why even bother, I wonder, helping people when nothing ever changes?

"What were you saying about leaving?" I ask. I can't keep the frustration out of my voice.

"Ah yes. I'm packing up shop and renting the place out. So I'm gonna need your help boxing everything up and getting it off the shelves, and after next week, that's it. Finished. Done."

"But—we need you!" I protest.

He shakes his head. "The store ain what these people need."

"What about that little boy?" As I say the words, I feel like a hypocrite. I don't care. We can't lose Mr. Rahming. Not him, too.

"Michael? His ma don't have no one to watch him in the summer. Some days he come up here for tutoring with Ms. Taylor, some days he goes by his auntie. After he leaves, know where he heads? Halfway into town to wait for his mummy to get off work, so they could go by his grammy and eat."

"So that's why you gave him the free nuts."

Mr. Rahming waves me away with a hand. "Them nuts ain nothing. That boy don't need nuts here and free chips there. He needs a home where his mother can earn a good living, not the couple pennies she making down at Tropic-Save. She stopped in here the other day, say she going to the hotel's job fair this coming weekend. Hopes to get hired in at the gift shop. Pay would probably be two, three times what she makes now, and she'll be so close to home. That's what people need through here. Opportunity. Imagine what this place could be. A bike shop renting out scooters. A local café when people want to get a taste of something outside the hotel. Someplace that brings even more jobs. That's what these boys like your brother need. When he comes back, he doesn't need a little corner store. Anyway," he says, getting up. "Sorry I won't have work for you myself anymore, but if you don't have plans for after you graduate next year, you should check that job fair too. Good money for your family. Let me go get you some boxes. You might as well start packing the shelves up now."

He heads into the back room, leaving me alone with the news. I set my cleaning rag down and look out into the street. What's happening to my home? I hate to admit it, but what Mr. Rahming says seems true—Toons has been looking for a job for half a year now, and people being able to pay their own bills is better than them having to take the small bit of charity others offer. Angel could probably make the laundry business lucrative—people could drop off work uniforms for a wash and press, and she'd have more clients than she could keep up with. She could put in two washers before she knew it and hire a couple people to help me. Instead of giving away food to kids shy on their lunch money, we could sell five-dollar sandwiches to guests on their way to rent scooters and explore the island. We might even get rich. But something about it just doesn't feel right to me. I know the hotel's coming, but does it mean that everything is about money now? Were Angel and Mr. Rahming wrong about what's important all this time? I look down toward Nia's house. For a moment, I forget that she's not here. Forget that we're not friends anymore.

The screen door opens, then clanks shut. I turn my head to see who's come into the shop. It's a young guy in black pants and a blue button-up shirt with badges on the sleeves and a chest pocket, a navy tie slung over his shoulder. His round face is covered with a hat that seems out of place with the serious uniform, like he's trapped between two worlds, one where he's reporting for work, and one where he might break into a ball game. *Baseball Cap.*

"What do you want?" My hostility rears up in an instant.

He slides the cooler open, taking out a bottle of water, then sets it on the counter without a word.

"Who's that?" Mr. Rahming calls from the back. He pokes his head around the office door. "Oh, I thought that was Paulette. What you need today, son?"

"Afternoon, Pops." His voice is soft and low, as if he's been saving it up all day and isn't sure how to use it now. "I just come for some water."

Mr. Rahming nods. "KeeKee, ring him up, please."

I take his money and make change as he opens the bottle and takes a long swig.

"Sun hot," he says, taking his change from my outstretched hand.

"Hard work, helping to destroy stuff."

He looks at me with a frown. "Why you on my case?" he asks.

It dawns on me—he doesn't have a clue who I am. He has no idea I'm one of the people he chased off the beach weeks ago. "This street is my home."

He takes the cap off, lifts it slightly, then settles it again. "And this street is my job." He takes the bottle and disappears out the door. I stare after him, thinking.

"KeeKee?" Mr. Rahming asks, coming up to the counter. "You okay?"

"How can guys like the ones behind the hotel bring jobs the community needs, but be so bad to the actual people?"

"That young man isn't behind the hotel, Kimberly," Mr. Rahming says, setting a few empty boxes down beside me. "Any more than you're behind me closing up shop."

As I start to stack cans into the boxes, I turn things over in my mind. I don't know if I agree with Mr. Rahming—jobs aren't the only important thing for our street, and we do still need a corner store, a place where the people who live here or who just pass through can come for more than a bag of chips and a cold drink. But maybe he's right about one thing. Maybe Baseball Cap isn't the enemy. Maybe he's someone who could actually help.

NIA

At the end of our last session of the day, I hang back while everyone else clears out. Faith catches my eye, hesitating.

"I'll catch up with you," I say.

She gives me a sympathetic look. "Good luck."

"Good luck with what?" Ms. Rose's voice is cheerful behind me. I take a deep breath and turn around. The room is emptying, all the other groups clearing out as well.

"Ms. Rose, can I talk to you?"

"Of course." She gestures to a couple of chairs. We sit opposite each other. She leans forward, waiting for me.

Speak, Nia. You can't back out now. "I don't think I'm . . . doing too well here."

"It's only the first week. You'll find your feet." Ms. Rose's voice is warm with encouragement I don't deserve. I swallow hard.

"It's not that. I—I'm not a poet. I took someone else's poem without her permission and I used it on my application." Saying the words out loud doesn't make me feel lighter. Instead, I feel a hundred times worse. Hearing it makes it true, not only for Ms. Rose, but also for me.

"You stole another girl's work?" The warmth is gone, replaced with disappointment.

"Yes," I say quietly. I want her to tell me I'm awful, tell me I don't belong here and that I'm a no-talent fraud, kick me out, send me back to Pinder Street to spend the summer eating bad food and sitting in the dark.

"Why would you do something like that?"

All the shame I've been toting around comes pouring out of me as tears. I cover my face with my hands, but more and more tears just keep coming because the truth is, I don't have a good answer. I wanted to get away from Mummy, but she's overbearing, not cruel. My life wasn't in danger. We have food in our house to eat—it sucks, but I never went to bed hungry. And I had a best friend—a sister—who loved me always. I didn't have to do this. I did it because I wanted to.

Ms. Rose rests a hand on my shoulder, waiting for me to catch myself. When I look up at her, she squeezes my arm gently. The kindness in her touch makes me feel even worse—I don't deserve anyone being nice to me.

"I'll go pack my bags," I say, getting up.

"Wait, Nia. Not so fast." She fishes a tissue out of her bag. "Sit down and dry your eyes. I want you to answer that question. Why would you do this? Tell me."

"I just wanted to get away and . . . I didn't feel like I was good at anything."

"I'm sure you're good at something. What do you like to do, really?"

I shake my head. "Mostly I just sit at home. My mother makes me do a newspaper, but I hate it."

"Well, you could even have submitted that, Nia. At least it would have been something you did yourself. Whose work did you steal?"

I look at the floor. "My best friend." I look up at Ms. Rose. "You must think I'm the worst person in the world."

"I'll be honest with you, Nia. I'm disappointed. You didn't just cheat your friend, you cheated yourself, the other girls who earned their way in here, and you cheated me. I was excited when I read that poem—I thought, wow, the girl who wrote this is really passionate. I'd like to meet her and work with her."

Ms. Rose's words make my heart sink. "You didn't just pick the application because of Mr. Wright?"

She looks surprised. "I chose who I wanted to work with. I read through every single application for the grade ten and eleven girls and picked who I thought deserved to be here. It's too late to see if another girl wants to come this year. So we have to make the best of it. Here's what you're going to do. I want you to go away and think about what you *really* want to do while you're here."

"But I'm not creative!" I protest.

"You put all kinds of imagination into finding a way to get here. That's creativity. It's deceitful and lazy, but it took some creativity. I want you to put that type of energy to good use. Figure out a way to make your time here count, Nia. Really count. And second, I want you to decide how you want to make things right with everyone you've wronged. Your friend, your classmates, your teacher, and yourself. I want you to do this properly, so I'm giving you some time. You have a week."

Ms. Rose gets up and starts tidying up for the day. I gather up my bag and step outside. I should feel lighter after coming clean, but now there's an even bigger problem in front of me. How do I find a place for myself here? And how can I ever get KeeKee to forgive me?

19

EVE

The door to the male ward is propped open. Images parade across a silent TV screen. There, in a bed under a window, on the far right. I stop as I near the foot of his bed.

"Eve!" Daddy struggles to sit upright. He is draped in the hospital gown, a faded blue. I can tell the cotton is scratchy and stiff. He is thinner. Too thin. "Oh, it's good to see you." Breakable thin.

Good to see you too, Daddy. The words are just past where my throat begins, stuck like too much dry bread. Daddy waves me closer, the pale vein of an IV snaking into his hand. The tube makes a flapping sound as it hits his gown. "How are you?" I choke out.

"Better, now that you're here. Sit." He pats the bed. There's too much space for me when I lower myself next to him. "Give me the news. I hear Mr. Rahming's closing up shop. Renting out to some big shots."

"You heard about that?"

"Miss Rolle. Loves to gossip." He leans back into the pillows. "What else is happening in the neighborhood?"

"They cleared away all the trees and started building already. I guess everyone's just going on with life. There's a lot of construction guys coming through, but they just mind their own business."

Daddy nods. "You must be busy, cooking and whatnot. Your mother's always here, I know she doesn't have time to do it."

"No, people keep dropping off food like . . ." I catch myself before the words come. *Like somebody died.*

"How is your mother? I'm worried about her, Eve."

The words I can't say clump up in my throat then, pressing. They come out as tears, more tears, tears that shake my body, tears I can't catch, tears that rattle and squeeze those words till choking animal sounds are coming out of me.

"Just give her a minute," I hear Daddy say to the man in the bed next to his, "this my oldest, she carries a lot for us." He says it so softly it makes me cry harder because I don't deserve it, his gentleness, his patience, his pride.

"I have to tell you something," I say between my tears. "It's about Mummy."

He strains to sit up in the bed. "What is it? She's not sick, is she?"

"It's something I said." I try to swallow away the lump in my throat. "I said something to her about having had so many kids. Something bad." The tears start pouring all over again. Nothing feels worse than knowing I let my father down. Than knowing he's about to summon up energy he doesn't have, to tell me how awful and disrespectful and rude I am, how he's disappointed in me. I squeeze my eyes shut, wiping away the tears. I feel something warm touch my cheek. I open my eyes to find Daddy's hand, gentle and big, calloused where each finger starts, cupping my face.

"Oh, Eve," he says. "Have you asked her to forgive you?"

"She doesn't even want to hear anything I say."

He pats my face, then takes his hand away, reaching over to the side table for a tissue.

"Eve. Look at me, now."

I bring my eyes up to Daddy's. They are wet, not as wet as mine, but damp. "People make mistakes."

"I don't want to let you down."

"Stop. Stop beating yourself up, now. Apologize to your mother and move on. You have enough on your plate, Eve. And listen, do your best and acknowledge when you're wrong. Do that and you could never let me down."

"I feel like all this is happening because of what I did. I said it, and right after is when you . . ." My words peter out. "And then they started cutting the trees down and—"

"Stop." He brings one hand to mine, then the other. Cupped between his palms, my hand feels so sure it's secure. "Let it go."

The nurse comes back around. "Visiting hours just about up," she says, a little sadly, like she wishes she didn't have to kick me out. She moves on to the next bed, and Daddy squeezes my hand tight. When he releases it, I see him, just for a moment, wince with pain.

"Let me fix your pillows," I say, reaching to fluff them up. Daddy smiles at me.

"You're a good girl, Eve," he says. "Ask her to forgive you, and forgive yourself, too. Trying to force yourself into perfection is only going to leave you bent out of shape."

On the way out, I look back and see him leaning back into the pillows, small and shrunken again. What would I do without Daddy? If something happens, how will I make it without him?

KEEKEE

A week and a half after Sammy took the washer and Nia left, Angel has so many work requests she brings in one of her friends to help her out all day—ironing, hand-washing delicates, repairing buttons and reattaching snaps. Some days Eve comes with her family; other times, like today, she shows up alone. We're a few hours into the day when there's a knock at the door. I answer it and find two girls waiting outside.

"Can I help you?" I ask.

The taller of the two nudges her friend, then steps forward, reaches into her bag and hands me an envelope. I stare at it, then at her. "What's this?"

The shorter girl speaks up. "Me and my cousin, we wanted to give you something. I heard you stopped giving supplies out. We wanted to help."

I look from the neatly folded envelope to their faces, one lightly sprinkled with acne across her forehead, the other dark and smooth. I'm speechless.

"Are you gonna start up again?" the shorter girl asks. "We sent all our friends to you last year, if they needed anything. I mean, my mummy usually has pads and liners in the cupboard, but she had to go to Andros last year to look after my aunt, and I ran out one time at school, and I didn't have any extra money on me."

"I don't know," I say. "I guess, maybe." The taller girl shifts her weight, glancing back at the road, and her cousin takes the hint. "Anyway, guess we'll see you."

When I close the door, I see Eve watching me. "Well, that was a surprise," I say.

She lays a polka-dot shirt across the back of the sofa and stretches. "Really?"

"All the years we've been here, no one's ever come to *give* something. I don't even think I'm supposed to take money. I mean, it's different when you're ironing and stuff, but the pouches are supposed to be like . . ."

"Charity?"

"No. More like goodwill, I guess. A service for the community."

"Would you do it if Angel didn't make you?"

"Thing is, it was my idea, in the beginning. We had this family show up at the house. People usually come in the night, you know? But this time they came in the middle of the day. I remember it was summer, and there was a picnic at the beach, everyone was there, music and tables set up and everything. I was like eleven, and I had just started getting my period. I had it then, so I couldn't go swimming, and I got tired of just sitting on the shore watching Nia and you and Faith and everyone else having fun in the water. I decided to come back to the house and just be by myself. I came around the corner and into the yard, and right away, I saw a woman with three kids waiting on our doorstep. I recognized them, the mummy had lost a couple jobs and they'd been evicted a few months before. I turned around when I saw them, half because I figured I'd get Angel and half because I didn't want to be bothered right then. The girl saw me. She was the oldest, and she came over, walking fast. I think she was thirteen or fourteen. She looked really embarrassed, and she asked me if I could lend her a pad, because they'd run out and she didn't want to stress out her mummy, and she was using paper towel, but that wasn't going to last much longer.

"I remember she looked like she wanted to disappear. And the way she said *lend.* Obviously she wasn't going to return it, but she didn't want to have to say *give.* Like they were having to take too much charity already and she wanted to hang on to a little bit of pride. They stayed with us a couple nights, and after they went, Angel kept in touch with them for a while. The kids would come and get breakfast before school sometimes, even though they lived a little way away. I kept thinking about lending pads, and I convinced Angel to buy an extra pack so next time the girl came by, I could give her a few extra in a little bag. It just grew from there."

Eve nods. "Well, you gotta start doing it again. Everyone who knows about it thinks it's a good idea."

"Even your parents? I wouldn't think they approved."

"Why, because you give other stuff away too? Daddy said one time that he thought y'all were doing more good than harm, even when it came to passing out birth control. He said it to Mummy, though. I don't think he knew I was listening too." A more serious look crosses her face. "Has Toons texted you again yet? What are you gonna do about trying to get Faith's phone back?"

Before I can answer, the front door opens and Angel comes in with two of her girlfriends. They set down buckets of takeout chicken and corn on the cob and French fries. While they sit at the table, talking for the hundredth time about who Toons might be staying with now, we take up food for ourselves and go outside.

"I had a couple ideas," I say. "Remember the guy who was working security that day on the beach, who chased us? The one wearing the baseball cap."

Eve chews at a cob of corn. "What about him?"

"He was just doing a job, right? So maybe he doesn't really care all that much about whether we go on the beach or not. Maybe if we approach him right, he'll let us get through and take a look."

"You actually think her phone's still there? All the building they're doing, there have to be fifty people on and off that area every day. Someone would have found it."

"I just have to see for myself," I say.

Eve picks up a wing. "I guess it's worth a try. What else were you thinking?" She takes a bite. "Man, they put extra seasoning on this or something. This is *good*." She looks at my face and sees the idea that's beginning to form in my mind, and she grins.

We load up a plate with still-warm food, then cover it and head down to the beach. The construction area is bustling with activity, but Baseball Cap is nowhere in sight. Eve scans the horizon, then points.

"There's a golf cart coming," she says.

I straighten up, rehearsing my pitch in my head, but as the vehicle gets closer to us, I can tell it's an older man behind the wheel. "You think we should still try?"

"We're here." Eve takes a step closer to the locked gate. The cart slows and the guard, who looks about sixty, stops and gets out.

"You girls need help?"

"We brought you some food—can you let us on the beach?"

The guard looks amused. "For food? What did you bring, caviar? You know this is an active construction zone, I can't let y'all in here without proper footwear and hard hats. Plus, this is private property. If you want to go swimming, take the bus and go to Montagu, or try Yamacraw Beach."

Eve elbows me gently. "We should go."

"You're not wearing a hard hat," I point out. "How come *you* get to be here?"

The guard frowns. "Move along, girls. Go, before I escort y'all off the property."

"We're not even on their property," I grumble as Eve pulls me away.

"Let's come back and try again, see if the young guy is here," Eve says. I know she wants to console me, but it feels like a failure. If our plan didn't work with this guy, why would we have success with Baseball Cap?

Late in the afternoon, though, I do try again. The chicken is cold and I've thrown away the fries, but I grab two of Toons' car magazines and one of Angel's beers to sweeten the deal, and put everything together in a big paper bag. As I near the beach, hope washes over me. I see a figure leaning against the gate, facing the sea. He must hear me as I approach, because he turns around. Sure enough, it's Baseball Cap. He has a book in his hands, which he moves behind his back as I get close.

"I brought a peace offering," I say, holding up the parcel, a little surprised. Who would have thought he actually reads books?

He looks suspicious. "What's that?"

"Food, and something to drink. Can you open the gate?"

He looks behind him, but the beach is empty, the half-built hotel silent, the golf cart nowhere in sight. He sighs and pulls a set of keys out of his shirt pocket, then unlocks the padlock and swings the gate open. He steps forward to block me from coming in, but reaches out. I pass the bag to him. He rummages around, lifting the edge of the foil covering the plate, pulling the beer bottle out halfway, then tucking it back in.

"What do you want to come in here so bad for? It's not like it was before they started building."

I let myself look, really look, in front of me. The sand has already been moved around, some dredged to make a small lagoon, more piled up in other areas. The husk of Eve's church is dwarfed by the partially built hotel. There's no sign that trees ever grew here. Then I catch myself. I didn't come here for the scenery. I came here for the phone. "Can I just take a look around?" I say. "Even if it's not the same."

He narrows his eyes, not buying my line. "You could cause me to lose my job, and you think some chicken with the grease congealed on it and a cheap beer is the way to go?" He shakes his head, handing the bag back. "Don't think because you see me in this uniform that I'm an ass."

"I never thought that!" I protest, but inside I feel caught. I turn away and head back up the path, no closer to finding that phone and clearing Toons' name than I was at the start of the day.

FAITH

Thursday of my second week at camp, Joy shows up at lunch with three trays of donuts and a jazzy smile.

"Can I take this one out to talk for a moment?" she asks Ms. Rose, who nods, waving us on, icing sugar dusted over her cheek. I follow Joy out into the sunshine. The air is thick and still. It smells like rain but feels like the inside of an unbrushed mouth.

"You taking me home?"

My sister lifts her sunglasses up onto her head, smoothing her hair back. "Faith, I have some news." Her phone starts buzzing from deep in her bag. "Hold on." She retrieves it. "Hey. Yes, perfect timing. Hold on." She hands the phone to me.

"Hello?" I say.

"Hi, Faith." Daddy. "How you doin?"

My legs feel like overcooked pasta. I look at Joy. She bites her bottom lip, nodding at me. "I'm fine," I say. "How are you?"

"Busy, busy. Hands full these days. I called to let you know that I'm putting the house up for sale."

"For sale?" I feel like the bottom's just dropped out of my world.

"We need something new." Daddy doesn't miss a beat. "A fresh start. A new neighborhood, maybe."

"A new neighborhood? Why?" The words I've been carrying around with me for too long spill out of my mouth. "You don't want to be too close to your dirty work?"

"What are you talking about?"

"You're working with the hotel," I say. "Aren't you?"

"I don't know where you heard that." Daddy laughs uncomfortably. "I haven't officially accepted any job offer there, but if I did, it would be good for our family. Just like this move."

My heart sinks. KeeKee was right—he was in with the developer. "What about me? What about Mummy?"

"She's safest up at that place. You know that."

That place.

I turn to look out over the water. My mother dances barefoot. My mother soaks in the tub. My mother has slim feet and pearly toenails painted pale pink. My mother laughs until she almost passes out. My mother doesn't belong in *that place.*

"Faith?" Daddy says, his voice distant. I hang up.

"I'm sorry, Faith." Joy leans over to hug me and I twist away.

"You knew, didn't you?"

"Come on. I'm trying to keep you in the loop and protect

you at the same time. It's not always good for you to know everything that's going on right away."

"Did you know about him being in with the people building the hotel?"

Joy's shoulders sag. "I didn't want to upset you. I don't like it any more than you do, but so much was going on with Mummy and everything. It didn't make sense to worry you even more."

"I better go," I say. "Sorry." I walk fast, skirting around the hall and heading for our class space. The door is open, the room empty. I let myself into the back room, then close the door. I squeeze my eyes shut, hands over my face, blocking out the world. Behind my closed lids, pinpricks of light shift and whirl like tiny stars. I wish I lived on a planet that orbited one of them. Wish my problems could stay back here far away from me.

NIA

Ms. Rose scans my notebook, her face difficult to read. "I can see you put some work into this," she says, glancing up from the third page.

"I did." All last night, Faith and I brainstormed, then after she fell asleep, I wrote out my plan. I explained how I've always liked cooking, and since people need to eat every meal, I could help in the kitchen during class times for a week, and if the chef is happy with me, I could stay for the rest of camp. I have to come clean with Mr. Wright and Mummy. The hardest part of all will be apologizing to KeeKee.

Ms. Rose looks over my shoulder at the rest of the girls

enjoying the Friday beach party. "No other girls applied for the culinary arts so we decided not to run that segment this summer."

"I know, but I think I can make it work. If you'll give me a chance," I say. "Please."

She hands the book back to me, then nods. "We can go straight down to the kitchen and see if there's something you can do. I'll be watching you closely, though, Nia. Don't let me down."

After Ms. Rose leaves me in the kitchen, the lady in charge, Chef Forbes, sets me up in a corner to wash veggies for the next day's dinner, then takes off for her weekly trip to the grocery store. I scrub my hands at the huge metal sink, then start poking around in the cupboards. I pull a wide, low drawer out and gaze down at the rows and rows of tiny jars.

"What you doin?" Faith's voice, in the doorway, surprises me.

"This place is like heaven." I lift out a jar of what looks like actual gold dust. "Turmeric. Can you believe it?"

Faith grins. "I guess not?"

"Oh! They have cardamom! Tarragon?" I reach in and pull out a bottle of cloves. "You know what this is?"

"Dead twigs?"

"Look, the cinnamon is like a little paper scroll. This place is my dream," I say.

Faith joins me by the sink and picks up the scrub brush. "You might need to dream bigger."

"You have these in your kitchen at home?" I open up a

jar and take out a nutmeg seed, the mace wrapped around it like a lace glove.

"Yeah, no big deal. My mummy used to cook."

"Lucky you. My mummy spreads and slices."

"Classy," Faith says, but I'm too excited to take offense. I open a cupboard that houses grains and flours.

"Buckwheat . . . quinoa . . . guinea corn. Hey, you think I could make something?" I pull out a jar filled with a deep-purple flour. I think it's grits milled from purple corn.

Faith hoists herself up onto a stool. "Aren't you supposed to be in punishment?"

"I'm supposed to be making up for stuff, yeah." I close the cupboard and open another. "But look—toasted sesame oil. How you think that tastes?"

"Seedy, I guess," Faith says as I fill a heavy-bottomed pot of water to boil. I can't resist—this kitchen was *made* for cooking.

"Help me wash these carrots." I run my fingers over the huge gas range. The middle burner is big enough to accommodate a whole caldron. "Wow . . . I always wanted to cook on real fire."

"Please don't blow us up," Faith says, but she slides off her perch and starts scrubbing at the sink. I slice two carrots into thin sticks with a knife that glides through them like they're ripe melons. When the water bubbles, I stir in the purple meal, then get the carrots sautéing with some garlic and a cardamom pod. I open a can of chickpeas, then drain them and toss them in avocado oil with a tiny drizzle of the rich brown sesame oil. It smells *really* good in here. The grits are cooking up creamy and thick, gorgeous as gems, and the carrots are getting caramelized, the spice making the air fragrant. Soon, it's time to assemble plates, with pats of butter melting into the grits, the carrots piled on the side. Faith hovers over my shoulder, impatient to taste.

"I can't believe you're like a gourmet chef."

"I wish." I scoop the chickpeas on, then add tomato slices. We sit at the counter. I pause, taking in the plate—deep-purple base, swimming with melty yellow, rich orange, red, light brown. "I think something's missing. Green onion, maybe."

"Well, I'm hungry." Faith dips a spoon in. "Girl, how much butter you put in here?" she asks, but I don't answer and she doesn't care, it's creamy salty bliss. "You ga have me busting out my leotard."

"You like it? My mummy doesn't want me to cook. Apparently I'm supposed to use my brain."

"And this isn't using your brain?" Faith scoffs. "I bet you if you made this for her, she'd be begging you to cook dinner every night."

I sit back and savor the toasty, nutty flavor on the chickpeas. "Mummy said cooking wasn't an art so I didn't even think it was an option. I should have submitted a recipe. Then KeeKee and I would still be friends."

"Think she'll forgive you?" Faith asks.

"I don't know. It's not just the poem—she was past upset when she found out about Mr. Wright being my daddy. And I don't know if anything can make up for that."

Before Faith can answer, the sound of a door opening makes both of us freeze. I get up first, hurrying toward the sound—it must be Chef Forbes with her hands full of groceries. I should have thought to save a sample for her in case she got back early. I push the two-way door open carefully and clap my hand over my mouth to stop myself from screaming. There, with a delivery trolley loaded up with boxes and a grin on his face, is Toons.

FAITH

When Nia gets up, I savor the moment in the kitchen, the room bright with midday sun, air thick with the scent of lunch, the comfortable clutter of empty dishes and pots, the shape of our stories softening the air. A memory flashes into my mind: Eve's kitchen, a sink full of dishes behind us, backs to the window so no one sneaks up. *I got a secret, I whisper. She turns her head so her ear is so close to me I can feel its fuzz. I tuck my secret into her and she laughs. Her mother's voice from somewhere else in the house, are we washing up like she told us to? Eve spins around and I grab the dish soap, squeezing too much into the sink. Bubbles froth up under the tap's stream, and she grabs a handful, blowing them at me. Hundreds of iridescent spheres bump into my face, gilded with rainbows and filled with air.*

"Faith." Nia's voice is a tap on my shoulder. I shrug it off, hanging on to my reverie a moment longer. "Hey!"

I turn back to ask what's taking forever and there he is, Toons, my Toons, leaning against the metal shelves with sun in his eyes and a smile curving his lips and a deeper brown to his skin and his hair braided low. He seems smaller and older and earthier and then I'm falling into him and he's big enough to be just right.

"Hi," he says, and his voice is my rhythm and his breath is my beat. He takes my hand, pulling me outside the kitchen and around the side of the building, then through a thickness of big-leafed trees with weedy trunks, then soft sand underfoot, then an opening out to the full length of beach, and when he kisses me I taste peppermint gum and early mango and when I pull away to make a home for myself on his shoulder, he lets me and I know my cheek on him and his hands on my back, still, just holding, are more love than all the hip-rocking and piano-key-banging in the pink-bellied-peppermint world. I pull away first.

"How you just up and gone? I thought—"

"KeeKee ain tell you I said I safe? I couldn't text you, your phone—"

I don't want to bad-mouth his sister, not when he's here, in front of me, in a khaki uniform, shirt tucked in and pants belted, but looking like bare feet and a quiet beach and every single summer of my life. "It's lost," I say, "but it doesn't matter, I could see you're safe." His grin on my grin is waves hitting rocks, is wide sea stretching under horizon for miles.

"What you doin here? What happen to your mummy? Tell me."

"I don't even think you have the time. What, you're delivering groceries now?"

He nods. "Working. I'll explain. Meet me out here tomorrow. Eleven."

"But . . . they have a schedule here."

He gives me a grin that could light dusk. "Find a way."

20

EVE

Ruth dives onto the bed, belly first. "I'm bored."

"You can help me put stuff away," I say, looking over at the line of bits and pieces on the bed—a doll, three books, a tiny bottle of perfume, mismatched socks. I expect her to flake out, but instead she grabs a pile of underwear and hands them to me.

"Hey, how come Faith doesn't come by anymore?"

"I don't know what's up with Faith," I admit. "I haven't talked to her since just before summer break."

"But you're best friends." Ruth wads up a pink striped sock with a yellow one and tosses it into Esther's open drawer. "Y'all talk every day."

"She's going through a lot with her mom. Maybe she just wants to be left alone."

"Nobody wants to be left alone." Ruth spritzes a dab of perfume onto her wrists and sniffs, disgusted, then intrigued. "Put that with my makeup for me?"

I open her drawer and reach under the bras. As I hide the perfume away, I remember the red rhinestone lipstick. I push the clothes out of the way and lift it out of the jumble of tubes and pencils and compacts.

"Lost something?" Ruth asks.

"Borrowing," I say as I head to the bathroom. I set the lipstick down on the counter. As I clean up, my eyes keep going back to the tube, its rim of cut glass glinting and winking at me.

We should have a picnic instead of church every week, I think, as I watch the men open out long folding tables that are quickly covered—old cloths that flutter like eager birds, then bowls of potato salad and dishes of steaming chicken that weigh them down in the soft breeze. Way more people come to the picnic than make it to any service, and they come with trays of fried snapper and sliced tomato, cobs of hard native corn boiled long but still chewy, pans of brownies and plates of homemade coconut candy and fudge that I eye from behind Mummy, till she shoos me away. KeeKee and Toons and Angel are here, and Riccardo, with his daddy who's usually out on a fishing boat with his brother, who's only a little taller, but much wider, and with the same gap-toothed smile. Faith's family comes late, like Nia and her mummy, and the two of them dare each other to raid the dessert table till Nia darts forward and comes back with four wide, dark brown cookies that smell of burnt sugar and spice. KeeKee runs over, led by instinct, and we stuff our mouths with cookies. Guilt washes over me as I chew, but cinnamon and ginger takes over and I wish Nia had grabbed four more.

When, finally, we take up food and sit in clusters on old sheets or retired towels spread on the sand, Daddy smiles,

*pleased at the expanded congregation. Later, when the food
is done, some people head home in the twilight while others
settle in for round two of the party. A cluster of men set up for
dominoes under the trees and Riccardo's father builds a fire to
keep sandflies at bay. The boys from the Junkanoo shack a few
streets over appear, toting drums as big as they are, and lay
them near the heat to warm. Young couples lurk in the shadows and older women scold them toward the light, chasing
them as if they are reluctant moths. The tide has pulled back
far, staying out late too tonight. Nia has gone home, along
with KeeKee, whose belly protested when she swam after eating eight pieces of fudge, but Faith is still here. Daddy is settled
on an upturned milk crate, talking church business with two of
the deacons, but Mummy has Ruth over her shoulder, asleep.
She beckons me over. "Ten more minutes?" I plead.*

*"I'll watch them, I'll watch them," Faith's mother says,
her voice taut and low with concentration. Mummy frowns.
I know Faith's mother isn't exactly like other mothers, especially lately. Last week, she dropped Faith off to play after
school, then never picked her up again. When Daddy drove
Faith home, the lights were on in the house, music blaring
while her mother scurried around inside. She answered the
door with a paintbrush in her hand, and for a second, she
looked surprised to realize she even had a daughter. Sometimes she asks the same question three or four times—am I
interested in doing ballet in the fall? Wasn't I in her class
last year?*

*But it might hurt Faith's mother's feelings if Mummy says
no, and the bulge that later we'll call Esther hangs low in*

her belly. Anyway, Daddy's still here and there's not enough water to splash an ant in, let alone for me to drown. I watch my mother and sister disappear into the trees, as though through a magical door that leads to everyday life, where dishes have to be washed and bedtime waits. Faith twirls, and for a moment I can almost see an actual tutu float up around her in a cloud of bright-blue net. This is our own world.

"Now you."

When I spin, it's a flat-footed stamp, but it makes my ears ring and my head sing. Faith knows how to turn and turn without getting dizzy, she picks a single point and focuses on it every time she spins around, but she lets herself go and clomps in the sand too, until both our heads tilt and our legs stagger and we collapse, breathless with laughter.

I step out of the bathroom, dressed. I grab the lipstick. Ruth is back in the living room with the younger ones, the TV blaring. "Ruth," I say, "can you be in charge? I have to go out."

Ruth nods and I slip the lipstick and my purse into my church handbag, then step out onto the street.

"A-ti-shoo, a-ti-shoo, we all fall down," I say, giggles garbling my words.

"We dru-unk," Faith says, and my body tenses—I'm not allowed to pretend bad things, like being pregnant or shooting guns or getting drunk. Guilt tugs at me again, and stalls my laugh.

The sun is high, but in the west, a tired moon moves toward rest, like an era ending. I turn my back to it as I head for the main road. The sun's glare makes me squint, but I keep going, welcoming the brightness, letting it bring light to all the old memories.

"*Look up.*" *I raise a finger to the yellow crescent scaling the sky.*

"*Hello, moon.*" *Faith wriggles over so her head touches mine. I smell the salty film a day of swimming has left on her, on me. Pinpricks of light are opening in the dark, only the brightest visible against the moon's glow.*

"*Hello, stars.*"

"*Hello, stars,*" *Faith echoes, hollow, low, slow, and I wonder if she is mocking. But there is the side of her slim arm against the plump of mine. "If a person goes crazy, you think they could still see the stars?*"

"*Who crazy?*"

Faith rolls, once, twice, three, four times away from me, coating her whole body in sand. She lands flat on her back, giggling, her voice light again. She moves her arms and legs apart, something we've both seen children on TV do in places where snow settles on the ground. "Sand angel!" she crows, and freezes, her arms and legs stuck out, her head forming the fifth point.

"*Hello, star!*" *I say, and wait for her to say it back. Faith frowns at the sky instead, as if reading a message hidden there. "Say it back," I order, giving in to a rare bossiness that rises in me.*

Faith ignores me. "Hey, lie flat on your back and look up," she says.

"*I don't want no sand in my hair.*"

"*Who care bout sand in your hair?*"

My mummy, I want to say, but something stops me, a knowledge I can't completely place but would know by face, if it would turn around. A knowledge that lies in my chest like a stone, weighing down, seeking ground. A knowledge that makes it easy not to care that Mummy will come really close to saying a swear, then shampoo my hair three times and clear it out roughly, all the while calling out for God to grant her patience with a grown-behind eight-year-old child who knows better than to come home looking like a donut dipped in granulated sugar. A knowledge that whispers, don't talk about mummies tonight, don't you dare even whisper the word.

On the bus, I slide in behind an older woman reading a book. I reach into my pocket, feeling the ridges of the lipstick tube. I close my eyes, imagining Faith is beside me.

"I should be star, and you should be moon," Faith says when she speaks again.

"No, I want be star."

"But we need a moon."

"Moon ain always in the sky."

"Moon is always in the sky. It's just hidden sometimes."

"Na-ah."

"Ask your daddy. And God create the moon?"

Her question raises doubt—the moon and sun rise and set. How could they always be there but refuse to show their faces for large portions of time? "I guess," *I say doubtfully.*

"So how something God make could disappear?"

Things disappear, though, all the time. Mummy's good spatula, after the social. The last piece of cheesecake after the potluck. A dollar bill from off Daddy's dresser. The stray cat that lurked around the back door of the house every day for a month. But Faith's voice has a squeak to it, a desperate crack. For some reason, this means everything to her. In the distance, the men at the domino table collectively groan. Someone has made a bad move.

"Okay then," I say, giving in. "I could be moon."

"Hello, moon." Her voice is calm again.

I give in and flop back but keep my head up and crane my neck back to look at the sky. It is darker now than even a minute before, and it seems alive with pinpoints of light. Some seem to shift and change, glimmering louder and then softly, like Faith. Others are a whisper, visible barely, but bound to brighten as the night goes on. With all these types of stars, there must be one like me.

I reach forward, tapping the lady in front of me. "Excuse me, do you have a mirror in your purse?"

The woman rests the book on her lap as she checks her bag, then hands a small blue mirror to me. I hesitate, then Daddy's words ring in my mind. *Trying to force yourself into perfection is only going to leave you bent out of shape.* I slide the lipstick out of my pocket and stroke it onto my bottom lip. The bus clunks into a pothole and red smears up my cheek.

"Excuse me again . . . can I have a tissue, too?"

We drive on and I correct the mistake and slip the tissue into my pocket, then press my lips together. I look at myself in the bus window. I almost don't recognize myself, my hair pulled up in a high bun, my lips a vibrant warning. I reach into my bag for the lipstick and hold on tight, feeling like somehow, Faith is by my side, urging me on.

The walk to the gate is shaded and cool. I step through the automatic doors. To the left, a woman sits behind a desk. Her fingers dance across the keyboard faster than I can think. I walk up, smiling my brassy red smile.

"I'm here to see Mrs. Elaine Knowles, please."

The woman peers at her computer screen. "And you are?"

I look down the hallway closest to me. Is she down there? Or will they send me to the other one on the far right? Everything here is open, scrubbed so clean it doesn't even smell like hospital. "She's my best friend's mother," I say. "Faith? She's away so she can't come herself. I just wanted to say hi and—"

"Sorry. She's not available."

"But . . ." I fumble for words. Where do patients at a mental institution go? "I can't see her for a minute?"

"I'm sorry, sweetie, I can't give out information to anyone who isn't family. Ask your friend."

The woman goes back to typing as if I'm already not there.

"You really can't tell me anything?" I try again.

The woman looks up at me. "No, sorry. Honey, why don't you go to the ladies' room before you go. You got lipstick smeared all over your teeth." She points down the far hallway with a sympathetic smile. I can't walk away fast enough. I push the restroom door open and my reflection greets me. A dumpy girl, hair pulled back in a ponytail that's already starting to fluff out at the sides. My blue skirt rides an inch or two higher at the back. Circles of sweat stain the fabric around my armpits. I clean my teeth off as best I can and splash water under my arms and on my face.

I can't take no for an answer, not anymore. I let my parents brush me off when I knew something was wrong with Daddy, and where did that get me? I had a bad feeling about Faith sneaking around with Toons, and that led to trouble too. Even that first day on the beach, I knew Toons was about to do something stupid, something that would change our world, and I did nothing. I can't stay in the shadows anymore. I roll my shoulders back and straighten up, adjusting my skirt. I may have let Faith down by not recognizing how bad things were getting with her mother all this time, but I won't let her down anymore.

I step out of the bathroom and look up and down the corridor. A nurse pushes a patient in a wheelchair, heading the way I came in, then disappears into a room. I start walking down the hall, my back straight, my head high, like I know where I'm going, like I have every right to be there. Because I do. I see older women, and a few younger ones, men staring off into space and men conversing with the air. At the end of the hallway, just as I'm about to turn around and look for another wing, I glimpse a wide expanse of aquamarine fabric spread out on a bed. A full skirt. I peer through the glass panel in the door. I can't see the woman's face, but she sits perfectly erect, like a dancer. Like Faith. I tap on the door. No answer. She doesn't look up as I press the button to unlock the door and step in.

"Mrs. Knowles? Do you remember me?"

She doesn't answer or look up.

I step closer. "It's Eve. Faith's friend. I don't know if she's been able to come see you lately but . . ." My words falter. Her lips hang slack at one side. A stream of saliva drains down her face. I reach into my pocket and take the tissue out. I dab her face dry but there's no change in her eyes. As if to make up for her stillness, I feel tears gathering in mine. How did I not know? All this time, how did I not know?

I reach for the hand resting on the pooled skirt. The nails are the same as Faith's. The hand is her hand. I hold it tight and wonder if Mrs. Knowles knows I'm here. If she feels Faith in me.

Her other hand reaches across to pull at something. The damp tissue, stained with red. In the corner of her mouth, a droplet reappears. It lands on the skirt, deepening the blue.

"Excuse me!" A shrill voice cuts into the air. A nurse stands in the doorway, hands on her hips. "Mrs. Knowles isn't taking visitors. You need to leave."

I look over at the moon again, smaller as it continues to climb in the sky. Maybe it's not so bad, being the big one, the one that's sometimes the hugest thing on display and other times, so hidden people think it isn't even there. It glows its own way, changing a little every night, sometimes fading, sometimes growing. I look over at Faith to tell her I'll be moon now, and see her eyes fixed on the trees. I stare too. Her mother is alone, but she takes a few steps toward the church, then shakes her head and turns back. She does it again, a few more paces this time. The third time, she steps out of the shadows and her face catches the moonlight. No one is close enough for her to speak to, but her lips are moving. Faith turns back to me and she must see confusion on my face, but I only see something sadder in hers, a sort of acceptance, like this is strange but normal in her world, and I realize that even though we're best friends, there are things about her life I don't know, things she's never told me, things I wish I hadn't found out but can't unsee.

"Faith, watch this!" I close my eyes and lie all the way back and start rolling in the direction of the faraway sea, knowing this time, Faith will follow me. That's what it is to be best friends. To look by mistake and know when to turn away. To get sand through your hair all the way to your scalp, even if your mummy yells later on and hobbles around the house later on, holding her big belly and threatening to swat you with the wide-toothed comb. To know when it's time to roll in the sand.

I get to my feet, looking back as I head for the door. Faith's mother sits, her expression unchanged, but I think I see her fingers tighten around the tissue. I don't say it out loud, but I promise myself I'll be back.

21

NIA

Faith bursts through the door, a wide smile on her face. I look up from my notebook.

"Where you coming from, looking like chocolate sundae and extra pie?"

She plops down onto her bed and her grin stretches even wider. "I can't believe Toons is here." She looks at my notebook. "What are you doing, planning how to write your wrongs?"

"Nope."

"*Write?*" Faith says pointedly and giggles, delighted with herself.

"I had some ideas for dishes I could try in that fancy kitchen they have here. Snapper with a mango and fevergrass sauce. Or what if I boiled sweet potato and then baked it with—"

"Blah blah blah, food. I just spent half an hour with my guy."

"How'd he get to be yours? Isn't he with Paulette?"

Faith rolls onto her belly. "You know how to ruin it."

"I don't mean it like that. I really wanna know."

"Why?" She sits up, scrutinizing me. "Wait, I know that look. You like someone too." Faith leans over and snatches my book. "No way are we talking about cooking when we can talk about *cooking*. What's his name?"

"It's no one."

"I bet I can guess. Amos?"

"No way!"

"Somebody from school? Hmm, is it Henry?"

If I tell Faith it's Sammy, what will she think? What will she say? Will she even understand? She's beautiful, everyone knows it, she has a car, even if it's not technically working, she dances, and her parents aren't strict. If what KeeKee says is true, she has more experience than the rest of us put together in our craziest dreams. Would she even get how I feel when Sammy looks at me? "It's just someone I met around," I say vaguely. "What about you? Were you and Toons talking about that night?"

"Not really?"

"Were you, like, kissing?"

Faith tosses my book back to me. "If you wanna be secretive, I'm not telling you anything."

"Fine. I like someone, but he's somebody else's boyfriend. I don't know. We talked a couple times and he gave me his number. He probably doesn't even remember me."

"If he gave you his number, he remembers you. Did you ever call him?"

"No." I stretch out on my bed. Here, in this well-lit room with fresh air blowing in from the open glass door, the curtain puffing in the breeze, out of Mummy's reach, anything seems possible. Even that someone could be interested in me. "You think I should call?"

Faith shrugs. "I don't know him. But if you like him, probably."

"How did you know with Toons? I mean . . . he's been with Paulette so long, didn't you feel weird?"

She picks up a pillow, tossing it and catching it, tossing it again. "I don't really think about it."

"How can you not think about it?"

The pillow lands with a thump on my head. I grab my pillow and toss it. It ricochets off the wall.

"Ha-ha, missed me!"

I bound up to grab it and she wrestles it out of my reach. I race for the bathroom and she follows just as I get hold of her bottle of face lotion. "This should moisturize my feet real good!"

"Don't you dare!"

"Silky-smooth heels, here I come!" I chortle. And for a moment, for a minute, nothing is askew, nothing matters, not Mummy, Sammy, or KeeKee, not the man who's supposed to be my father, not stolen poems or Ms. Rose, not even redeeming myself. I feel something I thought I'd never feel again: light.

I spend Monday morning in the kitchen, washing, chopping, and stirring vegetables and pumpkin and rice to go with the barbecued chicken thighs in the oven. Half an hour before lunch, I start ferrying pans out to the dining area, setting them above the chafing dishes that stand ready. I've just covered the carrots and corn when I hear someone whisper my name. I look up and see Faith, ducked down by the water cooler.

"What are you doing?"

"I'm meeting up with Toons. Can you cover for me at lunch?"

"I guess."

"I'll be back before next session." She slips away and I step back into the kitchen. Chef Forbes nods at me as I come in.

"You know how to peel cassava?"

I shake my head. She takes a moment to show me, chopping the thick, waxed roots crossways, then using the knife to make a small cut through the skin, then using it to ease the peel free. She hands me the knife. "We got thirty pounds to go through. I want it started before lunch."

"What are we doing with it?"

"Boil, salt, oil. Too many people to get fancy here."

I start on the stack of cassava, dropping the naked slices of root into a huge bowl of cold water. "How would it be fried?"

"Messy."

"I wonder if it would be good, though. Like, crispy on the outside. Especially if you boiled it first, then shook it up a little bit. Tossed it in something with flavor. Lemon juice and garlic powder and thyme. Or black pepper and red paprika."

"Are you working as fast as you're talking?"

I shut up, then, but I don't stop imagining. I could get my hands on that spice cupboard again. What would ground ginger and turmeric be like? I could even try something with cinnamon and date sugar, and sprinkle dried coconut on top.

"Paprika at the end," Chef Forbes says, out of the blue.

"Really?" I look over at her, then back to the cassava, so she won't think I'm distracted and stop talking.

"Garnish. Little dusting of red. Minced parsley over top." Chef Forbes chuckles as she opens the deep freeze, then starts stacking ground meat on a side counter. "You never peeled cassava, but you already wanna be a gourmet."

"I just like to have fun in the kitchen. When I get the chance."

"So this wasn't the best punishment for Ms. Rose to put you on, then. What landed you in here?"

I clear the peel out of the sink and pile it into the trash. "I took something that wasn't mine."

"Don't try that in here. I watch my equipment and my ingredient levels close."

"It wasn't like that. It was more of an idea."

"Then don't let me ever hear you get famous for sprinkling paprika and parsley on cassava." Chef Forbes washes her hands, then disappears out front to check the buffet.

"Nia."

I turn around to see Ms. Rose standing behind me.

"How are things going in here?"

"Fine. Peeling cassava."

She nods. "Finish up, your father's here for you."

I forgot about the optometrist appointment I have this afternoon. Faith will have to make up her own excuses, I think, rinsing my hands.

• • •

The car ride is quiet all the way over the bridge and into downtown Nassau, but as we pull onto West Bay Street, Mr. Wright turns to me. "Excited to get yourself a new pair of glasses soon?"

I shrug.

"You hold silence almost as well as KeeKee."

Hearing her name so casually makes it somehow more real, him being her father and mine. I look out the window at the beach, so clean, the water so close, compared to Pinder Street.

"Should we, you know, discuss it?"

I turn to look at him, but his eyes are on the road as we follow a curve. "Did you talk about it with her?"

"Actually, KeeKee doesn't want to even see me," he says. "If I'm being honest. She's pretty mad. That's why, I guess. Honesty. It's key, right? To any relationship. So I want to be honest with you. Can we do that?"

Outside, we're passing nice houses, sleek, set far back. As we slow at a roundabout, I look up and into a second-floor window. There's a perfectly clear dining table, a vase with red daisies on it in a pool of sunlight. I wonder if I could ever live like that. Crisp. Clear. Proud. Curtains open, perfection within. Nothing to hide. I want that. Maybe a fresh start with Mr. Wright can bring me closer to it. "Okay," I say.

"Phew." He exhales. "I'll let you start. What do you want to ask me? Anything?"

Questions swarm in my mind. Why didn't he come and find me before? Would he even be in my life if he didn't think I wrote that poem? How did he and Mummy meet and why didn't they stay together? Did he love her more than Angel, or less, or just the same? I don't even know if I want to hear the answers. But he's right. If we're going to have a relationship, we have to be truthful. I turn to look at him. "I want to tell you something first." He looks surprised but nods. "I did something, just before we met. There was this poem KeeKee would recite. It was so good. It was perfect, like music. She kept putting off her application, and things weren't that good at home, and I really wanted to get away from Mummy, even for a little while, and she wouldn't let me go to the camp."

"Yes?" He looks over at me as we slow for a stoplight. I swallow and carry on.

"I recorded KeeKee once, when she was practicing her poem. Then I wrote it down and put it on my application. I never thought I'd get in, I never thought I'd actually get to go. I knew Mummy would never let me, and then you turned up at the house and—"

"Wait a minute." The light turns and we start moving again. "What do you mean she was practicing her poem?"

"Well, you know how she never writes her poems down, she just says them out loud." It hits me. "You never knew that." Another turn and we ease into a shopping plaza. As Mr. Wright parks, I let that knowledge sink in. All those years in KeeKee's life, and he didn't know one of the single most important things about her. He doesn't even know her.

"We're here." He shuts the car off. "You actually recorded her without permission, then claimed her work as yours?"

"I'm not proud of it," I say.

Mr. Wright sighs. "We'd better head in now. I promised

your mother I'd get this eye test done on time. You know you have to tell her about all this, right? And I don't know how you can make it up to KeeKee."

"I know." As I get out of the car, I look over at Mr. Wright. I scour his face for some sign that I belong to him, but I can't recognize anything of myself. Maybe what I inherited from him isn't eye shape, or mouth, or a laugh. Maybe we're both the sort of people who hurt those we love to get what we want.

Ahead of me, Mr. Wright pauses with his hand on the door to the office. "Know what?" He turns to look at me. "I don't know how I'll make it up to KeeKee either. But I promised myself I'd try. I made the same promise to myself to fix things with you."

As I follow him in, I wonder if we might be alike in a different way, instead: both imperfect, but trying, now, to do right.

KEEKEE

Day five of going down to the fence, of rattling the gate. Of Baseball Cap ignoring me. I get back to the yard, sweaty and annoyed. Down the road, a van is parked outside Mr. Rahming's store. Paulette comes out of the store with three boxes and lifts them in.

I grab a rag and start wiping down the clothesline, just for something to do.

"Hello?"

The voice behind me is small, but when I turn around, the girl is my age, maybe a little older. Her jeans skirt fits snugly under a tunic top, and a bag is slung over her shoulder. "Hey," I say.

"Somebody told me I could get . . . you have stuff here?"

"We don't do that anymore."

"You don't?" She lowers her voice. "My friend told me you could help me with the . . . with a couple—"

"Sorry."

"I can pay you." She pulls a ten-dollar bill out of her pocket. "Is this enough? Please?" When I hesitate, she reaches into another pocket and pulls out a five and three more singles. "I don't know who else to go to."

"Why can't you go to the clinic?"

She looks down, and as she does, I see it. Shame, helplessness. Fear. She's afraid. Someone told her she could get condoms here and she was too scared to go anywhere else. "I—let me check inside," I say. "Wait here."

Inside, I rummage through the kitchen drawers, then the bathroom cabinet. I check the bedroom, but I cleared everything out too well. There's only one place left to look. I take a deep breath. I close my fingers around the doorknob, feeling its cool. Then I turn it and push. The door swings open easy, as if it's been waiting for me. The room is dark. The air seems old, as if the windows haven't been opened since Toons was here. My lungs tighten as I stand in front of his bureau, half expecting the mirror to reflect his face back at me.

I look, really look, at the room for the first time since the three days I holed up in here. His favorite jeans are draped over the open closet door. A bottle of cologne stands at the front of the bureau, cap off. The bed is half made. Wait. I walk over to the bureau and open the top drawer. A jumble of boxers greets me. I rummage through. Nothing. I check the next drawer down, undershirts. The next down: T-shirts and socks. My fingers find a small square, foil-wrapped. I feel the firm O rolled inside, then pull the package out.

Outside, the girl seems smaller. She stands awkwardly on the grass, arms folded over her chest. As I walk up to her, her eyes search my face anxiously.

"Sorry, I only have one today." I slip it to her. She takes it and tucks it in her bag.

"Thank you. You don't even know how much I appreciate it." She turns to go.

"Hey, can I ask you something?"

She turns around, her face a question.

"Why? I mean, is someone messing with you? Or, like, is it your boyfriend?"

Her eyes dart back to the street. "I have to go."

I watch her disappear down the street.

"What do you think you're doing?" Angel's voice startles me and I turn around to face her. Sunlight brings a gold haze to her smooth brown skin, makes her beautiful. But my mother is angry. "We don't ask them why. If you make someone explain why they need your help, you're doing it for you, not for them."

Her words finally click a missing puzzle piece into place, completing the picture, and for a moment, I'm so embarrassed I want to run and hide. I hold my breath as she stares at me, studying me, as if she's searching for something she likes, something she wants to believe is still in me.

Right then, I know what I want to do with this summer. Something that no one can steal from me, because I'll be giving it away for free. For real, this time.

"I want to do the pouches again," I say. "But differently."

Angel smiles, then, the first real smile I've seen since Toons was taken away. She holds out her arms and I step into her embrace, feeling the heat of the day on her skin, letting it warm me—but just for a moment.

"I have to do something important," I say, pulling away before I want to.

"Are you going down to the beach to harass that poor guard again?" Angel calls after me. "You were just there!"

I speed-walk, then jog, then run, dialing Eve's number while I move. "Meet me at the beach," I say as soon as she answers, then keep going. As I come down the path, I see Baseball Cap crouched down, a book in his hands again. He looks up as I approach.

"Oh, come on," he says. "Give it a rest!"

"What are you reading?" I ask, panting. He hesitates, then flips the book over to show me the cover of a history textbook. *History?* Ironic, but there's no time to dwell on that. "Are you studying?"

"You have a problem with me educating myself? Should I just stand here and stare into space the whole shift?"

"No, I'm asking. Are you taking classes?"

He looks exasperated. "I would like to, but my grades weren't that good leaving school."

"Okay," I say. "I know someone who can help. She's just up the path, she's a tutor and she can help you brush up and get better grades so you can take your classes and . . . I'll help you, you don't have to explain anything to me, but *please*, I have to get on the beach. I have to look around."

He looks interested but not totally sold on the idea. "What's so important? What are you looking for?"

Trying to negotiate and bribe hasn't gotten me what I need so far. "A phone," I say finally. "Remember there was a boy that some men beat up and carried away awhile back? That was my brother. I know those guys were probably your bosses or hired by the people you work for, but my brother didn't do anything to deserve that, and people think he set that fire to the church, which he didn't. The only way he can come back to home is if his name is cleared. He got video of what really happened on that phone, but he dropped it when those men took him. Can you just help me? Please?"

Baseball Cap closes his book, studying me. "What type of phone was it?" he asks.

"Rose gold, with rhinestones on the case, and a tiny crack on the top left side." Eve's voice comes from behind me. Just in time.

Baseball Cap looks at us for a few moments, then unlocks the gate. He steps aside, making a way for us to come through.

"Thank you," Eve says. Baseball Cap slips a hand into his back pocket, then holds something out to us. The phone.

My hands are shaking as I take it. "You had it all along?"

"Found it on my patrol that night." He lowers his voice. "I don't have anything to do with those guys. What if I'd been near the church? What if someone was in there?" For a moment, Baseball Cap actually looks afraid. Suddenly, he seems a lot like Toons. I throw my arms around his neck and hug him gratefully. "Okay, okay," he says, awkwardly, patting my back, then picks up his book again. "Now, you mind?"

At my house, it's agonizing, waiting for the phone to charge up enough to turn on. When the screen finally flashes on and the phone chimes, I pass it to Eve. She puts in Faith's code and we huddle over it as she scrolls through. There's a video dated from that night, the last thing saved in Photos. I hit Play.

The image is blurry and dark, with a pinprick of glowing orange in the background. There's a huge flare of light, and in an instant, the pinprick becomes a blaze.

"Fire," Toons says on the recording. "At the church." The video zooms in to show four, five silhouettes run in front of the church, tossing gasoline onto the flames. The camera turns abruptly and my breath catches as my brother's face fills the screen. "You see that? I can't even . . . They look like they want blow up the whole church. And they still down there!" Then angry voices in the background, calling out. *He see your face? Get him, get him!* "They comin for me, they comin!" The image shakes as if he's started running. "This still recording?" His voice is frantic. Then the video cuts out.

Eve sets the phone down on the floor between us. She doesn't look at me. I feel like I might have to be sick.

"It doesn't explain anything," Eve says, rubbing her face as if she's trying to wash away what we've just taken in. "You can't see who set the fire."

I struggle to think straight. "We didn't need the video to see who did it," I say, sorting my thoughts out loud. "We needed it to show that it wasn't him. He was far off when the fire started. It clears his name." Eve is quiet beside me. "Oh—I wasn't even thinking, Eve. You had to see your dad's church . . ."

"It's okay," she says. "The church is a place, but there's only ever gonna be one Toons. And now that we have this, maybe he'll come home."

EVE

Tuesday afternoon, after Mummy gets home from seeing Daddy, she whips us all into action, setting Esther and Joe to measure out flour and sugar for pancakes while Ruth loads towels into the washer. Junior's babbling rings through the house from the living room, and I sweep and mop around everybody. I'm still shaken up from seeing the video on Faith's phone last night, but the homey buzz comforts me. At the counter, Mummy slices up pineapple while she sings an old calypso about a woman who spends the food money on alcohol instead of cooking oil and peas and rice. She catches my eye and smiles at me for what feels like the first time in years.

"You're in a good mood," I say.

"Yeah—is Daddy coming home today?" Esther looks up from the mixing bowl, a layer of flour dusted over her face. Her eyes shine hopefully.

Mummy turns back to the cutting board. "He was just in good spirits, sweetheart. It made me happy."

"When is he coming home?" I press her.

Mummy drops a kiss on Esther's head. "Go wash off. Joe, you too."

"But I'm not dirty," Joe protests.

"Go." Mummy's voice is all business now. When we're alone in the kitchen, she turns to me. "Why would you do that? Don't put me on the spot like that in front of them."

The same fury that made me lash out at Mummy before rears up in me. *Why not, when you never tell me anything?* I want to shoot back. I bite my lip, forcing myself to stay quiet. All the joy that was in my mother is gone. Her shoulders are slumped, and for the first time I see worry lines in her forehead. She looks away from me, and as she stands there, she looks so helpless. So small.

"I didn't mean to put you on the spot," I say. "But Mummy, you and Daddy keep shutting me out. I'm old enough to hear what's going on. You want me to be responsible and I can do that, but it's not fair for you to exclude me. I'm sorry I was rude to you that day, but please. Just tell me the truth."

Mummy sighs. "The truth, Eve? He's weak. He's lost so much weight. They say the chemotherapy isn't as effective as they'd hoped. I don't know if he can fight this thing. I don't know when he's coming home. I can't lie to you and tell you everything's going to be okay. I don't know, and I'm tired. We didn't want to say anything because we were afraid, okay?"

I rush toward her and she holds her arms out to hug me. "I'm scared too," I say as she hangs on to me. "But Mummy? Thanks for telling me." It doesn't feel better, hearing how things really are, but it feels clearer, like now, at least, we can go forward together.

• • •

After our late lunch of pancakes and fruit, I sit outside in Daddy's chair. Across the street, Mr. Rahming is directing Amos and Riccardo as they pile the last boxes of groceries into a van. The driver eases away, heavy under the load. Mr. Rahming waves at me. "You all right, Eve?"

I put on a smile as I walk across to Mr. Rahming. "I'm fine. Are you done?"

"I'm done. Hanging up my hat as of this moment." I must look grim because he pats me on the shoulder. "I'll still be around here. Y'all can't get rid of me that easy."

"How long before new people move in?"

"Well, don't make sense anyone starting up till the hotel's finished. At least a year, maybe two if they're delayed."

"Can I go in and take a look?"

He nods, extending an arm out toward the door. I pull open the screen door and step in. The shelves have been dismantled, and the room is naked, stark. The structure still stands, but what made it live is gone.

"Every time I think I got everything, I end up checking it over again." Mr. Rahming chuckles behind me. "You go ahead, I'm just in the back room." His footsteps rattle through the place. "Helps to go back, doesn't it? Say goodbye? Last day we were open, Paulette and I walked through this place and just remembered. We had a lot of good times here, my family."

As his footsteps fade away, I realize that's been missing for me. I never had that special farewell to the church. The day of the last protest was so public for someplace I went for rare privacy, and seeing the church being set ablaze on that video only made me feel farther away from my second home. Sometimes, goodbye is too hard to look in the face. Maybe that's why when Faith had to leave, she never said anything to me.

"Mr. Rahming, you think I can salvage anything from the church?" I call out, my voice echoing in the empty store.

"Boy, I don't know. That fire was pretty bad, you know. I don't think it's structurally sound to get into it, or safe to poke around, after what happened to Toons." He pats my shoulder. "You might have to just say goodbye and start anew."

Suddenly, an idea blooms in my mind.

"We need a new space," I blurt out. "Here. The church is gone, and we need someplace. We could fit chairs for meetings, and a table for people to play games or eat or talk."

"The new tenants—"

"How about evenings and Sundays? In the summer, maybe one day a week?"

Mr. Rahming scratches his head. He looks around the room, then at me.

"I'll clean it up myself," I say. "I can wash the windows down, the floors will look good, we can take donations to help with the light bill . . ."

"You've got yourself a deal, Eve." Mr. Rahming smiles and holds out his hand for me to shake.

22

FAITH

Toons leans back into the tree, eyes on the horizon. I stand, waiting for him to catch sight of me. He looks up, and our eyes meet. He tries to hide his smile in a smirk that bursts wide open, showing teeth. He wraps his arms around me, twirling me so fast my feet leave the earth, and the world is made of wind.

"I'm mad at you," I say when the breeze stops.

He slips his hand around mine and tugs me to a corner of the beach that's hidden by trees.

"Where we going? I only have till the end of lunch."

"Just over here." That coercing voice. A pang that reminds me of that day at the clinic, those other pangs. I swat him away.

"What happened that time isn't happening today."

He pretends to sulk. "I just said I was happy to see you."

"Yeah, well. Be happy with your pants on."

Toons sinks down onto the sand, then looks up at me seriously. "I didn't think I'd see anybody who looked like home ever again."

I sit down beside him. "What happened?"

"That night?" He shakes his head. "It was crazy. I went down to the beach, just to blow off some steam. Okay, so the gate was locked. I had wire cutters in my bag and I cut a hole in the fence—"

"It's true? You didn't set the fire, did you?"

"Listen to me. I snuck through, and I was heading to the church, just to clear my head, and as I got close, I heard something, somebody sneaking up on the church. Then I saw a flash of flame orange as they threw something. I started recording on your phone, but then they saw me. I dropped the phone on the beach while they was chasing me. Then a bunch of them grabbed me—"

I rest a hand on his arm. "I was there."

"All I could hear was my mummy, and KeeKee crying and begging them not to take me. We rode around for a while and I couldn't see where because I was on the floor. When we finally stopped, they dragged me out and just started kicking and punching. Telling me that they were teaching me a lesson. Teaching the whole street a lesson about troublemakers. Eventually I blacked out and next thing I knew, I was regaining consciousness outside Mr. Rahming's store. I crawled down to Nia's house, I didn't wanna go home and let Angel and KeeKee see me like that. I was worried the men might come back and hurt them, too. Nia and her mummy patched me up and then Mr. Wright came and got me. He let me sleep by him that night, and I guess he called around, found a friend who could give me a job over here so I could just lay low. I've been here since."

"Where do you stay?"

"The people I work for, they have a guest room with a separate entrance. They live over there on Paradise Island, so it's quiet. I'm lucky. Can't complain. It's safe."

"But it's not here." I reach out to touch his face.

He nestles his hand on my shoulder and his palm curls around the knob of my joint like we were made to fit.

"Who else knows?"

"Just you." His words vibrate against me. "I only talked to KeeKee for a minute here and there."

"What about Angel?"

"We haven't talked since . . . everything."

"Haven't talked?" I sit up, looking at him. "It's been like a month."

"You ain gotta tell me, I was there. Remember?"

"Yeah, and it was also the night my mother got sent to that place," I snap back. "Remember?" Suddenly, the air around us seems heavy. I don't want to fight with him. But I also can't let this slide. If my mother was worried sick about me, if my mother even remembered there *is* a me, I'd be on the phone to her every night, not leaving her to stew. I let out a long breath. "You're her son."

"KeeKee's been telling her how I am."

I lean into him again. His body is rigid. He's still annoyed. I don't care. He needs to know. "But she needs to hear from you. She needs to hear your voice. She needs you." I turn to look up at him. At first, he doesn't look back, but eventually, I feel him soften into me. He laces his fingers between mine.

"You don't know what it is to have someone take you in

and make you their child, and you let them down in the worst way you could."

"Did you set the fire?"

He starts to pull his fingers away and I clench his hand tighter, holding him.

"Okay," I continue, "so you didn't let her down."

"People think I did. And all that stress I brought on her."

I try to imagine my phone ringing. Answering it and hearing my mother. Hearing her laugh, open, full, flying-kite-wide. "Nothing in this world is worse than not being able to get in touch with someone you love. Trust me. Especially when you know they're right there."

"Well, what about you?" His voice is defensive.

"I already told you, my mother can't even talk on the phone anymore, and they said she can't have visitors."

"I don't mean her." Toons raises his eyebrows at me. I look away. "I'm talkin bout your daddy."

"Yeah, obviously. And it's not the same thing."

"It's exactly the same thing."

"I can't believe you're defending him right now."

"Why? He's your dad. He's worried about you."

"Because—" I stop in my tracks. If I tell Toons what my father did, will he still want to be with me? I look back at him, our fingers still intertwined, and I know what I have to do. "Because he's working with the developers. I think he knows about what happened to you, and the men who did it."

Toons pulls his hand away, covering his face for a second. He looks down at the sand. "Wow," he says finally.

"I didn't know. I mean, I should have seen it, and I know

you might hate me, I'm here at camp while you're basically in exile, and—I just want to get back home and Joy won't come pick me up even if I beg her. She thinks I should stay here and focus on me, but everything is a mess."

"Well. Me and your sister can agree on one thing. I think I should focus on you too."

Toons edges back over to me so our shoulders and arms touch. I hold myself still, feel the soft lift and fall of his breath. He shifts slightly and sends electricity all through me. The world starts to feel stable, right, as if, even here, with everything we both know out in the open, we can still be us.

EVE

When the sun is setting somewhere, it's rising someplace else. Later the same morning the church is knocked down, our old car eases up alongside the house. Mummy gets out.

"Hey, y'all!" she calls. Ruth doesn't move from the sofa, and I'm sure Mummy doesn't want me. "Eve!" she calls, more urgently this time. I almost trip over my feet hurrying out to the car.

She's around the passenger side. Even though she is bent over the open door, I can see around her. Thin legs, bedroom slippers.

"Just let me pull up on the door." The voice is the same, makes up for that frail body.

"Daddy!"

His eyes are larger in his face, but they light up when he sees me. "Oh, Eve, I didn't think I was gonna set foot in this house again."

"Of course you were." I hold his arm, trying not to feel how dry and loose the skin is around his bones. From Paulette's yard, the younger ones appear. Esther and Joe hang back, unsure of how to approach this smaller version of Daddy. "Go get Ruth," I say, to give them something to do other than stare. It takes minutes to make the journey from car to front door. When we step inside, Daddy leans against the wall, breathing heavily, but smiling.

"You're home!" Ruth springs up and nearly bowls him over.

"Get your father a chair, make some space." Mummy shoos her aside. She lifts Junior up and leans him toward Daddy. "Let the man breathe. Eve, set out fresh sheets. Ruth, you put on some tea. Joe, Esther, you all pick up these toys." She claps her hands together. "Come on."

"How come they sent you home?" I ask, easing Daddy's slippers off his feet.

"They say I'm stable enough for it. I can continue the chemotherapy as an outpatient." He holds up an arm, then rests it down again as if the effort has worn him out. "I need some home cooking to put regain my weight."

"What do you want?" I ask.

"Right now, just to lie down."

Mummy is at his side, then, helping him to his feet. As I watch him go, I feel like this is the trade-off, the reward for the price we paid. Maybe we had to lose the church to really appreciate getting Daddy back. The kettle whistles, then is silenced, and as the house's flurry of sound slowly drains toward my parents' bedroom, I turn back to look out at our street. There's a scratch at our door. When I open it, there's a bag hanging off the doorknob. There's no sign of anyone on the road. I look inside and see several bits of wood. At first it doesn't make sense, but then I see something else, something that glints. I reach in carefully and lift out a piece of stained glass, its edges broken, its body purple and bright. I hold it up to the light and let the world glow.

KEEKEE

After I knock on Nia's side door, I wish I'd gone around front. It feels too casual to stand and wait beside her kitchen window as if I'm there to see a friend.

"Just a minute," Mrs. Taylor calls. It's too late to go back now. The door swings open and I come face-to-face with Nia's mother.

All these years living side by side, I've almost never spoken to her one-on-one, and I know she doesn't like me. I guess that makes sense now. But I can't let any of that get in my way. I straighten up. "Good morning," I say. "Can I talk to you?"

Mrs. Taylor hesitates. "Is it about Nia? Did she call you?"

"No, I came to ask for your help."

She looks as though she wants to ask more, but instead, she steps aside. "Come in."

I almost expect it to look different with Nia gone, but instead, it's completely unchanged. I notice that Mrs. Taylor is dressed in a Tropi-Save cashier's uniform.

"I picked up a few hours," she says, almost self-consciously, then gestures at a chair. "Do you want to sit down?"

"No, thank you. I came because I need your help. I kind of volunteered you for something."

Her eyebrows go up. "What's that?"

"I needed something from the guy who works security at the beach. He wants to get into college, but his grades are bad. I said you'd tutor him if he gave me something that would help me get Toons home."

"You bribed him with tutoring from me?" Nia's mother looks like she doesn't know what to make of that.

"It's not like that," I rush to explain. "I saw him reading a history book, and I wanted to help him. I needed the information about Toons, too, though. I probably should have thought of some way to help him that I could do myself, but I don't know anyone else who's good with that stuff, and—I just need Toons to come back. Will you do it? Please?"

Ms. Taylor studies me for a moment. Then she reaches over and takes both my hands. She squeezes them. "When you see him, tell him to come by in the afternoon when his shift ends." Nia's mum looks like she wants to add more but doesn't. I open my mouth to ask if she's okay, if she's lonely here without Nia, then change my mind. I'm not ready to go there. Not yet.

Back on our side of the yard, Angel sweeps out the space that housed the washing machine, coaxing cobwebs from the corners, clearing off old dead leaves. I set a table up in the space and lay out the new stash of supplies—pouches, pads, condoms, ginger mints, and tiny slips of paper. Every window in the house is wide open, airing the place out. Toons' stereo is on, and his Motown mix blares, calling him home. From down the street, Eve waves at me as she guides her father across to Mr. Rahming's store. A car turns down the street. I recognize it before it stops alongside the yard. I lean the broom against the wall and head toward the front door. Too late. Angel has already seen my father getting out.

"I'm going inside, baby," she says, stepping around me and into the house. My father stands outside his car awkwardly.

"I come in peace." He holds out a sturdy paper bag. "Please, KeeKee. Take it."

I lift the bag out of his fingers and reach inside. There are two boxes in there. The first is slim and rectangular. I open it up and take out a chain with a large, flat heart pendant. I flip it over. There are tiny controls on it.

"It's a voice recorder. You can wear it as a chain. Nia—she's really sorry about what she did, KeeKee."

"She told you?"

"This week. I had no idea. There's something in there from me, too."

I open the other box and lift out a shoe box–sized chunk of metal, brick-heavy.

"That's a safe for whatever private or valuable items you have. Poems or . . . whatever." He slips his hands into his pockets. "Think you can forgive us? Forgive me?"

Otis Redding is singing about change coming. Old violins hang their notes in the air. Mr. Rahming is in front of what used to be his store, Mr. Armbrister is back home, and over the rumble of tractors down near the water, our street sings back, sad and strong and sweet. There's the sound of a door

369

being pulled closed and I turn to see Angel looking at my father. She nods at him, once, then pulls out the lawn mower. It sounds its *click-click-click-click-click* call, then starts up again. If she's able to keep moving forward, so can I.

"I can forgive you on one condition."

"What's that?"

"Eve's trying to turn the store into a place for her church, and for the community. Will you help?"

His face lights up. "Deal."

After I watch Dad pull away, I turn to go back inside and see Angel clinging to the mower with one hand, the phone in the other. Her shoulders shake. "Angel?" I reach out to touch her shoulder and she turns, her face wet with tears. I reach down and turn the mower off. "What happened? Is it Toons? The police called?"

She holds her phone out to me and I look at the number that's still up on her screen. My brother. He called her. I wrap my arms around her, I feel her relief in my body as her sobs shake me through to my bones.

"It happened, KeeKee," she whispers. "He don't hate me. He's coming home."

In a moment, a minute, an hour, I'll catch myself and tell her what Eve and I found. For now, I hold my mother tighter, know she feels, like I do, that everything's going to be okay, that nothing can separate our little family.

NIA

Once cleanup is done after breakfast and everything is on the go for lunch, Chef Forbes lets me work on a new dish to celebrate. Today, she peers over at me as I mix a handful of sesame seeds into the mashed pigeon peas.

"What you plan on calling that?"

I dust off my hands, then pull the Johnny cake out of the oven. The top is golden brown already. "You'll see!"

As I mix in green thyme leaves, then add minced garlic and ground sea salt, I wonder what Mummy would say if she could see me. I squeeze my mixture into sausages, carefully swathing each one in the paper-thin cassava shavings I've prepared. Pressing them tight, I lower them into a pan. Hot oil makes them sing. Lunch is starting when I finally finish. Chef Forbes is elbow-deep in replenishing the dishes of potato salad, so I put my sandwiches together myself, thick slices of Johnny cake spread with spicy guava and tamarind mayonnaise, corn chutney, and the homemade garden sausages.

"What's all this?"

I turn to look at Ms. Rose. "Pinder Street slam bam."

She sniffs curiously. "I might need to grade that for you."

I slice it in two and add my sapodilly slices, then arrange it on a plate. "What do you think?"

She nibbles, then bites off a chunk. She chews thoughtfully. "I think, Nia, you might be a poet after all."

The grin spreads up my face.

Ms. Rose slides another slice of bread onto her plate, along with a sausage. "I can see you're doing well with one part of your assignment, but it's been a week now. How about the other components?"

Suddenly, my appetite wanes. "I told Mr. Wright," I admit.

"Yes. We spoke after he brought you back from your appointment."

"I guess he told you he was disappointed in me."

"He did. But I was able to tell him how hard you've been working in the kitchen, and he agreed to let you finish the program out here with cooking as your area of focus." Ms. Rose pauses. "As long as you speak with your mother and she agrees."

My heart sinks. "I'm dreading talking to her."

"Well, it's difficult, but it has to be done." Ms. Rose gets up, taking her plate with her. "Let me know how it goes."

I wrap up the leftovers in foil, then start cleaning up after my meal preparation, while, on the other side of the kitchen, Chef Forbes sifts flour into an enormous bowl.

"Your mother hard on you?" she asks as I stack rinsed dishes into the dishwasher.

"It's not just that. I don't know what to say, or when to say it."

"I thought you decided on the truth," she says.

"I don't have a cell phone and there's a phone in the room but . . ."

"You girls have roommates, though, don't you?" Chef Forbes's tone is understanding.

"My roommate is cool. I knew her before, and we've gotten even closer being here together, but I guess I don't want an audience for this conversation."

"Understood." She measures in baking powder, then examines her recipe. "Sugar. Sugar. Looks like I'm going to the storage room." Just before her chef's hat disappears through the doors, she calls back, "There's a phone over by the sink, you know."

Alone, I dial our house number. I don't know whether our phone will have been cut off, but Mummy picks up on the third ring.

"Hello?" Her voice is familiar and distant all at once.

"Hey. It's Nia."

"Oh!" Mummy actually perks up. Is she—happy to hear from me? "I didn't expect you to call. How's camp?"

"It's good. It's . . . a lot happened."

"Your eye test went well, I take it. I spoke with the optometry office, they said the new glasses will be here in a week."

"Yes—it was good." I'm stalling, and I can't afford to. "I have to tell you something, and you might be upset, but—I did something when I applied to come here. I used KeeKee's poem to get in. But I told my teacher the truth, and she's giving me a second chance, and she's letting me stay and do cooking instead, but only if I tell you everything, and only if you let me."

There's a long silence on the other line.

"Mummy? Did you hear me?"

"I didn't raise you to be a liar, Nia. I was right, you're too young to be away from me. And you're doing *cooking*? I didn't agree for you to go all that way just so you could work in the kitchen like a glorified housekeeper. It's bad enough you're chasing men now."

"But Mummy, I'm good, I'm really good. I wish you could taste what I made today."

"I'm calling your father. I didn't want you to go to this camp in the first place, and now I find that you lied and stole?" Mummy's voice is shaking with anger. "I'm not rewarding dishonesty with a summer away from home. Pack up your things and get ready to come home."

Tears are already pouring down my face. I wipe at them, then escape as fast as I can. I grab the leftovers and walk all the way back to the room, which is empty. Faith's suitcase is open, clothes strewn around. I don't want to be here. I don't want to be anywhere. Mummy won't even give me a chance. She wouldn't care what I do, if it's not what she wants. Now she's talking about how I'm chasing after men. *Men.* Sammy's the *only* man I ever cared about. The only one I've ever even spoken to.

If that's what she thinks of me, I might as well give her a reason. I'm not just some baby to be shunted from parent to parent, dragged around to appointments, prodded and tested to see why I'm not growing up. I'm grown enough for anything. I'm grown enough to know it's time to get out of here. I dial Sammy's number, and wait.

I lean back into the passenger seat of Sammy's truck. I wish I could just close my eyes, but my heart is racing, especially when he smiles to see me.

"I didn't think you were going to call me."

I glance over at him. Soft stubble, concerned eyes. "I changed my mind," I say. "Where are we going?"

"You tell me, princess. Your camp kick you out or what?"

Outside, it's starting to rain, huge drops that splatter onto the windshield, each bigger than a quarter. "I just—I had to get away is all. Can we get something to eat?"

"Oh, so you want me buy you lunch?"

"Uh . . . never mind, I didn't mean—"

"I'm just playing with you." He laughs, easy tickle in my ears. "We'll go to Grass Roots."

The drive there is quiet. He plays music, I relax. We eat chicken in the bag, the paper sacks soggy with grease and ketchup.

"How you feeling?" he asks.

"Fine."

"You wanna go for a ride?"

I look at Sammy, then lean back in the seat. The sky's started to cloud over, but I feel the heat of sunshine on my face. "Yeah," I say with a grin.

Sammy stops the car outside a tidy square house. My heart thumps so hard I can feel it in my head. Should I be here? *Where else would you go?* I ask myself.

"So." He drums his fingers on the wheel. "This is my spot."

A dog barks in some hidden place. If I go in . . . my heart speeds up again. Am I ready? What will it mean? Does it have to mean everything? Can it just mean something?

"So, this is where you live?" I speak fast to drown out my thoughts. The rain is harder now, hammering the roof, drowning out my words.

"You wanna come inside?"

It's as dark as evening, though it can't be much past two,

and water's collecting on the road behind us, and I can't go back to camp, not now, not late, and by now I'll be in as much trouble with them as with Mummy. I have to go somewhere, and I don't want to worry about where that will be in three hours, or two. I could go in. His house looks comfortable, dry. I could stay just a little while. I don't have to do anything. Maybe a kiss. That might be all right. I turn to look at Sammy. His smile is smooth. His eyes are warm. And he wants me to, I know he does. I smile back at him. "Yes."

We run to the front door, rain pelting us while he fumbles with the lock. "Hold on," he says, and the keys slip to the ground. Drops sting my arms and legs and face. Then he swings the door open. "After you," he says. As soon as the door shuts, the rain feels half a world away. Inside is neat, the curtains drawn tight. "Oh, man, we gotta get you dried off." He laughs. "You look like a drowned rat, princess. You upset I had you out in all this rain?"

"No." I hover near the sofa and take off my glasses and dry them on my skirt, but that only smears the water.

"Come this way." He walks me to the bathroom, disappears, then returns with a towel and an oversized shirt, then closes the door. I lock it after he goes, then run the tub hot, full of water. It's been ages since I sat down in a tub, and never since we had a heater. I hold my breath, lie back, head underwater. I try not to think. I let a breath out and start to soap up quickly. I dry off and take some of the vanilla lotion, probably his sister's. Then I dress. When I open the bathroom door, the tub is still draining water.

"I'm in here." In the front room, he's lit a candle. The

orangey dim light reminds me of the house, its unreliable flicker, its heavy shadows cast longways. I feel like I'm all arms and elbows.

"You want come sit by me?" He reaches out his hand, his palm up. It seems wrong not to take it. I sit beside him on the sofa, and he leans over. I freeze as he moves his mouth toward mine, panicking. Things are slow motion and things are fast, and his tongue is small and rubbery and seems too hard for a mouth, for my mouth. A droplet of water falls from somewhere, hits my chest and rolls down the too-big shirt. I wish I was home and my throat is squeezed so tight I can't push my words through and I want Mummy, but she won't understand and I'm about to do everything she's warned me not to and his hands are around my waist now, and I want to be wanted. I should be here, be in the moment, but instead I'm remembering a day when I was by KeeKee while Angel did her hair.

KeeKee is tucked between Angel's knees, and I'm playing cards with her. KeeKee freezes, sensing danger. Angel's hand turns her head slightly. The point of a rat-tailed comb glides through her hair soundlessly, making a razor-sharp part. Angel holds the comb between her teeth as she begins to plait, a crown of a French braid straight across the front of KeeKee's head. She stops again, removing the comb, to part the back section in three.

"Y'all gotta be careful. Sometimes these boys want touch and want hold and want—"

"Hey!" KeeKee protests.

"I just tryin to warn y'all."

*I've heard this talk before, don't let nobody touch you.
Don't let nobody hug up on you. You don't need to be kissing
up people. I know how it goes.*

"If you getting in deep with a boy, you gotta be careful. If
you even think you're getting close, come to me. You understand? Before anything happens. Not after. Before."

"So you're always careful?"

Angel pauses while she holds the comb in her mouth. I
wait for her to scold KeeKee, to tell her daughters don't ask
mothers things like that. "Always," she says instead.

"Every single time?"

"Well." She finishes off the last plait. "I had you. So you
tell me. If you want what I got, a big-head girl with a smart
mouth, then you go ahead and make your choice." She points
the comb at me. "Same go for you too, miss."

"Mummy." KeeKee pulls away, mortified. "She's eleven."

"Yeah, and you're twelve. Store it up till you need it. You
think I could afford to wait till y'all eighteen?"

"You have any condoms?" I blurt.

Sammy pulls away. "You a virgin, right?"

"Um—yeah?"

"Well, we good, then."

"But—"

"Okay. Okay." He groans as he gets up, and I can hear
him rummaging around. I can change my mind, now we're
not touching. My belly aches. I stand up. My head is spinning.
I reach for the switch on the wall, turning on the light. Sammy
comes back in and his eyes widen. "Hey, what happened—oh,
what the hell! Girl!"

I look down at the floor. Between my feet lie four pennies of blood. I look back at the sofa. Red stain. "No! What just happened? Did we—?I didn't even—"

"You bled all over my house." His voice is disgusted. "Stupid little girl," he hisses as he throws a towel at me. "You don't know to put something on when you on your period?" He opens the door. Looks at me. Looks outside.

"What?"

"I don't want you bleeding all over my truck. Get back however you want to. No one invited you here anyway."

"You can't just—"

And then he pulls a hand back as if he's going to hit me and I grab my bag and my wet clothes and run out into the rain. The door slams shut behind me and I haul my soggy skirt back on, right there in full view of the street, and I want to disappear but instead I run out here in the rain and I wish I could have wiped them up, my four little circles left on Sammy's floor, partly because they belong to me, they came out of me and it feels wrong to leave them behind, but mostly because that's how much I feel I'm worth right now.

The bus driver is off duty, the sign turned around to CLOSED, when he pulls over and opens the door for me. Before today, I would have got on, no thought. I'm almost doubled over with pain.

"Miss. Come, get on, let's get you home."

I look up, but I can't see straight. I put out a hand to say no and something deep in a part of my belly I didn't know existed wrenches and I hear an awful yelp escape out of me. I have to trust whoever this driver is, and trust that, like Sammy, he'll be disgusted, so disgusted he won't do anything bad to me.

"Go ahead and sit down," he says kindly.

"I can't," I protest.

He reaches for something at the front of the bus and walks back to me, spreading a newspaper onto the closest seat. "You can't stand," he says. "Make yourself comfortable."

My legs feel weak and my head is woozy. I give in and sit down.

"Where are you trying to get to?"

His kindness makes me cry harder because I don't deserve to be treated this way.

"I have to take you to the police station," he says, "if you can't tell me. I'll give you couple minutes." He puts on the hazard lights and takes out his phone. "Hey, I ga be late tonight. No, a girl walking in all this storm. Need to try to get her home or wherever she's trying to go. Boy, I don't know. I will. Love you. Bye."

The gentle sound of his voice calms me a little, enough to say, "Can you take me to Pinder Street, please?"

"No problem." The hazard lights go off and the bus starts up, easing onto the road. "I got six sisters. I'm the youngest. You got any brothers or sisters?"

"No. Yes. I guess, sort of."

"My oldest sister, Elkie, she's my world, after my wife and my little boy. She always taught me . . ." The driver's words fade away as I try to blot out the pain. If only I can get home in one piece, I promise I'll be a better person. Promise I won't lie, won't take things. Won't sneak away. When we reach the far end of QE Highway, I grit my teeth. "I can get off here."

He waves as I cross the street, then starts turning around. It's stopped raining now, but the sky is still dark, the air full of the voices of hidden frogs. I step onto Pinder Street.

Things have already changed. Mr. Rahming's store is repainted a luminous yellow that glows against the night's will. At the bottom of the street, construction trucks are parked and waiting. The trees by the beach are all gone now, and there's nothing to hide, even from here, that the church building is gone. The skyline seems naked, except for the hotel, which has already gone up three stories. And then, there is home. The house is small. Was it always so shabby? I hope Mummy will be glad to see me. I hope, before the screaming starts, she'll try to understand. I step onto the porch, then turn the knob. I knock. No answer. I knock again. Again.

My back hurts now. I can feel it, too, the blood flowing out of me. Then, from down by the store, I see someone come out and start coming my way. KeeKee, alone, a laundry basket on one hip. I want to shrink as she approaches, to wrap myself up tight, to disappear. She doesn't seem to see me. She's three houses away. Her hair is in tight cornrows. Two houses. Her face seems longer, without its grin. I did that to her. One house away and her head turns. She keeps walking toward me and then I am hurrying across to her. She stops in front of my house and I throw my arms around her and hold on. She freezes, rigid, and my belly cramps again and I know she should hate me, but I need her to love me anyway.

"KeeKee, I sorry, I sorry, I sorry," I say, and I cling to her tighter and as the tears come, I feel her arms come around my back as my sister holds on to me.

KeeKee and I dump the ruined skirt and underwear in a bag, along with Sammy's shirt, and she loans me a clean, dry set of clothes. She sits on the edge of the tub while I perch on the toilet, and she shows me how to use a pad. In all that time Mummy was hankering for me to get my period, she never thought to teach me what to do when it came.

"Just open it, unwrap and take off the paper. Then you put the sticky side onto the crotch of your underwear. Line it up so you have enough front and back."

"How you know what's enough?"

"You'll feel when it's right. You have liners, normal pads, long, heavy, overnight." KeeKee hands me a heavy one. "Try that, just in case."

"You sure this is enough? It might not be enough. Shouldn't I put something over, like, my whole underwear?"

"No, it feels like cups and cups are coming out, but really it's more like a few tablespoons." She gets up.

"You mind staying?"

She hesitates, then nods. "Okay."

I arrange things, then pull the underwear up. The pad bulges against me, awkward and reassuring at the same time.

"How does it feel?"

"Weird."

"You get used to it."

"KeeKee—I really am sorry. For everything."

"Yeah. I know." She leans against the door while I scrub

my hands. "I just don't get why you had to do it, though."

I dry my hands. "Didn't you ever want something so bad you'd do anything to anyone just to have it? You ever just wanted to be someplace else that badly? Or to get away from home?"

"I didn't think I could. People always need something."

"Well, that's why I took your poem. I thought it was my only way out of here. But I was wrong. I'll never do anything like that again. I promise."

"Better not. So, what about—" She pauses, gesturing at the wet clothes on the counter. "Did you sleep by someone or . . ."

"Something almost happened," I say. A knowing look crosses her face, and I realize that she guesses it was Sammy. "But my period decided to save me from doing something really stupid. He wasn't a good person."

KeeKee nods, then opens the door. Voices greet us from the living room.

"Here they come now." I recognize Angel's voice. Then we round the corner and there, with her, is Mummy, standing by the couch. My mother wears a name tag that says TANYA, and a cashier's uniform, and a pair of loafers. She looks tired and sad, and when she sees me, she tightens her grip on her handbag.

"Nia," she says. "You came home."

23

FAITH

I slip away during lunch again. When I get to the beach,
Toons sits sprawled on the sand in a pair of swim trunks, his
folded uniform on one side, a plastic bag on the other. I sit
down beside him and slip off my shoes.

"Going swimming?"

He stands up, but doesn't answer.

"You going in the water?" I repeat.

He grins and reaches into the bag, then pulls out a swim
suit and tosses it at me. "We are."

"We who?"

"Come on."

Toons reaches for me and I duck, then scramble to my feet.
Then he's chasing me and I'm half-running, half-smacking him
away, sand kicked in the air, feet stumbling toward the water.
Bubbles in the surf break over our toes, the froth white and
warm. I laugh, surprised by the sound. It's been so long. His
fingers wrap around my wrist, and I let him pull me closer.
He kisses me softly. "Come on," he says. "Put the suit on. It'll
be fun."

I change behind a tree, then join him at the edge. He leads me deeper into the ocean. A wave lifts, the water sucks around me as it turns on the shore, and I swallow hard against a sudden lump in my throat. "This is as far as I'm going," I say when the water is up to my waist.

"Why?" he asks.

"When my mum first started getting sick, that's how we knew. She kept coming to the beach, swimming out in all her clothes. The last time, she was so heavy with skirts, they almost didn't drag her back in time. After that, I didn't want to go in the ocean anymore. I guess I can't trust anything that I love and that has the power to hurt me at the same time. Not Daddy, not Joy. Not even my mummy."

Toons looks at me, his eyes bottomless water. "What about me?"

"I want to trust you," I say.

"You can," he says, wrapping his arms around me. We wade into the water until it's at my ribs, then my chest, then my neck. I clasp my arms around him, holding on, as we go farther, farther. How am I here, floating on his strength, suspended in his eyes? So much his and yet he's . . . I try to push the thought out of my mind, but it pops up again. *He's not even mine.*

"Are you still with her?" I ask.

"What?"

"Paulette. Are you still with her?"

Toons tips his head back a second, exasperated. "I'm here with you. What you wanna ask me that for?"

Has he seen her since he left Pinder Street too? Does he hold her like he holds me? What stories does he carry that she wept into him and how can he have space for mine too? Questions flood my mind.

He looks out to the horizon. "I don't know why you going there. We out here, nobody else around, and—"

I pull away from him, struggling against the water. "Someone else *is* around, though," I say, pushing. Then he stands up. The water only comes up to his shoulders. "Are you kidding me? We weren't even in deep?"

He lifts his chin slightly, eyes on the shore. "We are now," he says under his breath.

"What you mean *now*? Just say you still with her or—"

"Faith, get out of the water."

My heart stops for what feels like a whole minute. Ms. Rose.

"And young man? You have ten seconds to get out of here."

I think fast. This can go one of two ways: either I get even deeper into trouble or I can rely on my father's pull to get us both out of it.

"I'm waiting," Ms. Rose calls. I stand up, glance back at Toons, water beading his face, droplets clung to his lashes like smooth, clear jewels. I give him a tiny nod; we're in this thing together. I walk through the water, feeling its pull against my body as I retrace my steps. Ms. Rose's scowl deepens as I step onto the shore. "I can't believe you girls. First Nia skips out on her session this morning, and now I find you out here with this boy?"

"Afternoon, ma'am," Toons says.

Ms. Rose ignores him, her gaze fixed firmly on me. "Care to explain?"

"I don't know where Nia is," I say, "but this is my . . ." I look back at Toons, everything familiar, everything comfortable, everything that is home. I can't betray him, or me. "He's my boyfriend. I snuck out to see him."

"Faith, what you doin?" he hisses, but I keep going.

"It's not the first time either."

"He does deliveries." The words spill out of me easily now.

"Unbelievable. Skipping sessions, sneaking around, lying. We can just call your parents to come get you today. And I'll have to notify your employers," she says, turning to Toons. He grabs his shirt.

"No matter what, just remember," Toons says, "I want you to be happy." He hurries away across the sand.

Wheels crunch on the driveway. As I stand up, I feel a pang of excitement; Joy's going to have a lecture for me, but this is what I wanted. I'm getting out of here. I swing my tote onto my shoulder as the car eases into view. Except it isn't Joy's car.

It's Daddy's.

He gets out, shaking his head at me, as if I've broken some unspoken agreement between us. "Get in," he says. I reach for my case and he wrenches it away from me. I slide in and wait while he loads the trunk. He slams it shut, jolting me. I wait for his door to clap closed, for my body to shift forward as we move. I hold my tote close to me and something pokes into my leg. I reach into the bag and my fingers close around something cool, hard, smooth. I ease out Mummy's photo. She looks back at me. From behind the cracked pane, I see, for the first time, that a few hairs have escaped her bun, that her smile is more fixed than joyful, that her gaze is a little vacant, as if she's imagining a world outside the one the photographer, even the other dancers, inhabit. She is not whole. But she is there, as much as she can be.

I sit up as my father gets into the car. His head is tilted down as if life's answers lie in his lap. His shoulders seem lower, though, not squared in his usual, sure posture. Then he sighs, and eases away.

We drive in silence over the bridge. Instead of turning left to head out East, we cut through the center of the island, then west. The road curves around and the ocean surges into view ahead of us. The beach is bare of trees, even the stumps gone. The hotel stands like a giant, angular statue, bare-concrete-gray, its window holes like sockets waiting for eyes. In an instant, I feel like we're back on Pinder Street, except we're in the wrong part of the island altogether. As we continue on, I turn back, craning my neck, willing the old neighborhood to appear behind me.

"Daddy?"

"What?" His voice is curt.

"I know what happened with Toons. I know you had something to do with it. I don't know what all, but I know. And I know you're mad that I got kicked out of camp, but you were wrong too. Really wrong." I sit back, waiting for him to retort, to lash back, to tell me I'm out of turn, anything that shows that he hears, that we're in the same conversation, in the same life.

"The new house is about five streets past here," my father says. "Not far."

I open my mouth to tell him I think it's weak to screw

over Pinder Street and then move as far away from it as we can get, then realize where we are. The new house is minutes away from Hope Springs. From Mummy.

I take a deep breath. "I need to go by and see her," I say firmly, then lean back. I can't change who my father is any more than I can heal my mother through memories. I save the rest of my voice for when it will actually matter. For when it can help others. For when it can change me.

The halls are empty as I walk. My flip-flops smack against the floor in an arrhythmic beat. At the door, a nurse stops me to report that my mother is getting into some fresh clothes, which I know means she made some sort of a mess all over herself, something has happened that is shameful, that mothers should not do, except should and shame do not exist here. I wait outside until the nurse pokes her head around the door and says, "Come in, please."

I step through the door and brace myself for all of it. Uncombed hair. Vacant eyes. A face turned away.

"Easy," the nurse says, as I take a step over to the bed. "Easy, Fay."

I don't know where she ever heard that name, but I turn to it. Not toward the nurse, but toward my mummy. A name can change you in the softest ways. A name whispered in a cozy bed. *Fay-Fay, honey-sweet-sugar-lovey.* A name that belongs to a voice that belongs to a time that belongs to all of us— Daddy, Joy, my mother, and me. To strong arms and sculpted calves. To big shoulders and hands that toss and catch. Swung around in the water, legs dragging slow, and laughter, whole and free. I wrap my arms all the way around Mummy. She is limp, but she's warm, and inside her, there is life.

In the still, quiet room, I pull away and rise to my feet. I stretch out an arm. "Come on, Mummy," I say. "Let's dance. Remember that?" She reaches her hand out toward me, and from behind her quiet eyes, I see a hope, a stir. I take her hand and gently tug. She doesn't move, so I come and sit back down and wrap myself around her.

I don't hear the door open, don't hear footsteps at all. I just know that a third pair of hands is there, one on Mummy's and one on mine. I don't turn to look at Daddy. I don't think I can. But right now, I, we, move, feet in place, but bodies swaying and shifting a little, in some strange kind of way, and together.

EVE

In the middle of Daddy's second night back home, he wakes up in a cold sweat, incoherent and dizzy. The ambulance takes him away, with Mummy riding alongside him. Mr. Rahming drives the rest of us to the hospital to wait.

The waiting room is quiet at three a.m. My siblings sleep in a pile while I watch over them, one eye on the stairs, desperate for news. Finally, Mummy appears. I scramble to my feet.

"How is he?"

She shakes her head. "He has an infection. He's going to have to stay in here until it clears up, at least a few days. He wants to see you."

I follow her to his room, a much smaller, private one now. Machines beep quietly around him. I approach the bed.

"You found Eve, love?"

"It's me, Daddy."

"Oh." He turns farther to look at me. "You look like your mummy."

I want to say something back, except I have no one to compare him to, not even himself before he got sick. He seems even more frail than when he came home just days ago. What I really want to ask, right or not, is if he's going to be okay, if he's coming back home again, if this is something we can ever come back from. But I can't ask any of that. That type of clear, sharp question belongs to the pastor who walks tall, who calms a whole congregation, who washes clean in the evening and falls to his knees at night. The person in the bed can't even hold up his own head. The machines click and plip, speaking for him.

"Come sit down here," he says. I sit. "Close your eyes. We can't talk if you see me like I am. Go on."

I close my eyes.

"All right now."

It doesn't work. His voice is different, weaker. He carries on anyway.

"Now, I need you to take care of some things. Just till I get out of here. I know you do so much, Eve. I know it takes a toll on you. Can you hold it down just a little longer?"

"Of course."

"First, watch Ruth. She's acting all good now, but I don't know if that girl has her head on straight. I can't have her starting to run wild like that other one who used to come around."

He takes a long, labored breath. "Second, the little ones. Be patient with them, all right? I know they get on your nerves sometimes but they look up to you."

The way Daddy's talking scares me. I want to tell him to stop talking like this, that we're going to laugh at all this morose talk one day.

"You hear me?" His tone is urgent.

"Yes." I force the word out finally.

"And last, Eve." I feel fingers on my knee. I reach for them and grip onto Daddy's hand. The skin is dry and cool. I hold on. "Last, be big, Eve."

I pull my hand away, opening my eyes. Daddy's eyes are still closed, but a smile pulls at the edges of his mouth. "Big, Daddy? Really?"

He opens his eyes then, a mischievous grin, and he's himself, we are in front of the house under the tree, we are in the kitchen, we are at our table. "You heard me. Big. Massive. Gargantuan. Don't let anyone overlook you."

This Daddy, the one who's always been my friend, lets my brain unfreeze and I remember there's something I have to tell him. "Daddy, the new church? The one I'm setting up at Mr. Rahming's space? It's gonna be ready soon. Someone left some scraps they salvaged from the church, and there's a piece of stained glass in there. I'm gonna hang it in the window so it catches the light."

"Well." Daddy sounds pleased. Tired out from all the talking but pleased. "Then I think it sounds like you're going to keep things together till I get back home."

"Of course," I say.

He leans back, closing his eyes again. "All right."

I close my eyes too. And, right now, it is.

24

NIA

Mummy closes the front door behind us. I put my bag down, bracing for a tirade to begin. Instead, she walks to the table and pulls out a chair. She sits, her back to me, but I can see from the way she holds herself that she's tired. Her shoulders are hunched, her back rounded. I wait for a moment, but she says nothing. I ease my feet out of my shoes and tiptoe to the hallway.

"Your teacher called from the camp." Her voice is even more wrung out than her body. Her tiredness is so deep it stops me in my tracks. I look back at my mother, her feet crossed at the ankles, one behind the other. "Said you disappeared after we spoke on the phone. Then your . . ." She takes a moment to compose herself. "Your father called me at Tropi-Save and asked if you came by the house. I just started there last week, and I had to walk off the job. I was up and down the streets looking for you in that rain. Where were you? Where did you go?"

In my weeks away, our little house has shrunk. I feel too large, and my secrets can't be kept inside me any longer, and I don't know if they'll fit in this place I used to call home.

Mummy doesn't even sound angry, just worn out and confused. I don't want to lie.

"I called Sammy."

"Nia." She sounds so heartbroken I want to cry. "Why would you—"

"Nothing happened, Mummy. I mean, it might have, but it didn't. I was there at his house—"

"His house?" She cups her hands over her face. "You went to that disgusting man's house? He couldn't even treat Angel, a grown woman, decently, let alone—"

"I got my period."

She lowers her hands and looks at me.

"I didn't do anything with him. Honestly. I caught the bus back. KeeKee was here and she helped me out with a pad."

The room feels even smaller now. If I just reach my arm out, I could sweep the hulking old computer aside, knock away the filing cabinet and refrigerator, the dining table, the apartment-sized stove. I wait for Mummy to respond with something, anything. Slowly, she pushes my chair out with her foot. I hesitate, then sit down opposite her, waiting, not knowing what will come next.

"I was working as a teacher," she says, finally, "when I met your father. It was raining hard, like today. Water in the parking lot, two feet deep. He was the last person who came to pick up a child, this one little boy, Anthony, maybe four at the time. He was young, just early twenties. In one arm he had this baby, maybe six months old. She launched herself at me like she thought I was a mummy or an auntie, someone who knows better than to drag a baby out in the rain. Of course, I took her. She was so excited, she ended up grabbing my glasses right off my face, and then dropped them, and they broke.

"You know my eyes are worse than yours, even then, so I couldn't see to drive home. The man said his name was Tim, and he offered me a ride to the optometrist, and then home. The glasses place was closed by the time we got there, but the lights were still on. He knocked on that door and held that baby up and pointed to that little boy until the doctor let him in. He told her it was his niece's fault, and convinced her to put together a new pair for me right then. By the time we were done, his niece was asleep on my shoulder, and I was hooked. Thirty-three and my first real boyfriend. I was hooked. Months in, he said he loved me and I believed him. Everything was perfect, until my mother caught sight of me coming out of the bathroom in a thin housecoat, and saw what every mother can see.

"Once I told him I was expecting, he stopped coming around. When I called for him at his job, his coworkers stuttered and made up excuses. I went up there and it was the same, people looking off to the side, scurrying for the door when I came in, until one of them, an older woman, said to me, loud enough for the whole room to hear, 'Stop coming here, sweetie. He's taken. Have some pride.'"

"Angel. She stole him from you."

"I'm getting to it," she says, slowly. "I lost my job—a church school didn't want a pregnant, unmarried teacher on staff, and parents were beginning to talk. That's when I started tutoring. A few of the mothers felt sorry for me and brought their kids to me after school, but it wasn't much work. I stopped looking for your father, then. But when you

395

came, he came by the hospital to meet you. He was better then, for a little while. He came by often, he brought you clothes, kept food in the house since I couldn't work. When you got old enough, he'd pick you up for an afternoon and give me a break. It was good, for a while. I kind of let myself forget about the other woman, whoever she was.

"It was an accident that I found out who his other woman was. Really, a pile of tiny accidents that led to one bad day. One night, you cried for 'Angel.' Another day I saw in his truck a flyer of the cabaret show, but he was so smooth when I asked him about it. 'My cousin in the show, she asked me to put up some posters.' That's what he told me. Then I saw a picture in the newspaper. The same show, and there was a picture of a woman. Angelica Hepburn. Best cabaret dancer they had at the Old Fort Hotel. Slim and big-bosomed and much younger than me.

"I left you in the house with Granny and went down there one night. I was hell-bent on catching her. I waited till the show was over, then snuck backstage. There he was, he had her by the arm, not rough, but his voice was hard, and he was telling her all kinds of things. How she was a mother, this was no thing for her to do. Did she want her daughter to learn from her? She said she didn't see the shame, it was honest money. I don't remember even saying a word, but he saw me and it must have showed on his face. She turned around and gave me a look like a dog had thrown up in her fluffy red shoes. 'Her?' That's all she said. 'Her?'"

"That was Angel?"

"Yes." Mummy runs a hand over the table. "I just remember feeling so, so mad, and so small, and so low. I just charged for her. He tried to get between us and I pushed him right out of the way. I never even got to her. She stepped backward and right into a lantern. It overturned and there were flames everywhere. It was quick, someone threw water, and she was crying, just an awful sound, and he started yelling, 'You out your mind? You trying to kill my wife?'"

Wife. The word sits in the middle of the table between us. Angel wasn't just another girlfriend. He was married to her. We sit in silence together. Minutes pass before Mummy speaks again.

"I was scared to show my face. I was scared to even try to look for work. Your granny passed around that time. I lay low, tutored the few children who came. Then, one day, there was activity at the house next door. First time since I could remember, someone was over there, painting, sweeping, moving furniture in. I just went out to hang out my clothes and I was almost knocked down. It was that little boy. The one Timothy came to pick up, that day we met. Little Anthony. Hurled himself at me."

"Toons?"

Mummy nods slowly.

"A woman called for him. I heard her voice and I knew, and I couldn't move. There I was, you in my arms and the boy almost bowling me over trying to hug me, and my daughter's father's wife who I caused to get burned is calling the boy's name. Then she came outside. She had on pants, but no top. Big chest, bright-pink bra. The little girl—KeeKee—was following her out and when Angel turned around to pick her up, I could see her hand was bare—no wedding band anymore. Worst thing was the raw, pink skin right across her back, left shoulder all the way down to her waist.

"By the time she was better," Mummy carries on, "she had a new boyfriend, the one before Sammy came along. There were always people coming and going in that house—all hours of the night. Toons didn't live with her then, you know. He'd come to stay when his real mother was having a rough time, then go back to her. He was always back and forth. But there were others, too, coming and going all the time—children, women, sometimes even men. I didn't know what kind of gig she had going."

"What about Mr. Wright?"

"Your father? I think he was ashamed. After Angel moved in, he just didn't come around. I knew she'd told him to stay away."

"How come she had to move in right beside you?"

Mummy shrugs. "After everything happened, I couldn't go back to work, so I never left the house I grew up in. Angel's house was in her family for some time, but it was a great-aunt or something, so we didn't know each other when we were young. At first I thought she did it to spite me, to make sure I could never forget what I'd done to her, but really, I think it was just unfortunate chance. We both needed a place to live, and Pinder Street is just where we both landed. Before you were even old enough to walk, KeeKee would trot over here, looking to play. Barely a year between the two of you, and she picked up and decided she was gonna be big sister to you. Maybe Angel felt it was right for you two to grow up together. Much as I didn't like it, she was always good to you."

A million questions are tangled up in my head. How could she act, all these years, like Angel was so wicked and loose?

Had she been scared Angel would try to do something to her in return? Then the most important question rises to the top and takes shape. "How come you told me this?" I ask. "Today?"

Mummy reaches both her hands across the table. I take them, feel her squeeze mine tight. "The way you lied on that application, the way you went and snuck around with Sammy?" She shakes her head. "I want you to choose better. But I can't expect you to be an honest person unless I'm truthful with you too. And, more than anything, I don't want you to repeat my mistakes."

The room seems a little larger, with the words I've been waiting for finally out in the open. But I don't want Mummy to think what I did was her fault. "I'm my own person, though," I say. "From now on, the choices I make are mine. But I'll try to be honest. And smart. Okay?"

She nods. "Okay. Now, speaking of choices, did you make amends with KeeKee?"

"I think so. At least, I made a start."

Mummy leans over and gives me a long hug. When we separate, she reaches over to my bag and starts to unpack it. "What's this?" She holds up the plastic bag of food.

I smile. The sandwich is only from earlier today, but it feels like it's from another lifetime. I want to remember the freedom, the creativity I felt in that big kitchen on Paradise Island. I want to bring it into my life here. "Slam bam, Nia-style," I say. I get up and get two plates and two glasses of water. Together, we sit and eat. And this time, there's nothing in the world I'd rather be eating than a cold sandwich at home, across from Mummy.

25

EVE

It's past nine o clock when I push open the door to Mr. Rah-ming's store, but I find it buzzing with activity. Mr. Wright opens out a tall silver ladder while KeeKee fiddles with a wire-less speaker. Old-school reggae blasts out into the space. Then I do a double take—that's Nia kneeling over an open toolbox.

"You're here!" I exclaim as I hug Nia. I look tentatively at KeeKee, but she seems genuinely happy to have Nia back.

"I was just telling the girls that up there, we want to put in reinforcements." Mr. Wright points at the exposed rafters. "See, we'll use one of the pieces of salvaged wood from the old church to reinforce the existing structure." He holds out a chunk of wood. It doesn't look like much, a dark chunk, time-worn but, miraculously, not weather-beaten. He points to the ladder and Nia drags it over to the area we need to work on. "Who wants to do this part?"

"Eve should do it," KeeKee pipes up.

I roll my shoulders and stretch for a second. "Okay."

"I'm gonna walk you through it. You go ahead and get up there," Mr. Wright says. "Now, you'll need some glue on there—Nia, it's over by the door. KeeKee, see if you can find nails and a hammer."

I climb up, and they pass the wood and tools to me. Following Mr. Wright's instructions, I position the chunk of wood up where the two parts of the highest beam in the ceiling connect. The glue holds the wood so I can line up the nail. Then I hammer, driving metal through both pieces of wood.

"Pull on it," KeeKee calls up.

I tug. "Feels like one."

"They call that sistering," Mr. Wright says, and heads back out to the van. The three of us stand there a moment and let the word sink in. Sistering. Like making separate parts into family. Like us.

The door opens again and I turn, expecting to see Mr. Wright again. Faith grins at me, then looks outside.

"Come on," she says, and Toons squeezes past and inside.

KeeKee hurls herself at her brother so hard he almost falls over. Toons is laughing, and then she is too, and their voices are a sweet song that rises and echoes, christening the space. Off to the side, Faith slips over to Nia.

"What happened?" Nia asks her. "You get catch?"

"Yeah." Faith keeps her voice low. "By you-know-who." The shape between them has changed in these past few weeks; they share secrets now. A note of sadness rises in me, and I let it lift up and fall away. Faith's new tie with Nia doesn't have to shake our bond. Time, distance, fights and flights and sick parents don't have to break it either. Not unless we let it.

Toons ruffles KeeKee's hair and she bats his hand away, then turns to Faith.

"You got him to call Angel," she says. Faith nods. "Thank you."

Toons makes his way over and gives me an awkward hug. "You all right, Sis?"

There's only the faintest flutter inside me as I hug him back. "Of course. I'm not the one who's been adventuring and whatnot." I let him go. "You plan to stay?"

"Sort of. Mr. Wright got me a job and I wanna keep working. I'll sleep up this way though." He looks around. "Looks like we got a new spot to sing in, hey?"

"Yeah, the acoustics are good," I say, and Nia hoots like a confused owl. An echo bounces back down to her, and soon we're all shouting up into the corners, and the building rings with life all over again. Mr. Wright returns with more supplies and we keep working to strengthen the beams, joking in between. Nia slips home for a bit and comes back with her mother in tow, and a steaming dish of rice with some corn and sweet potato fritters, and creamy sauce she says is called aioli on the side. KeeKee and I bring plates and cutlery across from my house, and we dip into the food together. Mr. Wright heads into the back room and Nia's mummy steps over to the Munroe's.

"So what you doin with this place?" Toons points at me with his fork. "Y'all making another church?"

I look around. "Yes. And more. I want it to be whatever people need it to be, just like the last place was."

"We should have dance classes in here," Faith says.

Nia reaches across to help herself to more fritters. "We need long tables and chairs. We could do potlucks."

"I was thinking," KeeKee says. "What if we got some type of container, and I could put pouches in there for people to take as they need."

I look over at her. "You're gonna do the pouches again?"

She slips her hand into her pocket and takes out a small cloth parcel. "I revamped them a little bit. Some people never picked up their laundry, so I cut this out of an old sheet that was clean." The pale blue cloth is tied neatly into a bundle just a little bigger than a deck of cards. She tugs at a few points and it opens up to reveal two pads and a little piece of paper. Nia reaches over and picks up the scrap.

"'Slow tide rising, night disguising,
if you ever start surmising
that you're worth less than the starlight
that you mean less than the moon,
remember, girl, we love you
and better's coming soon.'"

She looks over at KeeKee. "You wrote that? I mean . . . you *wrote* it!"

KeeKee nods. "You can keep that one. I mean, I have other ones that have other stuff in them too . . ."

"Nope, this is good, thanks!" Nia tucks the pouch into her pocket.

There's a tap on the open door and Paulette peeps in. I feel Faith freeze beside me as Toons gets up to greet her. They step outside together. I have a feeling they have a lot to talk about. Once they're gone, I tap my shoe against Faith's.

"You okay?"

She shrugs. "Kinda have to be. Right?"

I don't know what that means, but maybe she doesn't either, yet. I leave it, for now.

Bellies full, we lounge in a sort of circle. Nia says, *"Remember when we used to play twee lee lee?"* That gets us on our feet, clapping each other's hands, turning left, then opposite each other, voices linked *gotta rock those people all night long, huffin and a puffin and a singin their song, all those boys down Peter Street, listen to the song goin Sesamee Street* the words a path we've always known and always will. The acoustics make us sound like eight girls, sixteen, thirty-two, a whole country of girls. A world. *Mother's in the kitchen cooking rice, father's in the backyard shootin dice, brother's in jail for tellin tales, sister's round the corner sellin fruit cocktail, gotta rock, rock, around the clock.* We start over again and again, fingers stinging, hands flying, song breaking down time, chanting fast and then faster, and as long as we keep going, this way, our way, is sure, is safe.

Out the open door, I see Mummy's car pull up to the curb. The others are in the car too, but she steps out alone. She holds her body wrong, one shoulder too high, hand over her mouth to keep words from spilling out. Someone is sitting on my chest. I break the circle, my palms tingling, voices tapering off as I run to her, my footsteps and the sudden slam of my heartbeat drowning out everything else.

"Eve!" Mummy's voice cracks as I reach her.

Daddy? I try to force the question out but my throat is

too tight. She pulls me close and even before she whispers *He's gone,* I feel my heart break open. Feel the air tear apart as someone screams *No.*

NIA

Doors open up and down the street, first one neighbor, then another. They come to Eve and her mother, surrounding them, until we can't see our friend anymore. Mummy is there, Angel too. They guide children out of the car, move the family into their house, supporting them.

KeeKee speaks first. "What now?"

"I don't know," Faith says, bewildered. "I don't know."

They sound like I feel—small, lost, unsure where to put my feet. Slowly, we start to tidy up the space. None of us says a word.

Then there is a sort of sigh. We look toward the open door.

"I—I left my keys." Eve.

Faith is beside her in a second, hugging her. KeeKee joins in, wrapping her arms around both of them. I hold on to whoever I can.

When Eve pulls away, her face glistens, saltwater wet. She turns around and walks outside. We follow, sure of the destination. Near the end of Pinder Street, it comes into view. Between a sky-slicing crane and the growing hotel, something beckons us closer. Cut through the yard, duck under the clotheslines, hop the fence and take the old path. Welcome the shift and give of earth that blends into sand. We near the second fence, and guard pauses, then adjusts his cap and, divinely guided, unlocks the gate. We step through. A security light casts a glaring beam that cancels out the stars. Eve doesn't seem to notice. She slides her feet out of her shoes and keeps walking. Something calls her. It calls us all.

One by one, we follow her down the shore to the water, and step into the breaking waves. The sky grows light, now, where it lies down against the water, first pale blue, then lilac, then pink. Behind us, the light flickers off, and farther down the beach, another, and another, until we are in the nearest thing to darkness the beach will ever see. I take Eve's hand, and Faith wraps an arm around her other shoulder. KeeKee leans against me. Water laps our ankles as it eases toward the shore, sucks away at the sand we stand on as it pulls back out to sea. Our feet stay firm here, though, rooted, no matter what. A sliver of red crests the horizon and stretches over the water, illuminating our skin. Together, we face the sun.

ACKNOWLEDGMENTS

Thank you to my wonderful agent, Rachel Letofsky, and my talented editor, Catherine Laudone, for helping to guide this story to publication.

Thank you to my family for supporting me through this book's journey, and in life.